Ask Me No Questions

SHELLEY NOBLE

Ask Me No Questions

A Tom Doherty Associates Book • New York

This is a work of fiction. All of the characters, organizations, and events portrayed in this novel are either products of the author's imagination or are used fictitiously.

ASK ME NO QUESTIONS

A Forge Book
Published by Tom Doherty Associates
175 Fifth Avenue
New York, NY 10010

www.tor-forge.com

Forge® is a registered trademark of Macmillan Publishing Group, LLC.

Library of Congress Cataloging-in-Publication Data

Names: Noble, Shelley, author.
Title: Ask me no questions / Shelley Noble.
Description: First edition. | New York : Forge, 2018. | "A Tom Doherty Associates Book."
Identifiers: LCCN 2018034242| ISBN 9780765398710 (hardcover) | ISBN 9780765398703 (ebook)
Classification: LCC PS3614.O253 A93 20118 | DDC 813/.6—dc23
LC record available at https://lccn.loc.gov/2018034242

First Edition: October 2018

Printed in the United States of America

0 9 8 7 6 5 4 3 2 1

To Charles,

who knew how to spin a tale

ACKNOWLEDGMENTS

It takes many hands to take a book from idea to novel to published book. Many thanks to my agent, Kevan Lyon, and editor, Amy Stapp, and Zohra Ashpari and my entire Forge team.

Ask Me No Questions

England 1907

Lady Philomena Dunbridge's father slammed the newspaper on the tea table. "This is an outrage."

Lady Phil stared at the headlines. Dowager? *Dowager*?? How could they call her a dowager? She was barely twenty-six years old. It was the twentieth century; no one her age should be called dowager. "It's shameful," she agreed. It was probably the first time she and her father had agreed on something since . . . um . . . she couldn't remember a time.

"Fine answer to have in hindsight." A cloud of spittle exploded past his lips.

"How was I to know he was going to drop dead of a heart attack?"

"What? What are you talking about?"

"The newspaper, my deceased husband. I refuse to be called 'dowager.' I couldn't agree more."

"Mad. Are you mad? Did you read the rest of the headline?"

Well, to be honest, she had stuck on the dowager part. She read it now. "Dowager"—her eyes stuck on that hateful word—"Countess, Lady Philomena Dunbridge Discovers Murder Victim, Solves Crime—Leaves Stymied Metropolitan Police Scratching Their Heads."

She smiled reminiscently. Actually, a child could have followed the clues left by the murderer. But men did tend to get caught up in the wherefores and whatnots.

She pulled the paper closer to read the article. Her father snatched it out of reach.

"And that's the best of the lot." He barely flicked his head toward a stack of newspapers on his desk.

She didn't think he'd appreciate her taking them. No matter, she could pick them up at the newsstand on her way back to the Savoy Hotel. She had no intention of staying under this roof and being scolded like a child. Her parents had given up that right when they'd married her off at seventeen to a man she hardly knew and wished she'd never seen.

"It's one thing the scandals you've caused with your less-than-discreet behavior. Those affaires could be forgiven considering the state of your husband. But this. *This*. Have you no care for your family's name?"

Actually, she hadn't cared much for her family since they'd married her off to the Earl of Dunbridge.

"This time you're going to have to pay the price."

Good heavens, hadn't she been paying the price for seven years of a loveless, cold marriage to a man who had no feelings, including the intimate kind, unless it involved whips and madams, or so she'd been told? Any self-respecting married lady would make sure she led her own, more compatible life. They had to.

"So what will it be?"

"Pardon me, sir?"

"Which do you choose? The dower house with a suitable companion, return home and live as a spinster with your family, or . . ."

"Yes?"

"There is always your great-aunt Sephronia in Yorkshire."

Those were her choices? It didn't seem quite fair. But she couldn't expect her current lover to put her up forever, and besides, she was getting bored. The dower house was crumbling and moldy, and the suitable companion would be equally moldy, she had no doubt. And she had no intention of living as a spinster, under this roof or any other. And as for the crazy old lady in the back of beyond . . .

"Well?"

There seemed to be only one choice. "I believe, sir, that I shall go to America."

1

"*Ay, Dios mío.*"

Philomena Amesbury, Lady Dunbridge, glanced at her lady's maid, who stood beside her, clutching the rail of the SS *Oceanic*, her eyes wide.

"Only speak in English or French, Lily," Lady Dunbridge reminded her. "And try not to gape. It's merely another large city, much like London."

The steamship had slowed to a crawl as tugboats navigated it up the busy Hudson River toward Chelsea Pier, and it was a remarkable view. The skyline of tall buildings passed before them like Edison's motion pictures, just as exciting and more than a little daunting. Lady Dunbridge could sympathize with the girl's amazement.

Lily bobbed a satisfactory curtsey. "Pardon, madam."

Not bad, Philomena thought, considering she'd been a lady's maid for less than a week, after Lady Dunbridge had snatched her from the jaws of the London immigration police who had caught her attempting to stow away on the ship.

At the last minute, Lady Dunbridge's own maid had refused to board. Stuck between a rock and the deep blue sea, and after much argument from her traveling companion, Preswick—her devoted if somewhat long-in-the-tooth butler—and promises from Lily not to run away the minute they landed in New York, Lady Dunbridge had paid her passage. Admitting defeat, Preswick spent the seven days at sea transforming the girl into a semblance of a lady's maid.

He'd done an excellent job with a very apt pupil.

Lady Dunbridge smiled encouragingly at the young woman, who was now her servant and confidante.

She was a tad too exotic looking for a lady's maid, dark hair and flashing eyes with a Renaissance painting complexion, which appealed to Philomena.

She'd stubbornly refused to tell her name—Philomena decided to call her Lily because of her complexion. Nor where she'd come from—certainly not the slums of London or Barcelona—or her age. She was possibly younger than she looked. Regardless, she was younger than Philomena, who was leaning closer to thirty than twenty.

She was a little rough around the edges but not vulgar, and very willing to learn. Most surprising, she was fairly fluent in three languages. Now if she kept her promise not to bolt as soon as they landed . . . "Speak in English or French . . . but listen in Spanish."

Lily frowned, then flashed her a grin. "*Oui, madame.* I understand completely."

Ah, thought Lady Dunbridge. *There was hope for this trip yet.*

The ship finally maneuvered into the wharf and the engines were cut, the constant rumbling giving way to the clatter of carts and carriages on the uneven paving stones. Newspaper boys and urchins cried for coinage. A marching band was playing, and she caught a glimpse of placards rising above the heads of people waiting on the street. Burly dockworkers hefted trunks and crates to their backs and lugged them through the waiting crowd, while cart boys darted in and out of the bystanders with a dexterity that belied their small statures.

There were even two automobiles, one black and one yellow, the latter she knew from Bev's letters must belong to Reggie Reynolds. Of course, Reggie would want to show off his new automobile. He had promised to meet them at the pier and drive them to the Reynoldses' brownstone on East Sixty-Eighth Street, while their coachman conveyed her servants and baggage in the town carriage.

The wind whipped up, rustling the ostrich plumes of Philomena's hat, and she held it to her head with one hand while she tried to catch sight of Bev or Reggie. It was impossible in the crush of people.

The captain approached her and bowed. "Lady Dunbridge. It has been a great pleasure to have met you. I hope you enjoy your visit. May I?" He offered his arm and personally escorted Philomena and her entourage of two to the gangplank, where the purser urged everyone toward the pier and the *carte de visite* agents. The captain kissed her hand before bidding her *adieu*.

But at the bottom of the gangplank, Lily balked. "What if they won't let me in? What will I do?"

"Just be calm and look lovely," Philomena reminded her. "You have a perfectly acceptable *carte de visite*."

Preswick humphed.

"A somewhat unorthodox *carte* . . .

And perhaps not altogether legal?" he added.

Philomena shot him a warning look. "It was drawn up, albeit hastily, by a member of the immigration service." At least she was fairly certain he worked for that branch of government. "No matter, where there's a will . . ." Lily certainly had the will; Philomena had merely given her the way. They should get on just fine.

They stopped at a customs desk and had their *cartes* stamped—including Lily's. Philomena sent the two off to claim the baggage and hire a carter to bring their trunks to the carriage. Then she followed the other passengers through the dark wooden reception hall to the street.

As she stepped out from the tall, wide arches, she was hit with a cacophony of sound and a sea of faces. Old and young, clean and dirty; friends meeting friends, families hoping to find their relatives—all were intently watching the opening to the wharf, seemingly oblivious of the traffic and noise around them.

Bev, petite and naturally blond, stood at the very front, accompanied by a servant, liveried in maroon and gold.

Philomena's smile widened. She was always amused by these American affectations, but she loved Bev, and if Bev wanted a driver who looked like he just stepped out of some moldy aristocratic castle—hers, for example—Bev should have him.

She was dressed in the latest mode as always. Lady Dunbridge's own plumed hat paled beside the clamshell Bev wore rakishly angled over one eye. Its green and beige aigrette feathers made a delicious comment on the turquoise bolero jacket and skirt she was wearing with such panache. Philomena remembered seeing its sister design in the Paquin showroom on her last trip to Paris. *No longer behind the times, these Americans.*

Phil raised her hand to wave. Bev waved back, then abruptly turned away and hurried off in the opposite direction and quickly disappeared from view.

Taken aback, Philomena looked to the servant, who was staring after his mistress. He roused himself and hurried to Philomena.

"Lady Dunbridge?" The driver yelled as the band marched closer and the noise grew louder.

"I am," she yelled back.

"Mrs. Reynolds has"—he darted a look in the direction Bev had taken—"has gone to fetch Mr. Reynolds and the auto. I'll wait here and transport your trunks and servants in the carriage." He gestured over the crowd to a well-appointed carriage in the care of two footmen.

"Thank you . . ." she shouted.

His voice rose over the nearing oompahs. "Bentley, ma'am."

"Bentley," she acknowledged at the top of her lungs. His name rang out in the sudden quiet as the band tumbled to the end of what Philomena now recognized as "Onward, Christian Soldiers." "My butler and maid should be arriving short—"

A pop, like a champagne cork, cut through the air. Someone

was already celebrating. Except the pop was followed by a high-pitched, piercing scream. Not champagne—a gunshot.

"That's Mrs. Reynolds!" Bentley spun on his heels and ran through the crowd toward the yellow touring car.

"Bev!" cried Lady Dunbridge. She lifted her skirts and raced after him.

They had to fight their way through the crowd, half of whom were fleeing in all directions. The band and sign-carrying women marched past, cutting off their progress.

"The Women's Temperance Union," Bentley said as he danced around the edges of the parade looking for a way through them. The music started up again. Bentley plunged through. Lady Dunbridge plunged in after him.

When she made it to the other side, her hat was pitched forward due to coming into contact with a tuba, the nest of ostrich plumes covering both eyes. And she'd lost a button from her kid glove where it had caught on the stick of one of the placards.

A crowd was pressed around the touring car, but there was no sign of Bentley or Bev. Philomena pushed the ostrich plumes from her face and squeezed through to the front.

She was met by a horrible tableau.

Reggie Reynolds was sprawled across the backseat, one foot on the floor, one arm dangling down from the seat, and his head cradled among the skirts of a woman's lap. Blood oozed past his vest, edged the lapels of his sack coat, and spread across the white shirt beneath.

Bev clutched the open automobile door and stared at the scene.

"Why? Why did you do it, Reggie?" cried the woman in the auto, who was looking decidedly pale and awkward beneath her wide-brimmed platter-sized hat. "Why did you kill yourself?"

"Murderer!" Bev cried, and reached out as if to reclaim her husband, who seemed to Philomena beyond reclaiming.

The woman shrank back. She was rather pretty, with light

brown hair poufed in a pompadour style. One sleeve of her pastel walking suit was smeared with blood where she was clutching Reggie. And when Philomena looked closer she could see the splatter of what must be blood across the bodice. Her stomach hiccupped in revulsion.

The crowd pressed in. Questions and speculations tumbled through the group.

"What's happened?" "Is that Reggie Reynolds?" "He's got a nag running at Belmont next week." "A real winner, they say." "Witness the evils of drinking!"

"It's that Florodora girl. What's her name?"

"Mimi LaPonte."

A Florodora girl. So this was Reggie's latest mistress. Leave it to him to be found dead in the arms of a cheap chorus girl from a popular stage play. She certainly looked the part. Blond—not natural—expensively but not entirely tastefully dressed. Her tears flowed freely, streaking her makeup. She didn't attempt to extricate herself from the body.

"And that must be his wife!" All eyes turned to stare at Bev.

"She musta' shot him."

"Nah, it was the girl. She musta' done him in."

"Oh, why, Reggie, why did you kill yourself?" the Florodora girl repeated.

Just in case anyone had missed it the first time, thought Philomena. She'd had enough experience to recognize an opportunist when she saw one, even if she was pinned by a dead man and covered in his blood.

The crowd moved closer to the car and Philomena broke from her stupefaction. She grabbed Bev. At first she fought, then realizing who it was, cried "Phil," and collapsed against Philomena's new spring coat.

The band was mercifully quiet as the members and the parading temperance ladies reversed course to get a better look. As soon as Philomena's ears stopped ringing, she heard a series of whistles converging on the area. The Manhattan police, no doubt. She was thinking fast; neither she nor Bev could afford to be found in a situation like this. Neither of them might have the best of reputations, but it was paramount that they keep what they had.

"Come. Now." Philomena pulled Bev back from the automobile.

"This way, my lady." It was Bentley. He took Bev's other arm.

"She's getting away! Stop her!" someone cried.

The trio sped up, right into the dark, brass-buttoned coat of a New York City policeman.

"Now where do you think you'd be going—miss—misses, uh, you three?"

"My friend has had a terrible shock. Her husband has been ki—injured, and she's feeling faint and needs a place to sit," Philomena said at her haughtiest, then looked around for an escape route.

Another patrolman skidded to a stop next to the first. "Not so fast."

Philomena noticed the piece of offal beneath his feet and turned up her nose at the smell. It worked to good effect. He blushed red, then stepped back and scrubbed the sole of his shoe against the rough surface of the brick paving stones.

Bev roused herself. "Do you know who you're talking to? This is the Countess of Dunbridge."

The men exchanged looks.

"Dunn't look old enough to be no countess," the younger one said.

The older one shook his head. "And sure she is. These society types are always pulling tricks to get out of trouble. Well, your highness, you three just go stand over there with this here officer and wait until you're called for." He nodded abruptly, and the younger man herded the three back toward the auto. The area around it had been cleared and the crowd was being held back by several more uniformed men. The whistles must have summoned every policeman in the neighborhood.

Bev was leaning heavily against Philomena. "Stay swooning until I return," she whispered, then thrust Bev at the coachman. She needed a closer look.

She had no intention of being enmeshed in a scandal on the day of her arrival, but at this point she didn't see how to avoid it unless she deserted her friend and kept moving. But that meant Bev would be left to the mercies of the police who, if they were anything like the London constabulary . . . She just couldn't do it. Which meant she would have to do something about it herself. Bev's husband had either been murdered or had killed himself sitting in a public thoroughfare in the company of his mistress for all the world to see.

Typical of a man.

Bev would need her support when the gossip became brutal, as it was sure to do.

She'd known Bev since they were girls at the same finishing school in Paris. Had it really been ten years ago? Phil had adored Bev's American bravado and had introduced her to Paris society. As young girls, they weren't invited to the adult soirees and balls, so together they discovered the Parisian demimonde.

Now Bev was but a pale memory of that girl, and Phil didn't have the heart to desert her.

No one was even guarding Reggie's body. They were too busy trying to keep the onlookers at bay. The crowd was becoming more voluble by the moment, calling for the arrest of someone, anyone, the mistress or the wife, either one of them would do, or both.

Philomena didn't for a minute think Bev killed Reggie, though as far as she was concerned she had every right to. Everyone had affairs, but good breeding insisted on discretion. Reggie flaunted his, made headlines with them, while Bev sat humiliated at home. But how to make certain suspicion didn't fall on his wife?

"Ugh!" Philomena pulled her skirt back, eased herself out from the restless crowd, and slipped past the distracted policeman who was trying to contain them.

She was immediately accosted by two more men in uniforms. "Sorry, miss, you can't come no closer."

"I'm a friend of the family. Are you sure he's dead?"

"Well . . ."

"You should call for a doctor immediately! He might still be saved!" She warbled this out, clasping her hands together to her bosom like a heroine in a play put on during a country house weekend.

"Is there a doctor here?" one of the policeman shouted, swiveling his head.

"Are you daft, man?" jeered a bruiser leaning over his handcart. "He's a goner for sure. Just look at him."

The group surged forward. The police pushed them back.

A clerk in a bowler hat craned his neck to see. "Oughtn'ya go see? Maybe he ain't dead."

"If I say he's dead—" The bruiser knocked the man's hat to the ground. When he leaned down to pick it up, another man punched the bruiser in the jaw. He fell back, dominoing into the people behind him.

It was a match in a tinderbox. Others took up the cudgels, the remaining policemen rushed to help, and Philomena hurried to the auto to get a better look inside.

The Florodora girl had been removed—or had removed herself. Now both doors were open. Reggie lay alone across the leather seat as if he'd fallen asleep or, more likely, passed out in a drunken stupor. He didn't appear to be breathing, though truth be told, she'd only said that to distract the guards.

Philomena inched a little closer, peered at the backseat, scrutinized the floor. If he'd shot himself, what happened to the pistol? She saw no evidence of one, not in Reggie's hand or anywhere in the enclosed space. Had the Florodora girl shot him? Did she still have the pistol? Or was she disposing of it while they all stood around doing nothing?

Then she spied a small black handbag lying on the floor in the far corner. She might be able to reach it if . . . She leaned into the auto, felt along the floorboards, shuddered when her arm brushed against Reggie's lifeless leg. She stretched out her hand . . . just a little farther. A large hand appeared before hers.

Philomena gasped, snatched her hand back, and glanced up to find a pair of glinting black eyes staring back at her. A man crouched at the other side of the automobile. Their eyes locked over Reggie's body, then abruptly the man stood, ducked his head, and melted into the crowd.

"Wai—!"

Before she could react, she was grabbed from behind, fingers encircling her waist, and she was yanked backward out of the automobile.

A fine situation for the Countess of Dunbridge.

As soon as her feet touched the ground, she whirled around with her Parisian reticule swinging. She had to stifle a yelp of surprise when her wrist was gripped, stopping both her bag and her person in their rotation, and she came face to chest with her would-be assailant.

"Pardon me, madam, but you have no business here. This is a crime scene, if you will kindly step back."

Philomena did step back, but out of surprise and disgust. The man was filthy and he towered over her. He wore a drab, wrinkled Mackintosh and a slouch hat pulled down on his forehead, leaving nothing of his face visible but a morning-after beard. He looked absolutely disreputable, but he was barking orders at her with the authority of the Lord Chamberlain.

"Just who are you, sir?" she demanded, gathering what aplomb she could manage. Where were all those policemen who had just been milling about when she needed one?

"I was about to ask you the same."

She took another cautious step back. "Are you with the police?"

He reached inside his Mackintosh with a dirty scraped hand and pulled out a metallic shield. "I'm Detective Sergeant John Atkins."

Considering the state of his hands, she decided to forgo good manners and didn't offer hers. "I'm Lady Dunbridge . . ."

"So I've been told," he said drily as he returned his shield to his pocket. "And may I ask what you are doing here?"

"I just arrived on the SS *Oceanic* from Southampton to visit my friend Mrs. Reynolds. And I would be quite grateful if I were allowed to take her home. Her husband is dead and she's naturally in shock."

He motioned her away from the crowd. "I have a few questions."

"Which she'll be glad to answer once she's recovered. Shall we say tomorrow morning? I doubt she will be receiving visitors." She smiled condescendingly. "Ten o'clock? Thank you. You're very kind." She didn't give him time to answer, but called out, "Bentley, help your mistress back to the carriage. I'll join you shortly."

She turned back to Detective Sergeant Atkins. "Before you begin your inquiries, I think you should know there was a man who was taking an inordinate interest in the scene. I believe he was going to steal a handbag from the automobile, before I interrupted him."

"Handbag?"

"Yes, black, with a lovely confection of sequins and onyx."

"A handbag in the auto? A man? Where?"

"In the far corner on the floor. He was standing on the other side of the automobile. Over there." She pointed back to the auto, and when the detective turned to look, she took the opportunity to slip away.

2

Lily and Preswick were waiting by the Reynoldses' carriage. Bentley quickly ordered the footman to hire a cab and accompany them and the baggage to the brownstone. Then he fairly pushed the two ladies into the carriage.

"Whew," Philomena said as the door closed on them. She reached across Bevvy, who had collapsed against the seat, and pulled the curtains shut as the carriage jolted forward.

"But we can't just leave him there," Bev moaned.

"I'm afraid we don't have a choice."

"But what are they going to do with him? And what about the touring auto?"

"I don't have the slightest idea."

"We should go back." Bev reached to alert the coachman.

Philomena grasped her sleeve. "And stand there for however long they take with people pointing at you and crying, 'She did it!'? Newspaper reporters are probably already on their way, with their photographic equipment."

Bev moaned louder.

"I'm sure the automobile and Reggie's body will be fine. And we can expect to see that policeman first thing tomorrow morning, if not before."

"What policeman?"

"Well, he said he was a policeman, a detective of some sort; he wasn't wearing a uniform and he was disgustingly dirty." And if he didn't look any cleaner in the morning, Philomena would have the servants turn him away.

"Oh, no. Do I have to talk to him?"

"He'll have questions. And you are Reggie's wife, though I suppose under the circumstance, the past tense would be more apropos."

"Why would Reggie shoot himself? He had a horse running at Belmont next week. A big race. It must be that awful woman. She must have killed him in a jealous rage. That detective should be talking to her."

"I'm sure he is," Phil said soothingly. "But since no one knows for certain and you *were* standing over the body, it would behoove you to stay calm. And hope for a verdict of suicide or murder by persons unknown."

"Verdict? It won't go to court, will it?"

"Hush. I have no idea. Though I do think you should ring up your solicitor when we get to the brownstone."

"My solicitor? I'm not sure we have one."

"Everyone has a solicitor, or at least a man of affairs."

"No, they don't."

"Well, I'm sure Reggie does—did. And I know your father must. Hopefully his services won't be required."

Philomena ardently hoped they wouldn't. From a purely selfish standpoint, she couldn't afford to stay out of society for the length of a trial. Lily and Preswick were dependent on her, and she couldn't depend on Bevvy's generosity or her introductions, because Bev would now be in mourning for months.

Philomena was just out of her own mourning period, eighteen tedious months of it. And she hadn't even liked her husband, even if he was the Earl of Dunbridge. She'd gotten a title but little else from that arrangement.

Bev had scrunched up against the opposite side of the carriage and rested her head against the squabs. Her eyes were closed. At least she'd stopped crying and Philomena left her alone.

She sat staring straight ahead in the semidarkness of the carriage. She was dying to catch a glimpse of the city—she hadn't visited since before her marriage—but she didn't know if they'd been followed and she certainly didn't want to end up on the pages of a scandal sheet.

The carriage stopped after an interminable amount of time.

"Are we there?" Bev asked, rousing herself and managing to look beautiful and ravaged at the same time.

After a prolonged wait, the door opened and Bentley let down the steps. Two footmen ran down the brownstone steps to trundle them into the house. Philomena didn't even have time to notice the neighborhood or the residence, just that it was made of brown rectangular stones, hence the term "brownstone," she surmised. *So no marble palace for the Reynoldses.*

A bit of a disappointment, but no matter.

A butler stood by the open door. Bev's maid was waiting with the smelling salts. Bentley must have alerted the household before he let them out of the carriage. A good man, Bentley. Philomena would give him a substantial tip when she said *adieu*, which might be sooner than she expected, considering the circumstances.

Bev waved the maid aside. "Go away, Elmira. I don't need smelling salts. What I need is a cocktail. Tuttle?"

The butler bowed, followed Philomena and Bev into the parlor, and shut the double doors behind them.

"I suppose you've heard the ghastly news," Bev said.

"Yes, madam. Bentley informed us, and on behalf of the entire household, may I offer you our profound condolences."

"Thank you. Do we have ice?"

"Yes, madam." He went about making drinks.

Philomena pulled the pins from her hat and tossed it on the sofa next to her. She found Bev staring at her.

"Is something wrong?"

"No, I'm just always amazed at your hair. The color is so . . . so . . . Remember Monsieur André the drawing master said you looked like you'd stepped straight from a Titian painting."

"Monsieur was drunk most of the time, or he would have

noticed that my hair is mostly mahogany and only hints at his favorite Titian red in the sunlight."

"I think he was in love with you."

Philomena puffed a French expletive. "I think he was in love with having all the young girls dote on him."

"He was definitely that."

Bev was silent until Tuttle had handed them glasses and left—reluctantly, Philomena thought—the room.

"They all think I killed him."

Philomena almost choked on her drink. She looked over the rim of her glass and perused her friend's face. Should she pooh-pooh the idea or be honest? Best to get it over with. "Did you?"

"Good heavens, Phil, how could you even think that?"

"I don't really, but you didn't answer my question."

"How could I kill him? I loved him." Bev paused and took a healthy gulp of her martini. Sighed. "I loved him, but I didn't much like him anymore. We still had some fun, when he wasn't out carousing with Miss Potts."

"The woman in the auto with him?"

Bev nodded. "Mimi LaPonte. Real name Mildred Potts. A chorus girl from a variety show.

"Ugh! It's all so awful and I'm so glad to see you. You look wonderful. And out of mourning at last." She sniffed. "I've made such grand plans for your entertainment. What on earth was Reggie thinking of to get offed at a time like this." Bev dabbed her handkerchief to her nose. "Oh, Lord, some friends are coming over for pretheater drinks. We thought an evening at the variety would be entertaining. There's the Langham ball on Friday and the opera. And the races, of course."

Bev emptied her glass. "I suppose we'll have to cancel tonight's get-together. But how will we reach them all? Tuttle, I need Tuttle."

Philomena found the bell and rang for the butler.

"Why don't you let Tuttle and me take care of the guest list and you go upstairs for a rest?"

"What? Oh, no, I need another martini."

The butler appeared in the doorway. Without pausing, he crossed the room and made another round of drinks.

As they waited for him to finish, Philomena leaned over to her friend. "You should ring up your solicitor before your second martini."

Bev shook her head. "You said we have until tomorrow."

"I can't be certain. I told the police officer you would receive him in the morning."

"Tuttle, do we have a solicitor?" Bev asked as she took a martini from the tray.

"Of course, madam, but I've taken the liberty to telephone your cousin Freddy. He might be more useful at this point than the solicitor."

Bev's teeth clinked against the martini glass. "Do you think so? Freddy?"

"Yes, madam, at this juncture. Though I will ask Mr. Brangle to come to you tomorrow if you wish."

"You're right, of course, Tuttle. Thank you. But the guests for this evening?"

"Mr. Freddy said he would take care of it. And that he would visit you around six o'clock. He isn't able to get away from meetings before that."

"Yes, well. Thank you, Tuttle, that will be all."

"Who is Freddy?" Philomena asked as soon as Tuttle left the room.

"Reggie's cousin. He's some pooh-bah at City Hall. Totally dissipated, which is what happens if you hang around Reggie for any length of time. But he's a dear old thing." Her voice caught. "Freddy will know what to do."

With their second drinks in hand, the two women grew silent and Philomena looked at her surroundings. It was an odd assortment of old family furniture, she guessed, mixed with newer pieces, several lovely *japonais* lacquer pieces, artwork ranging from what appeared to be a Gainsborough to several rather naughty pen-and-inks. There was the usual Turkey carpet on the floor and an electric chandelier overhead. It all felt vaguely modern and yet . . . displaced.

"I suppose I shouldn't be surprised that Reggie met his end violently. You should see some of the characters he hung out with. And the women, and the way he spent money."

Philomena remembered Reggie as mildly charming, but already looking a bit worse for wear when she'd met him last year at Ascot, where he had a horse running. Not a hunting man, Reggie was a racing man, and evidently had the stables to prove it.

"He just bought that new touring auto. First of all his friends, he said. That was Reggie for you, fast drinking, fast driving, fast living. He did everything fast." Bev sighed. "Even during the times he should be going slow . . . If you know what I mean."

Philomena spluttered into her drink. "I believe I do."

"The big nitwit didn't get that some things require attention, not a hell-bent-for-leather gallop to the finish line."

"I wonder if Miss Potts felt the same way."

"She'd better. That would be the last straw."

Philomena could sympathize with both women. She'd had a few lovers whom she would have gladly murdered for their lack of prowess where it counted most. But at least she had been able to pick and choose. Poor Bev was stuck with Reggie. Well, no longer.

"Mimi LaPonte, my *derrière*." Bev finished her second drink. "And now I'll have to be in mourning for a year or more; my family are such sticklers."

"They always are," Phil said under her breath.

"Pardon?"

"Nothing, just thinking about families."

"And how will I introduce you to Manhattan society if I'm stuck at home in widow's weeds?"

Yes, how indeed? Phil pushed down the bubble of panic that was mixing with her martini. She had money enough to keep herself and her two servants for a few lavish months, thanks to her grandmother's foresight in leaving legacies to the Hathaway girl children. Her dowager's—she shuddered at the word—allowance was barely pin money. The earl had squeezed what was left of his estate dry before he died. The heir was an abstemious Methodist.

Manhattan promised to be as expensive as London, and she couldn't afford to cut corners if she meant to start a new life in society.

She'd planned on staying with Bev and Reggie as long as they would keep her, and she was sure Bev would still welcome her, but that didn't really relieve the problem of getting out and mingling.

Well, the situation might resolve itself if they carted Bev off to jail.

But she couldn't let Bev be arrested. She'd seen the inside of a jail once when she'd befriended a suffragette who had chained herself outside the Exchequer's residence on Downing Street. Bev would never survive prison. Phil would just have to do something to ensure her freedom—even if she had killed her odious husband.

Bev finished her drink and showed all the signs of lying down for a rest. Philomena took the glass from her hand and returned both glasses to the drinks cabinet.

"Come on, what you need is a nice hot bath and a lie-down before Cousin Freddy arrives."

Bev let Philomena pull her from the sofa. She was as malleable as warm wax and for a minute Phil was afraid she was going to have to call for assistance, but Bev roused herself.

"I'm a terrible hostess. You must be fagged to death. We'll both have a lie-down, then dinner at home."

Upstairs, Philomena deposited Bev with her maid, who was waiting patiently in her boudoir. Then she made her way to her own room, where Lily was pacing the carpet with the look of murder in her eyes.

"Well, well," Phil said. "This is probably not what you expected when you agreed to be a lady's maid."

"Was he murdered? Madam," she added as an afterthought.

"Possibly. Probably. Does that frighten you? I promise, I'll keep you safe."

"It doesn't fr-r-r-ighten me," Lily returned, rolling her *r*'s in the way she did when emotion got the better of her.

The sound grated on Phil's ears. "Then what disturbs you?"

"That other maid. Elmi-r-r-r-a. She has airs. And she is an American."

Phil laughed. "Oh, my dear, Americans are allowed to have airs, too."

"Bah."

"What are they saying downstairs?"

"How should I know, when they shut up the minute I come into the room?"

"Well, never mind. Downstairs people are usually higher sticklers than upstairs. It will take some time for you to insinuate yourself—as certainly you must—into their midst." She tapped her ear. "*Comprends tu?*"

"*Oui, madame. Je comprends* very well. I am to spy for you."

Phil took a deep breath. "I was thinking of something a little more subtle than that."

"Yes, madam. I understand that, too, but they are very annoying."

"Be patient. Now pour me a bath, please. All this tramping about on the streets of New York has left me dusty and not quite the thing."

Lily slipped through the dressing room and into the bath beyond. The sound of gushing water began soon after and Lily returned to help her out of her dress. "You will be going out this evening?"

"No, but there will be at least one visitor in connection with Mr. Reynolds's demise, so I will need to dress for dinner. But I think . . . something demure."

"Do you have such a gown?"

"Don't be sarcastic, Lily. You must at least pretend to be servile."

Lily dropped to her knees. "Oh, I am. I owe you my life. Sometimes I forget who I am now."

And who were you before? I wonder. One day hopefully Lily would trust her enough to tell her story. Until then . . .

Phil smiled. "Not that servile. Please get up. I'm sure you would have managed on your own, but I think we do quite well together."

"Yes, madam. Very well."

The bath was indeed hot and filled the deep marble tub. Phil slid into the water with a satisfied sigh, leaned her head back on the rim, and closed her eyes.

Deliciously hot running water. Another good reason for living in Manhattan.

Lily came behind her and began to pour water over her shoulders. "I think it was in poor taste for her husband to die where all could see."

"I completely agree," Phil said. "But we shall keep all opinions to ourselves in this house and everywhere. I believe Mr. Reynolds was acquainted with some none-too-savory characters. We don't want to incur any hard feelings."

"Humph." Lily came to the side of the tub. "I am not afraid." She pulled up one side of her dress. "I have this." A wickedly long knife was strapped to her ankle.

"Good heavens," Phil exclaimed. "What if someone were to see that?"

"They would run away very fast."

Phil sat up and rested her elbows on the side of the tub. "That or slit your throat while you leaned over to retrieve it. Besides, it's extremely unladylike, and you should find a better place to keep it."

"Where do you suggest, madam? My linen dr-r-rawer?"

"I was thinking perhaps your thigh."

Philomena was downstairs when Freddy Beecham arrived. She'd dressed in an at-home dinner gown of muted rose silk moiré.

The only black gown she owned was an exquisite silk cut velvet with hand-embroidered borders designed by Worth. Definitely not mourning wear and not to be wasted at home on Reggie's cousin.

Freddy stepped into the parlor and looked around until his eyes settled on Philomena. He dipped his chin in her direction. "You must be Lady Dunbridge," he said with a slight nod, and strode toward her. "Poor Bev has been so looking forward to your visit, and now this. How is she?"

Philomena held out her hand and he kissed it lightly. "I expect her to come down shortly. She was still dressing when I stopped by her room earlier."

"Ah, yes, well." He turned slightly, his gaze taking in the drinks tray. "Care for a drink? I could use one myself. Terrible, terrible business. I'll just pour if you, um, your ladyship doesn't mind."

"I don't mind at all. And please let's not stand on ceremony. Call me Philomena."

He relaxed visibly. He was a tall, stout man and younger than Phil had been expecting, after Bev's "dear old thing," maybe late thirties or early forties with light brown hair parted slightly off center and pomaded to each side. He'd evidently stopped at home before coming here since he was dressed in evening wear. A quick "strategy meeting," a couple of drinks, and he'd still make the theater by curtain time.

"Freddy," said Bev, gliding into the room and looking romantically pale in an elegant black gown. Not a mourning dress by any stretch of the imagination. Low cut in front and trimmed in jet and deep carmine glass beads. She looked stunning.

Freddy obviously thought so, too. He hastily put down the glass he'd just picked up. He rushed to meet her and took both her hands in his. "My dear."

"Oh, Freddy." Bev melted against his chest.

"There, there," he said, patting her back. "Buck up. We'll see this through."

"How? What are we to do? There will be such a scandal. And Papa will be mad as nails. He warned me time and again to take Reggie in hand. But there's no dealing with either of them."

"I know. You just let me handle this."

"Will you, Freddy? Can you fix it?"

"Well, for the most part. I can at least focus the attention elsewhere. At least for a while." He glanced at Philomena, lowered his voice. "There isn't anything particular I should know?"

Bev pulled away far enough to look up at him. "I don't understand."

Philomena did. She wasn't the only one who wondered if somehow Bev had managed to kill her husband or arranged to have him killed. Everyone knew America was filled with gangsters ready to murder for payment.

"You don't own a pistol, do you? Don't say a word. Only if you do, have one of the servants dispose of it immediately. And don't be stingy with your appreciation."

"But I don't own one."

"Well, then, nothing to worry about."

They both told Freddy their versions of what had happened. He nodded and hmm'ed and fixed them all another drink. "I'll see what I can do to make this as painless as possible. I'm honored, Lady Dunbridge—Philomena—to have the ear of several influential men in the government as well as the police force. I'll see that the situation is treated with sensitivity and discretion."

"Indeed." *Bribery* is what he meant, she had no doubt. He was already calculating whose palms he could anoint. So no minor official, then.

It was a good thing that Philomena had spent time in country houses and on the hunting field with some of the more interesting political figures of the realm—and their wives. She'd learned quite a bit about how to stanch rumors and stop speculations. Not that she always bothered when it came to her own indiscretions.

The English lords used power or the withholding of power to achieve their ends. Americans, it appeared, resorted to money.

Phil understood the allure of money, but she didn't trust it as much as she trusted power. So she would leave Freddy to pay off whom he would and wait to see how long it would take John Atkins or the newspapers to uncover his schemes.

For herself and Bev's sake, she thought they needed a little more activity.

The doorbell rang, followed by muted voices.

"It's probably Marguerite," Freddy said. "I dropped by home on my way here and she stayed behind to telephone the guests to cancel the party."

A woman hurried in. "Oh, my poor dear Bev. I'm so sorry." She took Bev into a hug.

Very affectionate, these Americans. Phil wasn't sure she would enjoy being mauled by everyone she knew.

Introductions were made. More drinks were passed around, this time by Tuttle.

Philomena had no love for Reggie Reynolds. Well, in truth she hardly knew the man, but it did seem that everyone was acting very cavalier about his death.

Marguerite Beecham took a seat next to Bev on the sofa. She was very petite, dainty almost, with deep golden hair and large blue eyes, and like her husband was dressed for the theater. She took one of Bev's hands. "I telephoned or sent around notes to everyone I could. We'll just have to turn the others away."

Bev nodded and slipped her hand from Marguerite's in order to dab her handkerchief to her eyes. "Thank you, Marguerite, you're so kind."

"Not at all. Do you have any idea of who Reggie might have invited without your knowledge?"

Bev shook her head. "Tuttle will just have to turn them away with our apologies. Lord, we have canapés and crudités enough for an army. I suppose the staff can have them for their dinner and we'll just have to throw the rest away."

"Well, anything that can be kept, they should refrigerate. You're bound to have a crush of condolence calls."

Bev sank back again. "Phil, you should go to the variety with Freddy and Marguerite."

"Nonsense," Freddy said. "None of us is going. We wouldn't dream of leaving you alone at a time like this, unless of course the countess . . ." He ducked his head in Phil's direction.

"No indeed," Phil said. Besides, she wanted to hear more about how Freddy was going to "handle" things and whether that extremely coarse, not-to-be-trusted police detective would make a surprise visit.

The four of them were sitting in the parlor when the doorbell rang for the third time. There was a commotion in the foyer and four people burst into the room—two couples, all dressed in the latest mode and smelling of L'Origan *parfum* and bay rum.

Tuttle followed them in.

"Tuttle said you weren't at home, but we had to give our condolences in person. Our poor, poor Bev. We just can't believe it." They clustered around Bev, making soothing noises with a little too much gusto.

Bev motioned to the butler. "I think you'd better bring up some champagne. I suppose . . . the grand cru."

"Yes, madam." Tuttle took his leave.

Philomena followed him out as Freddy began passing around cocktails.

Another group swept past her. A footman stood rigid and open-mouthed at the door.

"I'm sorry, Mr. Tuttle," he stammered. "They just pushed past me. There was nothing I could do."

"Go to the cellars and bring several bottles of champagne. The grand cru." Tuttle sounded like he might choke on the words. He turned to Philomena, and she realized that he was waiting for her to give him orders.

"I don't think we'll be rid of them easily. Perhaps you should ask Cook to serve the canapés. I believe we're having a wake."

Another group arrived before he could get away; this time they poured into the foyer, dropping coats and top hats wherever they could. Almost a dozen in all rushed into the parlor. "Look who we picked up on the sidewalk outside. They said they'd been turned away. Nonsense, I say. Where's Reggie?"

Philomena and Tuttle exchanged looks, then he bowed and hurried away.

Philomena returned to the parlor, where the noise level had risen as the news of Reggie's demise spread to the newcomers.

"Shot, you say?"

"Good heavens, a robbery. Getting so you can't walk the streets."

"The Florodora girl? She didn't—Oh, sorry, Bev."

Bev waved a languid hand.

At least they weren't accusing Bev—yet.

"We'll give him a sendoff. Here's to Reggie. A fine fellow."

Those who had glasses raised them. "To Reggie."

"Who are these people?" Phil asked Bev when she managed to get close to her.

"I don't know half of them. This is just like Reggie to invite all these strangers and not be here to greet them."

Phil cut a look at her friend. Reggie wouldn't be greeting guests ever again. At least not on this mortal plane. Perhaps Bev was suffering more from shock than Phil had realized.

Someone claimed Bev's attention and Phil moved away.

She broached the subject to Freddy.

"Not much we can do at this point, except remind them of curtain time and hope they take the rest of these folks with them. Reggie was always doing this—bringing home people, his cronies from the track or the gentlemen's clubs or God knows where. He had no regard for how it looked. No regard at all. Stupid, selfish man. And to do this to such a lovely girl as Bev. I wouldn't blame her if she had—" He broke off. "Sorry. Forgot what I was going to say."

—If she had killed her husband?

As Philomena was returning to Bev, she noticed one of the guests standing by the French window. He'd come in with the last large group. She'd noticed him right away. His manner was not the insouciant carelessness of Reggie's friends—refined yet possibly dangerous. She reminded herself she was at a wake. But really, murder or suicide, an alluring man was an alluring man. She caught his eye and tilted her head, acknowledging him and letting him know she'd seen him and that it would be appropriate for him to introduce himself, but he turned away and was lost among the revelers who littered the floor.

In England she might suspect him of giving her the cut direct. Then she turned and saw him watching her, only to turn away again. Odd, but she'd never learned to understand the manners of these Americans.

The champagne flowed freely. Occasionally she'd see her intriguing guest standing near one group or the other, but he never came any closer to her. It was just a tad lowering.

Tray after tray of hors d'oeuvres were served and eaten. The "mourners" became more boisterous.

Bev sat on the couch, letting Phil mingle with the guests as titular hostess.

As the evening wore on, she found herself getting annoyed at their elusive guest. She must have met every other person in the room, some of them twice, and yet he always managed to elude her.

As far as she could tell from a distance, he was just what she liked. Tall but slight, with dark, slicked-down hair. A well-kempt mustache that could be easily dealt with if the occasion ever arose—she *did* despise hairy kisses. The earl had nurtured his carefully, and his kisses always left her mouth feeling as if she'd just eaten waxed fruit.

She pointed him out to various people, but no one seemed to know his name.

"Must be one of Reggie's turf friends," said one of Bev's friends.

"Must be someone his wife knows," said Reggie's friends.

" 'Fraid I don't know the family. We're friends from the club. Reggie said to come on over tonight."

"Which gentleman?"

"There." But he had stepped from view.

Was he doing this on purpose? Some kind of titillating game? Normally Philomena would enjoy this kind of cat-and-mouse dalliance. But it was beginning to feel like work, and that was no way to begin a flirtation.

At one point during the evening she spied him standing much closer to her than usual as he leaned over to light a cigarette. She wove her way past the inebriated guests to where he'd been standing only to find nothing but the lingering aroma of an unusual and exotic tobacco.

Oh, yes, Phil thought, an evasive and exotic tease, like its owner.

Unfortunately, any furtherance of their acquaintance would have to wait. Bev was looking fagged to death. Phil needed to call an end to the wake.

She enlisted Marguerite, who agreed that the evening was setting the wrong tone and went off to find her husband and ask him to rid the house of the partygoers.

Philomena found Bev back on the sofa. She squeezed in beside her. "I'm going to send these people away, you're exhausted."

"Yes, please."

"But first, who is that man?"

"Which one?"

Phil pointed discreetly to where the mysterious gentleman had just appeared. He was gone again. She perused the room, but this time she didn't catch sight of him.

"It doesn't matter. I'll just get rid of your guests." Phil took a glass and ice tongs from the drinks table and clinked the crystal for silence. At last the conversation died down.

"Thank you for coming to pay your condolences. But I'm sure you all have plans for the evening, and Mrs. Reynolds is very tired. The butler will see you out. This way please." She started herding people out of the room. Marguerite took the cue and ushered a handful of guests toward the door. Freddy stood in the foyer thanking everyone for their kind visits while Tuttle and the footman doled out hats, coats, and scarves as quickly as they could.

At last they closed the door behind the revelers.

"Bev is exhausted. I'm sending her to bed."

"Right, right," Freddy said. "What an untenable situation. But what could we do? It would have been impolite to turn them away."

Of course, Freddy didn't have to pay for the liquor and food.

Marguerite took her coat from the butler. "I'll come to see Bev tomorrow."

The door finally closed on them, and Philomena returned to Bev. The room was filled with mountains of dirty glasses and plates and overflowing ashtrays. A shambles.

She turned to find Tuttle standing in the doorway. "We're expecting the police detective in the morning."

"Yes, my lady. I will make certain the maids pay particular attention to the cleaning and airing."

"Thank you, Tuttle. That will be all."

Bev poured two more glasses of champagne and sank onto the sofa. "I thought they would never leave. Did you ever find your mystery man?"

"No," Phil said thoughtfully. "He must have left before the others."

"Poor Phil. I'm sorry to have ruined your first day in America."

"It's not your fault."

"Hmmm." Bev closed her eyes.

What a mess, thought Philomena. She crossed to the French window and looked out into the night. She should be out there making her way in the world, going to the theater, taking New York by storm.

A light flared on the street. Someone lit a cigarette, leaned against the lamppost, and . . . stared up to her window. She peered back at him. Surely it was the man from the party. But what was he doing there?

A thief who planned to come back and burgle the house? He'd not get past her. She marched to the front door. The footman scrambled out of his straight-back chair to open it for her.

She stood on the stoop looking up and down the street. It was empty. The man, of course, was gone.

3

Birds. Lady Dunbridge swore she could hear birds.

"No!" She stuffed the pillow over her head. So it hadn't been a bad dream. She was at the grouse shoot at Henley-on-Thames.

And she actually thought she'd made it to New York. The bit about the murder and the wake must have been the delectable dream.

"Madam."

Madam?

Phil turned over and pulled the pillow off her face. Blinked against the light streaming through the window of . . . Bev's guest bedroom. She sat up, dislodging the pillow to the floor.

"Oh, thank God!" she said with a sigh of relief.

Lily stood at her bedside, holding a cup of hot coffee.

"It's Lily," Phil said with enthusiasm.

"And who else would it be?" Lily handed her the cup and Phil leaned forward while Lily replaced the pillows behind her back.

"No one at all. Excellent. It must be morning."

"It's past nine o'clock. And old slouch face has been sitting in a chair outside your door since seven."

"Who?" Phil asked with a raised eyebrow.

"Mr. Pr-r-reswick," Lily said.

"Now, Lily. It's thanks to Mr. Preswick that you, and I for that matter, are starting life in the United States."

Lily looked at the floor.

"He may be slow and not quite up-to-date in his thinking,

but he's very loyal, even to you. That's the best quality you can have in a friend or a servant or a master."

Lily looked up through long black lashes. "I have to like him?"

"Yes."

"He thinks I'm a wh—"

"I'm sure he doesn't. But—did you say past nine? Good heavens." Phil set down her cup and pushed the covers away. "That unkempt policeman is going to be arriving here soon. Tell Preswick I'll talk to him later. I must get dressed. Is Bev up? Tell him to ask the butler—the other butler—what's his name . . . Tuttle, to have—Oh, it's too complicated. Find me something to wear. The maroon-and-eggplant China silk, I think. I'll be right back. I have to make sure Bev's awake."

"But you hate that dress."

"I'm meeting the police. I need to look *formidable*." She slid off the bed, pushed her arms into the sleeves of her dressing gown, her feet into her slippers, and rushed out of her room, past Preswick, who sprang from the straight-backed chair that had been placed near her door. To guard her chamber? There wasn't an even remotely interesting male in the house.

She sped down the hall to Bev's room.

A quick knock and she opened the door. As she suspected, Bev was fast asleep in a gigantic four-poster bed beneath a persimmon satin comforter. Phil strode to the bellpull and rang for Bev's maid.

"Wake up, Bevvy," Phil cajoled, using her school days nickname.

Bev moaned, turned over.

"Come on, Bevvy, look alive. It's time for morning prayers."

"Nooo. Madame Floret will make us write 'I am a sinner' one hundred times if we're late. Tell her I'm sick."

"Bev. Wake up. That police detective will be here any minute and we haven't even breakfasted."

One of Bev's eyes opened. She saw Phil and closed it again. "I'd rather face Madame Floret than your rumpled filthy policeman."

So would I, Phil thought, but there was no hope for it. "Oh, good. Here is Elmira."

"Yes, my lady?"

Better manners than her own servant, who refused to say "my lady" and when forced to do so, managed to roll the words despite the absence of any *r*'s.

"Please see that Mrs. Reynolds gets dressed and comes downstairs immediately. I'll be in the breakfast room."

Elmira curtseyed and turned to Bev.

Philomena left them to it.

But Phil was not allowed to breakfast in peace. She dressed in the despised maroon gown—why she'd let herself be talked into buying it was beyond her memory—and descended the stairs to find two butlers standing in the foyer.

If she hadn't been so preoccupied with Reggie's death she would have foreseen this problem. Preswick was not about to cede his duties to his mistress even in someone else's house under the control of someone else's butler.

She attempted to nod once, taking in both men.

"Preswick, the police should be here any minute, but we shall speak later. Tuttle, I'll be in the breakfast room if he arrives before Mrs. Reynolds comes downstairs."

"Yes, my lady. This way, please."

They hadn't gone two steps before the doorbell rang.

So much for breakfast or even a cup of coffee.

Preswick started automatically toward the door. But Tuttle turned on his heel and caught up to him.

They stood eyeing each other while the doorbell rang again. Tuttle gave the extraneous butler a sharp look intended to put him in his place. But Preswick wasn't so easy to intimidate. And while the two butlers stared at each other, the footman opened the door.

Phil saw it all, and though she tried to duck into the parlor before the detective entered, the butlers were blocking her way. So instead of standing at the French window of the parlor looking *formidable* when the detective entered, she was caught running across the middle of the foyer floor.

She froze and straightened up to her most dignified manner as he stepped into the hall. She was relieved to see that he was wearing a familiar but clean overcoat and hat.

"Detective Sergeant Atkins," Tuttle announced superfluously.

"Good morning, Detective." Phil smiled graciously, in a manner any dowager would be proud of. Her stomach growled, echoing through the foyer with humiliating clarity.

The detective nodded slightly. "Lady Dunbridge, I'm afraid I've interrupted your breakfast."

"Not at all." She hadn't even had a full cup of coffee.

He removed his hat and handed it to Tuttle.

All thought of breakfast flew from Phil's brain.

My, my, she thought. Could this possibly be the Detective Sergeant Atkins from the wharf? *That* detective had been a dirty, uncouth derelict. *This* detective looked like one of the rugged Wild West cowboys on the covers of the imported dime novels that were so popular among the staff at Dunbridge Hall.

He was tall with a firm jaw, thick hair, something she was particularly fond of, and clean shaven, something else she was extremely fond of. All that was missing was his faithful steed, and she was tempted to take a peek out the window to see if perhaps . . .

He shrugged out of his overcoat, which he gave to the footman. Beneath it, he wore a well-cut suit.

Her stomach growled again, but she didn't think it was over eggs and toast.

"Shall you use the parlor, my lady?" Tuttle asked, stressing "my lady," for the policeman's benefit, Phil was sure.

She led the way, the skirts of her train rustling with superiority. Really, he was the most gorgeous man. Too bad he was a policeman. Yet, this was America. Much more democratic in their notions than the English.

Come to think of it, the possibilities were endless.

"Lady Dunbridge, I must apologize if I frightened you yesterday. I was in the vicinity on another case. 'Undercover,' as we say in the force, and that is why I was called to the docks to take charge of the situation."

"But you are here today."

"Well, the Reynoldses' address is in my jurisdiction."

"I see." So they were not to be rid of this troublesome detective, a delightful and frightening circumstance. A sliver of panic put an end to any notion of the policeman's charm, leaving only the fright. What was she thinking? Why had she overslept? Why hadn't she refused the guests from last night?

What if there was still evidence of the wake? She quickly glanced around the room and saw that Tuttle had been true to his word. The room was clean; there was the merest lingering odor of tobacco, but that might be normal for American drawing rooms.

"Please be seated." She indicated the wing chair and seated herself on the couch.

The detective sat without hesitation and looked totally comfortable. Well, he was extremely appealing and he did have the upper hand, she had to admit. She sincerely hoped that Tuttle was informing Bev that the detective was here and waiting for her to make an appearance. Phil didn't think it was her place to play hostess in a murder investigation.

She waited. Something she'd learned from her father, not the kindest of that breed, but a consummate master of wielding power. Never speak before your petitioners. Let the weakest begin the attack.

"I see the Reynoldses' servants did an admirable job of cleaning up after last evening."

Phil blinked. Well, she hadn't expected that approach. And how the deuce did he know? She lifted an eyebrow.

"You received quite a number of guests last night."

Well, Papa, what now? He's doing all the talking and I feel like the person of weakness.

The detective sergeant cocked his head.

"There were a number of close friends who wished to pay their condolences."

"Quite a number of friends."

"Mr. Reynolds was a popular man; he had many friends," Philomena answered. This inanity could go on all day and she'd hoped to get some idea of what he wanted before Bev arrived.

"Evidently, and very lively ones."

Phil gritted her teeth. He was goading her. Well, let him goad. "Do you make a practice of spying on the bereaved?"

His expression didn't change, but Phil hadn't existed in society for nearly a decade without learning to recognize the change in temperature. And the air around him had definitely gotten cooler.

"I had men watching the house . . . for your safety."

"Do we need protecting?"

"That's what I'm trying to ascertain." He smiled, but it wasn't reassuring in the least. "I was hoping to speak to Mrs. Reynolds this morning."

"I'm afraid she's still deeply in shock."

"Good morning, Detective Sergeant," Bev said from the doorway. She looked ravishing in a midnight blue tea gown shot with silver strands and embellished with a filigreed shoulder cape.

She glanced at the policeman, then to Phil, and widened her eyes.

Phil could have kicked her shins but had to settle for a meaningful look, which she was afraid Bev missed completely since she seemed smitten with the detective sergeant.

"I'm so sorry not to be down to welcome you, but I . . ." She finished the statement by lifting the back of her hand to her forehead, creating a perfect picture of mourning and loss and leaving the detective sergeant an unobstructed view of her inviting décolleté.

On second glance, Bev did look awfully faint, and the detective and Phil moved at the same time as Bev swayed on her feet. Together they led her to the sofa.

"I do beg your pardon," Bev said, holding on to both of them and pulling them closer as if she were about to impart a secret. Phil fervently hoped she wasn't about to confess.

"Would you mind terribly, Detective Atkins, if I asked Tuttle to bring coffee? I'm feeling just a little . . ." She fumbled in her sleeve for her handkerchief and dotted her eyes.

For the first time since she'd arrived, Phil wondered if her friend was showing her true colors. Or giving them a run. She was brought to mind of a night during their youth when they were returning after curfew to school. They were a little tipsy, or perhaps they'd been rip-snorting drunk—it was hard to remember. They had hiked up their skirts to climb the school fence when they were stopped by a gendarme. Bev had whipped out her handkerchief and begun a story of a party where they had been drinking punch not knowing it was spiked and they were so afraid that Madame Floret would be disappointed in them. It was a total lie. They were always in trouble. But whether he'd believed them or not, he'd helped them climb the fence and, with an admonishment to be more careful in the future, watched until they were safely bestowed inside.

Once coffee was served and Detective Sergeant Atkins had been persuaded to take a cup, he took a notebook from his pocket. "I'm afraid I must ask you some questions about yesterday," he said. "Normally I would bring an officer to record our conversation, but I thought you might prefer more privacy."

Phil didn't miss the tightening of his jaw as he finished the sentence. Had he been instructed to be discreet? Was this evidence of Freddy's handiwork so soon?

"Thank you." Bev didn't simper. She didn't have to; Phil was fairly certain poor John Atkins was caught.

John Atkins cut Phil a look.

Well, perhaps not entirely caught.

"Can you tell me what occurred at the wharf?"

Bev rolled her eyes upward as if she were about to recite sums. "I was there to meet Phil's ship—my friend Philomena Amesbury, Countess of Dunbridge."

"And why did you leave your position there?"

"I realized that Reggie hadn't seen us, so I went to tell him to drive closer."

"And when you arrived . . . ?"

"When I arrived, Reggie was dead and that . . . and Mimi LaPonte was holding him in her arms." She covered her face with both hands, looking so pure and innocent that Phil moved to put her arm around her.

Atkins seemed oblivious of her discomfort. "So he was dead when you arrived at the car."

"She said he was," Phil snapped, leaping to Bev's defense.

Atkins plowed on. "Was he, Mrs. Reynolds?"

"Yes," Bev said, lowering her hands and clutching her handkerchief.

"And did you hear a shot?"

"I . . . yes, I must have. It just sounded like a loud pop. I was startled for a second, like one would be, but I didn't think anything of it."

"Can you describe the scene?"

"What?"

"Really, Detective Sergeant, is this necessary?" Phil asked. "I arrived shortly after she did. I can describe the details if you insist."

"Thank you, but all in good time."

"I just saw Reggie lying there, covered in all that blood. His head was in her lap and she was caterwauling that he'd shot himself." Bev straightened up. "Why? Why would Reggie shoot himself? I won't believe it. His thoroughbred Devil's Thunder is scheduled to run at Belmont in just a few days. He's favored to win. That . . . woman must have shot him. She must have forced her way into the auto and shot him."

"Are you acquainted with Miss LaPonte?"

"Only by reputation. Wives and mistresses don't tend to run in the same circles, Detective."

It was the first time since Phil had arrived that Bev showed that streak of bravado that had served them well in their many schoolgirl scrapes.

"I don't suppose they do. Did your husband own a revolver, Mrs. Reynolds?"

"Of course he did. Several, in fact. He needed the protection. It was sometimes necessary for him to carry large sums of cash on his person."

For instance, when he won at the racetrack, Phil thought. *Or for his mistress's allowance.* He must have been supporting her. Phil would have to ask Bev once the policeman was gone.

"He carried it in his coat pocket at the ready."

"Did you see a pistol when you looked into the car?"

Bev shook her head. "Only Reggie and all that blood."

Detective Atkins nodded and scribbled something in his book.

"Did you find a gun in his pocket?" Philomena asked.

"I'm not at liberty to say."

"It must have been," Bev said. "He always carried it when he was out on the streets."

Phil wanted to warn Bev to be more careful in her answers. She didn't think Bev was a murderess, but as the scorned wife, she might appear to be. They should have prepared better for this visit, but since neither of them had ever been involved with a police investigation—discounting that little misadventure back in London, and that certainly didn't count—they hadn't anticipated what questions he would ask.

"But if it was in his pocket . . ." Phil frowned at the detective.

"I didn't say that it was. Regardless . . ." He cast Bev an apologetic look. "If he killed himself, he didn't live long enough to return it to his coat."

"Ah." They hadn't found a pistol either. "So an unknown assailant must have murdered him," Phil said.

"Unknown as of now, but I have two very possible suspects."

"Oh, really, Detective Atkins. You can't imagine that Bev—Mrs. Reynolds shot her husband, so unless you think this Florodora girl did it . . . Do you?"

He opened his mouth.

"And don't say you're not at liberty to say."

"She did do it." Bev jumped up from the sofa. "I know it. That . . . that . . . woman killed my husband."

"Do you own a pistol, Mrs. Reynolds?"

Bev, who had crossed to the window, spun around. "Me?"

He didn't answer, merely raised his eyebrows

Her hand came slowly to clasp a cameo that hung around her neck on a thin gold chain. It was an elegant gesture and had the effect of drawing both Philomena's and the detective's attention to her graceful neck.

"No," she said tentatively. "Reggie once . . ."

Philomena's breath caught. "Another cup of coffee, Detective Sergeant?" she said, standing. Unfortunately, it was too early for cocktails. Heaven knew Phil could use one.

A slow smile curled his lip. Philomena couldn't tell if he was amused or going in for the kill.

"Are you attempting to distract an officer of the law?"

"I beg your pardon? I was being polite."

"Manners don't usually come into play in a police investigation."

"Fortunately, I have never had the occasion to be involved in one."

"Until now." He handed her his cup.

His hand was steady. She was afraid hers might not be, but she took the cup.

"Are you also questioning Mimi LaPonte?"

"We questioned her yesterday."

"And I suppose—"

"As soon as I conclude my conversation with Mrs. Reynolds, you'll have your chance to enlighten me, but for now . . ." He turned back to Bev. "Were you aware that your husband had a . . ."

"Mistress?" Bev supplied for him. "Quite a few. Is Miss Potts aware she wasn't the only one?"

Atkins blinked, either at her candor or because this was news to him. "Would you care to enumerate?"

Bev trilled a laugh, though it sounded a shade hysterical to Phil. "Detective Atkins, I lost count ages ago."

"Miss LaPonte—"

"Potts," Bev spit out.

Atkins's mouth twitched. "If you will. Miss Potts says he promised to leave you and elope with her."

"Rubbish," Bev said, but Phil noticed the two bright slashes of pink that sprang to her cheekbones. She was certain Atkins was aware of them, too.

"It's more likely just the opposite," Phil interposed. "He told her he wouldn't leave his wife, they argued, and she shot him. Did you ask her that?"

"I believe I'm the one asking the questions."

"And they're lovely questions, but perhaps you're asking the wrong people."

The detective's nostrils flared. Phil knew she had just crossed the lines of civility. Which she didn't mind doing on occasion. Only she didn't want to antagonize Detective Atkins. He might just hold their future in his hands.

"I beg your pardon, Inspector."

"Detective Sergeant."

"Of course. My apologies, Detective Sergeant. But if it wasn't suicide, and you don't think this Miss Potts killed him, then it obviously was murder by some ruffian in the crowd. With all the commotion and the crush of people and that marching band, anyone could have walked up to the automobile and shot him. I believe an anarchist murdered your president Mr. McKinley in much the same manner."

"We are considering all possibilities."

"Surely there were witnesses. And where was the driver during all this? Reggie was not dressed in motoring clothes, so he must have brought a driver. Maybe he's your anarchist."

The detective sighed and stood to take his forgotten coffee cup from the butler's tray.

"Lady Dunbridge, you have just demonstrated the problems with witness testimony."

Phil frowned. "I wasn't a witness. I didn't arrive until after I heard the shot."

"So I was told, and I would be much obliged if you would give your statement when I finish with—when my conversation with Mrs. Reynolds is at an end."

Phil tried not to smile at that. He was definitely watching his wording—and chafing beneath the need to do so—which meant he must have been ordered by someone higher up to tread lightly, and he didn't like it.

"And when did you arrive at the auto, Mrs. Reynolds?"

"What?"

"Where were you when the shot was fired?"

Phil opened her mouth to speak.

Atkins raised a hand to stop her.

"I—I don't know," Bev said. "I went to get him and he was lying there."

"And where were you, Lady Dunbridge?"

"When the shot was fired?"

He nodded.

"With Bentley. But we were right behind Bev—Mrs. Reynolds."

"How did you know to run to the automobile? Was there any reason to think someone would be shooting at Mr. Reynolds or his wife?"

"Bentley started running and I followed—" She saw that she

might be leading Bentley into trouble. If the American police were anything like the London constabulary—and it looked like they might be—they would love to blame an underling for wrongdoing rather than a member of the upper crust. She rapidly thought back to the events at the pier. "I believe he recognized Bev's scream."

Atkins turned back to Bev. "Did you scream? You didn't tell me about that."

"I screamed? Yes. I must have. I really—"

"She was probably too distraught to really know what was happening at that point," Phil said desperately. "But yes, she screamed. When we arrived at the car, she was barely supporting herself by holding on to the car door."

He shot a quelling look at Phil. "And did you open the door, Mrs. Reynolds?"

"Why . . . yes. I did. I saw that he'd brought that odious creature with him to pick up my friend. The nerve of the man."

"Bev," Phil warned.

"So I yanked the door open, and there he was, just lying there, with his head on her lap and blood—" She broke down.

Phil patted her hand but didn't take her eyes off the detective.

"Now we begin to get somewhere," he said.

"Yes," Phil agreed. "And Mimi LaPonte just sat there until she started crying, 'Reggie, why did you kill yourself?' She repeated it, more than once, very loudly. I wonder if it was the actress in her? She seemed determined to make us all hear her."

"Lady Dunbridge."

Phil barreled on. "Reggie was wearing a suit, not motor clothes. So where was the driver? I didn't see him by the car. Why wasn't he there trying to aid his master, um, employer?"

"The police are investigating."

"And the man I saw?"

Atkins shrugged slightly. "If he was there, he'd disappeared into the crowd by the time we went after him."

"He was there, all right. And the bag?"

"What bag?" Bev asked, rousing herself.

"There was a purse on the floorboards."

"Gone, probably snatched by a petty thief in the excitement. If there was a bag."

"There was a bag. I described it to you. And you lost it? It may have been important."

"Like I said, a petty thief, most likely, taking advantage of the commotion."

At that moment the double doors burst open and a stocky man, wearing a checked suit and bowler hat, burst into the room. "I came as soon as I heard." He saw the assembled occupants and skidded to a stop.

Phil caught a glimpse of Tuttle, Preswick, and the footman standing in the doorway.

"I'm sorry, madam," Tuttle said.

"It's quite all right," Bev said, and waved a dismissive hand. Tuttle closed the doors.

"This is Mr. Bobby Mullins, my husband's—my late husband's—stable manager."

"And right-hand man," Mullins said.

"And welterweight boxing champion in 1894," Atkins added. "You've put on a little flesh since then, Bobby."

Boxing. It was a universal truth that anywhere men met, boxing was sure to be the subject of conversation. And he certainly had put on a couple of stone if he'd been a welterweight. He was midheight and thick set. His suit barely buttoned around his middle.

Bobby recognized the detective and snatched the hat from his head, displaying a bush of carrot orange hair that seemed to defy the pomade that had been generously applied. "Constable Atkins."

"Detective Sergeant these days."

"So, is it true? Did somebody off Reggie?"

Bev gasped.

"Oh, sorry, Mrs. Reynolds." Mullins glanced over to the detective sergeant, then back to Bev. "I don't think you should be answering no more questions until you can get Freddy over here."

"It's all right, Bobby. I believe the detective sergeant is almost finished. Pour yourself a cup of coffee and have a seat."

"I'm almost finished for now, though I will be needing to speak to you all at a later time. Just one more question for Lady Dunbridge. Do you own a pistol?"

"I do," Phil said. "Though it was packed in my cases at the time. Besides, I have a witness."

"Oh," Bev said. "I'm sure the detective didn't mean to imply—"

"Not at all," Atkins said smoothly. "Though it does seem odd that a countess would own a pistol and you, Mrs. Reynolds, the wife of a, shall we say, cosmopolitan man about town, don't."

Bobby's cup clattered on the butler's tray.

Atkins shifted to Bobby. "Want to say something?"

Mullins shook his head.

"Are you sure? Withholding information is a serious offense."

"Just that she—" Mullins broke off, gulped his coffee. His eyes flitted to Bev and then to the floor.

"Does own a pistol?" Atkins asked.

"Well, yeah. Reggie gave it to her two Christmases ago. But it don't mean she shot him."

"Is this true?" he asked Bev.

"Well, yes. I'd forgotten all about it. I've never even used it. A horrid thing, I don't know why Reggie thought it would be a good present."

"That's right," Mullins said. "It were a pretty little thing, but she didn't want it and told him to take it away. He weren't none too happy, but he locked it in his desk drawer. It's probably still there right where he put it. Too girly for a man to use."

Atkins turned to Bev. "I'd like to see your husband's desk."

"It's in the library. Tuttle has the key. I'll ring for him."

"The study is kept locked? Isn't that rather unusual?"

Phil thought so.

"No. My husband always kept his study locked when he wasn't using it. He handled a great deal of cash and didn't want the servants to be tempted."

"I see."

Atkins suggested they might stay in the parlor while he looked over the study, but neither Phil nor Bev nor Bobby Mullins was having any of that. The four of them followed Tuttle to the back of the brownstone and waited expectantly while he unlocked the door.

Tuttle crossed the darkened room and opened the drapes, allowing the light to flood in. They all crowded through the doorway and stopped.

A man sat at Reggie's desk, one hand inside the top drawer.

"Who are you?" Bev demanded. "What are you doing in Reggie's chair? How did you get in?"

"He's going for the gun!" Bobby cried, and pushed Bev behind his substantial bulk.

"Nobody move," Atkins ordered. He drew his own gun from inside his jacket and aimed it at the man as he strode toward him.

Just as he reached the desk, the man nodded slightly, then abruptly fell forward, his forehead making a dull thump when it hit the desktop.

Bev screamed.

Phil stared in disbelief.

Atkins returned his revolver beneath his jacket and checked for the man's pulse. Shook his head slightly.

Careful not to touch anything, Atkins looked in the drawer, on the desk, and then on the floor around the man's feet. "Well, well, what do we have here?" He pulled the handkerchief from his jacket pocket and knelt down. When he stood, he was holding a small pistol.

"I don't suppose you know who owns this?" he asked.

"It's mine," Bev said, and crumpled to the floor.

4

What a dilemma, Phil thought as she let Bev collapse. Bev had always been the consummate fainter. And this was no different. Whether real or feigned, shock or hunger—God knew neither one of them had touched much food in the last twenty-four hours—or sheer theatricality, Bev was on her own.

This situation was rapidly getting out of control. A scandalous public death was one thing, but an unknown murder victim in one's library was more than just coincidence.

Phil was half aware of Tuttle rushing to help his mistress, Bobby Mullins inching backward toward the open door. Only Phil and Detective Sergeant Atkins were actually perusing the intruder.

The detective, after an initial instinctive move toward the fallen damsel, collected himself and pointed a finger at the retreating Mr. Mullins, who froze in his steps.

"I never saw him before in my life. I swear it."

"I don't believe you can see him now," Atkins returned. "I was merely going to ask if you'd kindly help Mrs. Reynolds back to the parlor."

"Criminy. She's out cold."

Atkins lifted his eyebrows, and Mullins quickly but not too gracefully hauled Bev into his arms.

"And wait there until I call for you," he added as Mullins staggered his way through the open door, followed closely by Tuttle tut-tutting and wringing his hands.

"Tuttle. Is that your name?"

"Yes, sir," Tuttle said, coming to a halt in the doorway and turning on his toe like an act from the Variety.

Oh dear, thought Phil. He *is* upset.

"Please send for Mrs. Reynolds's maid, then be so kind as to have one of the footmen stand guard on the door to the library while I contact the proper officers to investigate the scene."

"All but one of the footmen are off this morning, sir. The other is stationed at the front door. But there is a telephone on Mr. Reynolds's desk. He just had it put in a few months ago. You may use it."

The extra footmen off? The day after a death in the family when they would be needed more than ever as legal, clerical, and condolence calls would be made. Or had they merely been hired for last night's festivities? The Dunbridge estate hadn't come to that, but Phil knew plenty of houses that were mere shells whenever they were not being used for entertaining.

Was it possible that Bev and Reggie might be in financial trouble? If that were the case, things were looking bleak for all of them.

"One more thing, Tuttle."

Tuttle stopped midturn. "Yes, sir?"

"Did anyone have access to the library since yesterday when Mr. Reynolds left the house?"

"No, they did not. Mr. Reynolds handed me his key like he always does."

"He must have trusted you."

Tuttle didn't bother with an answer, but his look was what one might call quelling.

"And no one came in during the wake."

"They did not."

"The maids this morning?"

"No. I decided that under the circumstances we would leave the library as Mr. Reynolds left it."

"Good man."

"The decision was in deference to Mrs. Reynolds's feelings."

And not for your convenience, was the implication, and Phil had to give this American butler credit where it was due. He'd handled the detective admirably.

Atkins nodded slightly. "That will be all."

Tuttle bowed and left the room.

Phil sighed with relief. Tuttle had weathered the detective's questions without a blink.

Atkins glanced at Phil, who had lagged behind. "I'll need to speak with both you and Mrs. Reynolds . . . later. Thank you."

Phil peered around his shoulder for a glimpse of the body. "Detective Sergeant, there is a dead man in Mr. Reynolds's library. I must insist that you have him removed at once."

"All in good time. Once I complete my investigation, which I can't do until you return to the parlor."

"Investigation? What is there to investigate? One of Mrs. Reynolds's guests must have come in to use the telephone and had a heart attack."

"You heard the butler. The library was kept locked. He squeezed in through the keyhole, perhaps?"

She gave him a dour look.

"Thank you for your refreshing observations, but now if you would just—"

He reached for her, but she slipped deftly out of reach. Really, all those years gracefully evading the lechers of London society were already coming in handy in Manhattan.

"Detective Sergeant. In Mrs. Reynolds's absence, the duty of hostess falls to me. And I couldn't possibly leave Reggie's library unattended."

She gave him the dowager stare. "Don't you need someone to identify the poor soul?"

"Are you suggesting I call Mrs. Reynolds back in here?"

"Heavens no. Bev is much too upset. But I'm willing to take a look."

"Pardon me for saying so, but I was under the impression you had only arrived in the country yesterday."

"Yes, but he might have been present at the par—wake last evening." She bit her tongue. That would mean someone would have let him in, and Tuttle was the only one with the keys.

"And you would remember him?"

"I never forget a face."

Atkins bowed slightly and moved so she could see.

Phil swallowed, stepped closer, and peered at the man. His head had fallen to the side, leaving half his face exposed. Nondescript brown hair with thick sideburns, rough-shaven cheeks, and one side of a bushy handlebar mustache.

Not their mystery guest. She let out what she hoped was an unnoticeable sigh of relief. That would have been a disappointment.

"No, sorry, I've never seen him."

His jaw tightened. Phil could imagine him grinding his teeth. The detective, handsome or not, certainly wasn't accepting his place in the social strata.

"Mrs.—Lady—Dunbridge, thank you. Now I really must insist that you leave. A crime scene is not a place for amateurs."

"Amateurs?" Phil turned, rustling her formidable eggplant gown. And then she stopped dead. "Crime scene?"

He tilted his head. "Crime scene. Now if you will . . ." This time he gestured at the door and stepped toward her. She stood her ground.

"A thief, then. Who . . . broke in through the window? And then had a heart attack? I suppose it's possible." She slipped around the opposite side of the desk. The windows were nearly floor to ceiling in the French style and opened inward. "I suppose he could have broken the latch and climbed right through." She pulled back the drapes.

"Don't."

One glance had been enough to tell her the window was shut and the lock was still intact. But not so the glass. One rectangular pane was missing, and cool air wafted into the room. "Aha!"

"What? Leave that alone."

"See for yourself, Detective Sergeant."

"Don't touch anything."

She was getting a little irritated at these Americans with their fast cars, blatant love affairs, crime every time she turned around, *and* who felt they had the right to give her orders.

He reached over her head and, using the back of his hand, he pushed the drapes farther aside.

"Ah, yes, fingerprints. So you subscribe to that theory?"

He glared at her. "Fingerprinting is not a theory but a scientific method of identification."

She lifted her chin. "True, and there may be fingerprints," she explained. "Though I doubt you would find any on the drapes. The windowsill perhaps, or the desk but—"

Atkins beetled his eyes at her. A scowl became him. "What do you know about fingerprints?"

"I had the pleasure of meeting Sir Edward Henry at the Grosvenor ball several seasons ago. He invited me to a lecture he was giving at the Royal Society the following day, about whorls and loops and some such as I recall. Charming man."

Now she wished she'd paid more attention to the talk than to Sir Edward's equally charming secretary, who was devastatingly handsome and a bit of a flirt, the consequences of which she missed a good portion of the lecture.

"Why does that not surprise me?"

"I haven't the faintest—but why do you need fingerprints? You have the culprit and his fingers right here."

He cocked his finger toward the door. "Out."

Good God, things were rapidly deteriorating. She didn't know what Bev had gotten herself into, but she needed to find out before things became even more complicated, as from the looks of things, they promised to do.

She should have grilled Bev about the situation, except all those people descending on them the night before had made it impossible. As soon as she could get a moment alone with her friend, she would do just that. If there was something Bev wasn't telling, she needed to know it now. Before John Atkins did.

Since she was still standing at the window, with the dead man and desk between her and the door, she took a moment to peer at the victim's back and the jeweled dagger on the desk by his head.

"Of course, the dagger. There were two of them. A falling-out among thieves. But the window is locked. Why would they break in the window and then lock it behind them? And how did the other man get out?"

"Good question, which I will try to answer if you will just please vacate the room."

"There's no need to raise your voice, Inspector."

"Detective Sergeant."

"Oh, forgive me, I forgot. It's just like a stage play," she extemporized, while she made a quick search of the body and the desktop, stopped at the tiny hole in the man's jacket.

She peered closer and saw the dark corona around the hole, and noticed the faint odor of singed fabric for the first time. She'd seen the same type of burn when Bernie Oglethorpe dropped his loaded target pistol and shot a hole through his trouser cuff.

The man was shot, not stabbed, and Bev's pistol was found at his feet. Oh, yes, the detective sergeant was way ahead of her. And she knew right where they were both headed.

"So now you must look for a second thief?" she said, her mouth so dry she could hardly form the words.

Atkins didn't bother to answer, merely took her elbow and propelled her across the floor and out the door.

"My lady," Preswick exclaimed. He must have been waiting for her just outside the door, the dear.

"It's quite all right, Preswick. The detective sergeant was just accompanying me to the parlor."

Still holding her elbow, he trundled her down the hall. Tuttle was standing by the parlor door and, after a brief glance at Phil, opened the door.

Atkins stopped her on the threshold. "I don't trust you, Lady Dunbridge."

She looked up at him, tilting her head, attempting a gesture of question mixed with innocence and mild flirtation. "Why on earth not?"

"Humph." He dropped her elbow, waited for Tuttle to see her into the parlor, and strode away.

Phil stood with her back to the door, wondering how on earth she'd gotten into such a situation and why she didn't have Lily pack her bags. They'd be perfectly happy at the newly opened Plaza Hotel. Then she saw Bev lying on the sofa, her eyes closed, the dark lids making her complexion appear even paler than usual, and she relented. Loyalty, friendship—and, she had to admit, curiosity—won out over self-preservation every time. The more fool she.

Elmira knelt beside the couch chafing Bev's hands. A tray holding smelling salts and other preparations was set on the floor beside her. A few yards away, Lily looked ready to pounce. She held a small vial cradled in both hands. Phil didn't own smelling salts; she hadn't needed them once she realized that slightly easing her stays did wonders for breathing and the circulation.

"What have you there?" Phil asked her thunderous-looking lady's maid under her breath.

Lily opened her hand briefly, then covered the vial again. Phil's Radiant *parfum*.

Lily gave her a slight one-shoulder shrug. "I couldn't find a r-r-r-estor-r-rative."

"But didn't want to miss out on the action?"

Lily made a perfunctory curtsey.

Bev opened one eye, saw Phil. "What the devil is going on?" she whimpered. "Reggie murdered. A stranger dead in his library. And on an empty stomach. How am I expected to cope with this without my breakfast?"

"An excellent question." Phil rang for Tuttle and directed him to have breakfast served. She nixed his idea of serving Bev from a tray brought to her room, though she had no doubt they'd be plagued with the detective sergeant before their final cup of coffee. Bev needed to take command of the situation. And she couldn't do that from her sickbed.

"The morning room, my lady?"

"No, Tuttle, I believe the dining room." Morning rooms with their comfortable, gardenlike intimacy tended to invite confidence, something she wanted to avoid at all costs, at least until she could figure out what on earth was happening and to counsel her dear, outspoken friend to be discreet.

"Yes, my lady." He cut his eyes toward the door.

Oh, dear, what now? Phil thought and followed him into the hallway, only to find Preswick standing at the ready. The two butlers glared at each other.

Phil sighed. This would have to be dealt with. But not now. "What is it, Tuttle?"

"The police sergeant has called for additional support and several officers have arrived and are in the library."

"I see. Nonetheless, Mrs. Reynolds needs fortification."

"Yes, my lady. However, Cook was forced to return most of the dishes to the kitchen. She will need time to prepare a fresh repast."

"That's to be expected, Tuttle. Tell her we much appreciate her forbearance."

Tuttle bowed.

"Oh, Tuttle. The newspapers?"

"The morning edition of the *Post* has arrived, and several of the others that Mr. Reynolds had delivered to keep track of the racing news, but I took the liberty of keeping them in my parlor. Away from sensitive eyes."

"Excellent. Please make sure that Mrs. Reynolds doesn't see them. At least not until the . . ." She nodded in the direction of the library.

"Yes, my lady."

He bowed and walked away, only slightly raising his nose at Preswick as he passed.

Phil hurried over to her ruffled butler.

"My dear Preswick. Patience. Have you been apprised of the situation?"

"Yes, my lady, and if I may say, my lady, you have no business consorting with murderers and Florodora girls if you plan on entering New York society."

"How true, but unfortunately, it seems to be out of my hands. Are they making you comfortable here?"

"Yes, my lady. Mr. Tuttle has given me the use of his parlor, though—"

"Excellent. I'm sure you and Tuttle will get on famously."

"Yes, my lady."

"Good. Later you and Lily and I must have a private few minutes."

Preswick bowed and creaked off after Tuttle. Now to get Lily off her high horse and into the other servants' confidences. Phil might not have any intentions of leaving Bev in the lurch, but it was best to know your enemy—and your friends—and make contingency plans.

She returned to the parlor, where Elmira was still chafing Bev's hands. Lily looked on with an air of bored derision. No doubt she would have plenty to say later, but mercifully she held her tongue.

By the time Tuttle returned to announce that breakfast was ready, Bev was sitting up and Phil had apprised her of "the Dead Man in the Library," a title arch enough to appear in one of the serial dime novels that were sold on every London street corner.

She dismissed Elmira and Lily, handed Bev over to Tuttle, and excused herself. "I thought I'd invite the detective sergeant to join us after his investigation is complete."

Bev groaned. "Must we?"

"We must. So prepare yourself."

As soon as they were gone, Phil hurried down the hall to the library, only to find the door shut.

Phil quickly looked down the hall, then leaned into the door and pressed her ear to the wood. The voices were muffled and she was about to move away when one of the voices, not Detective Sergeant Atkins's, became louder.

"I told you."

"And I'm telling you."

Phil instinctively moved back. That was the detective sergeant's voice. And he was angry. So who was he talking to? Not a constable.

She knelt down and tried to look through the keyhole, but it was blocked by the key. She could have stamped her foot in frustration.

Without warning, the key was turned in the lock. Phil barely had time to stand up before the door opened. She grabbed her skirts and practically threw herself behind a conveniently placed potted palm.

Made a note to always place potted palms in strategic places in her new domicile.

She held her breath and peeked out.

A policeman stood with his hand on the knob. He was enormous, his back straining at his uniform. One arm flexed as he raised a massive fist toward the open doorway.

"Don't cross me or you'll be sorry."

"This is my jurisdiction."

"Reynolds was offed in mine. And I've been given the go-ahead."

A disgusted snort from Atkins. "I just bet you have. Stay away from this brownstone and its residents."

"Stay out of my way." The man didn't bother to close the door but strode angrily toward the foyer.

The footman jumped from his chair and rushed to open the front door.

Phil stepped out from behind the palm—which she noticed was in dire need of watering—and marched on only slightly shaking knees to the library door.

It closed in her face.

"Well, in for a penny . . ." She needed to know who that man was and how much of a threat to their well-being he actually was. She knocked.

After a few moments, Atkins opened the door.

The were two slashes of ruddy color across his cheekbones. Fire in his eyes. It made a shiver run up her spine.

"I believe I told you—" He broke off. "I beg your pardon. I will try to end this inconvenience as quickly as possible. If you will please return to the parlor, I will be with you shortly."

Definitely upset, Phil thought.

"Who was that man?" she asked.

"No one you need to worry about."

"It sounded like he was threatening you."

His eyes narrowed. "A person in my occupation is used to threats."

"But not by other policemen." It was a guess. They had been talking about jurisdictions, and if the other man had been given the "go-ahead," what else could she surmise?

Interesting. Bev's family were Knickerbockers. Her father was the head of one of the largest New York publishing houses. But Reggie's family, as far as anyone knew, had neither clout nor lineage. Reggie lived by his charm and his wife's money. Neither were royalty, not even in the American way of mimicking the peerage, and they certainly didn't warrant special treatment on that count.

He glared at her—definitely off his game—and started to close the door.

She slipped in front of it. "I came to invite you to join us in the dining room when you're finished," Phil said, trying to catch a glimpse of the room, which was virtually impossible with the broad-shouldered Atkins in the way.

He merely inclined his head, stood his ground, and waited until Phil was forced to retreat. She'd barely stepped into the hallway before the door was slammed behind her.

The situation was escalating and she couldn't get any answers from the angry, tight-lipped detective.

This time she did stamp her foot. And wishing she hadn't bothered wearing the hideous eggplant dress, she walked demurely down the hall to breakfast.

Bev was sitting at the far end of the long dining table, looking lovely but forlorn and staring at a plate of eggs, ham, and tomatoes. Tuttle stood statuelike at the sideboard ready to pour. When he saw Phil, he pulled out a chair at a place setting next to Bev. He poured coffee, and when Phil said she would serve herself, he started to withdraw from the room.

"And bring me the morning papers," Bev ordered.

Tuttle cut a look toward Phil.

"Do you really want to put yourself through that this morning?" Phil snapped, still unsettled from the overheard altercation.

"Can you think of a better time?" Bev asked petulantly. "Before the vultures descend in person to gloat?" Bev laughed rather hysterically. "I can just see them now, lined up to make their conscience calls. Only the very decent and the horridly upper crust will be satisfied with leaving a card. And I might as well prepare myself, because you can bet they're all devouring the news over their morning marmalade and toast." She shuddered. "Damn him," she added as she speared a piece of tomato and carried it to her mouth.

Phil sat down and kept one ear out for John Atkins. She didn't intend for him to leave without explaining a few things.

The news was not kind. It ran the gamut from bare facts to outrageous speculations.

"Mr. Reginald Reynolds was found dead in his touring automobile at the Chelsea Street pier at nine thirty Wednesday morning. The cause of death was a bullet wound to the heart. There was one other passenger—" Phil lowered the paper and peered over it to Bev, who was hidden by the *Sun*.

"Why those no-good . . . Listen to this." Bev's voice rose from the other side of the newspaper. " 'Horse breeder and suspected racketeer Reginald "Reggie" Reynolds was found dead Wednesday as he waited for his wife, Beverly Reynolds, née Sloane, who was at the pier for the arrival of her friend, the Dowager Countess of Dunbridge, off the SS *Oceana*.

" 'He was discovered by Mrs. Reynolds, in the back of his new Packard touring motorcar, sprawled across the lap of Florodora girl and purported mistress, Mimi LaPonte. An investigation is under way.' "

"Disgusting," agreed Philomena. *And why must they always call her dowager?* "What's this about racketeering?"

"Piddle. He was no such thing. He often put side bets on the horses. Everyone does. And he never bet against any of his own. The idea is preposterous. Reggie's purpose on earth was the win; to be bigger, richer, splashier than everyone else." She slapped down the paper, rattling her cup and saucer. "I'll have Freddy sue them."

"I think," Phil said, "you and I should have a heart-to-heart before this goes any farther."

Bev looked up. "Well, of course. But I don't quite understand. You're not thinking of leaving me?"

Phil folded her paper and put it down. "Of course not, but Bev, your husband just died in a most inglorious way."

"You don't have to remind me."

Phil glanced toward the closed dining room door. "An unknown man has just been found dead, murdered, in your library with the pistol Reggie gave you for Christmas. This is not looking good."

"Murdered? That man in the library? With my pistol? No. It can't be. He must be a friend of Reggie's and had a heart attack."

"That's what I was hoping, but he has a bullet hole in his back. Detective Sergeant Atkins is still in there looking for clues."

"Of how the man broke in?"

"That, too, but for more than that. I don't suppose you recognized him?"

"The dead man?" Bev shook her head. "I don't know half of Reggie's friends. Besides, I couldn't see his face even if I had wanted to. Which I didn't." She picked up her crumpled newspaper and rattled it at Phil. "Why is this happening? I don't think I can take it . . . I know—We'll motor up to Saratoga, take the waters and stay for the races. Get away from this nonsense."

"Bev, pull yourself together. You're in no position to flee the scene, so to speak. You're under investigation."

"I am not."

"Well, you're a part of the situation, and I don't think the police would appreciate your leaving. Besides, your automobile has been impounded."

"That's right. They still have our Packard." She grabbed the delicate dinner bell and rang it until Phil was afraid the clapper might fly off. Tuttle appeared before the last clamor had died away.

"Tuttle, I want you to go tell that detective that I want the dead man out of my house immediately."

"I believe they have already called for the coroner's wagon, madam."

Bev's lip quivered. "I want him out now! And I want my motorcar returned. They can't just keep it, they can't just keep upending my household. Tell him I'll need it by this afternoon."

"Yes, madam, but—"

"I said now, Tuttle."

It was then Phil noticed that the salver Tuttle was holding contained a telegram.

"Madam."

"What, Tuttle?" Bev snapped.

"A telegram." He thrust out the silver salver.

Bev looked at it as if it were the Hydra.

"You'd better open it," Phil told her.

Bev snatched it off the tray, hesitated, then tore it open.

Phil watched as Bev's expression turned from anger and impatience to sheer horror. "My father's coming."

She tossed the telegram at Phil, who picked it up and read. *Horrible news. On way from Boston. Arrive soonest.*

"Just what I needed." Bev pushed her chair back and stood.

"Where are you going?" Phil asked.

"To tell that detective to take himself and that dead man off my premises. I can't have Father finding him here. He will be in such a rage as it is. He never liked Reggie." She stalked to the door, nearly knocking Tuttle over in her consternation.

Phil hastened to stop her. "Bev, you can't order these people around like that. They'll take offense, then make life hell. Try for some finesse." Not that it had helped her much. Atkins already seemed determined to find fault with them. Still, it wouldn't do to destroy what little sympathy he might have, which was bound to happen if Bev continued to threaten and humiliate him.

"Oh, no? Reggie's dead. He left me to deal with who knows what. Humiliated me. Made me a laughingstock. Now one of his cronies has been murdered in my library. I've had it. No more."

"Bev, please calm down. You don't want to get in more trouble."

"Oh, don't I? Watch me."

She threw the doors back and stormed out of the room and right into a stretcher carried by two of the coroner's men. The stretcher wobbled, the men stumbled, Bev screeched, and the stretcher toppled its load onto the carpet. Two dead eyes stared up at them. In death the face was pale and bloated.

"Bev?"

"Never saw him in my life."

Elmira and Lily were running down the stairs. Other servants appeared in the doorways to other rooms. John Atkins came striding toward the debacle, eyes narrowed, and his mouth as tight as any mouth Phil had ever seen.

He took in the scene at one glance and turned on Philomena.

She braced herself; she'd been the brunt of worse anger than his. The earl was a bitter, drunken sod. She'd quickly learned not to quail before it.

"Is this your doing?"

Phil didn't even get a chance to defend herself.

Bev turned on him. "Don't you dare speak to Phil that way! I was the one who ran into that stupid stretcher! Bumbling idiots. I'll never be able to wear this dress again." She burst into tears.

"Mrs. Reynolds," the detective began.

"Don't talk to me. I'll have your head on a plate. Get out. Get out and take these stupid men with you. Get out. Just go away. And don't you dare leave that—that thing on my carpet."

The two coroner's men stooped and clumsily tried to roll the deceased back onto the stretcher. It was such an awkward moment that Phil had to stop herself from bending down to help.

"That 'thing' was a human being," John Atkins said in a voice that would have made Phil think twice, but it had no effect on Bev.

"I want my motorcar. Now! Do you hear me? You have no right to keep it. I want it now!"

"It will be returned at our earliest convenience," Atkins said drily, but Phil could tell he was holding on to his temper. She didn't blame him. Bev was acting like all the people they couldn't stand.

"How dare you. I'll have you know—"

Phil thrust Bev at Elmira. "Take your mistress upstairs. A calming draft would be in order."

Elmira nodded, but her eyes were round with fright. She obviously had never witnessed Bev in full throw before.

"Lily will help you."

Bev wrenched away. "I want you out now. Do you hear me? Or I'll report you to your superiors."

"Elmira, please," Phil said. Elmira and Lily took each side of Bev and practically dragged her up the stairs.

The attendants managed to return the body to the stretcher, hastily threw a cover over it, and headed for the door. Tuttle raced to be there before them.

That left Phil and the detective sergeant alone in the foyer.

"Well," she said. "Surely you deserve a cup of coffee before you go."

"I deserve to be unimpeded in my investigation of two murders."

"I agree. And with the all the excitement you still haven't had time to question me. Let's have our coffee in the parlor, shall we?"

5

With Bev safely bestowed upstairs, and the body gone, Philomena began to breathe a little easier. Perhaps this wasn't the time to panic but to re-collect herself. And what better way than a tête-à-tête with the detective who seemed determined to take charge of the rapidly expanding case while being thwarted at every turn even by his own associates?

She gestured toward the parlor.

The detective hesitated. Most likely because he, too, was evaluating the situation. How strange it was to come to America expecting to make a splash by enduring a few balls and soirées and then settle down to a life of delightful excess, and instead to be embroiled in a situation from which her reputation—such that it was—might fail to recover. And yet . . .

Bugger it. "Really, you're safe from me. I'll even have Tuttle bring a fresh pot." She turned away, making the most of the stiff fabric of her skirts, and walked into the parlor.

She rang for Tuttle, but it was Preswick who appeared moments later. Phil bit back a laugh at Atkins's expression. A thimblerig of butlers. It was delightful.

"The detective sergeant is staying for coffee."

Preswick gave her a pointed look, and gave Atkins the evil eye, before bowing and leaving the room.

"That wasn't—?"

"Tuttle?" She shook her head. "I'm afraid that at the last moment I couldn't leave poor Preswick behind, and he came to hold my household while we're here. So we have a surfeit of butlers at the moment. Won't you be seated?"

She sat, wondering if she was expected to carry on small talk under these circumstances.

"And so here we are again," he said, walking not to a chair but to look at the artwork that adorned the walls of the parlor. "An odd assortment of paintings."

"Yes. I thought so myself. A combination of the Louvre and Chabanais brothel."

"Well, one thing I'll say for you, Lady Dunbridge, is you're never at a loss for an opinion."

"So my mother used to tell me."

"Are you planning on making an extended stay in New York?"

"Well, that depends."

There was a moment of silence, while he waited for her to continue and she thought of reasons at this point to stay or to go. She wouldn't return to England, so stay she must.

"I'd planned to visit with the Reynoldses while I acquired a domicile in the city. However, I find my plans somewhat, shall we say, off track."

"Is this your first visit to America?"

"Since I was a child. The earl disliked travel. He didn't really like London overmuch. He much preferred his country seat."

"I could see where that might be stifling for someone of your . . ."

"Shall we say energy?" she finished. "Ah, here's coffee."

This time it was Tuttle at the door. He carried the tray to the coffee table and set it down. "Will there be anything else, my lady?"

"That will do, Tuttle."

He bowed and left the room.

"Cream, sugar, Detective Sergeant?"

"Black, please. Do you think Mrs. Reynolds murdered her husband?"

Phil nearly dropped the cup. She made a mental note to never relax around this man and safely handed him his coffee.

"Heavens no. Bev enjoys life, and can be a little reckless, but she isn't mean-spirited."

"Mean-spirited? Perhaps not, but I was thinking more in terms of unhinged."

"Oh, no, that's just Bev's personality. She's always given in to the dramatic." Not to mention that her flights of hysteria had gotten them out of many a fix as girls. She'd perfected them since, if her outrage this morning had all been an act.

"If it isn't an inconvenience, Lady Dunbridge," he said, "can we just cut to the chase?"

"Another turf lover, I see. Do you hunt?"

He put his coffee down and stood, startling her. He walked four long strides away and turned. "Lady Dunbridge, I know what you're doing. My mother was a master of it. But I don't appreciate it. Someone killed Reginald Reynolds, someone murdered the as-yet-unidentified man in the library. Things are not looking good for your friend Bev."

"I don't know what you mean."

"Of course you do. You're either stalling so that you can find out just what is going on before you decide whether to stay and abet or cut ties and move on. Or you already know what went down here and are trying to keep me off the scent. Either way, you're obstructing the investigation."

Phil trilled a laugh she was far from feeling. "You flatter me, Detective Atkins. I haven't a clue as to what is going on." She gave him her steadiest look. "After all, I'm a woman alone in the world, in a strange country. I must take care of myself—and my reputation."

He shook his head. "You are something else, Lady Dunbridge. But so am I. Thank you for the coffee. You can tell Mrs. Reynolds that I'll return when she's up to answering some questions, unless she'd rather come down to the station. And if you have any ideas about going into the library to satisfy your curiosity, forget it.

I've had Tuttle turn over both keys. He has a receipt. Good day." He bowed and strode across the room.

She hurried after him but made it only as far as the front door before he stopped abruptly and she nearly plowed into him.

"Who was that man you were, um, consulting with in the library?" she asked.

"His name is Charles Becker; he's the sergeant in charge of the Tenderloin District and an unsavory character. I suggest you give him a wide berth."

"But what was he doing here?"

"It's best you not concern yourself with the progress of the investigation."

"How can I not?"

He grabbed her wrist, shocking them both.

He dropped it just as quickly. "My apologies. But you need to listen. You may know your way around the drawing rooms of London, Lady Dunbridge, but I know the streets of New York. Don't even attempt to get in the way here."

He trotted down the steps to the sidewalk, where he turned long enough to tip his hat at her, then strode off down the street. He was gone before she could come up with a retort. But he'd thrown down the gauntlet. What could she do but accept the challenge?

I shouldn't have done that, she thought as she stood in the foyer. Never let your temper get away from you. Though she suspected that John Atkins had just succumbed to the same weakness. She could still feel the marks of his fingers on her wrist. That was one unhappy detective.

How soon would he return to badger them for more answers? And what to do? Should they telephone Freddy? Would he know what to do, if anything, about this Sergeant Becker? From the little she'd seen and heard in those few brief minutes, she had no doubt he was mean and dangerous.

She needed to consult with Bev. God forfend that the ever-ready Elmira had already doped her mistress beyond reach.

Phil hadn't much cared for Reggie, the little she'd seen of him, and Bev would no doubt be better off without him. But she certainly didn't want Bev to be tried for murder.

But it could be ruinous to interfere. What to do? It was one thing to defy parents, English tradition, and the censure of society by running off to America with a butler and a maid. It was another to embroil oneself in a murder investigation. It was exhilarating, but frightening. And there was no room for fear in her new life. It would take the top of her game to survive.

There was no other choice. She would not go back. She couldn't fail. Strength and staying on top was the only way to succeed. And quite frankly, her loyalties aside, she had never felt so stimulated in her life.

She lifted her detested eggplant skirts and ran up the stairs.

Bev was lying in bed, her hair down and spreading across the pristine pillows.

Phil leaned over and shook her. "Bev, wake up. This is no time for the vapors. I need you."

Bev opened one eye. "Is he gone?"

"Yes, for the time being. But he says if you don't answer his questions, he'll take you to the station."

Bev bolted upright. "I can't go to a police station. The last time Reggie and I got hauled in, Father said he'd cut off my allowance if it ever happened again."

Phil stared. "You've actually been arrested?"

"Of course not. We were just taken in for drunk and disorderly. That was before they realized who we were. But Father got wind of it, and all hell broke loose."

"Well, it's about to break loose again. And I think it might behoove us to telephone Cousin Freddy about the discovery of this new victim and ask his advice."

Bev reached for an enameled bell by the bed. Elmira appeared in the doorway of the dressing room.

"Go downstairs and find Tuttle. Have him come here at once. And be discreet."

Elmira didn't blink, but curtseyed and departed.

"I pay her a fortune," Bev said. "She's good, but a tad mercenary. Most servants are more than willing to exchange gossip for a few pennies from the local scandal sheets. But not to worry, I make certain to pay her more. We understand each other."

Bev plumped the pillows and leaned back. "You won't desert me, will you, Phil? I know you're eager to get on with your life, and I can ask one of my friends to escort you to all the society functions."

She sucked in a sob and her bottom lip protruded in a pouty expression that Phil remembered well. "While I'm sitting here in my widow's weeds."

"Better here in widow's weeds than in your local jail wearing prison garb."

"The Tombs? I can't go to prison, I didn't do anything."

"What tombs?"

Bev waved her hand in the air. "The prison downtown. It's where you go before they send you upstate to Sing Sing, an awful place where they have the electric chair."

"You terrify me," Phil said. "Bev, did you kill Reggie?"

"How can you ask that?"

"Because your life depends on the answer."

Bev closed her eyes, then opened them again. "Between you and me, I sometimes felt like it. I'd had enough of him. He constantly humiliated me in front of the whole town, the whole world. My father is so angry about it he can barely look at me." Her eyes widened. "You don't think—No he wouldn't."

Daniel Sloane was the most mild-mannered, superbly educated man of Phil's acquaintance. Until he wasn't. She remembered several occasions when he'd become irate at Bev's shenanigans, as he called them, paced and blustered and threatened to take her out of school, but nothing had come of it.

Could he become angry enough to murder his son-in-law? Ridiculous. Besides, he had been in Boston.

"Why didn't you divorce Reggie? Divorce seems to be very popular these days."

"For the same reason you didn't divorce your odious earl."

"How could I? He was a peer and I would be an outcast. Surely America is a little more lenient than that."

"We don't have a peerage in a royal sense. But it still exists here, for all our modern ways. My family is old New York. My father would never have allowed it." She laughed, a hollow sound that made her sound old and jaded. "He put up with all our nonsense, the scandalous parties and yachting orgies, the racing and betting, even Reggie's affairs."

"And your affairs?"

"I didn't have any."

"You?"

"Well, maybe a few. Like I said, Reggie wasn't very . . . attentive in that department. He had a roving eye, and roving everything else, and once he started flaunting his behavior before the world, I decided I would not sit at home alone and be the proper, cheated-on wife while that bounder had all the fun. Perhaps it wasn't the smartest choice. But at least I was discreet." She sighed. "What's done is done. And now . . . ugh . . . Father will probably insist on two full years of mourning."

"I don't envy you."

Bev grasped Phil's hand. "I know what you must have gone through. But please, Phil, don't desert me."

"I told you I wouldn't. But I think we need to do something and not depend on the police to find the murderer. They can be awfully slow to the post. And I'm sure Atkins is being held back from really going after you because of pressure from someone. At first I thought Freddy was planning to bribe him."

"Phil," Bev began.

"Don't put on shock for my benefit. You forget I moved in the top circles. We're not quite so blatant, and money isn't always involved, but I know bribery when I see it. And I can recognize a man who is chafing under it, and that is our detective sergeant. I wouldn't be surprised if he breaks rank before the investigation is over.

"There was another policeman here this morning. He was arguing—threatening, actually—to take over his case. Becker, I forget his first name."

"Oh, Lord," Bev said sitting up. "Becker, here? In this house?"

"Who is he?"

"The most cutthroat, greedy, ruthless, bribe-taking cop in the city. And ugly as sin. He always reminds me of a giant fireplug."

"Fireplug?" Phil laughed. "He did look like a fireplug."

"The ugliest. But he's never been interested in Reggie before."

"Well, apparently he's interested now."

"I'll call Freddy."

"Bev? How high does Freddy's influence go?"

"Oh, Lord, I don't know. He knows people."

That sounded awfully vague to Phil.

"Well, you don't have to worry about me," Bev said. "I'm not about to be cowed by Detective Atkins or Charles Becker. I can hold my own. Lord knows I've had to."

"But if they come after you?"

"Let them come. I didn't kill Reggie or that man in the library. Or anyone else. So set your mind at ease." Bev leaned back and stretched. "Now, no more worrying. This will all be over soon."

"I hope you're right. Now, if we can just convince the detective sergeant."

Bev wiggled her shoulders. "I'm sure you have your ways."

"I don't believe my ways will work any more than yours have so far."

Bev sighed. "Such a loss. That face and those shoulders wasted on a policeman."

"True," Phil agreed, glad for the distraction. "Like a dime novel cowboy. Without the horse."

"True. A pity, really. And the New York police department does have a horse brigade. I'd love to see him mounted."

"I would, too." Phil cut Bev a sideways look. "And I'd be happy to oblige."

Bev laughed, then slapped her hand over her mouth. "Phil! How absolutely naughty of you, but I completely concur. That chest, those arms—"

Phil threw a toss pillow at her, which Bev hugged to her chest. They were laughing when Tuttle knocked on the door.

"Yes, madam?"

Immediately sober, Bev asked him to telephone Freddy and advise him of the latest development.

"I suppose you pay him a fortune, too," Phil said as soon as the butler was gone.

"Alas, yes." Bev lowered her voice. "But I trust Tuttle more than . . ." She tilted her head in the direction of the dressing room.

Phil nodded. A loyal lady's maid was worth her weight and more. A maid who could be bought was no better than a politician.

Phil didn't have to warn Bev to be careful. She evidently knew the full measure of her Elmira. Phil wished she could say the same for her own Lily. And yet there was something about the girl. Would she give up Lily for someone with brilliant references?

Not for all the tea in China.

With Tuttle in charge of apprising Freddy, and since Bev had no personal secretary, Bev and Phil embarked on all things funereal. The dressmaker was summoned and arrived shortly after to take measurements and pick out patterns. Phil unbent far enough to allow a gray taffeta silk visiting dress to be made with an accompanying black-trimmed pelisse. It would soon be too warm to wear the pelisse anyway. A funeral dress was decided on by Bev, and suddenly taken up with the idea of the latest in widows' fashion, she ordered several other dresses.

As soon as the dressmaker departed, Bev and Phil began making lists and preparing the announcement while Tuttle ordered black-edged cards from the stationer.

Detesting every moment, Phil put on a brave and practical face, knowing her experience would help to make the situation for Bev much less painful than her own had been.

By the afternoon post, undertaker and stone-carver advertisements filled the silver salver. Mr. Brangle, Reggie's solicitor, made arrangements with the police to release Reggie's body to a reputable undertaker he knew personally.

Freddy telephoned to say he had reserved Saint Bartholomew's Church for services, which would be followed by a processional to Green-Wood Cemetery. He advised Bev not to insist on a private ceremony. Reggie was a popular man and his friends would feel slighted. And would probably show up outside the doors of the church in a rowdy state of inebriation.

Neither Bev nor Phil much cared for their feelings, but Bev acquiesced. "We don't want a drunken brawl over the casket," she said. "Father would have a fit."

Phil wrote the obituary and funeral times for the newspaper. Marguerite called several times offering to help, which Bev graciously didn't accept, but with such heartfelt gratitude Marguerite could not take offense.

Or at least shouldn't, thought Phil. After Marguerite's second telephone call, Bev finally agreed to let her choose the flowers and the casket blanket, and hung up with a "whew."

Phil didn't know quite what to make of Marguerite Beecham. Lovely, demure, sympathetic. Phil didn't trust those people. In her experience, benign people were invariably found to slowly disappear into nothing or to have a dastardly hidden agenda. She didn't take Marguerite as the disappearing type.

Though to be fair, Marguerite had given her no real reason to distrust her.

By late afternoon, Phil was more than willing to return to her room for a lie-down before dinner and the arrival by Daniel Sloane.

"I tell you, Lily," Phil confided as she soaked in a hot tub, "this house is teetering on the brink of something. I'm just not sure what."

"Scandal," Lily said, letting the word roll off her tongue.

"Well, murder of one's husband and then an unknown murder victim in the library does lend itself to speculation."

Lily rolled her eyes to the ceiling. "The mister was a gambler as well as a r-r-roué."

"I'm not surprised," Phil said, thinking of the odd assortment of furniture and artwork. Maybe it wasn't the Reynoldses' eclectic spirit that replaced old valuable artwork by modern, less expensive furnishings. Lord, she'd seen enough of that in the great old houses of England. In the gradual depletion of artwork in her own rambling old mausoleum of a castle. In the paste jewelry worn around the necks of a multitude of impecunious duchesses and countesses.

"He consorts with not-so-savory characters."

Phil perked up. "And you know this how? I thought the staff became mum when you were nearby."

Lily gave her that brief flash of smile. "Stupid ser-r-rvants. I go where I want. They do not always see."

"Ah. How clever of me to hire an invisible lady's maid." And what worked one way could also work the other. She liked Lily for her spunk and her bravery. But she would do well to follow her own admonishments to Bev. Be discreet until she knew Lily to be trustworthy and true.

She shook it off. Ridiculous. The girl was one in a million.

Which made Phil think of racing odds. Was the man in the library a thief after Reggie's winnings? Possibly one of Reggie's racing associates?

What else would he be doing in the library? And when did he break in? What if he'd been dead for days? Well, maybe not days, but for a day. And who shot him? And why was his hand still in the desk drawer?

Who knew murder could be so complicated?

Phil and Bev sat half the evening drinking martinis and waiting for the arrival of Bev's father. Evidently it was taking him longer than expected to return to Manhattan. By ten o'clock Phil was ready to climb the walls. She was used to being bored at Dunbridge, especially being in mourning, but there was a whole world of excitement just beyond the doors of the brownstone. And here she sat, getting tipsy from good gin but for no good reason.

Finally, at eleven, Bev took herself off to bed. Phil would have gone to the library for a book if she'd been able to get in. But the detective had taken the only two keys.

She went upstairs to find Lily sitting in the dressing room.

"Do you spend all your time here waiting for me?" Phil asked. "They have an intercom here if I need you."

"No. But Elmira went up to her mistress so I came, too."

"Ah."

"Are you ready for bed, madam?"

"I am not." Phil paced to the window, looked out, not really expecting to see anyone. She didn't, except for a constable who seemed to be assigned as their personal bodyguard. Did they really need a bodyguard, or was the detective afraid that they would try to run?

She dropped the curtain with a huff.

"What is it, madam?" Lily asked, returning from the dressing room with Phil's nightgown folded over her arm.

"This is so infuriating." Phil paced back to where Lily was standing by the bed. Looked at her from head to toe. "We really must get you new clothing."

Lily smoothed down her apron. "Is that what is annoying you, madam?"

"No, no, but it must be rectified. Tomorrow. Regardless of dead men and obnoxious detectives, we must get you clothing. We'll take Preswick. He'll know best how to outfit a maid."

Lily made a sour face.

Phil stopped her with a motion of her hand. "What bothers me is this situation we find ourselves in. Two murders: Reggie's and the body in the library. What an absurd thing to say; it sounds like something out of a dime novel. And now Detective Atkins has taken the keys so that none of us can get in. And I don't have a thing to read."

"He is not stupid, that one."

"No, I'm afraid he isn't. Which of course could be a good thing." Or very bad if he decided Bev had killed her husband.

"Do you need to get into the library for a book?"

Phil raised a skeptical eyebrow. "And if I did?"

Lily shrugged one shoulder.

"I don't suppose you have skills in opening locked doors?"

"Perhaps."

"Then let us go."

"Not yet, madam. There will still be servants about."

"Oh." Phil returned to the window. Her lady's maid was an enigma, but could she really open locked doors? Phil could hardly wait to find out. She looked out the window again. The constable was still there. Only now he was talking to someone. A man in a dark overcoat.

She pulled aside the drapes and peered around the edge. A match flared in the night, and the man in the overcoat walked off down the street without looking back. Phil peered after him, which was ridiculous. Just because the deliciously devious Mr. X lingered under the lamppost the night of the wake didn't mean he'd return. Though the idea was intriguing.

She kept watch for a while longer, listening to Lily rummage in the dressing room, doing whatever maids did. The constable never left his post except to walk a few feet to either side of the lamppost and back again.

Finally, Lily returned and said, “This would be a good time to fetch your book, madam.”

Lily stuck her head out the door, looked both ways down the hallway, then motioned Phil to follow. They tiptoed down the stairs like two thieves in the night.

They had every right to be here. And Phil *did* need something to read.

Downstairs was dark, something Phil hadn’t taken into account, and she didn’t dare turn on a lamp for fear of alerting the constable outside or waking Tuttle or Preswick. She stood blinking, waiting for her eyes to adjust to the lack of light, when she felt Lily’s fingers on her wrist and she was being pulled into an even darker passage.

Phil tried to move as stealthily as possible, but what with dead people and police investigations and funeral preparations, she hadn’t had time to change her attire all day and now she cursed her stiff, noisy skirts.

They stopped abruptly at the library door. She felt Lily kneel down.

“What are you doing?” Phil whispered. “I can’t see a thing.”

“Not necessary,” Lily whispered.

Phil peered into the darkness. Heard Lily’s steady breathing. And a click. Lily stood, the door opened.

Phil considered her lady’s maid with ever growing interest and admiration. “I don’t suppose I should ask where you learned that particular skill?”

“No . . . my lady,” Lily said, and pushed her mistress inside.

6

Phil stood perfectly still. The library was pitch-black except where the drapes were slightly parted, and a tiny sliver of moonlight cast a wedge of light across the desktop. But beyond the heavy desk, all was in shadow, the bookshelves towered over her, and Reggie's reading chair was posed like an amorphous nighttime monster.

Phil shook her herself. This was no time for lurid imaginations.

Lily eased the door closed. "What are we looking for?"

"I don't know, but we'll need some light." Phil moved toward the desk, her hand outstretched. "Damn, I wish I had a torch. We'll just have to turn on a lamp. Pull those drapes fully shut."

Lily seemed to glide, phantomlike, toward the window. But when she got there, instead of pulling the drapes closed, she opened them wider. "The windowpane is cut out."

"Yes. The inspector—I mean detective—and I discovered it yesterday. We think the thief cut it out in order to unlock the latch."

Lily studied the latch. "But the latch is painted over. He did not come through here."

Phil groped her way over to the window and looked at the lock more closely. Had Atkins noticed that and chosen not to point it out?

Of course. He had no reason to include her. She frowned at the latch. From the tail of her eye she caught movement below them and stepped back into Lily. "There's someone down there."

Lily pressed in beside her. "The constable. Do you think he saw us?"

They both stepped from the window simultaneously.

"We have every right to be here," Phil said, with more calm than she actually felt. "I'm just looking for something to read."

"And did you break into the room, too? Because the door was locked. They'll arrest me."

"They absolutely will not."

"How will you stop them?"

"I'll tell them I did it."

"But you don't know how."

"You'll teach me as soon as we get upstairs."

She and Phil pressed their faces back to the window. Phil leaned into the casement and tried to search the tiny patch of garden below.

"Do you see anything?"

Lily shook her head. "Are you sure someone was down there?"

"I thought so, but most likely it was just shadows." Phil turned from the window and sucked in her breath. Wordlessly, she pointed to the hulking shadow standing in the far corner.

"It's a coatrack, madam. A jacket is hung on the hook." Lily's voice quivered slightly, and Phil wasn't sure if it was from relief or laughter.

"So it is," Phil said, chagrined at her own imagination.

"Are you sure he was a thief? What is there to steal in a room filled with books?"

"Bev said Reggie kept large sums of money here. See if you can find a safe."

Phil leaned over the desk to open the center frieze drawer, stopped with her hand two inches from the drawer pull, then snatched her hand away. "Wait!"

Lily's hand was already reaching for her skirts and the knife hidden at her leg.

"Fingerprints," Phil explained.

"What, madam?"

"How stupid of me. That detective will look for fingerprints, if he hasn't already. We can't touch anything."

Lily turned both hands over and studied her fingers. "Then how are we to find anything?"

"I don't—" The sentence stuck in her throat.

Across the room, there was a soft click and the doorknob began to turn.

Lily turned to Phil.

"Fingerprints be damned," Phil said. "Lily, the door!"

Lily whirled around. A Meissen vase sat on a pedestal table a foot away. She grabbed the vase with both hands and lifted it over her head, just as the door opened.

"Not the Meissen!" Phil hissed as Preswick stepped into the room.

There was a moment while Phil watched in horror as Lily juggled the vase as she tried to change direction. And for a precarious moment Phil was sure the priceless antique would crash to the floor, destroying it and rousing the entire household.

But she should have known better. Without a hitch, Preswick shut the door, walked over, and plucked the vase away just as it began to fall. He placed it carefully onto the pedestal and turned in full butler disapproval to confront the miscreants.

"My lady," he said at his blandest.

"Ah, Preswick, you startled us. What are you doing here?"

"I noticed that Lily had not returned to her chamber." He paused to give Lily his sternest look. Instead of being cowed like a good—and Phil might add humble—servant would, Lily thrust out her chin and glared back at him.

"I thought perhaps something might be amiss. And so I took the liberty of—"

"He decided to spy on me," Lily snapped.

"See here—"

"Not now, you two," Phil said, coming closer to them.

"I had no need to spy on you. I merely did the obvious."

He gave Phil a deadpan look. "I supposed you would not be able to resist the challenge of a locked room, and here you are."

"Actually, I'm glad you came, Preswick. You'll know much better than either of us what to look for."

"Look for?" Preswick said, momentarily startled out of his butler demeanor. "And may I ask, my lady, how you managed to enter this room? Tuttle was very irate that the inspector had confiscated the only two keys, thus preventing the chamber maids from doing their work."

"Yes, well. We were forced to stoop to a bit of . . ."

"Lock picking," Lily supplied, and Phil could have stepped on her toe. Preswick would be outraged. "My mistress needed a book to read."

Preswick didn't bother replying, merely looked down his rather formidable nose. It made no impression on Lily. At least not outwardly. Phil had thought she had as much sangfroid as the next person, but her maid could give as good as she got.

And for some reason that made Phil a little sad.

"Yes, I know, Preswick. Very unbecoming activity for the Dowager Countess of Dunbridge. But needs must. That detective sergeant is not being cooperative. And I'm afraid he may suspect Bev of both murders. And yes I agree that being involved in two murders isn't good for my reputation."

But certainly advantageous when needing bits of gossip to drop. A certain entrée into female inner circles. She could dine for weeks on tidbits from the investigation without humiliating Bev or giving anything away.

Preswick bowed slightly.

"So the sooner we discover who the murderer is and save Bev from someplace called Sing Sing, I promise you I will send her off to the Continent and we three will repair to the more elegant environs of the Plaza Hotel.

"But for now we must avail ourselves of every . . . legal-ish . . . means necessary to find the real culprit. Agreed?"

"If you say so, my lady."

"Good. We've just discovered, well, actually, Lily pointed it out to me, that the thief couldn't have entered through the window because the latch is painted shut. He must have cut the glass"—she motioned him over, showed him the cut-out space—"then realized he couldn't get in without breaking the lock, though I don't know why he would suddenly become so fastidious. A cut pane, a broken lock. What's the difference?"

Phil frowned. "That would mean someone had to let him in."

Preswick nodded ever so slightly.

"But Tuttle is the only one with the keys."

Preswick didn't bother with a nod.

"Not Tuttle. Reggie must have had a key."

"Which he left with Mr. Tuttle when he left the house. He was afraid of pickpockets and such."

"Preswick, you're a wonder. How did you find this out?"

"Merely in conversation, my lady. Mr. Tuttle has a very fine brandy that he was gracious enough to share with me."

"He didn't happen to confess, did he?"

"Certainly not, my lady."

"Someone must have stolen one of them."

"Mr. Tuttle kept them on his person at all times."

Phil reluctantly continued. "Then someone else had to let them in . . . Unless . . . they were already inside when Reggie left for the docks." Which suddenly put Bev back as the main suspect.

"Did the inspector question him?"

"All of the servants, my lady."

"Not you and Lily?"

"Very briefly."

"So he could have been lying dead all through the wake. Ugh." Phil shivered.

"Perhaps your ladyship would like to retire to your room now?"

"Not yet, Preswick. We're here; we might as well look around. Only—"

"Then a moment, please." Preswick eased Lily and Phil out of the way, pulled the drapes shut and overlapped them where they met. Then he moved to the desk and turned on the lamp.

The sudden light was startling. Even more startling to see Preswick dressed in full regalia down to his white gloves and looking as neat as if it were midday instead of midnight.

He moved to turn on a floor lamp next to Reggie's wingback chair. "Is that not better, my lady?"

"Yes, it is, Preswick. And how clever of you to be wearing your gloves."

"Thank you, my lady. And I suggest if you plan to make a search of the library, you wear these." He reached inside his jacket and pulled out a pair of pristine white gloves and handed them to her. "They might be a bit large but will be adequate for the purpose."

"Preswick, I'm amazed. How did you know we would need gloves?"

"I didn't. One always carries a second pair in case of spillages and whatnot. Unfortunately, Lily must use her apron."

Lily shot him a sour look but held her tongue. They were making progress in that direction, at least.

Preswick's Adam's apple traveled up his thin neck. "What are we looking for, my lady?"

"I'm not certain. But something that could tell us . . . Oh, I don't know, Preswick. Important documents, money. Where would Mr. Reynolds be likely to keep important papers?"

"His desk or a safe, my lady."

They all looked at the desk. It was the first time Phil had actually looked at it. It was massive mahogany kneehole desk with heavy carved plinths of leaves and grapes, and a brass inkstand that appeared to be built into the desktop.

The desk at Dunbridge Castle had a similar stand, which didn't make sense at all to Phil. What if you needed to move the ink closer to you or use the entire surface of the desk?

"Heavens, but Reggie was a messy businessman." Papers were

stacked high, his blotter was covered with doodles and figures crossed out and rearranged.

There was a heavy ashtray, piled high with ashes, cigar butts, and a small square of paper, which on closer inspection turned out to be a candy wrapper.

Phil donned the gloves and pushed the offensive receptacle to the far edge. Then, trying not to think of the dead man who had recently used it, she sat down in the desk chair and started on the first stack of papers.

"I'll look for the safe," said Lily.

"You," Preswick said, "will look under cushions and pillows. I will look for the safe."

Lily made a guttural noise in her throat. "Yes, Mr. Pr-r-r-reswick."

Phil pushed away the first stack of papers, which consisted mainly of racing forms and track schedules, and started on another. There were recent bills, lots of them, letters from creditors, IOUs, and personal letters, but none to or from the notorious Miss Potts.

She hadn't expected to find the pistol. Atkins most certainly had taken it. Finding a gun on the floor next to a man who had been shot to death was pretty damning evidence.

Really, she hoped they discovered his name soon. She couldn't keep naming people according to the alphabet. Mr. X was quite enough for her.

She moved on to the frieze drawer above her knees and felt a bit squeamish when she pulled it open.

With slightly trembling fingers, Phil reached inside, trying not to imagine the man's hand making the same movement, or his head hitting the desk with that decidedly sickening whack.

The drawer was a jumble of pens, pencils, a pair of scissors, a receipt book, a bottle of ink, rubber bands, and a container of paper clips. Several more bills were wadded up and Phil pulled them out, dislodging a dyed rabbit's foot.

Oh really, Reggie, Phil thought. He should have taken it with him. A silver matchbox, more pens. More papers, which she riffled through, hoping for something interesting. Only more bills. And a set of keys.

She felt under the desktop. Nothing taped there. Slid off the chair to her knees and perused the bottom of the drawer. She knew a thing or two about hiding secret missives and couldn't help a reminiscent smile as her fingers ran over the wood.

Nothing hidden there, either.

She reached for the top drawer on her right. It was locked, but one of the keys she'd found in the frieze drawer opened it.

Frankly, she would have hidden the keys better if it had been her desk. Why bother to lock it at all?

It wasn't her desk, but it was very like one she knew quite well. "Preswick?"

"Yes, my lady." He returned the painting he'd been looking behind and faced her.

"Isn't there a desk much like this one in Dunbridge Castle?"

"Yes, my lady, something very similar. A very popular style during the Tudor period. The fourth earl was said to have used this desk writing his great tome of the family's participation in the preservation of royal family. The earls of Dunbridge were a scholarly lot . . . until recently, I believe."

"Quite," she agreed.

"Though I believe we should hurry. It's getting on three o'clock and the servants will be up soon."

Phil returned to her search, moving more quickly now. How she thought a visiting countess, a lady's maid, and a butler could find something that a trained detective couldn't was pure folly. Of course she'd done just that once in London, but that had been so much simpler than this. She didn't even know what she was looking for. She just knew that she couldn't sit by while her childhood friend—for all her faults—was accused of murder.

The second drawer yielded more of the same: bundles of papers held together by rubber bands.

Again, Phil patted the inside of the drawer, felt beneath it.

And found nothing more except that Reggie was in debt to numerous people, some with unsavory names like Toots Kelley, Mosey Grimes, and Roach Pendergrass, and a few copies of formal promissory notes to more respectable-sounding creditors. All in all, Reggie Reynolds was seriously in debt.

Would Bev be responsible for them? It could break her.

Phil returned the bundles of papers to the second drawer, quickly opened the bottom drawer. A liquor bottle. A box of unopened cigars. And nothing else.

Phil moved to the left set of drawers. Mainly old racing magazines and several pairs of binoculars. It had been a fruitless endeavor. Was that because there was nothing here? Or that the second intruder had already taken whatever he and the dead man were looking for? But then how did he get out? Unless whoever let him in, let him out. And that could only be Tuttle.

What was she missing?

"Ah, here it is," Preswick said, interrupting her train of thought.

Both Phil and Lily stopped to watch as he pulled at a large painting of dancing nymphs. The painting swung from the wall on a set of hinges to reveal a wall safe.

"Of course," Lily groused. "It would be under a picture of a bunch of naked ladies."

Preswick turned back to his mistress. "I don't suppose we know the combination."

"No, we don't." Phil shot a hopeful glance toward Lily.

Lily made a face and shook her head.

Phil sighed. It had been a long shot, and quite frankly she was relieved that her unorthodox lady's maid wasn't also a safecracker.

"Perhaps it's unlocked?"

Preswick tried the handle. "I'm afraid not, my lady."

"Thank you, Preswick. Clever of you to find it."

"I've been butler for many years. One learns these things."

One does indeed. Phil looked from her butler to her lady's maid, who was showing grudging respect toward Preswick for finding the safe.

The best of both worlds, she thought. She was sensing a future for the three of them. If she could just get into society and make a start.

Preswick returned the painting and brushed off his gloved hands. "I think we should leave now."

"Just one more second." Phil knelt down and crawled into the kneehole, running her hands along both sides of the desk.

"Are you looking for the mechanism to open the secret compartment?" Preswick inquired.

Phil banged her head as she scrambled back and to her feet.

"Of course," Phil said. That explained the earl's curious reactions when she'd sometimes entered the library unannounced. *A secret compartment.*

"Many desks of the Jacobean period had one. It was a turbulent era. These particular desks were made to conceal secret documents pertaining to the Crown, the church, what have you. Quite ingenious. The desk at Dunbridge Castle had one that was particularly complicated."

"Do you know how to open it?" Phil asked.

"If I may?"

"Please."

Preswick sat down. With Lily and Phil both leaning over the desktop to watch, he opened the frieze drawer, felt around, not the underneath of the top but along the inside of the desk frame. Phil heard a click, but nothing popped up or sprang loose.

Preswick ran the tips of his fingers over the ornate carving of the desk frame and down the front of the desk until he almost disappeared from view.

"Aha," echoed the disembodied voice.

"Did you find it?" Lily blurted out.

"Almost," came the reply. Preswick's head appeared over the

edge of the desk, making him look very much like Lewis Carroll's Cheshire Cat. The rest of him was still stretched beneath the surface.

"Now if your ladyship would indulge me by pulling the brass part of the inkstand toward yourself."

Phil closed her fingers around the holder and pulled. At first nothing happened. Then Lily pushed a stack of papers aside and the whole pen and inkstand rotated to the right, exposing a dark hole in the desktop.

Preswick pushed himself back into the chair. "Well?"

Phil stuck her nose practically inside the opening but saw nothing. Now, praying there wasn't a mousetrap waiting for her, she stuck her hand and arm through the hole and felt inside. All she got was dusty fingers.

She pulled her hand out. "It's empty."

"Ah, well, I dare say the Reynoldses didn't even know about it. Most people don't."

"How did you?"

"Having been butler to the earl's family for many years, I was occasionally called in to witness certain documents . . . And now, my lady, we really must go."

Preswick insisted Lily and Phil wait for him by the door while he turned off the lamps, then groped his way across the darkened room to let them out. He waited only long enough for Lily to relock the door, and without comment preceded them up the stairs.

He paused briefly on the landing to check the second floor, then motioned them down the hall—and followed them into Phil's boudoir.

Phil stretched broadly. "Oh, I am tired."

"No doubt, my lady," Preswick said, and made no move to leave.

"No scolding tonight, Preswick. You'll have ample time tomorrow. We're going shopping in the morning. I need an appropriate funeral hat and Lily needs a new uniform and an entire new wardrobe."

"Shall I accompany you, my lady?"

"But of course, the proprieties, Preswick."

Preswick unbent enough to raise on eyebrow. "Quite. If that will be all."

"Yes, Good night. And I'll send Lily up to her bed *tout de suite.*"

Preswick bowed and reached for the doorknob.

"One other thing, Preswick. How did you know we should use gloves to search the office? Not from being a butler?"

"No, my lady, but I've been a longtime subscriber to the *Strand.* And Sir Arthur Conan Doyle's stories of Sherlock Holmes are favorites of mine. It was elementary. Good night, my lady."

"Who is this Doyle person?" Lily asked when the door closed behind him.

"A man who writes about a famous detective. Pure fiction." Though Preswick did seem quite knowledgeable about investigative techniques.

A butler who knew about fingerprints and secret compartments, a lady's maid who could pick locks and carried a stiletto. And Phil, merely a dowager before her time. It was a lowering thought. She turned for Lily to unbutton the suddenly not so formidable-feeling purple gown.

7

"You're dressed for going out," Bev said the next morning as Phil joined her for breakfast. Phil was wearing a pale moss green walking dress with a matching brown twill jacket, one of her favorite ensembles. On a day like this, she needed the extra flair it always gave her.

"Yes. I bought this on my last trip to Paris, do you like it?" Phil turned around.

"Love it. I'll come with you."

"Bev," said Phil patiently, "you're in mourning. You can't go shopping."

"Oh, Phil, this is the twentieth century. The modern woman goes to the salons. We even shop in the department stores—the upper floors, of course. We dine with other women in public restaurants." She dropped the triangle of toast she was holding.

"But not while they're in mourning."

Bev pressed the back of her hand to her forehead. "I'll die of boredom."

Phil had a good mind to say better from boredom than from the electric chair, but somehow her wit was running a little too dry even for her this morning. "Well, at least wait until after the funeral."

As it turned out, no one was to go shopping that morning. Phil had just left the breakfast room and was going upstairs to ready herself for the excursion when the front bell sounded and Tuttle appeared from the back hall to hurry toward it.

A brief indecisive moment and Phil decided to leave Bev to

her own devices. She'd had quite enough of Detective Sergeant Atkins for one week. She lifted one side of her skirt and hurried up the stairs.

She reached her bedroom without being summoned. She felt just a little guilty for going shopping while Bev was stuck home being interrogated by the police, but one look at Lily's limp and spot-cleaned uniform told her where her loyalties must lie.

"Fetch my hat, Lily. The brown messaline with the rosettes and feathers. Then put on your coat and—"

There was a tap at the door. Lily went to open it.

A housemaid stepped inside. "Begging your pardon, my lady, but you are requested downstairs."

"That policeman again?"

"No, miss—my lady. It's Mrs. Reynolds's father, Mr. Sloane, and another man is with him."

Phil sighed. She wasn't really looking forward to seeing Bev's father, either. He was bound to be upset. She'd had a not very congenial discussion with her own father before leaving for the "colonies," as he quaintly called them, and wasn't eager to repeat the experience.

"Tell her I'll be down directly."

The maid bowed and withdrew.

"I'm sorry, Lily, it seems we are going to have to postpone your new wardrobe for a few minutes longer." With a quick look in the mirror, she left the room.

Naturally, Preswick was waiting outside the door.

She smiled slightly but didn't stop. At the bottom of the stairs, she'd adjusted her smile and her attitude and stepped into the parlor.

Daniel Sloane had been standing by the unlit fireplace, but he turned when Phil entered the room.

He was tall, rather thin shouldered, but fit for a man in his middle fifties. Two wings of silver were brushed back over his darkish-brown hair. As publisher of one of the oldest bookselling firms in the city, he would have held a certain cachet even without his considerable fortune and pedigree. And his manly good looks made him a favorite at every dinner and ball.

"Ah, Lady Dunbridge. A pleasure as always, but unfortunate for you to visit us in such trying times."

Phil held out her hand. "Unfortunate times, but I'm glad that I could be here for Bev . . . erly in her time of need." She smiled benevolently at Bev, whose cheeks were almost as flushed as her eyes were red. Another day of crying was upon them. Not from missing Reggie, to be sure, probably from the inevitable chastisement from her father.

"Allow me to introduce Mr. Everard Carmichael, Esquire. Everard is our family solicitor."

Philomena inclined her head to Mr. Carmichael, a slight, bespectacled man with thinning hair.

"It's a pleasure, Lady Dunbridge."

"The pleasure is mine," Phil said, wondering how soon she could politely make her exit.

She looked toward Bev for a clue as to why she had been summoned.

Bev jumped as if she'd been goosed. "I told Papa that you knew better than I what happened the day of . . ." She trailed off, circling her hand in the air as if to stir the nasty memory away.

"If you wouldn't mind, Lady Dunbridge," Sloane said, and gestured to the couch.

So it was to be a morning without shopping.

Bev sat in the chair usually reserved for John Atkins, and the two men pulled up secondary chairs. Phil was alone on the sofa as if she were holding court. *Absurd.*

Sloane cleared his throat. "I've already spoken to Beverly on this point, but I shall reiterate it to you for I'm sure you will be in agreement."

Phil doubted it, but she gave him her almost undivided attention. She was keeping one eye on Bev for clues of what to say and what to agree to. They'd perfected this years ago at school, but Phil was rusty. She'd have to be careful.

"That no more should be said to that detective—or any other policeman, I might add—without our solicitor present."

Carmichael's mouth moved a minuscule amount, which Phil took as a reassuring smile, and nodded.

"Not that we think Beverly or you have anything to do with Reggie's unfortunate demise."

Phil cut a look to Bev. He thought Phil might be involved? Surely he jested.

"I think that is wise advice," Phil agreed. Though she would make her own decisions about John Atkins.

Sloane seemed to relax a tad. Relief at having gotten his way? Which Phil thought was probably a rare occurrence when dealing with his daughter and her deceased husband. Or relief, because he actually thought Bev had killed her husband?

"Which reminds me, Beverly. Please do not have Freddy intercede on your behalf in this case.

"It was brought to my attention when I returned home late last night that he has already been meddling." He paused to say to Phil, "I've been in Boston at a book exposition and returned to New York as soon as I could. And before I had time to hand my hat to the footman, I was summoned to the telephone.

"It was someone whose name shall remain anonymous but who is the secretary of a powerful member of the mayor's office. He was not amused at Freddy's antics. He'd actually offered this particular secretary money to keep tabs on the investigation."

"I'm sure he was just trying to help," Bev said, looking mortified.

"I have no doubt Freddy means well, and he does have a minimal amount of clout among the lower orders—the beat men, the sergeants, the clerks—which is good as far as it goes, but in this instance he may have overstepped. He could do more harm than good if he continues."

He leaned ever so slightly toward Philomena and said in a confiding way, "Reggie had a reputation. It's common knowledge that he was heavily in debt."

"Was he, indeed?" Phil said, trying not to think about the bundles of unpaid bills she'd discovered the night before. Did Bev's father know about even half of them?

"Yes, some paltry things, others not so. In fact, he owed rather substantial amounts to several people who'd rather not be dragged through the yellow press. All lent in good faith; no reason to sully their good names."

"Of course not." Perhaps the lowlifes weren't the only ones getting impatient for Reggie to pay up. Was one of them willing to kill Reggie and make him an example for others in the same situation?

"If Freddy will just not muddy the waters, I have every confidence that the killer will be brought to justice forthwith. I don't want to alarm either of you, but it might be better if Beverly returned home to me until her period of mourning is over. Lady Dunbridge, you of course are welcome also."

Here was something not anticipated. And not to Philomena's liking at all. A quick glance at Bev told her Bev was about to throw a fit. Good. Phil would just sit back until Bev reached her peak, then she'd step in to save the day. She had no intention of wiling away her days in a house of mourning overseen by Daniel Sloane. And she was pretty sure Bev would balk.

"Ridiculous," Bev said.

"I'm sorry, dear, but I must insist you close the brownstone."

"You can't do that. You don't own it. You gave it to me as my wedding present."

"So my daughter would have a nice place to live, not so your husband could squander his as well as your money, sell off the artwork and antiques and replace them with this cheap modern pornography. Some of those pieces were your mother's favorites, bless her soul. And I shudder to think what he's done with my library."

Phil thought first of the naked ladies on the painting that concealed the safe. There were plenty of others, and though some of them were painted by the masters, she wondered how many had been there in Daniel Sloane's day. He might be pleased to see his desk hadn't been sold, but he wouldn't be pleased to find the number of bills it held. He might, however, be able to tell them what was in the safe. If he was willing to share, which Phil doubted.

"Beverly, have the servants pack your bags. You're coming home now."

"I most certainly will not. I'm not going to leave my home because Reggie was so inconsiderate to be killed in public. I could kill him myself for that."

"Don't even hint at such a thing," Sloane said. "The sooner they arrest this Florodora woman the better, but until then, I think it's better that you live discreetly under your parent's roof."

"I won't. I'm a woman, not a child. And I have a life. And I have a houseguest."

Sloane glanced at Phil. "Are you certain that Lady Dunbridge wouldn't rather be staying with some other friends who could show her about society instead of remaining in a house of mourning?"

Bev blanched, shot a worried look to Phil.

Here was her chance. Just be understanding and quietly make her exit. "I assure you, Mr. Sloane, that I consider it my duty as a friend to support Bev in her hour of need." She sat back. There, she'd done it, sealed her fate and possibly the future of her two servants. But she couldn't desert Bev now.

Thank you, Bev mouthed.

"Admirable, I'm sure," Sloane said. "But I must insist. Go upstairs now, Beverly. Take what you need for a few days. I'll send someone over for the rest of your things. Don't argue. I've brought Carmichael here to go through Reggie's papers. He's a busy man. I sent to Brangle for a copy of the will."

"Well, I'm not leaving and you can't see the papers," Bev said defiantly. "The police took both Tuttle's and Reggie's keys and locked the door. No one is allowed to enter until the detective sergeant is finished with his investigation."

"Outrageous! We'll just see about that." Sloane leaped to his feet.

Was he planning on breaking down the door? And why was it so important to get to the will today? Reggie wasn't even buried yet.

Carmichael made a deprecating cough. "Sir. I'll talk to the commissioner this afternoon. Get this all sorted out."

"See that you do. In the meantime, I'll just have to demand the keys from this detective what's-his-name."

The door opened. Tuttle stepped inside. "Detective Sergeant Atkins to see you, madam."

Atkins, obviously having learned how to outwit the recalcitrant rich, didn't wait to be fetched but stepped into the room the moment he was announced.

Phil fairly slumped in relief; she was half expecting Sergeant Becker.

Sloane stepped forward and for a moment Phil thought he might actually attempt to push the detective out the door. But he merely stuck out his hand. "I hear you're in charge of investigating the death of my son-in-law. What news have you brought us? Have you caught the infamous villain who did this?"

Atkins shook hands. "The matter is still under investigation."

Sloane glanced at Carmichael. It seemed to Phil that he was a little chagrined. "I will, of course, help in any way I can, but I'd appreciate you not upsetting my daughter, she's very much in shock. She's only downstairs today because she insisted on doing her duty to those wishing to pay their respects."

Phil could have told him Atkins already had Bev's measure, but she just sat back to watch the battle of wills.

Atkins nodded slightly. "I wouldn't think of upsetting Mrs. Reynolds." Lord, Phil didn't know how he managed to keep a straight face. Bev had pulled out all the stops with the beleaguered detective. "But I do have an investigation to run. And this is the scene of a crime."

"Crime? Here? I thought he was killed at the pier."

Atkins looked taken aback, but only for a split second. "I understand you have just returned to town and may not have heard. This residence was the scene of an additional murder."

"Who? How?"

"As yet we don't know his identity. And as for the rest, the details are part of an investigation."

"Preposterous."

He looked at Bev, who merely shrugged. "He was sitting at Reggie's desk."

"At Reggie's desk?" He turned on Atkins. "A burglar? A burglar managed to break into my daughter's house? What do we pay you people for?"

Atkins merely clasped his hands behind his back, Phil thought more in order to hide his clenched fists than withstanding Sloane's storm of protest.

Carmichael interceded. "As you can understand, the family is much upset."

"Upset? When a person isn't safe in his own home. What was taken? When did this take place? Why wasn't I informed?"

"An officer was sent to your residence as a courtesy and was told you were out of town."

"I was in Boston. I took the train back last night." Sloane paled several shades. "You don't mean someone in this household shot the intruder? Bully for him. I'll give the man a raise."

"I wouldn't be too previous if I were you." Atkins shifted ever so slightly. "The complete circumstances of the incident here and those surrounding the death of Reginald Reynolds are still under investigation."

"What?" The one word exploded into the air. Philomena was surprised it didn't send the chandeliers to tinkling. "Let's not mince words, Atkins. Either Reggie's mistress killed him or a thief did. As to the other business, the intruder got what he deserved."

"As I said . . ."

"I don't give a damn what you said, I—"

The door opened. Tuttle stepped in, as stoic as ever except the slight dilation of his eyes. "Mrs. Tappington-Jones . . ." he intoned in his perfectly modulated voice.

There was a profound silence as detective, publisher, and solicitor stared open-mouthed at the butler. Philomena barely resisted the urge to laugh out loud.

Beside her, Bev stifled a snicker.

Phil caught her eye, willed her not to start laughing. This onslaught had all the trappings of a Restoration comedy.

". . . has come to pay her condolences," Tuttle finished and eased himself aside as a tall, buxom woman swept in.

Daniel Sloane strode toward the newcomer. "Hilda, how kind of you to come."

She gave him her hand, which he pressed a little convulsively, Phil thought.

"I came as soon as I heard. I am so sorry, Daniel. How is our Bev holding up?"

"Our Bev" looked as if she might choke on chagrin or derision, it was difficult to tell. There was a story to be had about Mrs. Tappington-Jones.

The woman dropped Sloane's hand and pivoted toward Bev, all of a piece, somewhat like a luncheon epergne. Though on second thought it was her gold visiting suit and fruit-trimmed hat more than her shapely person.

"My poor girl." Mrs. Tappington-Jones wafted toward them.

Bev rose at the same time, and for a split second, Phil feared a collision of heads.

But Mrs. Tappington-Jones held up at the last minute, then clasped both of Bev's hands in hers. "My poor, poor girl. Arthur sends his deepest condolences."

"Thank you. Won't you sit down?" Bev motioned to the occasional chair next to the sofa and Mrs. Tappington-Jones sat.

Carmichael cleared his throat.

Sloane, who had been glaring at Atkins, was startled into action. "Well, we menfolk will leave you ladies to visit. Thank you so much for coming to support dear Beverly in her hour of need."

How many times had she heard that terribly inadequate phrase? Phil wondered. Bev's hour of need was about to turn into a year of unrelenting loneliness.

Mrs. Tappington-Jones smiled at him, letting the remnants of her expression slide over Carmichael and Atkins, as she turned back to Bev.

Sloane gestured Atkins toward the door. Atkins had no choice but to follow. Carmichael lingered only long enough to nod to the ladies, then he followed them out.

"Ah, child, what a terrible tragedy. I know that you are *désolé*." Mrs. Tappington-Jones looked sympathetically at Bev. "But at least you have a dear friend to support you."

Phil doubted if Hilda considered Reggie's death or Bev's widowhood a tragedy. And Bev was anything but *désolé*.

"Thank you, Hilda." Bev sniffed, looked sad. "Forgive my lack of manners. Lady Dunbridge, may I introduce a dear friend of our family, Mrs. Tappington-Jones."

They did their how-do-you-dos perfunctorily. Since Hilda Tappington-Jones had come in instead of merely leaving her card, she wasn't here for expressing condolences. She came for the "dirt."

"I don't know what you must think of us, Lady Dunbridge, but Bev and I can both assure you that New York is a wonderful place to visit. And Bev, I'm just sick to death about what happened to Reggie. I couldn't wait until after the funeral to let you know, that anything, anything I can do, please let me know."

She paused to smile at Phil. Phil knew where this was going, and she wasn't about to look a gift horse in the mouth.

"Well, there is," Bev said. "I'd promised to introduce Philomena to society and here she sits in the midst of tragedy and she hasn't left the house once. I'm afraid I have been the worst hostess ever known."

"No one blames you in any way," Mrs. Tappington-Jones assured her. "And I would be delighted to have Lady Dunbridge join us for social occasions." Another smile at Philomena. "In fact, I would be honored if you'd come and stay with us while you're here. I know Daniel will want Bev home with him until she's feeling stronger."

Bev visibly gritted her teeth.

"That is so very kind of you, Mrs. Tappington-Jones, and I do appreciate the offer, but I feel I can't totally desert Bev. I just ended my own mourning, and I know how lonely that can be. I would however, be honored if you might show me about, as it were. Perhaps introduce me to a few people."

"Oh, my dear, it would be my pleasure. Everyone is quite aware of your arrival and will be so disappointed if you shun our society."

"I wouldn't think of doing anything to disappoint," Phil returned.

"Then it's decided, and you must begin by joining Arthur and me at a little dinner party we're having on Thursday for a visiting Austrian dignitary."

Phil smiled, dipped her head. *Well, it was a start.* "I gladly accept. Thank you."

"Excellent. None of us would want you to miss out on the festivities." Hilda sighed. "I declare, this new idea of parties all the time keeps one busy from sunrise to the wee hours year-round. But I suppose it's better than the way we used to do things, crammed all in between Christmas and Lent. It absolutely fagged one to death.

"But no going back. Progress will out. Now I must take my leave. I'll ask Daniel to accompany you. That way he can't say no. He's become such an old hermit since your mother died."

“Excellent idea,” Bev said. “I’m sure he will enjoy it immensely.”

“Well, I must be going. Don’t hesitate to call for anything you need. And Lady Dunbridge, I expect to see you on Thursday. Bev, stay seated and rest. I’ll have Tuttle show me out.”

As soon as she was gone, Bev let out a sigh. “She’s rather effusive, but we must put up with her. She was Father’s mistress at one time, and I believe they still catch a quick one now and then.” She waggled her eyebrows. “My father, imagine.”

“I want to hear all about it, but not now.” Phil went to the door and poked her head out. “The coast is clear. I suggest you run upstairs and have a case of the vapors until Atkins takes himself off.”

“Okay, but what are you going to do?”

“If I’m to meet society, I must take my maid shopping. She’s not fit to be seen.”

8

A few minutes later, Phil trundled Lily and Preswick down the front stairs to Bev's town carriage. She couldn't wait to get away, just for a few minutes. This was not how she envisioned her first few days in America; she would be a good friend but, really, even good friends needed respite now and then.

Bentley was waiting for them at the curb. Phil paused long enough to nod to the constable who was standing across the street.

Phil climbed into the carriage, followed by Lily and Preswick, though he balked at riding inside. She just hoped he could hold on until they established their own living arrangements. And even then it wouldn't be the same as running a full household. She hoped he would adjust to their new life.

Bev had given her the names and addresses of several salons with an introductory letter, but Phil was not shopping for herself today. Tuttle had given them the address of a shop that clothed domestic workers and several nearby shops where they would be able to buy the girl an acceptable wardrobe.

As they drove away, Phil caught a glimpse of the policeman, hand in the air, hailing a cab. Oh, Lord, he was going to follow them all afternoon.

It seemed to take an inordinate amount of time to go the few blocks before turning south onto Third Avenue. The traffic, smells, and noises were just as bad as in London. No wonder Bev had merchants come to her.

They inched down the avenue and had just passed Sixtieth Street when the carriage stopped for the umpteenth time.

Phil looked out the window to see if they were still being followed by the constable, but it was impossible to tell in the crush of vehicles. They were surrounded by motorcars, carriages, drays, and handcarts. Pedestrians scooted between them, taking their lives in their hands to catch the trolley car or merely to cross the street.

Even the sidewalks were crowded with shoppers and workers pushing their way up and down the pavement, skirting around the street venders, avoiding elbows, and dodging shopping bags.

They inched forward and stopped again.

Preswick seemed content to look out the carriage windows, but Lily was having a hard time containing her anticipation of buying new clothes.

Phil sympathized. She was impatient also. Outside her window, a huge building rose several stories. A steady flow of women, children, and men entered and exited with abandon. All carrying parcels. And Phil and her companions were confined in an unmoving carriage.

"Preswick, what is that building?"

The butler leaned over and looked out the window. "It appears to be a department store. Bloomingdale's according to the sign."

"Bloomingdale's. Excellent. The Harrods of the West. We'll start our shopping there." Phil knocked on the ceiling. "Bentley, we'll get out here."

Bentley pulled the carriage to the curb.

"You may return for us in three hours," Phil told him.

"Very good."

"He'll probably still be here in three hours," Lily said.

"Very likely," Phil said. "Shall we go inside?"

"Oh, yes, madam." Lily reached for the door.

"Lily, mind your place," Preswick ordered.

Lily threw herself back against the seat. "I beg your pardon, Mr. Pr-r-reswick."

"Come along, Preswick." Phil opened the door and was almost

out of the carriage while the groom was still letting down the step. Lily bounded down behind her.

"Your ladyship, wait. What are you doing?" Preswick climbed down behind them.

"We're going to a department store." She didn't know whether she or Lily was more excited. In her former life, *affaires de coeur* were expected; rubbing shopping bags with the great unwashed was strictly taboo.

But no longer. As Bev pointed out, it was the twentieth century and the peerage of England was very far away. She'd be completely unrecognized here.

She quickly looked around. The policeman who was following them got out of a hansom cab several carriages back. Honestly, what did John Atkins think she could possibly do on a shopping excursion? No matter, they'd stop at the lingerie department first. That should deter his efforts.

"Come quickly, before he sees us."

"But my lady."

Phil took off toward the entrance. Unfortunately, she didn't see the older gentleman stepping out of the hansom cab that had stopped just in front of them.

"Oof," Phil said, practically knocking him over. He was tall but rather frail, stooped in the shoulder with a full gray beard and wearing a bowler hat and a worn morning suit.

"I beg your pardon, madam," he said, doffing his hat to reveal a head of coarse bushy gray hair and releasing the faint aroma of an unusual scented pipe tobacco.

"No, it was all my fault and I do apologize," Phil said. "Are you all right?"

"But of course. It is not every day I literally run into a lady of such quality."

He spoke with a faint accent, Romanian or Hungarian.

"Nor I to meet a gentleman so delightfully unexpectedly." No reason not to return his compliment. This was America.

He nodded, she nodded, and Preswick whisked her away.
"Quite, Preswick."

"My lady?"

"You were about to chastise me for talking to a total stranger on the street. I was a little excited. But I did almost run him over. I hope the poor man is all right. And he had such a twinkle in his eye that I couldn't resist. I promise to be more discreet in the future." She looked back for the victim of her enthusiasm, but he had disappeared into the crowd.

"Then come let us see what this Bloomingdale's has to offer." They joined others climbing the wide marble staircase just inside the entrance, passing others carrying parcels, some accompanied by a porter or maid, coming down the stairs on the opposite side.

"Where to begin," Phil said, once they reached the first floor and saw that it stretched as far as the eye could see.

Lily for once was speechless.

They wandered up and down the aisles of glass display cases containing everything imaginable. Phil had ventured into Harrods several times, even purchased a few minor items, and ridden the "escalator" there.

Even Preswick was impressed by the array of goods on sale. They wandered from floor to floor, taking in all their surroundings. On the third floor, they stopped to listen to a phonograph that played all the latest songs on hard round discs. The rows and rows of premade clothing were daunting, but at the end of an hour they had purchased Lily two day dresses and a walking outfit, stockings, underthings, and a pair of shoes. Just as they were leaving, she spied an elaborate parasol. Her delight was catching. So even though she would rarely be able to use it except for her half day off, once she knew her way around well enough to have a day off, Phil gladly bought it for her.

They stopped to eat lemon ices on the street and Preswick led them to a much smaller establishment, where domestic uniforms were sold.

But Phil had seen a small book emporium two doors down. She'd been chastising herself ever since the discovery of the dead man in the library for not having listened to Sir Edward's talk on fingerprinting. Here was a perfect opportunity to rectify that oversight.

She left explicit instructions with Preswick on what to buy, and though he tried to convince her to wait for them, when she explained that she need to buy some books and Lily must have new uniforms, he acquiesced.

"And don't be miserly, Preswick, if you please," Phil told him under her breath. "Uniforms, underthings, stockings, and day wear for when she is working. And Preswick, nothing but the best for a servant of mine."

"But of course, my lady."

Having safely extricated herself from an hour of toil, Phil headed straight into the bookstore. The proprietor sat on a stool behind a counter, stroking a fat orange cat who was stretched across an open book the man was obviously trying to read.

The man slid off the stool. "May I help you, madam?" Standing, he was no taller than he had been when sitting at the counter, a little over five feet tall and dressed in a brown suit and bow tie.

"Yes, if you please. I'm looking for a book on fingerprints."

He blinked. Rolled his eyes toward his eyebrows as if the catalog of his inventory was written on his forehead.

He smiled, dipped his chin. "An unusual request, but I do believe I may have something that would interest you. This way, please."

He led her down a narrow aisle between two towering cases that ran the length of the store. At the back the entire wall was one floor-to-ceiling bookcase with a ladder that ran on tracks from one end to the other.

He moved this halfway along the case, then climbed to the top shelf, where he touched the spines of several volumes until he came to a slim volume, which he pulled out.

"Here is the *Classification and Uses of Fingerprints* by Sir Edward Henry," he said from his lofty perch. "Is madam interested in other forensic tomes? I have several."

"Yes," Phil said, "I am."

He nodded, then holding on to the ladder with one hand, he stretched himself as far as possible and jimmied out two more volumes, before tucking all three under his arm and climbing down to the floor.

She followed him to the front of the store, where he pushed the cat off to the side and placed the books on the countertop.

"Here is Dr. Edmond Locard's paper on what he calls the 'exchange principle,' the fact that a criminal always leaves something behind when he commits a crime. Like your fingerprints. But also other things—footprints, hair, clothing fibers." He smiled deprecatingly. "I happen to be a crime buff myself. I'm afraid it's written in French."

"My French is excellent," Phil said. And if she had gaps in her understanding, she had no doubt Lily could help with the translation.

"And this other one?"

"And this is a must-read for any gentleman—or lady—interested in investigation. Dr. Gross's *Criminal Investigation, a Practical Handbook.* It's quite thorough on actual investigative techniques, though I must warn you, it can be rather specific. Actually, perhaps it isn't appropriate for a . . ."

"It sounds perfect. I'll take all three." To these she added the latest edition of the *Strand,* which had a Sherlock Holmes story advertised on the cover. She was fairly certain Preswick hadn't read it, though he would never suggest buying it in her presence.

The door opened, a little bell tinkled, and another customer entered the store. "With you in one moment, sir," the proprietor said, and rang up Phil's purchases.

"No hurry at all," the newcomer said in a slight European accent.

The door closed, and a moment later Phil caught a whiff of exotic tobacco. She turned around. It was the old man from the hansom cab.

"Ah, what a double pleasure this fine day," he said, his eyes twinkling. He quite reminded her of a favorite professor from Madame Floret's.

He made his way over to the counter. "Ah, I see you are a reader of Sir Arthur's. If I might suggest a title that might interest you?"

Phil smiled. She'd always had a soft spot for delightful but lonely old men. "Please."

"Do you have the *Memoires of Sherlock Holmes*?"

"I certainly do," the proprietor said, and hurried off to the shelves. He returned a minute later with a rather large book.

"I think you would rather enjoy 'The Adventure of Silver Blaze.' One of my favorites," said the old gentleman.

"Thank you," Phil said, and nodded to the proprietor to add it to her bundle.

"My pleasure. Now, my good man, can you direct me to the history section."

He tipped his hat to Phil and disappeared into the rows of bookshelves, while the proprietor saw her out of the store.

They returned to the brownstone so laden down with parcels that the footmen were called to carry them inside.

"It looks like a fruitful excursion, my lady," Tuttle said, and closed the door behind her. "Mrs. Reynolds is in the parlor. Mrs. Beecham is here."

"Tell them I'll be down as soon as I rid myself of this hat." And these books, she added silently. She'd practically had to wrestle the footman to keep him from carrying them. But she insisted on carrying them herself. It was one thing for a lady to indulge in the occasional novel, but forensic enlightenment? Disgraceful.

Phil was sitting at her boudoir mirror when Lily burst into the room.

"Did you have your tea already?" Phil pulled the last pin from her hat and tossed the hat into Lily's agile hands.

"No, but I wanted to tell you. The servants were having their tea when I came in. They were talking about their mistress. And wondering whether she was going to be taken off to jail."

"Idle speculation."

"Maybe, but they said there was a ter-r-r-ible row after we left. And Mr. Sloane told that inspector-r-r—"

"Detective sergeant," Phil corrected.

"That detective ser-r-r-geant that he'd see him in hell before he accused his daughter of murder."

"Oh, dear." Phil stood for Lily to unbutton her visiting dress. "I think the aquamarine tea gown for the afternoon, Lily."

She followed Lily into the dressing room. "Is Detective Atkins still here?"

"I do not know, they shut up when they saw me."

"Oh, dear. Here, help me into this dress and then run downstairs for your tea before they finish. Time to slip them a morsel. Grease the wheel so to speak. *Capisce*?"

"*Sì*. What shall I tell them?"

"Well . . . that we were followed by the police on our excursion today and we had to give them the slip."

"But we did not. That silly one was always nearby, and he bumped into the manikin and tried to apologize. *Stupido*."

Phil chuckled. "Well, that's a good tale, they'll enjoy the laugh.

"Meanwhile I'll go down to Mrs. Reynolds and find out just what happened while we were gone. And tonight will be a night of study."

As soon as Phil was dressed and her hair had been tidied, she sent Lily on her way to the kitchen, and she took herself to the parlor, hoping not for tea but for one of Bev's cocktails. Even a glass of sherry would suffice, though she really hated sherry.

Another good thing about America, she noted, as she went down the stairs. Ladies weren't stuck drinking sherry and tea but indulged in cocktails and whiskey and soda and all manner of things. Yes, once they were past this murder business she thought she would enjoy living here very much.

Phil found Bev and Marguerite Beecham sitting on the parlor settee. Tuttle stood at the drinks cabinet mixing cocktails, though not martinis. These had a distinct pink tint to them. The things she'd missed while being in black for the last year and a half. Well, no more.

"Phil, there you are," Bev said. "Look who's here."

"Good afternoon, Lady Dunbridge."

"Do call me Phil. Lady Dunbridge reminds me that I'm actually a dowager, and I find that so lowering."

"Phil. And you must call me Marguerite. Did Bev send you to the incomparable Madame Grayard?"

"She did give me an introduction," Phil said, taking a seat in what she'd come to think of as the detective's chair. She rather liked the idea of her in the detective's seat.

"Oh, Phil, don't keep us in suspense. Did you see Madame Grayard? Did you order fabulous things?"

"Actually no," Phil said, taking a glass from Tuttle.

"Pink gin," Bev said by way of explanation.

Phil took a sip. "Interesting."

"So where did you spend the last several hours if not at Madame Grayard's?"

Bev and Marguerite must have started on the pink gins awhile back, their cheeks were flushed and Bev at least seemed a little giddy.

"Well, actually, we stopped at one of your department stores. Bloomingdale's. Fascinating. We had to get my maid Lily some new furnishings," Phil explained to Marguerite. "She lost most of her luggage on the voyage over."

"I've heard there have been increasing problems with theft," Marguerite said.

Phil had never heard that, but she nodded. "Then we visited the domestic goods shop, ate ices on the street. Scandalous but delicious." She decided not to mention the bookstore. She held up her drink and considered its color. "And this drink will probably go straight to my head, since besides the ices, we never stopped to eat."

"That's no problem. I'm rather peckish myself. Tuttle, please bring us a tray of hors d'oeuvres. We're all absolutely starving."

"Yes, madam." Tuttle strode out of the room.

"Even a trip to Bloomingdale's would be better than the way I spent today."

"With Marguerite here to entertain you?"

"Oh, she just arrived a little while ago."

"I would have come earlier, Bev, if I'd known you needed me."

"I know you would and you're a dear for keeping me company when you must have a thousand things to do. I was just about to tell Marguerite about Hilda Tappington-Jones's condolence visit this morning."

"Old crow," Marguerite said. "What did she want? To smirk over Reggie's death or use it as an opportunity to flirt with your poor father?"

"It was a condolence call," Bev said. "And she was perfectly civil . . . when she wasn't making eyes at my father. It was rather depressing."

"Well, I hope you're not going all sentimental over that philandering husband of yours."

"No, but I do prefer the wake the other night. Reggie's friends were all so droll . . . most of them." Bev sighed.

"Well," said Marguerite, "whoever did shoot him did you a favor."

"Really, Marguerite," Bev protested.

"Oh, don't get miffed. I'm sure Lady Dunbridge is in your confidence." She looked at Bev for confirmation.

"Of course she is."

"Then not to put too fine a point on it, we all know what Reggie was and how he spent his—and your—money. How he was constantly humiliating you with his affairs. Have you had a chance to look through his papers?"

Phil frowned. A rather abrupt non sequitur. Of what concern could Reggie's papers be to Marguerite?

Bev shook her head. "Father was here with our solicitor, Mr. Carmichael, but that Atkins fellow wouldn't allow them to get into the library. I don't care how swell the guy looks in a suit, he's trouble. And he and Father had such a dustup. I think he wanted to take me to jail."

"Did he say that?" Phil asked.

"Not exactly. But he asked all sorts of impertinent questions, and I didn't have you here to put him in his place." Bev turned to Marguerite. "You should see Phil in action. Wonderful."

"What kind of questions?"

"I don't know. Stupid stuff. And he still won't let anyone in the library because it's still a crime scene, and Father threw one of his mightier-than-thou fits, which have often quailed the entire publishing world. It didn't seem to have much effect on that detective, which it should, because he could easily find himself out of a job.

"Then he finally left after threatening to put a guard on the library door, unless we all wanted to vacate the premises, and Father said absolutely not. That it was his daughter's house and that I would stay here as was my right. So I didn't even have to fight with Father to stay here. John Atkins did it for me. Which I suppose I should be thankful for, but really not if he's going to send me to prison.

"I shudder to think what they'll find. Reggie had to borrow a large sum from me just last week. He said it was to increase his bet on this new horse of his, Devil's Thunder. That we would be rich after the race. Of course we're already rich. Rich enough for me, anyway."

"Maybe not for Miss Potts."

"Ugh, don't mention that name. If I ever see her again, I'll wring her neck."

"Bev," exclaimed Phil.

"Well, I will."

"Fine, just don't say it aloud." Phil tilted her head toward the closed door. "Sing Sing?" she whispered.

Bev shuddered. "It's just a nightmare, Marguerite. And yesterday they found a dead man in the library."

"A dead man? How awful. Was it a burglar after Reggie's money?" Marguerite turned to Phil. "Reggie always kept a large amount of cash in the safe. The whole world knew. Very irresponsible, if you ask me."

"I guess," Bev said. "He said he needed quick access to it. For his racing and betting cronies. They were always coming and going at all hours. And no doubt for that cow he kept on the Upper West Side."

"I take it you're alluding to the mistress," Phil guessed.

"That odious Mildred Potts, I refuse to call her Mimi LaPonte. She was a human sponge when it came to Reggie's money."

"I hope she's not planning to get her hooks into Freddy now," Marguerite said, and snapped her teeth, which completely spoiled Phil's former impression of her being a meek and docile woman.

"Is there any chance of that?" Phil asked.

"Oh, Reggie's not the only philanderer in his family. And I'm not sure that Freddy didn't dip his wick in that pot of wax. He was certainly chummy with that whole gaggle of cheap tarts. After all, it was he who introduced Reggie to her, for which, Bev, I'm eternally sorry." Marguerite sighed. "Though it did pave the way for you to see more of Otto Klein."

"Wait," Phil said, glancing toward the door and leaning forward. She lowered her voice. "I thought you said you hadn't had a lover recently."

Bev shrugged one shoulder. "Well, not recently, I guess."

"What do you mean?" Marguerite said. "You gave him his congé?"

"I'm afraid so. But it was a few weeks ago. He wanted me to leave Reggie and run away with him to Prussia, of all places. It sounded so morose. He did not take it well."

"A few weeks ago?" Phil asked.

"About three. He was getting to be a bore, one thing I could never say about Reggie. And you were coming and I wanted to be free to frolic."

"Oh, my God."

"What is it, Phil? Are you unwell?"

"Maybe. Please tell me Otto wasn't the man in the library."

Bev's eyebrows furrowed. "In the . . ." Her hand came to her mouth. "Oh, heavens no. Why would he be?"

"I have no idea. But Bev, if there is any other little thing you haven't told me, now would be an appropriate time."

"I don't understand."

Phil wondered when her friend had gotten so dense; she remembered her as smart and witty. Several years had passed, but surely . . . "There are two murders associated with this house, one of which was your husband. The identity of the other remains to be seen. Any way you consider it, you are involved."

"You don't think they suspect Bev of killing her husband?" Marguerite's expression flashed with something that Phil thought was more than concern. Fear? "That's ridiculous."

"I'm not privy to what they think, but I can tell you this, Detective Sergeant Atkins is no dimwit, and he won't be bought. At least not yet."

"Well, Father will put him straight there," Bev said.

I wouldn't bet on it, Phil thought. "Well, until then I think we should all be discreet."

"Well, I really must be going." Marguerite put her drink down and opened her bag. She rummaged around and pulled out a piece of peppermint candy.

She unwrapped it and dropped the wrapper in her empty

glass. "So the servants won't gossip about me drinking in the afternoon." She made a droll expression and slid the peppermint into her mouth.

"Until tomorrow, then. Freddy and I will be here at nine." She leaned over and kissed Bev's cheek. "I'll see myself out."

9

When Philomena retired to her bedroom later that night, she found Lily dressed in her new maid's uniform. The books she'd bought that afternoon were stacked neatly on a card table placed near the reading lamp in the window alcove. A tablet of lined paper and several pens and pencils had been placed in front of one of the two chairs set at right angles at the table.

"You've been busy this evening," Phil said approvingly.

"Yes madam, my lady."

"I see you didn't bring a chair for Preswick."

"He said he would not sit in the presence of ma—my lady."

"You know, Lily. I'm growing quite used to madam, rather than my lady. We'll never get Preswick to change, but if it isn't too difficult to remember, you may use madam when we are alone."

"Yes, madam."

"And you must make allowances for Preswick. He's been a butler for many years. And he did know about the secret compartment."

"Yes, madam."

"So let us begin." Phil sat in one of the chairs and gestured for Lily to sit in the other.

"*Classification and Uses of Finger Prints.* Let us see what they are and what we did wrong the other night in the library." Phil opened the book, looked up. "How well do you read, Lily?"

"In which language, madam?"

"English."

"Well enough, madam."

"Excellent." And one day Lily might actually drop a clue about who she was and why she was willing to serve as someone's lady's maid when she'd obviously been educated for more. "Yes, well . . . 'The employment of finger prints in many branches . . .'" She turned a few pages. "Ah, here it is, 'Finger Prints Part I.'"

The funeral was held the next day. An overcast sky and incipient rain exemplified everyone's feelings and boded no good. The funeral attire arrived early that morning, and when Phil met Bev at breakfast the two of them looked as morose as the gray clouds gathering outside.

"Lord, I hope it doesn't rain," Bev said, pulling at the crepe ruching around her neck. "I swear whoever decided that a widow should be tortured for two years just because her no-good husband died should be shot."

"True," Phil said, thinking Bev looked rather tragically elegant in her funeral dress, but for the fact she was munching on a piece of toast and reading the *Tribune*.

"Well, the good news is we won't have to put up with that annoying policeman anymore. They've taken the husband-stealing Mildred into custody."

"For murder?" Phil asked.

"For 'questioning in the death of Reginald Reynolds.' And for not cooperating with the police. So there."

Phil, who had just picked up the coffeepot, put it down again. "They said death and not murder?"

"Yes. Though we all know she did it."

"Bev, no, we don't. And if they've only taken her into custody for not cooperating . . ." She let the sentence trail off, hoping maybe Bev would take the hint. Alas, it was not to be.

"Well, I say she did it." Bev rattled the newspaper as she turned the page. "Here's something much more interesting. Black hats are back in favor this season. I suppose I should be glad seeing how I may be wearing them for some time."

While Bev read aloud about the latest Paris fashions, Phil poured herself coffee and helped herself from the sideboard buffet.

Daniel Sloane arrived a few minutes before ten to accompany his daughter to the church in his closed carriage. Philomena followed with Freddy and Marguerite. The servants were conveyed in two carriages, Tuttle, Elmira, Preswick, and Lily driven by Bentley, the head coachman; Cook and the lesser staff were crammed together in the second carriage, driven by an understableman.

It began to rain almost the minute they entered the carriage. "Good thing we didn't bring Reggie's touring car," Freddy said, and breathed out a chuckle.

Marguerite shot him a fulminating look, reached in her bag, and brought out one of her peppermint candies, which she pushed into his hand.

Looking sheepish, Freddy unwrapped it. It took some doing—it seemed to be stuck in the paper—but at last he popped the candy in his mouth and shoved the wrapper in his pocket.

Marguerite scowled at the closed carriage window.

Phil didn't blame Marguerite. She gotten close enough to smell the liquor on Freddy's breath this morning. Though she supposed he should be forgiven for a fortifier before his cousin's funeral. If it had been up to her, she would have had Tuttle serve cocktails to all before they piled into the carriages of the cortege.

"Have the police returned the automobile?" Phil asked, risking Marguerite's further disapproval.

"So I've been told. I haven't seen it myself."

"Where does he house it?"

"At a garage on Fifty-Eighth Street."

"And when he wants to use it, he has to go ten blocks to retrieve it?"

"No. He merely telephones around and has someone drive it over."

"And that person would also be his driver, if he wished."

Freddy frowned at her. "Oh, no, Reggie always drove. Sometimes I wondered if he didn't like motorcars better than his horses."

"Or his women," Marguerite said caustically, provoking surprised looks from both Freddy and Phil.

Certainly better than his wife, Phil thought.

It was fully raining by the time the carriages arrived at the church. They were shown up the steps by the undertaker's lackeys, holding large black umbrellas over their heads, which may have kept the gentlemen dry but did little to keep the ladies' skirts from trailing through the puddles.

The sidewalks were packed with people, seemingly oblivious of the downpour. Umbrellas were raised only to have them jerked down again by someone standing behind whose view was cut off.

Murmurs rolled through the crowd as the servants passed to be seated in the back pew but were soon replaced by rustling anticipation. "Is that her? Is that the wife?" as Marguerite and Phil, huddled under their umbrellas, hurried inside.

"That's her comin' now!" A roar of cheers and boos resounded as Phil reached the vestibule.

She turned to see Bev, head bent and leaning against her father, stumble on the steps of the church.

"Did you murder him?" came a cry from the crowd, which was quickly muffled as the yeller was dragged away by a squad of policeman.

Daniel tightened his hold on Bev and she managed to stay on her feet.

"Buck up, Bev! We know you didn't do it! Three cheers for Reggie and Bev!"

Daniel Sloane steered Bev into the church, and the doors shut on the cheers behind them.

Phil took Bev's free arm and gave it a squeeze. "It's almost over." She knew it wasn't anywhere near being over. A person could grow old at a funeral service, catch pneumonia while waiting for the casket to be lowered into the ground, and as for the ensuing mourning period—cruel and unjust.

As they walked down the aisle, the church doors opened and shut again on shouts and pinpricks of driving rain. There was a ripple of movement and murmurs behind them. Phil had to concentrate on not turning around, to see if Mildred Potts, the now notorious Mimi LaPonte, was free and had dared to make an appearance. It would be the height of poor taste to do so, but no one had ever accused the Americans of being tasteful.

Fortunately, she had Lily and Preswick sitting in the back pews with the household servants who would be her eyes and ears. Though Preswick would never admit it, butlers were the world's best spies. They knew everything there was to know about their masters and the masters' households.

And Lily? Who knew? She was an enigma, and Philomena wasn't about to press her into telling her story. She didn't want to scare the girl into running away. She was turning out to be an excellent companion, and if her hairdressing left a little to be desired and Phil's undergarments weren't perfectly folded, at least they were clean and well cared for.

Phil didn't want the girl to feel threatened and "do a bunk," as they said in the East End. Beautiful and alone, without Phil's protection, she would be susceptible to every undesirable villain in the country.

The one time Phil had asked if she had family or friends here whom she would like to contact, she'd given an emphatic no. And Phil had left it at that.

They made their way slowly down the aisle to the front pew, Phil on one side of Bev, her father on the other. Marguerite and Freddy sat on the pew farther down. The church was packed to capacity, which would account for the crowd outside. Phil hoped there would be no more outbursts during the service. Whatever their relationship had been, Bev was certainly filled with emotion this morning.

Was it a coincidence that someone had killed Reggie on the day she arrived? And why in a public venue? Someone had managed to kill a man in Reggie's own study. Why couldn't they just have killed Reggie there, too?

Of course, that would even more strongly point to Bev as the potential murderer.

The eulogy began. The preacher's voice was kind, but the man he described sounded nothing like the man Phil had met. Did Reggie really have a heart of gold?

And if he did, why was he dead? And who . . . ? And . . .

The congregation stood; Phil stood with them, sat down again.

Was the murderer sitting somewhere in the church behind them? Sorry for what he had done? Or smirking that he had gotten away with it?

How she wished she could turn around and peruse those faces, but she kept her head bowed, while the preacher's words droned into a distant buzz.

Organ music startled her from her thoughts and she realized the service had ended. She stood mechanically with the others. The pallbearers took their places on either side of the ornate casket, and Phil recognized Bobby Mullins as one of them. He was someone else she should talk to, because if the initial meeting with detective Atkins was any indication, Mr. Mullins knew more than he was telling.

Atkins didn't strike Phil as the type of policemen who would resort to bribes or bullying; Freddy's attempt certainly had no effect on him. But Mr. Mullins wouldn't be forthright without some incentive . . . A lady had her wiles, after all.

The pallbearers lifted the casket with precision and began their slow, arduous journey to the back door.

Bev and her father filed out behind the casket. The Beechams followed. Phil joined the precession, her head bowed but her eyes searching the mourners. What wonderful things veils were, she thought, as she studied the crowd. She didn't know what—or rather, whom—she was looking for. But it wouldn't hurt to look. Who knew what little discovery one might stumble across.

For instance, there was more than one comely young lady, whose handkerchief found its way beneath her veil to stanch the flow of tears. Evidence that Reggie's stable didn't limit itself to horses.

Was one of them Mimi LaPonte? Phil would never forget that face as she stared down at Reggie's bloodied body. But today she couldn't see faces, just a sea of veils. Veils made an excellent disguise.

The back pew was empty, the servants having been scuttled away to prepare for the return of their mistress. John Atkins was standing at the very back, hat in hand, head bowed, eyes roaming, and Phil swore their eyes met, even though there was no way he could have seen hers beneath her veil.

She looked in his vicinity for Charles Becker but didn't see him among the crowd. She hoped Atkins had won out and they wouldn't be bothered by the "Fireplug" again.

Then she passed out the door and into the carriage that would make the interminable drive out to the cemetery and back.

Marguerite looked straight ahead, dry-eyed, her thoughts shuttered. Freddy sucked nervously on a peppermint and kept jiggling his foot at random intervals until Phil wanted to physically hold his knee still.

How could anyone think with that kind of distraction?

Was Freddy Reggie's only relative? Bev had never mentioned his family and Phil hadn't at the time been interested enough to ask. She was interested now. If he was, was Freddy expecting to inherit? Was Mimi LaPonte?

The will was to be read that afternoon, and Phil was determined to be by Bev's side. Curiosity? Yes. But she knew how confusing wills could be.

Codicils and entailments, therefores and whereofs. Phil had had no one with her at the reading of the earl's will. And though she imagined Daniel Sloane would be present, she wouldn't let Bev go into that lion's den alone.

"I thought that would never end," Bev said, as she tore the pins from her hat and tossed it on the foyer table. "Tuttle!" She headed for the parlor, unbuttoning her coat as she walked while Elmira followed literally in her footsteps trying to ease it off her shoulders.

Phil allowed Lily to take her coat and hat and smiled as she acknowledged Lily's eyes widen and return to normal. *The girl had news.* Excellent, but for now one of Bev's excellent cocktails was definitely in order.

Daniel Sloane, Mr. Carmichael, and Mr. Brangle, Reggie's attorney, had repaired to the billiards room, a room Phil hadn't known existed until that moment. They certainly managed to pack a lot of rooms into the rectangular brownstone.

Phil passed Elmira on her way out, carrying Bev's coat in a haphazard fashion. Bev was already sitting on the settee, legs stretched out along the cushion, her hand held desultorily in the air waiting for Tuttle to place a long-stemmed glass between her fingers.

She looked like a nymph in repose, though her eyes were red rimmed, and Phil had heard more than one sob being suppressed by a handkerchief held in a tight fist.

Phil tried to think back to Dunbridge's passing. The only tears she'd shed were tears of relief. The earl had been less than virile, which had made him vicious. And he'd taken out much of his frustrations on his wife. Phil would never forgive her parents for being so enamored with his title that they had refused to listen to the warnings of their friends.

Something she supposed she had in common with those poor American girls thrust at effete peers just because their fathers were willing to pay for it. It was a lowering thought. But no more. The tables were turned, and as soon as this terrible business was over, Philomena Amesbury, née Hathaway, Countess of Dunbridge, would take Manhattan by storm.

For now she took the glass Tuttle was holding out to her.

"How clever of Freddy and Marguerite to reserve Sherry's for the funeral luncheon," Bev said. "Good food and wine and a toast to send Reggie off, another for the grieving widow, and they'll be on their way. They'll wonder why I'm not there. Or maybe they've already forgotten me."

"Do you care?" Phil asked, surprised by this bit of reflection from Bev.

"Well, I've been running with that crowd for so long."

"No reason not to run with them, as you say, though the expression tends to remind one of the hunt. Just get rid of the lowlifes. They can't be that entertaining."

"They're not. I just hope I haven't become one of them."

They sat for a while, had another cocktail, and waited for the reading of the will.

"Listen, Bev, when they call you in, lean on me and say you can't do without me."

"I can't."

"Thank you, but I'm worried that in your bereaved state you might not understand all the bequests."

"You think Reggie is going to cheat me even in death?"

"I'm sure your father will prevent that. But it helps to have a second pair of ears for things we might not expect." Like not only all the entailed land but also the contents of one's castle even when those contents were part of your dowry or were given to you as gifts. Phil had learned life's lesson the hard way and would be living a dire existence in a crumbling dower house save for her grandmother's foresight. Eccentric maybe, but no fool, Almay Grandison Hathaway. Phil missed her sorely and hoped to do good by her.

She raised her glass to her memory.

They were called into the dining room at three, Bev admirably clinging to Phil's arm and begging her not to leave her. And

Phil thought maybe it wasn't all an act. There was a formidable panel already sitting at the table. On one side, the two lawyers and Bev's father, and on the other, cousin Freddy and Bobby Mullins.

Bev's grip tightened on Phil's arm. Phil gave a reassuring touch of her hand.

Tuttle stood just inside the green baize door, in his capacity as butler and to accept the usual death gratuities for the household.

The gentlemen rose when Bev and Phil entered. Both lawyers looked askance at Phil but didn't demur when she helped Bev to be seated then sat down beside her.

Phil waited with her heart in her throat, half expecting Mildred Potts to pop in at the last minute demanding her fair share.

The men returned to their seats, except for Mr. Brangle, who cleared his throat. "Before we begin the reading of the will, let me express my condolences for your loss." Mr. Brangle bowed in Bev's direction.

"With your permission I have asked Freddy Beecham and Robert Mullins to attend the reading. Though they are not direct beneficiaries as such, Mr. Reynolds has left instructions to be given them at this time."

Freddy started, swallowed convulsively. So no inheritance for Freddy. Mullins was expressionless. Not a twitch of his beefy countenance.

Brangle looked the most distressed of the three, and Phil wondered, *Ah, what evil lurks in that shiny bald pate?* She gave Bev's hand another squeeze. It was all she could do.

"Very well," Bev said.

And so it began.

A sum was left to Tuttle with an additional amount granted to the staff to be divided as per instruction by Tuttle.

"Thank you, Tuttle, you may leave us now," Brangle said.

Tuttle bowed and left the room, but unless Phil missed her guess, not so far as to be unable to overhear what came next.

Phil had every confidence that her own servants would have found a spy hole through which to listen to the proceedings.

"'As for my remaining assets, to include moneys, establishments, and stables . . .'" Brangle named several stables and their locations. "'The stock, including . . .'" He named several racehorses. "'Their progeny and all things owned by the entity known as Holly Farm, I leave entirely to Beverly Sloane Reynolds.'"

"Oh," Bev exclaimed, and burst into tears.

Phil handed her a hankie, which she had at the ready. At a reading of a will, there were bound to be tears.

"'I strongly advise Beverly to retain the services of Freddy Beecham in the role of financial adviser, and Robert Mullins as stable manager for a period of six months, at which time she may decide to sell or continue the business under her own aegis.'"

Bobby's head snapped toward Bev, a combination of surprise, anger, and perhaps fear, an expression intense enough to make Phil flinch. Fortunately, Bev was looking at the table's shining surface. Freddy sat stone still.

"This ends the reading of the will. However"—Brangle cleared his throat—"before we adjourn, there is one more item. Gentlemen, this is a private matter and I would ask the two of you to leave us to that end." It took a minute for Freddy and Bobby to take the hint, but finally they pushed back their chairs, bowed, and left the room. Mr. Sloane didn't make a move to leave.

Brangle shifted uncomfortably. "A duty I would rather not perform. And highly unusual. But I was instructed by Mr. Reynolds to deliver this to his wife on the fourteenth of this month, and since it is now the fourteenth, I feel duty bound to honor his request."

He pulled another envelope from the briefcase and handed it across the table to Bev.

Bev took it with a trembling hand, tore open the flap, and looked at the document. For document it was.

She read. "What is this?" She read again. "I don't understand."

"Let me see that." Daniel Sloane reached across the table and snagged the document from Bev's hand. "This is a divorce decree. This is outrageous."

Brangle nodded. "A rather odd situation."

"Odd?" snapped Sloane. "I'll say it's damnable. Just what are you trying to pull?"

"Nothing at all. I'm merely following my client's requests."

Sloane rose from his seat. Carmichael laid a hand on his sleeve. "Perhaps if we let Mr. Brangle explain."

Sloane sat down.

"Thank you. Mr. Reynolds came to me last week with two requests. One was to change his will and the other to start divorce proceedings against his wife. And that is what I have done. Though the second does seem somewhat redundant as things stand."

"But where is the new will?"

"I've just read you the new will. He came to me, said he had to divorce his wife, and then changed his will to leave her everything."

"That makes absolutely no sense." Sloane slumped back in his chair, seemed to collect himself, and sat up. "Well, there you have it. Reggie was in financial straits, and seeing no way out, he must have decided to—"

"He could have come to me. Or you," Bev said, glaring at her father. "No. It doesn't make sense. Reggie would never kill himself, if that's what you're implying. He always had a plan B."

And, Phil thought, divorcing his wife was his plan B? It wasn't like being divorced was any less scandalous than being the widow of a suicide or murder victim. Besides, Reggie didn't seem like the kind of guy who would go out of his way to have his wife avoid scandal. On the contrary, he was more likely to create a scandal for the pure fun of it. Daniel Sloane was right, none of this was making sense.

Sloane roused himself. "Do the divorce papers negate the will? I'll have it struck down."

"Not at all," Brangle said. "The will is actually dated later than the divorce papers. And I have a letter on file signed by Reggie to that effect. Now if there are no further questions, I will take care of disseminating the funds to your butler, and the rest is yours."

He bowed. Sloane jumped up to see him to the door.

Freddy and Mullins were waiting for them in the parlor.

"Oh, bother," Bev said under her breath, and moved forward to Freddy, who clasped her hands in his.

"I just want you to know you can count on me. I know the ins and outs of Reggie's affairs. I can at least relieve you of that aspect of his loss."

"Thank you, Freddy. I know you loved him, too. This must be so hard for you."

Freddy nodded. Sniffed manfully.

"And me, too," Mullins said, working the rim of his hat. "We're gonna have a crackerjack race. Devil's Thunder is in top form. You just put your money on Thunder and don't worry about a thing. I'll take care of things for you."

"Reggie always depended on you, Bobby. I know I can, too."

"Well," Freddy said, "we'd better get back over to Sherry's. Marguerite's playing host on her own."

"Be sure to thank her for me, both of you, all of you."

The two men bowed. Tuttle showed them out.

"God, I thought they'd never leave," Bev said. "Come on."

"Where are we going?" Phil asked, hurrying after her.

"Upstairs to take off this horrible itchy crepe."

"You really shouldn't. You're a widow. It would be unseemly."

"Phil? That doesn't sound like you. When did you become such an old fogey."

"Since someone killed your husband."

"Oh, pooh. You heard Brangle. Reggie divorced me first. Whether he planned to run off with Mildred Potts or not, he was thinking about me. Making sure I wouldn't be responsible for his debts." She stopped, frowned. "He *divorced* me. He would never want to see me wasting away in black.

"Good old Reg. As soon as I've changed, we'll have a toast. To Reggie. Now I'm no longer a widow but a very relieved divorcée."

And murder suspect, thought Phil, but she declined to mention it.

10

Phil was surprised when John Atkins didn't manifest himself at the reading of the will. And she had to admit she was a little disappointed that he hadn't arrived by the time they took themselves to bed. Though considering the outcome of the reading, perhaps it was better that he stayed far away.

She'd spent the day pondering the odd juxtaposition of the will and the divorce decree. But he had left Bev with all their assets. Generosity and a thought for someone else were not qualities she would have associated with the bombastic and freewheeling Reggie.

She suspected Atkins had opted for the luncheon at Sherry's, which Phil would have been glad to attend herself if only for a change of scenery and because Sherry's was famous for its coq au vin, which she adored. And annoyance aside, she would really like to know what he found out, why he was at the funeral, and if the police had settled on Mildred Potts as the murderer, why he'd bothered to come at all. He seemed to be spending a lot of time on Reggie's murder when supposedly there were several murders a day in this city.

But when she awoke to a sunny day the next morning, she was glad he had stayed away. She'd had vivid dreams of murder and blood, of her mother and father dressed in rags beseeching her to return home. And of Dunbridge rising from the grave shaking his fist and crying, "If you'd only given me an heir . . ." She woke up before she'd heard the rest of his accusation.

She blamed the dream on the rather lurid descriptions in one of the forensic science books she and Lily had read before going to bed. On the harrowing story Lily and Preswick told of listening to the reading of the will by sticking their heads into the dumbwaiter at the third floor. And perhaps, on a wee, very wee, soupçon of guilt for not giving the earl an heir.

Though she was fairly certain it was not her fault. *Oh, the times she'd thought of England and endured.*

As morning slid into early afternoon, Phil thought they might have one whole day free of investigation. She was correct—and relieved. But by the third morning without an appearance by the determined detective, she was ready to climb the walls from tedium.

Phil had thrown off any semblance of mourning and was wearing one of her tea gowns by Poiret, a delicious combination of patterned silks that reminded her of something a geisha might wear—if France had geishas.

She and Bev sat in the parlor, reading . . . more or less. Bev's book lay open on her lap while she drummed her fingers on its surface. She was dressed in black, but *sans* crepe ruffles and trim. And she looked quite youthful and frail as well as beautiful.

It had taken some persuasion and the heretofore unknown skills of Lily as a dressmaker—really, the girl never ceased to surprise—to create something that didn't make Bev look, in her words, like an "absolute fright," but that would be appropriate for entertaining condolence calls.

It wouldn't do to appear flippant until the dust cleared and Detective Sergeant Atkins was a dim, very dim, memory.

Since they were quite alone, Phil had brought down Dr. Gross's *Criminal Investigation,* which was considerably easier reading than Sir Edward's *Finger Prints.* Still, she'd covered it in an embroidered handkerchief ostensibly to "protect the edges" but really to protect it from prying eyes.

"It's just too quiet," Bev said for the third or fourth time that morning. She pushed her book off her lap and walked to the window, something else she'd been doing all morning.

Phil looked up from her book. "You'd rather have your father, Freddy, and Bobby Mullins falling over each other trying to get into the library? What's so important about the library anyway?"

She certainly hadn't found anything of note. Just lots of notes of the IOU variety.

"Hey, now. Who is that?" Bev craned her neck to see out the window.

A little thrill bubbled inside Phil and she got up to join Bev at the window. "Where?"

"Oh, nobody. He's gone. I guess he was just walking by and went through the park just there."

Phil peered into the well-manicured park. No one was there.

"Well, I suppose I shouldn't be surprised," Phil said, uncharacteristically disappointed. She hadn't really expected to see the elusive Mr. X again.

She did, however, see John Atkins striding up the sidewalk toward the brownstone.

She crushed a twinge of consternation mixed with anticipation. "Oh, not him again."

Bev pressed her nose to the window. "That face, those shoulders—wasted on a policeman. I wonder if he can waltz?"

"Oh, Bev, do pay attention. He's not just physically fit, he's intelligent."

"Not to worry, my dear. I like intelligence just fine as long as it doesn't get in the way of passion. And once he's gone, we'll have a drink."

They quickly returned to their seats.

When they heard the doorbell, Bev's book was once again opened. Phil's book had been stuffed beneath the cushion of her chair and the nearest magazine was open in front of her.

Unfortunately, it happened to be a book of French pornography; it quickly went the way of her book on investigation, so that when the detective sergeant entered, Bev looked primly serious and Phil was twiddling her thumbs. They both stood, Phil with more alacrity than Bev.

He made his condolences to a wanly smiling Bev, and nodded to Phil. They stood facing each other before Bev said, "Do sit down, Detective Atkins. Phil, come sit by me and let the detective have the comfortable chair." She held out her hand to Phil, who had no choice but to take it and sit down next to her.

To her chagrin, a corner of her magazine peeked out from beneath the cushion. She could only watch as Atkins pulled it out and glanced at the cover. Without comment he placed it on the side table and sat down—on her book of investigation techniques.

"I came," he said, looking somewhere between the two women, "not only to pay my condolences but also to return Mr. Reynolds's possessions.

"And to tell you that the intruder has been identified as a two-bit bagman for the west side. Sergeant Charles Becker of the Nineteenth Precinct closed this aspect of the case. Hopefully he won't bother you again, but if he does, do not try his patience. I'm sure you will be perfectly safe without my police guard; however, I would caution your staff to be ever vigil about doors and windows being kept locked."

He couldn't be more stiff if he'd been reciting from a book. A muscle twitched in his jaw.

Phil wasn't certain what a bagman was, but it sounded ominous. She was also dying to ask if they suspected someone of his murder, but she didn't dare set him off in that direction.

"But who killed him?" Bev asked.

Phil had to stop herself from groaning.

Atkins didn't answer at first, though he did look like he might erupt. "They've decided much as you have, Lady Dunbridge," he said, practically choking on the words. "A falling-out among thieves."

"Ah." She decided not to ask him how the other thief escaped. Not with his frown daring her to mention it.

"What about Mildred Potts?" Bev asked.

"Miss Potts has been released."

In for a penny, in for a pound, thought Phil. "Does this mean you are now pronouncing Reggie's death a murder by persons unknown?"

The detective glanced at Bev, who was studying her hands. "The police have decided to follow another lead."

"The police? I thought you were the police."

He smiled somewhat bitterly, and Phil added outrage to her indignation. She should be used to how wielded power worked. Among society it could be brutal and often was, but somehow to see the same type of power in play when justice and lives were involved, and even if this time it might work to Bev's advantage . . . Well, it just didn't seem right.

"I am only one small part of the police. They've decided to concentrate on searching for the driver of the automobile."

"He still hasn't appeared?"

"Not only has he not appeared, no one seems to know who he is. Do you, Mrs. Reynolds?"

"What? No. We didn't have a usual driver, just a coachman, and he never learned to drive. Reggie always drove unless we were going someplace formal. Or the weather was inclement. I don't know where Reggie found drivers. I suppose from the garage or one of the stable boys."

"Then for the time being our driver must remain a mystery man," Atkins said.

Mystery man? It seemed their life was suddenly replete with mystery men. Well, at least the driver's absence would take their attention from the only suspect left, Bev.

"Then can I have the touring car back?" Bev broke in.

Oh, Bev. Why did she have to mention the bloody touring car?

"I'll have someone bring it around." He reached inside his jacket and pulled out a packet wrapped in brown paper. I've been authorized to return Mr. Reynolds's personal effects. A few dollars, a money clip, a watch, cuff lengths, handkerchief. Here is an official list of his possessions. Please check to make sure you receive them all. There was also a suitcase, which is now in possession of your butler.

"I thought you would not want the clothes he was wearing, but they can be sent if you so desire."

"Good God, no," Bev said, taking the packet.

"You will notice we have had to keep two pieces of evidence that are on the list. His passport and two steamer tickets to Buenos Aires."

Phil heard Bev's sudden intake of breath. Though it was hard to think Bev could be surprised by anything her often errant and now blissfully out-of-her-life husband might do.

And she didn't miss the barely perceptible look of satisfaction in the detective's eyes.

"I take it you and Mr. Reynolds weren't planning a trip abroad?"

Bev looked at Phil. She might not be surprised by Reggie's antics, but she still smarted under the humiliation. And who could blame her?

Phil narrowed her eyes in warning. *Stay calm.*

And she saw the moment Bev gave up all pretense.

"No, we were not."

"So we might surmise—"

"You can surmise what you like, Detective Atkins. Everyone else will."

Phil leaned forward. "Why would he leave the week before his big race?"

"That is a question I've been asking myself." Atkins shifted in his seat, frowned. "I don't suppose you have any theories?" He lifted one hip and reached under the cushion.

Phil popped off the settee. "No, I don't. Neither of us does. Will that be all, Detective Inspec—Sergeant?"

The detective pulled out the book she'd so hastily hidden.

Phil sat back down.

He took his time reading the cover, then opened it. Closed it again. Placed it on the table on top of the French pornography.

Phil had the good sense to blush. Not that she could have stopped the wash of heat up her neck and face if she'd wanted to. The French pornography didn't bother her, but being found out studying something clearly none of her business did.

"Interesting reading material," he said to Phil.

"I have eclectic tastes." Heavens, that didn't sound right. "One never knows."

"Evidently not," he said, and stood. "Good day, ladies. You should have your auto back today."

"And the keys to the library?"

Phil was going to strangle Bev before this investigation was finished. "The dust, Detective Sergeant. The parlor maids are complaining."

"I can't say. Sergeant Becker is now overseeing the case. He'll no doubt return them to you when he sees fit." He bowed to both, and without waiting for Tuttle he headed for the door.

He stopped as he reached it. "Oh, by the way, Mrs. Reynolds. Who inherits Mr. Reynolds's estate?"

"I do, naturally."

"I see. Thank you." Another nod. And he was gone.

"I'll see him out," Phil told Bev and rushed after him.

"Is the investigation over for Mrs. Reynolds?" she asked as they reached the door.

"Not at all." He tilted his head, looked her square in the eye. "I think we are both people of the world, Lady Dunbridge."

She nodded.

"I don't know what you're playing at."

"I assure you, I'm not playing. But I do like to keep myself informed."

"My hands have been somewhat tied. I don't know if that's your doing, or someone else's. Charlie Becker is a dangerous man. He'll think no more of throwing Mrs. Reynolds—or you—in jail if he wants and then ransom you to Daniel Sloane. My advice to you is don't cross him."

"Then why are you turning us over to him?"

"I have no choice, but I'll tell you this. I won't be muzzled. There were reforms made in the department when Roosevelt was here, and I intend to follow them whether anyone else does or not.

"And don't think you can thwart me with your amateur armchair theories. You obviously have a wide range of interests, but don't let the current rage for detective stories beguile you into thinking you can prove your friend innocent if she isn't."

"I've never read a detective story in my life," Phil said indignantly. "But I might start." And she would begin tonight with "The Adventure of Silver Blaze," which the nice gentleman in the bookstore recommended.

"For your own good, stick to shopping and afternoon martinis. It's a lot safer. Good afternoon."

"But you don't think Bev did it." She hated that she'd blurted that out, but she had to know where they stood.

"Passport, tickets, mistress, inheritance, missing pistol that happened to turn up here in the library next to a dead man. What do your studies tell you, Lady Dunbridge?"

A tip of his hat and he was gone, leaving Phil looking at the closed door.

This wasn't over, and she didn't know whether to be concerned or relieved. He'd been stymied by someone for some reason, but he didn't intend to let it go at that.

If Bev was innocent, and Phil believed she was, Atkins would be a good ally. Or he could be Bev's downfall. Either way, he wouldn't back off. Detective Sergeant John Atkins was a stubborn man.

He might be officially off the case, but she knew that while the police were going off in another direction, Atkins would keep coming back with one more request, one more question, gathering evidence and organizing a separate case from the one his superiors were following.

Passport, tickets, mistress, pistol, and now the inheritance and divorce. Step-by-step, like a game of Dots and Boxes, the detective seemed to be setting his aim on Bev, and the motives for murdering Reggie were slowly piling up at her feet.

Phil walked thoughtfully back to the parlor, where Bev was ringing for Tuttle. Phil was having trouble keeping up with Bev's propensity for cocktails. After a visit like that, a cup of hot tea would do the trick.

"That's why he wasn't driving," Bev exclaimed before Phil managed to sit down.

"Atkins?"

"Reggie, stupid. He was planning to run off to South America with that . . . that creature and wanted to make sure we had a driver to get us home."

"Oh, Bev." God forfend that Phil ever got that wrapped up in a man. Reggie was dead, and Bev was still trying to make him love her.

Bev's lip slipped into a pout. "If he wanted to go to Buenos Aires, why not take me? Surely I'm as much fun as Mildred Potts. And *I* would have paid our way."

Phil thought maybe she had paid for the trip anyway. "Do you really want to be on the lam with a dissolute gambler in South America?"

Bev sniffed. "Well, if you put it that way, no. But I just don't understand."

"Neither do I," Phil agreed. Actually, she could think of several reasons for divorcing Bev. She might be putting pressure on Reggie to drop his mistress. Mimi was most certainly pressuring him to leave his wife. Maybe he just got fed up and chose his mistress.

But why Mimi LaPonte? She seemed like an odd choice. Bev was beautiful, affectionate, fun loving, and rich in her own right.

Mildred Potts, on the other hand, was nice looking in a cheap way, probably knew how to have fun, but couldn't possibly have money. How much did a Florodora girl make? And why South America? That didn't make sense. Any woman worth her weight would have made him take her to Europe. Paris, Venice, Monte Carlo.

"Was it my fault?"

"What? Of course not. Why would you even think that?"

Because it was easier for a man to disappear in South America. Reggie was murdered. Perhaps he knew his life was in jeopardy and he was fleeing to stay alive. Would they come after Bev next?

"Because he wanted to borrow money and this time I said no."

"This time? Did he often borrow money from you?"

"Well, I'd hardly say borrow. Once you lent Reggie anything, it was more of a gift. And I just got tired of forking it over knowing it was going to that bitch of a chorus girl."

"As you should," Phil told her. "I'm sure he would have eventually bled you dry." Phil bit her tongue. Now, there was a motive for murder. Still, she couldn't draw her mind from the possibility that Bev might be in danger.

"It was always feast or famine with Reggie, only we always feasted regardless of the money on hand."

So Reggie had asked for money. In order to flee with his mistress. Something was not adding up here. Why leave before the race? If everything she'd heard about Devil's Thunder was true, Reggie could have made a killing on the winnings. Why not wait a few days and abscond with the prize money?

Bev blew out air. "Maybe he was so besotted he couldn't wait." Tears welled in her eyes. She pulled out a hankie.

It was possible that he was running from his creditors; Phil had seen the bills and IOUs piled up in his desk. But surely even the most notorious villains would have waited another few days for the race to pay off.

The police may have released Mildred Potts, but Phil wasn't

convinced that the driver had killed Reggie, and something told her John Atkins wasn't convinced of it either.

"Phil, what are you thinking?"

"Just . . . nothing."

Bev stood, dislodging the book from her lap. It hit the carpet and she kicked it out of her way as she crossed to the window and looked out. "Not a soul in sight, not even a policeman—not even some old Knickerbocker matron come to gloat at my misfortune. At this rate I might as well take up backgammon."

And why elope on the day of her arrival, at the docks surrounded by a hundred potential witnesses, instead of sneaking away quietly in the middle of the night? Take a cab with Mildred to the docks one night when no one is around to find him out until he was gone. The divorce papers wouldn't be delivered until he was out of reach.

Unless he didn't have time to plan ahead.

"Bev, how much money is in Reggie's money clip?"

Bev picked the clip off the side table and counted the bills. "Not quite thirty dollars. That wouldn't get him very far, not the way he spent money."

"Maybe the rest was in his suitcase," Phil suggested. Unless Mildred—or even the police—had helped themselves to it.

"In his suitcase? Reggie would never take money in a suitcase. Too easy to steal."

He certainly wouldn't have left without money unless he had it wired to a bank there. She thought back, tried to remember if she'd seen any bank books in Reggie's desk. No, they must be in the safe.

"Was Reggie really the only one who knew the combination to the safe?"

"Why?"

"I just thought that if everyone knew he kept money there . . ." Phil shrugged.

"He didn't tell *anyone*. He was very adamant about that."

"Too bad, they'll have to dynamite it to open it."

"Don't be silly. I'll open it before that. If they ever give us back the key to the library."

"What? You know the combination? How? Why didn't you tell the detective sergeant? I think you can be arrested for lying to a police officer."

"I didn't lie. I don't actually 'know' the combination. I mean Reggie didn't *tell* me. That's the truth."

"Then how do you think you know?"

"Well, consider this. Reggie is—was—a man and yet he never forgot my birthday."

"The combination is your birthday?"

"It must be. I told Reggie he should make it something he could remember. But being just like a man, he forgot everything that wasn't about money or the races—or my birthday. God knows I drummed it into his head often enough. It was the one way I knew Reggie would always remember to buy me a present. Aren't I clever?"

Phil jumped up. "You are indeed. Let's go see if he heeded your advice. I want to get a look at what's in that safe."

"But the police haven't returned the key to the library."

"Not to worry. First we're going to take a look at Reggie's suitcase and then I'll ring for Lily."

The suitcase contained just what the list said it contained—clothes, shoes, a modicum of jewelry—if you believed the police were totally honest and wrote down everything before they helped themselves to the contents. Which was possible; the case had definitely been searched.

Still, Phil and Bev searched thoroughly. They didn't find a dime or dollar bill anywhere inside even though Bev seemed to know all the places that might serve to stash hidden cash. Something Phil noted and wondered if Bev knew about the desk's secret compartment, now empty.

They stopped by Phil's bedroom, summoned Lily, who arrived huffing from a run up the stairs.

"Yes, madam." She blew out air. "I was downstairs . . . in the kitchen . . ."

"Oh, did we interrupt your tea?"

"No, madam."

"Well," Phil said, "we have a job to do that includes a hairpin. Shall we?"

Lily curtseyed. She must have been practicing; it was quite a good curtsey, except the situation was so droll that Phil had trouble not bursting into laughter.

They tiptoed down the stairs even though it was afternoon, and after checking to see that there were no servants about, they hurried down the hall to the library.

When the three of them were standing outside the door, Phil turned to Bev. "You must turn around and close your eyes."

"Why?"

"Just do it."

Bev turned around and put her hands over her eyes.

"Don't peek."

Bev shook her head.

Phil pulled out a hairpin and handed it to Lily. The girl knelt down. The lock clicked almost immediately. Her curtsey wasn't the only thing Miss Lily had been practicing.

"Thank you, Lily, that will be all."

Lily bobbed a jaunty little curtsey and was gone.

"You can look now." Phil turned the knob and Bev slipped inside. Phil locked the door behind them.

"How did you do that?" Bev asked.

Phil put her fingers to her lips. "All in good time, Bev. Now we must be quiet. We don't want anyone to know we're in here, and we must put everything back the way we found it." She reached into her pocket and brought out two pairs of gloves. Handed one pair to Bev.

Bev didn't ask, just put them on.

"Now to the safe."

"Should we be doing this?" Bev asked in a whisper.

"Probably not, but since we no longer have Atkins to depend on, we'd better start taking care of things ourselves."

"Okay, but we'd better hurry. Knowing Father, he'll come by early to visit before taking you to Hilda and Arthur's dinner."

"Oh, drat, the dinner. I'd forgotten. We'd better get to it."

Bev walked over to the naked nymphs painting and swung it away from the wall. Three manipulations later, the safe was open.

"It's empty!" Bev exclaimed.

"Shh!" Phil hissed.

Phil looked inside, ran her fingers around the edges. Not even a speck of dust. So if Reggie didn't have all the money he supposedly kept in the safe, who did?

Another rummage through the desk revealed the same stacks of bills and IOUs.

"I hope they don't expect me to pay all these," Bev said, and stuffed them back into the drawer.

So did Phil. She wandered over to the window. The gap where the glass had been broken was covered with a piece of cardboard. Not very secure, but until the library was freed, there was no way to make the repair.

"Bev, can you tell if anything is missing? It's possible they had the combination and stole the money, at which point one kills the other one, which makes a certain sense. But if the thieves couldn't get into the safe, what would they steal?"

"Paintings? They're the most valuable things." Bev looked around the room. "They all seem to be here."

"And the other thing, Bev. The window was locked, painted shut. They couldn't get in or out that way."

"I don't understand, how else would they have gotten in?"

Phil looked toward the door, then at Bev.

"Well, it wasn't me. I don't have a key. Besides, why would I break into my own house? And when was I supposed to do it?"

"I wasn't suggesting anything of the sort. But perhaps the staff or one of Reggie's close friends."

"Nobody had the key or the combination."

"That you know of. When was the last time Reggie was in the library?"

Bev shrugged. "The morning you came? I was running around getting things ready for your arrival. I left the house for a couple of hours to run some errands. I didn't notice. Why does it matter?"

"I don't know." Maybe she was wrong to think the two deaths were related. But how could they not be?

Phil stripped off her gloves. "I think we'd better finish up here."

But before they could leave, they heard the sound of a key in the lock.

Bev grabbed Phil's hand. Phil took a deep breath while she desperately searched for a lie as to why they were in the library. Half of her hoped it would be John Atkins. But what if it were Charles Becker?

The door creaked open, a man slipped inside.

Bev let out a squeak and cowered into Phil.

"Bev? Philomena? What are you doing here. How did you get in?"

Phil cleared her throat, looking for her voice. "Mr. Sloane? We . . uh . . ." She sounded just like the guilty schoolgirl of days gone by. She cleared her throat again. "We might ask you the same thing. Where did you get that key?"

Sloane looked at the key. "It was a spare I found from when I lived here. I saw no reason I shouldn't have access to my own library."

"Mine," Bev corrected.

"Regardless, that doesn't tell me how the two of you managed to get in."

"Clever Ph—"

Phil pinched her.

Sloane was only paying half attention to them. His gaze was constantly drawn away, and it was clear to Phil he was looking for something. To make sure his paintings were still on the walls? Or . . .

Phil made a stab. "Perhaps we can help you find what you came for," she said at her most imperious. She wasn't sure it would work on Daniel Sloane. He'd seen her at her least flattering and guilty moments.

He darted another look around.

"Phil is ever so clever and we've done an efficient search."

Sloane's eyes shifted to Phil. His eyebrows rose. She remembered that expression; it presaged a blistering scold.

But evidently not today. "Reggie had planned to leave me something."

"What?" exclaimed Bev. "You knew he was leaving?"

"No, no my dear." He rushed forward to reassure his daughter. Though Phil saw him cast a quick glance toward the inkstand. *The secret compartment.*

Interesting. She knew it was empty, but perhaps he didn't. So what did he expect to find there? And did it have anything to do with the murders?

Should she tell him and put him out of his anxiety? Perhaps not quite yet.

"Tell us what it is and we can help you look for it."

"Oh, nothing. Just doing a favor for a friend who was interested in being published."

"A manuscript?"

"No. No. It doesn't matter. Why don't you girls run along, and I'll just have a little walk down memory lane."

"Oh, Papa," Bev said, coming to stand next to him and sounding like a little girl. "You know there's no use in brooding over Mama. You should be living and having some fun. Come on, I'll have Tuttle fix you a nice drink while Phil gets ready."

Somehow, Bev steered him toward the door. Wax in her hands, thought Phil as she followed them out the door. Though

Bev's father did take a quick look back before she closed the door on the library, and he was forced to relock it.

Bev looked at Phil over his bowed head.

Phil shook her head. She had no doubt he'd be back. But for the moment she could only admire Bev's technique.

11

"Just remember when you're nodding over your *crème glacée*," Bev said as she watched Lily add the final touches to Phil's rather elaborate hairstyle, "that I told you so."

Phil had tried to get Bev to stay downstairs with her father; she wasn't sure that she trusted Daniel Sloane not to go snooping around the library on his own. But Bev was afraid he'd start asking questions, hence her sitting on Phil's bed making dire predictions for the evening.

"Then there's the interminable hour while the gentlemen linger over their port and ribald conversation and their wives sit demurely in the parlor with banal gossip and suppressed yawns," Bev continued. "Ugh. I'm sorry that this should be your first introduction to New York society.

"At least Hilda and Arthur generally have guests who are worth knowing and you'll probably start receiving invitations as a result," she added.

Phil motioned Lily away while she went over to kiss Bev on the cheek. "This too will pass, my dear. Then you can show me the town the way it should be."

"If I don't die of boredom first."

"You'll survive. I'm almost ready, go keep him company."

"You can watch the cobra circling her prey tonight."

"Does that upset you?"

"Not at all. If she makes him happy. He's eager enough. Though I can't imagine what he sees in that straitlaced matron."

Phil threw her a coquettish look. "Perhaps she's a fireball behind closed doors."

"The mind boggles." Bev started for the door. "Don't hurry, the preprandial conversation is always a crashing bore." She stopped. "Though I suppose I should thank them. They are one of the few 'haute' society couples who took a liking to Reggie. I think because he gave them good racing tips. Arthur Tappington-Jones is a member of the Turf Club. Lord, I can't imagine why else we were always invited." She slipped out of the room.

Phil came downstairs a few minutes later to find Daniel Sloane standing at the cold hearth with a drink in his hand. He put down his glass and strode across the room to kiss Phil's hand.

"You look lovely, Lady Dunbridge." It was said with charm and finesse, but she could tell he was agitated.

Which was unsurprising since Bev was sitting on the sofa looking like she'd just chewed on a castor bean.

Phil however was feeling à la mode. She was looking forward to getting away from the stress of murder, even for a few hours. Her new dinner gown perfectly fit her mood, a deep plum velvet cut over chiffon. Light enough to billow when she walked and yet with bit of dark rich fabric in keeping with the late bereavement. Monsieur Worth had outdone himself on this confection, if she did say so herself. Lily had also outdone herself in coiffure tonight, and Phil had topped the low curls with a very modest tiara of diamonds. She was a countess, after all.

"I almost wish I were going," Bev said. "You look exquisite."

"Indeed," her father said.

Bev sighed.

"You know, dear girl," he reminded her, "you're always yawning after the first hour at one of Hilda's soirées."

"I know. And it isn't Hilda's fault. But Arthur reeks of cigars and only has two subjects of conversation, Tammany Hall and the track. You can imagine Reggie and he got along famously."

"Well, yes." Daniel Sloane shot his cuffs, revealing large

oval blue opals fitted in gold. “Though I must warn you, Lady Dunbridge.”

“Please call me Philomena.”

Bev snorted. “Just call her Phil, everyone does.”

“I wouldn’t presume,” her father said, darting her a black look. “It won’t be an exciting evening. The Austrians are a cool lot, but I confess I wouldn’t mind having a few minutes with the attaché about the Hungarian situation.

“Father, please don’t be an old bore tonight. It’s Phil’s first night out.”

“I’m sure I will be entertained,” Phil said, and smiled at Daniel Sloane. She didn’t mind political discussions. The few newspapermen she’d been acquainted with were passionate, serious people. She had no doubt Daniel Sloane was one of them.

“Well, Bev isn’t altogether wrong, Lady Dunbridge. We dine too late, have too many courses, talk too long, and go home exhausted from the sheer length of it all.”

Phil laughed. “And you enjoy every moment of it, I have no doubt.” She took his arm and they went out into the foyer, stopping long enough for Lily to drape Phil’s evening cloak about her shoulders.

A carriage was waiting for them outside, and Phil thanked the stars that her dress wouldn’t have to withstand an open-air drive in a motorcar to dinner. She’d been in them before. They were quite exhilarating, but not when you were on your way to your debut dinner in America.

Mrs. Tappington-Jones’s intimate dinner turned out to be an affair for twenty people. Thank heaven Phil had worn her tiara—she wouldn’t want to be underdressed.

Conversation stopped as she and Daniel Sloane were announced. He was rather debonair in a slightly erratic way. Phil, on the other hand, looked ravishing. She accepted her hostess’s hand graciously. Nodded to her husband, a tall, barrel-chested man, with thinning red hair and, yes, the acrid aroma of cigars.

"Glad you could make it, Lady Dunbridge. Hear they've been keeping you under wraps since you arrived. Terrible business," Mr. Tappington-Jones said, then turned to her companion. "Well, Daniel. Glad to see you out as well. Black band is more than enough, if you ask me. Come, I want you and the countess here to meet the cultural attaché." He leaned closer to Daniel and said under his breath, "Only understand one in every two words he says, damn accent so thick you could cut it with a knife. But a pleasant enough fellow.

"Personal favor to the president. An honor, really. Don't always agree with the man. But after what he did with the Rough Riders and then how he stepped in after that anarchist assassinated McKinley, you can't fault him. Leastways not on everything. Lady Dunbridge?"

He offered his arm to Phil.

Daniel offered his to Mrs. Tappington-Jones, and they were trundled across the floor to meet the attaché.

Mr. Tappington-Jones leaned closer to Phil. "I dare say you've met the fellow. I know he makes several trips to England a year."

"Why, yes, we've met on several occasions." And she wouldn't mind if they never met again. The man was in his dotage, hard of hearing, and had the habit of looking down one's gown at the least opportunity.

"Well, good. Good."

And if Arthur Tappington-Jones thought she was going to entertain Heinrich Ganz all night, he was very mistaken.

A small group of people were clustered around the screened fireplace. A man in black evening wear stood with his back to her. He was taller than she remembered him. Actually . . .

"I've brought an old acquaintance of yours, Herr Schimmer," Mr. Tappington-Jones said.

The attaché turned to greet them, revealing the official red sash draped across his chest.

"My dear Herr Ganz" died on Phil's lips.

For a second Phil and the attaché stared at each other. Him trying to place her and where they had met, and her wondering who the hell he was. He was tall, with short-cropped dark reddish brown hair and a neatly trimmed beard and mustache. His eyebrows were bushy, which seemed out of keeping with the precision of the rest of his appearance. And the eyes . . .

Tappington-Jones, perhaps sensing something was wrong, interjected a hint, "Lady Dunbridge."

"Ach," the attaché said, "I don't believe I've had the pleasure. I'm sure I would have remembered."

"No, we haven't met," Phil said. "How absurd. Herr Ganz must have retired."

"Yes, that is it. I am Johann Schimmer, the new attaché. At your service." The attaché's eyes met hers for a brief second. They were a lovely shade of blue and twinkled humorously. But it wasn't their color; it was something else that gave her pause. She'd seen those eyes before. And she definitely recognized that scent of his tobacco as he bent to kiss her hand.

He bowed to Daniel Sloane. "I've been telling my friends here how much I admire their metropolis."

"Yes, lovely, isn't it?" Phil said. "I've only just arrived myself."

"Indeed? Are you making a long stay?"

Was she? Did she even have a choice? Phil inclined her head. "I think . . . perhaps yes."

Bev would have hated this small talk. Phil didn't usually care for it herself, but tonight she had ulterior motives, a phrase that had taken on new meaning since she'd arrived in Manhattan.

She really couldn't care less about the dinner. Conversations at table were usually desultory. But she looked forward to Bev's boring hour with the ladies after dinner. The best secrets were kept by the tightest-lipped women. All it took to get them to share was a little finesse.

"You must get out to Belmont track before you leave, Herr Schimmer," Tappington-Jones said. "Is Devil's Thunder still running this next week, considering the circumstances?"

"I imagine so," Daniel said with a slight frown. "We haven't discussed it. I'm sure Freddy will see that all is in order."

"Now, Arthur, no horse talk before dinner," his wife chided. "Honestly, during racing season these men have one-track minds." She tittered at her little joke. The men in the group smiled.

Herr Schimmer looked befuddled, then he laughed. "Ah, one-track mind, I see, ha-ha, you must forgive my lack of wit, my poor English, I'm afraid."

His poor English indeed. It was impeccable as far as Phil could tell, as were his manners and his charm.

"Ah, here are the Gringolds." Tappington-Jones made the introductions to the attaché, and Phil and Daniel Sloane took the opportunity to ease away.

"Seems nice enough, the new attaché," he remarked as they stopped to take glasses of champagne from a waiter's tray.

"Yes, but I had no idea Heinrich Ganz was leaving his post. I only saw him a few weeks ago and he didn't mention it."

"Perhaps it wasn't of his choosing. Things are a bit unstable in Europe these days. Between the Russians and their revolution and the situation in Serbia and Bosnia, I imagine the Austrian government is in a state of zealous preparation."

"For what exactly?"

"God only knows. Ah, I see an old friend and his wife. I'll introduce you."

It didn't take long for Phil to take the tenor of the dinner guests. The men were friendly to Daniel, commiserated with him over the death of his son-in-law. They were enamored of Phil, as she knew they would be—a title, a tiara, and a little subtle flirtation and they were hers.

The women, however, were more circumspect, as she also knew they would be. They obviously didn't approve of the Reynoldses' lifestyle and, by association, Phil's. Or perhaps her reputation had preceded her.

They were perfectly polite, glad to make her acquaintance—she was a countess, after all. Still, they couldn't help but let slip their disdain for the English peers all the while willing to give their eyeteeth—and their fortunes—to be one. And they were all afraid their husbands would go to bed that evening comparing them to the newest visitor. It would take some work to gain their confidences, but Phil gladly accepted the challenge. She had no doubt they were a storehouse of information.

She went in to dinner on the arm of Mr. Tappington-Jones and saw Herr Schimmer dart a quick smile toward her as he seated Mrs. Tappington-Jones at the far end of the table and took his seat next to her. Phil wondered what he thought was so amusing. He'd be yawning into his game hen before dessert was served.

The dinner was excellent and the talk was lively, and in spite of Hilda's admonitions, conversation kept slipping into enthusiasms for the next Belmont races. Phil rather enjoyed the races, but what she really wanted to know was their opinions of Reggie's horse and of the man himself.

She would have gladly stayed and shared a glass of port with the men, but she followed the other ladies out to the parlor.

"Let me introduce you to my good friend Mrs. Fielding." Mrs. Tappington-Jones guided Phil over to a small group of ladies already in conversation. They smiled tightly but invited the countess to sit, which she did.

"And how are you enjoying our fair city?" asked Mrs. Fielding, not without a bit of malice, Phil thought.

Phil smiled. "Well, I must say, it isn't quite what I expected."

"I dare say," said another lady.

"It must be such an imposition, being accosted by policemen at every turn."

And what had they been hearing? Phil wondered. "It's certainly not what I'm used to," Phil said at her haughtiest.

"We were discussing the upcoming nuptials of Louisa Langham's daughter. She just became engaged to Lord Abington. The wedding will be in London next year."

"Have you met the Langhams? They're forever traveling to England."

Looking for a title for their daughter, no doubt, thought Phil.

"She's such a lovely girl. So pretty, and petite."

"Oh, good," Phil said. "Then she won't end up like poor Consuelo, always having to look down on her husband."

One of the ladies tittered. "Oh, is Lord Abington a short man? Do you know him well?"

"We used to run in the same circles." Quite often, in fact, when he had partaken of a bit too much champagne. Fortunately, he'd never caught her.

"Is it true what they say about Consuelo?"

"Well . . ." Phil paused, inviting more confidences.

It took a few minutes of well-edited morsels on Consuelo's lack of love life before Phil steered them into the subject they were really interested in: Reggie's murder.

"Probably someone Reggie knew," said Mrs. Fielding. "He was known to consort with lowlifes. I don't know why Beverly put up with it. Such a disappointment to Daniel. No one would blame him if . . ."

"Really?" Phil said. "He seems like such a doting father."

"Oh, my dear, he was furious with her last year. You do know about the mistress."

"I've heard a little . . ."

"Well, they say Reggie wasn't her only, how shall we say, suitor?" said Mrs. Fielding.

"I believe we'd call it something else, Priscilla." The woman on her right, a Mrs. Rollins, pursed her lips.

Priscilla Fielding smiled slyly. "I'm sure I wouldn't know."

"Well, I would," said Mrs. Rollins.

"Do tell," Phil encouraged her.

"Well, what I mean is . . ." She looked around, leaned in closer. "My Phillip is on the council, and he said she was arrested one night in the company of several gentlemen, in less than acceptable clothing." She gave them a knowing smile. "Both her and the gentlemen."

"Poor Beverly." Mrs. Tappington-Jones sighed.

"Beverly Sloane reaped what she sowed, for all you say, Hilda," said one of the other ladies. "Marguerite Beecham is the one I feel sorry for."

"Marguerite? Don't be absurd."

"You're not saying that Reggie and Marguerite were lovers?" asked Phil.

"Shhh," Priscilla said, looking quickly around. "I'm not saying anything of the sort. What I'm saying is that Freddy is terribly in debt, and Marguerite blames Reggie Reynolds. There were words."

"What kind of words?"

"Between Reggie and Freddy. Marguerite told me herself. I caught her crying in the ladies' withdrawing room at the Claridge's ball. She told me—well, I had to prod it out of her, but we *are* third cousins, and I thought it was my duty to help if I could. I told her she should drop the Reynoldses before it was too late."

"What did she say?"

Yes, what? Phil thought, glancing toward the door where the gentlemen would be entering any moment. They all leaned closer, including Phil.

"She said she wished someone would drop Reggie for good."

"Well, she isn't alone," said Mrs. Fielding. "Did you hear about the Tennebaums?"

"Heard they had to sell the Fifth Avenue house."

"He's gone belly—has lost all his money"—Mrs. Fielding leaned over and whispered—"at the track. At least, Hilda, that's what your husband told mine at the club the other night.

"And Sophie is threatening to divorce him." Mrs. Fielding sighed. "Scandalous. And it won't make one jot of difference. It's hopeless for her now. Such a blot."

"You're too severe," Hilda said sharply. "People have lost fortunes and managed to survive in society."

But not many, thought Phil.

By the time the gentlemen joined them, Phil had gleaned

quite a bit of information about the people she had met. She felt inordinately satisfied. She'd learned much more than she'd given out, surely the sign of a good detective.

It was strange, but somehow even the ladies' gossip had centered around the track and betting. These Americans seemed obsessed with horses. Or gambling.

And from what they said, she would have to add Marguerite to the growing list of possible murderers.

Reggie might be responsible for Freddy's excesses, but he could hardly be blamed for the irresponsible betting of others.

The door opened, and hearty talk and a cloud of leftover tobacco entered the room. The tête-à-tête quickly broke up. "And here they come now," Mrs. Tappington-Jones said brightly. The other ladies began to disperse toward their husbands.

"I hope you didn't find all that talk of horses boring, Herr Schimmer," Hilda said, leading him toward the coffee table.

"On the contrary. Racing is the sport of kings. And how could one be bored knowing that such delightful company awaited us in the drawing room?"

Mrs. Tappington-Jones nodded graciously. Herr Schimmer took a cup, and when she turned to pour for the next guest, he made his way toward Phil.

"Holding court, Countess?"

"It does rather look that way. I seem to be a bit *célèbre*."

"I heard of the tragedy over the port. Sloane's daughter, I believe, is the widow."

"Yes."

And where was Daniel Sloane? She hadn't seen him enter with the other men.

"Will this mean I won't see you at the races next week?"

"What? Oh, I don't know. It would rather depend on the circumstances. Are you planning to attend?"

"I think I must see this 'sure thing' they were all talking about, no? Devil's Thunder. With a name like that, who could resist?"

"Is that what kept you all so long over your port? The odds on Devil's Thunder?"

"Guilty as charged. Some of the gentlemen are avid sports aficionados."

"Gamblers, you mean."

His eyes flashed with amusement and Phil felt a frisson of titillating interest. And of something else not quite so delightful. She'd seen those eyes before and not in any Viennese ballroom. Much more recently.

"Ah, Lady Dunbridge." Mr. Tappington-Jones stepped up beside Schimmer. "So glad to see you and the attaché renewing your acquaintance."

Schimmer nodded, his expression as bland as only a diplomat could master. Phil merely said, "Yes, it is."

"I've promised to take him to the races next week. Would it be untoward to expect to see you there? Perhaps we could make a party of it?"

"But of course. I, like Herr Schimmer, have a desire to see Devil's Thunder run." She enjoyed the races as a rule, especially when the earl wasn't among her party. Bev would probably have to stay behind, and she wouldn't like that at all, but Herr Schimmer might make an excellent substitute.

Daniel Sloane entered the parlor and came to stand by Phil. He seemed distracted; perhaps he was the one bored by the dinner conversation or chafing beneath his daughter's notoriety.

They left a few minutes after that. He hardly spoke during the carriage ride home. And when she asked if he was feeling unwell, he apologized.

"Sorry to be such boring company. I just heard some disturbing news at dinner. Oh, it's nothing to worry about. Just got me to thinking. Really, nothing at all."

He spent so much time telling her what it was not about that by the time he walked her to the door of the brownstone, she knew it must be something quite awful.

They stopped at the door. "Can't you tell me, as a friend?"

He shook his head.

"About this awful murder of Reggie?"

"No—no."

"Did you never find what he was supposed to have left you?"

"It was nothing. A book. A tell-all exposé of the peccadilloes of some of society's most prominent ladies. He came to me. He needed money. Reggie always needed money.

"He said a lady he knew had written it. I agreed to buy it. I'm not really interested in that kind of literature, but I was . . . I was afraid that perhaps there was something written about Bev in it. I know she likes to shock people, doesn't always know where to draw the line. I don't want any of her more lurid escapades published for the world to see."

"Certainly not. And you paid him?"

"Yes. I should have gotten the book first. He telephoned the day you arrived to say there was something he had to do, but he would leave it in the desk compartment, which you no doubt know about."

She nodded. "It isn't there."

Daniel turned to her, his eyes dark and turbulent. "We have to find it."

"I agree." Though really, how bad could the scandals be? In the wrong hands it could be embarrassing at most. And most scandal rags were willing to accept payment to keep a name unsullied.

He didn't come inside, and Phil went straight upstairs to bed. She had much to think about, including why everyone assumed Devil's Thunder would still run next week. Had anyone thought to consult Bev? Did she really intend to turn over the operation of the stables to Freddy and Bobby? Did she even have experience if she decided to take an interest? Would the jockeys and trainers ever accept a woman as their boss?

Bev wasn't stupid when she wasn't being flighty. She'd always had a good head for numbers. There was no reason that she shouldn't run the stables herself. But she couldn't do that until this murder was put behind them.

Phil rang for Lily and sat down at her dressing table. While she waited, she picked up the *Memoires of Sherlock Holmes* and turned to "The Adventure of Silver Blaze."

When Lily appeared a few minutes later, Phil could tell she was in a state. "What has happened?" she asked cautiously.

Lily rustled over to the dressing table. There was no other way to describe it. Her new apron was starched so crisply that it talked as it moved. Phil would have to suggest to Preswick that he have the laundry go lightly on the starch. A lady's maid must look prim, but she also must be able to sneak about in the dead of night without alerting the whole household.

Lily pulled the tiara from Phil's head, taking several strands of Phil's hair with it. "Why do they always blame the wife or the mistress?"

"Ah, the staff has been gossiping."

"Yes."

"And what is their opinion?"

Lily began pulling pins from Phil's hair.

"Leave me some scalp, please."

Lily's hands dropped. "I am sorry. I—"

"Do not throw yourself on your knees, just tell me what happened without scalping me."

"Yes, my lady."

Phil smiled. Whenever Lily used "my lady" in private, Phil knew that she was either contrite or being terribly sarcastic. Tonight, it had to be contrition.

"So-o-o-o," Phil urged.

"Most of them believe it was that mistr-r-r-ress. But a few, they think it was Mrs. Reynolds. I would fir-r-r-r-re them all without a r-r-reference."

"You don't think either of them murdered Reggie?"

"Lots of people could have mur-r-r-rdered him."

"True, though now they seem to be concentrating their detectival energies toward the missing driver."

"Ah, him. Always . . ."

"The lower classes are blamed for whatever the rich refuse to believe about themselves. I agree. Go on."

"You do?"

"Yes," Phil said, watching her maid in the mirror. "I think the lower classes may have an ally in Detective Atkins. I don't believe for a minute that he agrees with the new turn in the investigation. I think he still has his sights on Bev, unfortunately."

"Do you think she killed her husband?"

Phil thought about it. "No. I think she might have been driven to in a fit of rage. But not on the heels of my arrival. She went to have Reggie bring the auto closer. I arrived at the scene right after she did. She was in shock. And the timing is all wrong. How would she have the time to discover him with his mistress, fumble in her reticule or pocket for a pistol that she just happened to be carrying, shoot him, hide the pistol, and break into a feigned fit of shock?

"And it isn't like Bev to plan ahead. If she shot him, she'd be more likely to turn herself in and dance on his sorry carcass."

Lily sputtered out a laugh. Clapped her hand over her mouth. "Sorry, madam."

"Don't be. I think we could all use a little humor in this situation. Now tell me, what else are the servants saying?"

"The footmen think the mistress did it. Cook thinks it was the anarchists." Lily rolled her eyes expressively. "The two parlor maids keep mum, but the sculleries, they don't think Mrs. Reynolds did it, but they wish she had, because he was not nice to them, and he took advantage of the parlor maids and Elmir-r-r-ra, who no one likes."

"Elmira, too?"

"If I were Elmir-r-r-a, I would have killed him myself." Her hand touched the side of her uniform where Phil imagined the knife was now kept.

"No killing, Lily."

Lily grinned. "*Oui, madame.*" She bobbed a quick prim curtsey that made Phil laugh.

"Well, we can guess that Elmira in this case didn't kill him, since she was waiting for Mrs. Reynolds with the smelling salts when we arrived."

Lily puffed out air in the French expression of "it doesn't signify."

"They said this at tea?"

"Oh, no, madam. The sculleries don't take tea with the others. And they would be turned off for expressing such views. I learned it in the garden on the back steps. It's where they go to smoke cigarettes."

"No smoking," Phil told her.

"No, madam, it makes them stink."

"Yes, it does. Good work, Lily."

Lily finished braiding her hair. "Are we going to study about fingerprints tonight, madam?"

Atkins had disparaged her reading, had warned her off. She should get herself and her servants out of this quagmire before things became dire, which they might at any moment. And yet she was intrigued by the whole idea of investigation.

The books she and Lily were avidly studying were rather dry discourses, but sneaking down to search the library in the middle of the night, watching out for Mr. X, even gossiping with the ladies at dinner—those things had made her blood race.

No telling what she could find out by questioning the infamous Mimi LaPonte, who just happened to be out of jail for the moment. Perhaps a little visit to that not-quite-a-lady would be in order. Or furthering her inquiries into horse racing. There was a lead she hadn't begun to follow.

"Tonight, I think we'll skip the treatise and read something a little more exciting." Phil reached for the *Memoires of Sherlock Holmes* and opened it to "The Adventure of Silver Blaze."

"Isn't it interesting that the gentleman in the bookstore recommended a story about horses." She turned to the first page and read aloud, "'"I am afraid, Watson, that I shall have to go," said Holmes . . .'

"And so must we," Phil murmured.

"But where, madam?" Lily asked, sounding alarmed.

"Wherever the clues lead us, Lily."

"Ah, and are we to become detectives, madam?"

"Yes, Lily, I believe we are."

12

Phil came down to breakfast the next morning with her head filled with missing horses, lost fortunes, murder, and the Dartmoor fog. Bev was still abed and Phil was now eager to make plans to visit the stables. But when she picked up the morning *Times*, all thoughts of horses fled her mind. She grabbed the offending piece of journalism and hurried upstairs to wake her friend.

"Mimi LaPonte is going back on stage," Phil announced as she brandished the morning paper above Bev's groggy head. She stopped for a moment. "You look terrible."

Bev blinked at her. "Phil? Why are you dressed? Where are you going?" A yawn escaped and she blinked again. "What time is it?"

"It's almost afternoon. Are you feeling ill?"

"I didn't sleep well."

"Too many martinis, my dear. You should pace yourself."

"That was nothing compared to life with Reggie. Lord, the man could drink." She pulled a pillow over and propped herself up in bed. "So what's so important that you woke me up?"

Phil dropped the newspaper in her lap. "This."

Bev turned the paper around, snapped the pages straight, then scanned the page, finally settling on the article. "Well, that little—"

"Quite," Phil said. "And I suddenly have an insatiable urge to go to the theater."

"—bitch," Bev finished.

Phil frowned. "Was that directed at me or the detested Mildred Mimi Potts LaPonte?"

Bev's mouth almost reached a smile. "Mildred, of course." She pushed the covers away. "I'll come with you."

"You're in mourning."

"I'm a divorcée."

"Well, I wouldn't brag about it. Divorce may be the 'in' thing these days, but most of society will condemn you for it."

"And since when did you care about what society thinks?"

"Since you became the number one suspect in your husband's murder."

"Me? You heard Detective Atkins. They think it was the missing driver."

"The operative word being 'they.' He, however, doesn't think it was the driver. And I believe he thinks it's you."

"He couldn't."

"Just because you have a pretty face and flirted with him? Good heavens. What's happened to you, Bev? You have to know how to toe the mark in public, a boxing term, I believe, but very apt for our current situation.

"You aligned yourself with a man whose closest friends seem to be flash and fury without much substance except firearms and racehorses."

Bev's lower lip pouted.

"Well, is it not true?"

"You don't understand. We're the modern set."

"Perhaps, but Reggie's now part of the graveyard set."

Bev's mouth twisted. Phil went to sit beside her.

"Bev, I don't give a fig for mourning, and you can be as modern as you like, but you must put on a show at least temporarily if you ever want to be accepted in society again."

"Society is changing," Bev said stubbornly.

"I certainly hope it is, but until Atkins catches the real killer and society actually does change, think of your reputation." She patted Bev's shoulder.

"I'd rather have fun than a good reputation."

"Perhaps, and once the culprit is caught, you can dance naked on the table at Delmonico's if you want. But until then, please be the proper grieving widow."

"Ugh. A week. I'll stay in mourning a week. That should give him time to find out who really killed Reggie. And save my reputation."

Phil cast her eyes to the ceiling. "Good. Thank you. I, however, don't have a reputation to lose. Though being new to the local mind-set, I believe I'll borrow one of your veils for my visit."

"Then take the crepe silk. No one could recognize you behind that awful thing." She pushed the covers and Phil away and got out of bed, padded barefoot across the carpet to a bureau, and pulled out the bottom drawer. "It might be a little wrinkled. I was trying to hide it from Elmira. She's such a stickler."

She pulled out the crumpled black veil and gave it several good shakes. "There, as good as new. And you're welcome to it."

Phil just stared at the mess of material as her own mourning, such that it was, came flooding back. Putting on that veil was the last thing she wanted. But she also didn't want to be seen when she didn't know who was who and who was watching, and none of her Parisienne chapeau veils were anywhere nearly big enough to hide her face.

She reluctantly took the veil. Trying to ignore the chill that was slowly spreading over her, she sat down at Bev's dressing table to pin it over her hat.

When she was finished, she turned to Bev. "How do I look?"

"*Très dramatique.* The mysterious Madame X." Bev laughed. "To accompany your mysterious mystery man from Reggie's wake."

"I think we can give him up, alas. He seems to have lost interest," Phil said. "Wish me luck."

"Good luck with your interrogations."

"Really Bev, I'm merely going to hear her side of the story. And perhaps ask a few questions of my own."

"Ask her if he was good in bed."

"Oh, Bev, you're hopeless." Phil left the room wondering for the first time if trying to save Bev from this scrape would only postpone her getting into another—possibly as bad, perhaps worse.

She left the house a few minutes later without Lily and Preswick, both of whom put up numerous arguments about why she couldn't go alone. But in the end she'd had her way. Not that she wouldn't have appreciated their support, but she wasn't sure what she would encounter. If her meeting with Mildred Potts would be considered contrary to Atkins's investigation and if there were to be legal ramifications, she'd rather weather them alone than put her loyal servants at risk.

Bentley was waiting by the carriage when she came down the steps of the brownstone.

She hesitated. "Terrible business, Bentley."

"Yes, my lady."

"I don't suppose you know who was driving the touring car that day?"

"No, my lady. The police asked me. I always meant to learn to drive. Just never seem to have the time."

"It's quite all right, Bentley. Good carriage men are worth their weight in gold."

He smiled at that. "Thank you, my lady."

"Do any of the staff drive?"

"Not to my knowledge, my lady."

"Thank you, Bentley. I see that our ever-vigilant police guard has been removed from his place across the street?"

"Yes, my lady."

She stepped into the carriage. He pulled up the steps and closed the door, and soon they were headed downtown. Phil had rather enjoyed the notion of a police escort everywhere she went. But even knowing that she wasn't being followed didn't prevent her from feeling uneasy on the ride to visit the Florodora girl.

And she kept thinking of the lines from Shakespeare, "By the pricking of my thumbs, something wicked this way comes." It wasn't her thumbs that were feeling prickly. It was the back of her neck. It might just be the itchy fabric of the veil, but she had a lowering feeling that there was menace afoot.

So much so, that she kept looking out from the carriage to make sure she hadn't missed something.

They turned onto a wide boulevard past Central Park, where the trees and shrubs were displaying their greenery over a low stone wall. It seemed a poplar place as the entrance was crowded with pedestrians.

After a few minutes the carriage slowed at a traffic circle large enough to accommodate carriages, automobiles, and trolleys. Several streets created a pinwheel from the center, and Bentley turned the carriage down one of these. *Broadway,* Phil presumed.

This was a wide thoroughfare, lined by storefronts and peddlers selling everything imaginable. Traffic ran in fits and starts, as the trolleys passed them without slowing down only to stop suddenly to disgorge and take on passengers and speed off again. Several blocks later, they entered the theater district.

Marquees lined the street above double entrances, Unlit now, at dusk the electrified lights would line the avenue like a carnival or Guy Fawkes day.

After several blocks, Bentley turned the carriage to the left and they entered a narrow street. Here, too, theaters lined the sidewalks.

Just a few doors in from the corner, they came to a stop in front of a big brick building that rose several stories high, its façade broken by rows of faux windows.

It didn't look nearly so glamorous up close.

For an instant, Phil wished she'd brought Preswick along with her.

She'd never been backstage at a theater. She'd met several fine actresses and actors in society, but never a chorus girl, at least not formally, which according to Bev made her old-fashioned, something she'd never in her life been accused of.

Bentley let down the steps and helped her from the carriage. "Are you sure you don't want me to accompany you? The boy can handle the team until I return."

"I don't think that will be necessary, Bentley, but how do I find backstage?"

He pointed out a narrow metal door set back into the wall several feet from the main entrance.

It seemed early for Mimi to be at the theater. She was basically a showgirl, nothing against the profession, but not the most challenging of theater roles. After all, it was mainly a matter of putting on makeup and changing into her costume. And Phil had witnessed enough after-theater parties to know chorus girls could change out of costumes fast enough.

Bentley climbed back up onto box.

Phil stood on the sidewalk for another minute, gathering her courage. On the far side of the front door a stagehand leaned against the wall, smoking a cigarette. He seemed in no hurry to get back to work.

To tell the truth, she wasn't looking forward to going inside either. Which was ridiculous—that was why she'd come. She took another minute to practice, "Good afternoon, I'm the Countess of Dunbridge," wondering if the guardian of the stage door would actually let her in.

As she stood there, four women hurried down the street and converged on the stage door. When it opened, Phil converged with them, signed the call book, then scurried down the hall with the others before the doorman realized she wasn't really a cast member.

Her name was on the door: MIMI LAPONTE. Paid for by Reggie, no doubt. It was unusual for a chorus girl to have a private dressing room.

She tapped lightly and, getting no response, opened the door.

Two people were seated in front of a long mirror surrounded by lights. One was Mimi and the other was Bobby Mullins.

Mimi shrieked and jumped up. "Who are you? This is a private dressing room."

"Oh, I am sorry," Phil said, and pulled back her veil. What was Mullins doing here? Taking over Reggie's stables in more ways than one?

Bobby pushed to his feet, straightened his tie, and snatched his bowler from his head. "Countess, your, um, lady. What are you doing here?"

"Why, I came to see Mimi, of course. Lovely digs you have here, my dear."

Mimi shot Bobby a confused look.

So much for the advertised "beautiful, long-legged Florodora girls." Mildred Potts was at least a head shorter than Phil. She was voluptuous and pretty enough, but not beautiful to Phil's way of thinking, and with hair that couldn't possibly be her natural color.

Bobby kneaded the brim of his hat. "This here is the Countess of Dun-Dun—"

"Dunbridge," Phil supplied. "You know, I've never been backstage in a theater. This is delightful." It actually wasn't as bad as she'd expected. There was a table for making up, a chaise covered by a Moroccan tapestry and several throw pillows. A small table with the remnants of lunch. A hanging rack with a pink chiffon costume, and a wide-brimmed black picture hat and ruffled parasol. Phil recognized the costume from the advertisement bill.

Several large bouquets of white roses crowded one corner of the room. They looked quite fresh. All delivered today once the news broke that Mimi would be returning to her role as one of the *Florodora* girls?

Mimi was wrapped in a dressing gown of some shiny fabric that must be one of the new synthetics. Evidently Reggie's beneficence didn't go as far as the dressing gowns. Or perhaps that was her lucky talisman. Actresses were notoriously superstitious.

She was holding a crumpled sheet of paper in her hand. There were several other sheets of crumpled paper on the dressing table.

"I see your admirers are delighted to have you back."

"What do you want?"

"Just a little chat." Phil wandered over to the dressing table, picked up a bottle of eau de cologne, and sniffed. Wrinkled her nose and put it down again. She turned to face the other two.

"Shall we make ourselves comfortable?"

Bobby jumped as if awakened from a deep sleep, quickly looked around as if he had no idea where he was, and pulled up a chair for Philomena, tripping over his feet like an actor in a bad melodrama.

Phil sat.

"You're that friend of Reggie's wife what was at the docks that day." Mimi sniffed and groped for a hankie. "Poor Reggie."

"Yes, so unfortunate."

"Why are you here? I have to get ready for the matinee, and now this." She tightened her fist around the paper she was holding.

"A letter from an admirer?" Phil asked, thinking that John Atkins's methods of questioning a suspect were much more efficient. Perhaps it was time to use her more finely honed, drawing room skills.

She pulled her chair closer to Mimi's. "You poor dear. This must have been such an ordeal for you."

Mimi opened her eyes over her handkerchief. "Why do you care?" came the muffled reply.

"Well." Phil moved even closer, felt Bobby being drawn in, too. His presence was something she hadn't anticipated. And he was definitely nervous about hers. She'd have to deal with him later.

"If you've come here to accuse me of murder, you can hold your peace. The cops let me go. It was humiliating, the things they said, I can tell you."

"Do."

Mimi frowned.

"Do tell me," Phil added. "I can't imagine what it was like. Was it that Detective Sergeant Atkins? He's been annoying us to no end. He's had a guard on the house and everything. I had to, um, give him the slip just to go shopping yesterday. And today . . . well . . ."

Mimi flashed a look toward Bobby. "Did you see any policemen outside?"

"Naw, Mimi. They're done with you." He turned toward Phil. "They're done with her, Mrs. Countess."

"Are they indeed?"

"They'll never be done with me. Becker will hound me do death."

"Becker? I've heard he's a tough, um, cop."

"Tough?" Mimi laughed hysterically.

Phil hurried on before it became a full-scale breakdown. "How did you ever convince them that you didn't kill him?"

"I didn't kill him." Mimi burst into tears.

"Well, who on earth do you think did?"

"Not me. They think it was the driver. Seems they can't find him anywhere."

"Oh, that would be a relief to all of us."

Mimi cut off crying to stare at her. "It would?"

"What I mean is, then you and Beverly Reynolds would both be, um, off the hook."

"Well, I still say she did it. And I don't care if you are her friend and go running off to tell her. Reggie was going to leave her. We're were going to sail away that very day. She must have found out about it."

"You think she killed him?"

"Of course. She was insanely jealous. And if she found out—"

"Mimi," Bobby warned. "No use bad-mouthing Bev Reynolds. She and the countess here are good friends. She's staying at the town house. Begging your pardon, um, ma'am."

"Think nothing of it. We're both women of the world. Did

you tell the police your suspicions? I only arrived after Reggie, rest his soul, was dead. What a horrible experience for you."

Mimi nodded, and Phil prayed she wouldn't resort to more tears.

"What happened? Can you bear to tell me?"

She could and with dramatic flare. "There was such a crowd and we couldn't get through. And Reggie told the driver to go move them out of the way, and he was gone a really long time, and Reggie was getting fidgety. Kept looking around saying, 'Damn the man, where is he?' Then all of a sudden he says, 'I better find him,' and he started to get out of the touring car. Then there's this explosion and Reggie fell back and he . . . and he . . . died in my arms." She threw out those arms and looked down at her lap, which had the effect of opening her robe to display ample mounds of bosom. Phil looked away, but Bobby was mesmerized.

"So much blood, so much blood!"

"Oh, dear, how awful," Phil broke in before Mimi's account of the proceedings turned into a Lady Macbeth monologue. "Out, damned spot."

"What?"

"Such a spot you were in." Phil frowned, pursed her lips. "Don't I recall you crying out that Reggie had shot himself?"

"Well, yes." Another glance at Bobby. "That's what I thought at first. You see, Reggie always carried a pistol, so I thought that his pistol must have fired by accident."

"Was he holding his pistol?"

"I—I don't know. No. What does it matter? When I opened my eyes—"

"You'd closed them?"

"I must have, because when I opened them, she was standing in the open door."

"Was she holding a pistol?"

Mimi shrugged. "Yes, no, I don't know."

Phil had to discipline herself not to shake the silly woman until the truth fell out. She took Mimi's hand and patted it. "How awful for you. Mr. Mullins, can you see if there's tea in that pot still or perhaps a bit of brandy." She kept patting Mimi's hand while Bobby rummaged in a drawer and came up with a flask. "And I suppose that horrid Detective Atkins made you tell him every detail."

"He did." Mimi took the flask and sipped. "He started out such a gentleman, but he just wouldn't stop asking me things. Over and over again. And he's such a looker."

"Isn't he?" Phil said confidingly. "Who knew he could be so cruel? He was absolutely vicious with poor Bev."

"He was?"

"Yes. Then yesterday he came by and said they were no longer interested in either of you, because they can't find the driver and figure he did it."

Bobby snorted. "I bet my granny's teeth it weren't Atkins. Someone higher up pulled a fast one." Bobby fairly spit out the words.

Phil flinched. *Someone higher up. Higher than Becker?* So what was Atkins in all this? The honest policeman he claimed to be, or someone very smart at the game?

"Now, Bobby," Mimi said, "you know you don't want to go saying things like that about the cops. They just followed their noses and it led them to that driver."

"That ain't where it led them. But I'll tell you to both your faces, none of our boys woulda killed Reggie. He treated 'em good."

"Who was the driver? Do the police know?"

"No," Mimi said.

"You didn't tell them?"

"I don't know who he was. Reggie always hired a driver when we were together, so's we could get a good cuddle in the back, you know."

Phil tried not to imagine. "They're lucky that you were in the car. Being an actress, you are more observant than most people. I hope they rewarded you for giving them a good description of the man."

Mimi snorted. "Fat chance. Plus I didn't really notice him. I had more important things on my mind."

No doubt, Phil thought.

"He was wearing a driving coat and cap and goggles. Who could tell what he looked like? It could've been Bobby, for all I know."

"Oh, no it couldn't," Bobby said. "I've got an alibi." He shot a look at Phil. "Besides, me and Reg, we were like this." He pressed two fingers together.

"I didn't mean you literally, Bobby."

"If you're wondering, ma'am, I was at customs dropping off Mimi's trunks and things."

"And Reggie's?"

Bobby chewed on his bottom lip. "That's what I don't get. He said he didn't have no trunks or anything and to just take Mimi's."

Aha, Phil thought. That explained the one suitcase. But not Bobby Mullins's part in all this. If he played a part.

"Mr. Mullins, how did you know Reggie was planning a trip?"

"I didn't. The first I ever heard of it was that morning when he telephoned me and said to run around to Mimi's and pick up her trunks and deliver them to the dock."

"Reggie decided to go to South America that morning?"

"It was a spur-of-the-moment decision," Mimi said. "It was going to be our honeymoon. That's what he said."

"So what will you do now?" Phil asked. "Besides your career."

Mimi's grasp had crumpled her hankie and the piece of paper she'd been holding into one soggy ball. She tossed it aside.

"I don't know."

A knock sounded at the door.

Mimi shot out of her chair. "Who is it?"

The door opened and a messenger boy carried in a big urn of roses.

Mimi stepped back. "No! No more. I can't take this. Don't bring any more flowers backstage."

The boy dropped the flowers next to the others. Bobby flipped him a coin and he ran from the room.

Mimi seemed ready to start wailing again. Really, the girl was too melodramatic. Phil went over to the new bouquet to read the card.

"Good heavens. Were all these flowers accompanied by the same message?"

"Yes, they want to kill me!"

Phil half expected Mimi to throw herself on the chaise and cover her eyes with her arm, but she just didn't have the finesse of an Eleonora Duse or Ethel Barrymore.

But Mimi did surprise her. Instead of lying down, she flung off the Moroccan tapestry to reveal a packed valise. She yanked several garments off a coatrack and crammed them on top, rushed to the dressing table and swept the makeup into a bag, which she tossed onto the clothes.

"Mimi, don't lose your head. It's just people who are spouting off."

"Perhaps," Phil said, rereading the words on the card: *If you appear on the stage, you're dead.* A succinct sentiment, but an awfully expensive way to deliver it.

And who would send such a thing? Another jealous mistress who blamed Mimi for his death? How many did Reggie have? His racing cohorts, angry because they thought Mimi had killed their golden goose? Would they go for Bev next?

"I told Reggie it wouldn't work. They killed him, and now they're coming after me."

Good heavens, Phil thought as she realized this had taken a totally unexpected turn. "Who are *they*?" she asked.

"Nobody," Bobby snapped at the same time Mimi cried, "I don't know!"

Phil made a note to invite John Atkins to a nice dinner once this investigation was over. Who knew how hard gathering clues could be? She was quite ready for one of Bev's cocktails.

Mimi had frozen in the middle of the floor. Now she crumpled onto the chaise, then sat rocking and wringing her hands. Yes, a cocktail was certainly called for. Phil might never attend a melodrama again.

"Bobby, I beg you. You gotta get me out of here."

"Perhaps, Mr. Mullins, it might be better if she did take a few days off, just until the air clears."

"No. I mean outta Manhattan. Please, Bobby."

"Mimi, hon, the coppers told you not to leave town. If you do they'll come after you and try to pin Reggie's murder on you. But you can't stay in town without money. I already gave you what I could."

"But don't you have Reggie's money for the trip?" Phil asked. Surely she couldn't have run through it that fast.

Another look to Bobby. "There wasn't any money."

"There had to be. You don't go traipsing off to South America without cash, and the police didn't return any to Bev."

"How did you know where we were going?"

"It don't matter," said Bobby. "The coppers probably kept the money. They do stuff like that. Old Roosevelt tried to clean up the force, but as soon as he left it just went back to like it was. There's a few honest coppers, like Atkins, and you don't want to cross him, though I doubt he'll last. Good riddance, I say. Impossible to deal with honest cops."

"Indeed."

"I mean, you gotta admire the guy for hanging tough, but it'll get him killed before it's all over."

"Before what's all over?"

"Everything. Ain't nothing totally honest in this town. Just the way it's always been. Not gonna change anytime soon, if ever."

Mimi closed the suitcase, tried to snap it shut, leaned against it. "Ugh!" She pushed the top back, pulled off the top layer of clothes, dislodging a shiny black purse.

Phil reached it before Mimi did.

"How pretty," Phil said, and snapped it open it before Mimi could snatch it back. Empty.

"It got all mucked up the day that . . . the day that . . ." She sniffed.

"But you got it back," Phil said, stifling the urge to look inside.

"The cops found it on the street—damn dock trash copped it then threw it away. It only had my compact and lip rouge and a hankie in it. Now it's ruined."

Phil didn't comment.

"If you want it, you might as well keep it. I don't have room for it anyway."

"Thank you," Phil said, and tucked it under her arm in case Mimi changed her mind.

Mimi latched the suitcase and yanked it off the chaise. "I'm done."

"The hell you are." Bobby grabbed the suitcase and tossed it back on the chaise. "What will the countess here think of you, acting like a crazy woman?"

"I think she's frightened and needs someone who will protect her."

Mimi nodded emphatically and cast a grateful look at Phil.

Another knock at the door.

Mimi squeaked.

"Half hour, Miss LaPonte."

"Come on, old girl, I'll be out front and make sure nobody's got a gun. It's all gonna be fine."

The door opened and an older woman stepped into the room. "You'll have to leave now. Miss LaPonte must dress. Lord, girl, you been crying again? Nobody wants to see swollen eyes and a hangdog face on a Florodora girl." She pulled Mimi over to the dressing table and shooed Phil and Mullins toward the door.

Mullins escorted her down the hall.

"Did Mrs. Reynolds send you here?"

"No. We just read that the police had released Mimi and I wanted to find out how she fared. I think they are both perhaps victims." Phil lifted her eyebrows, inviting his response.

"Well, between you and me, they were both driving him crazy. A couple of demanding broads, begging your pardon."

"How so?"

Bobby screwed up his face. "Like all women. Wanting this, wanting that, wanting more of his time. Wanting him to stop seeing the other. This one"—Bobby jerked his head back over his shoulder—"always needing more money. She was never satisfied. I told Reggie to leave her and settle on his wife. She's a comely woman and classy, knows how to have fun without stoppin' being a lady, if you know what I mean."

"I do."

"I thought he meant to do just that. Pay Mildre—I mean Mimi—"

"Mildred will do."

"Pay her a lump sum and send her on her way. England, maybe. They need dancing girls there, right? Maybe that's what he was doing. He never said nothin' to me about South America. No way would he leave the boys in the lurch. And a lot of men got money on that race. Devil's Thunder is gonna make a lot of people money. I don't believe Reggie woulda cut out on us. He might want to leave town for a few days. Like maybe he was afraid Mrs. Reynolds might be on his back, ya know? I begged him to stick with his wife—she was a true one—but he couldn't follow nothing but his . . . well, you know how it is."

Alas, she did. "Did you tell all this to the police?"

"Hell, no. Pardon, your missus—ma'am. But you don't tell the police around here nothin'. Just pay your protection money and go on about your business."

They'd reached the exit door and he opened it for her. "Do you have a carriage waiting for you? Or you want me to hail a cab for you?" His step faltered slightly. "Do countesses take cabs?"

"I believe that if they want to survive in Manhattan, they must, but it was arranged with the coachman to return for me here."

He nodded to the doorman, shoved his bowler down over his bright orange hair, and they stepped out onto the sidewalk.

There was no carriage. She scanned the street to see if it was nearby and saw it coming toward her, stuck behind a slow-moving sanitary commission cart.

"Ah, here it is." As she turned back to Bobby, a man across the street struck a match and tucked his head to light a cigarette.

Hadn't she seen the same man outside the theater when she'd arrived? What was he doing across the street now? He certainly didn't seem to be in a hurry, and he would be needed for the matinee in a few minutes.

"Do you know that man?" she asked. "Over there with the cigarette."

Bobby squinted. "Can't say I do. Why?"

"He just for a moment seemed familiar."

"Don't think it would be anybody you'd know."

"No, you're probably right."

The carriage pulled up and Bobby helped her inside.

"Ma'am, you won't tell Mimi I said those things about her, she can be a right harridan."

"I didn't know you were friends."

"We're not exactly. But I was Reggie's right-hand man."

"I see." And Phil was pretty sure she did. "Will she be safe going on stage again?"

"I don't know, ma'am. Nothing makes sense to me."

He closed the door. The carriage took off, and Phil leaned to the other side of the carriage as they drove away.

Why was she not surprised when she found the street empty and no sign of man or cigarette?

13

"I'm beginning to agree with you, Bev," Phil said, bursting into the parlor and pulling off her veil. She tossed it to Bev, who was lounging on the sofa. "If we had a fire lit, I'd gladly toss this monstrosity into the flames."

"Oh, let's do it," Bev said, sitting up and slipping her stocking feet into a pair of satin slippers.

"Not yet. But I do agree. There is no sense in you being in mourning any longer than necessary. You would have thought Reggie, after choosing you, would have better taste in a mistress."

"Mildred Potts is a sow's ear," Bev said. "And Reggie was a rotter."

Well put, thought Phil. "Bev, stop it. You shouldn't say such things."

Bev propelled herself off the sofa. "What is wrong with you, Phil? You sound like an old prude. Is this what marrying royalty does to you?"

"Actually, just the opposite, my dear Bev. But the police are looking for someone to arrest. And if Miss Potts told them what she told me, and if they can't find this alleged driver, you might be the one they choose."

"They wouldn't dare."

"They would more than dare. I'm deadly serious. They need to arrest someone. So stop being a self-indulgent brat and start thinking about your survival."

Bev stopped cold, slowly turned back to Phil. "Is it as bad as that?"

Phil sighed. "I don't know, but it is certainly within the realm of possibility. That LaPonte woman would throw her mother under a trolley to save herself. She's hiding something—her guilt, perhaps, I don't know for certain. But she's definitely afraid."

Bev reached for the bell.

"And don't think your afternoon cocktails are going to solve the problem. You should start searching your mind for who would want to shoot Reggie. And why. And then we'd better seriously go about proving it, because if we don't, you'll be living on bread and water while you're waiting to be executed."

Bev sank onto the nearest chair. "I didn't kill him. Or the man in the library."

"Then who did?"

"I don't know."

"And you really don't know who he is?"

"I told you, no."

"And no one knows who the driver is or where he is. No one seems to know anything, not us, not Atkins, not even Bobby Mullins, who was Reggie's right-hand man."

"Bobby Mullins? When did you talk to him?"

"He was at the theater."

Bev sat up. "What's he doing at the theater when he should be at the farm taking care of my horses?"

"This morning he was trying to talk the inimitable Mildred out of leaving town."

"She wouldn't dare. Unless she's guilty."

"She may be guilty, but I don't think that is what's scaring her. And she was definitely scared. While I was there, she received a threat not to appear onstage. I guess Reggie had his admirers."

"He did. Too many, if you ask me. But I'm glad they're taking it out on her and not me."

"I suppose. But surely none of Reggie's friends will actually kill her for going onstage. She's in the chorus, for heaven's sake."

"I'm sure I don't care."

"And she was hiding a half-packed suitcase under a tapestry.

When the note came, she threw the rest of her belongings into it and slammed it shut."

"And?"

"And she gave me this."

"A purse? Really, Phil."

"Not just any purse, I'm certain it's the one I saw lying on the car floor the day of Reggie's death. The one the thief was trying to steal. I thought it might be a clue. But it's empty."

"Let me see."

Phil handed it to her, and she immediately began rummaging in the lining and seams. "There's nothing here." Bev tossed the bag onto the couch.

"I know. I thought there might be something. It was on the floor of Reggie's auto. But the thief stole it while I was arguing with Atkins."

"Then how did Mimi end up with it?"

"She says the police found it on the street and returned it." Phil picked up the bag, opened it, felt along the lining. "Whatever was—or might have been—here is long gone." She dropped the bag back on the cushion.

"So then what happened?"

"Then Bobby showed me out. He says Reggie would never have left before the big race. Not and leave all of 'them'—I assume he means his employees, stablemen, jockeys, and such—in the lurch with a big race coming up. Something about this just doesn't make sense."

"Something?" asked Bev, her voice growing slightly shrill. "How about nothing? Nothing makes sense."

Phil walked to the window, pushed back the curtain, and looked out. No policeman, just ordinary pedestrian traffic. A picture was beginning to emerge, but it was dim and the details were elusive. As she let the curtain drop, a chill ran up her spine. She quickly turned back, but no one was there—not that she could see. Nonetheless, one thing was perfectly certain. They were being watched.

"What is it, Phil? You look worried."

"Not worried, just at a stand. From the moment I set foot out of the house this morning, I felt like someone was watching me."

"Well, there are the constables Atkins put to guard us for some reason or another."

"They've been taken off the watch."

"Oh? Maybe they no longer consider me a suspect?"

Phil let that pass. She didn't think for a minute Atkins had come to that conclusion.

"But as I was leaving the theater, I caught a glimpse of a man across the street. He was lighting a cigarette and he looked so familiar that I thought I must have seen him before."

"Why didn't you hightail it across the street and ask him?"

Phil shrugged. "I was already in the carriage before I became suspicious. It was just a man lighting a cigarette. But then . . . well, when I looked out of the carriage, he was gone. Besides countesses don't 'hightail it' anywhere."

Bev laughed. "I think you're having handsome mystery man fantasies," she said. "Not that I blame you. You have just spent a terrible two years in black."

"Yes." Though it hadn't been all bad, Phil recalled with a little smile. Even dowagers needed a bit of fun. "I thought so, too, but remember the first day I met Detective Sergeant Atkins? He looked like a street bum because he was doing what they call an 'undercover operation.' A disguise to make him look different and to fit in. Hmm."

"You think the man you saw today was Atkins being 'undercover'?"

Phil thought back. "No. I would recognize John Atkins even if he was undercover." She gave Bev a quick smile. "This was someone else, and there was something familiar about him, the way he stood, something. At least I thought that at the time.

"Maybe it's just some strange hysteria or like one of those dreams where you find someone but when he turns, it is someone else."

"My poor Phil. I'm sorry to get you into this."

"Don't give it another thought. Now I have an idea."

"Do tell."

"I think we should tell Tuttle to say you are indisposed tomorrow and you and I will slip out to Holly Farm. I'd like to see Devil's Thunder for myself. Can you drive the Packard?"

"Of course, it's the twentieth century. And I think that's an excellent idea. Someone needs to look out after my investments. And that person is me.

"We'll go out in the morning. It's a two-hour drive. We'll stay at the farm overnight. It's quaint, but comfy. Not grand enough for Reggie, he only stayed there when he had horses running back to back. But I rather like it. We'll have a picnic dinner, then watch the training session the next morning."

"Sounds divine. Though I have no motoring clothes."

"Not to worry. I'll just have Tuttle call around for a duster and accoutrements. We'll have them delivered."

"Shall we take Elmira and Lily?"

"Elmira, no. She gets queasy, but Lily if you think she'll do for us both."

Phil thought she would do famously. "Two dusters and accoutrements."

"Wonderful. I feel better already."

"So do I," Phil agreed. She might be able to learn something from the stable boys, or if not, Lily certainly could. And with any luck Bobby would start taking his duties seriously and she'd get another chance to question him, too.

"It will be nice," Bev continued. "The ride will be a bit dusty, but the farm is quite lovely, if you don't mind nature."

"I rather like nature." And there was no end to the things she might learn.

At the crack of noon the next day, Phil and Lily, dressed in their linen driving dusters, met Bev downstairs for their drive out to

Holly Farm. Phil could tell Lily was excited. She'd hardly been out since they'd arrived in the city.

Once this unfortunate situation was over, Phil would make sure that she'd have plenty of chances to see everything Manhattan had to offer, like the library, the museum, and the park, which Bev said stretched for miles but Phil had seen only from the outside.

They would all go, Phil, Preswick, and Lily. They'd have a holiday, Lily would wear one of her new dresses, and Preswick, well, he'd never dispense with his suit and vest and tie but he might have some fun.

Yes, Preswick deserved a little fun. He'd volunteered to go with them today, though he detested the out of doors, because he considered it his duty to attend the "dowager." Only after explaining to him that she was afraid to leave the brownstone without someone she could trust there to make sure nothing nefarious happened, did he agree to stay behind.

He did insist on seeing them off himself, giving last-minute instructions to Lily as if they were about to embark on a safari in darkest Africa instead of an overnight jaunt to Long island. But at last Lily climbed in the back where picnic baskets, valises, and a box of wines and cordials enough for a fortnight were piled on the seat, conveniently covering up whatever stains might be left from Reggie's demise.

The driver who brought the auto around from the garage handed over the keys to Bev, who tipped him and climbed in the driver's seat. He ran around to crank the engine and the motorcar rumbled into life. Phil turned, gave Lily a thumbs-up—she had no idea if the girl had ever been in a motorcar.

Lily merely lifted her chin and sat a little straighter. They both adjusted their goggles, and they were off.

It took quite a while to get through Manhattan to the bridge that would take them to Queens, an outlying suburb, and then to Long Island, where Holly Farm was located.

"We could wait for the car ferry at Thirty-Fourth, but the bridge is more fun," Bev yelled from the driver's seat.

Phil gave another thumbs-up—the only gesture that seemed appropriate, since it was too noisy for conversation—and she sat back to watch the array of buildings pass by.

The bridge indeed was wonderful. With the expanse of sky above them and river below, they flew toward Queens on a highway that seem suspended by silver threads. The fact that they were really steel cables made no difference at all.

The speed and the wind, the blue sky above . . . Phil had a mad urge to stand up and spread her arms. However, she stayed put, clutching the sides of the car to keep from bouncing off her seat.

She glanced back to see Lily, looking somewhat like a bug in her goggles and cap, grinning and holding the basket of food steady.

As soon as they passed into Queens, the Manhattan hustle and bustle dimmed into a hum of activity, but more spread out, less hectic, a bit cleaner. And not nearly as interesting.

After an hour the houses became sparser and the sidewalks and curbs were replaced by trees and rolling green pastures. Phil felt a momentary jab of nostalgia for her childhood country estate in Sussex. But it passed quickly, shoved aside by the memory of Dunbridge Castle and its drafty rooms and nearly nonexistent plumbing.

She was in America. And free—more or less. The farmland was just as green as England, and there was Central Park, Broadway, and hot baths. If she could just see her way clear of this murder investigation, she saw a bright future ahead.

They sped past farmhouses and pastures enclosed by white rail fences, cows lowing in the closely cropped grass. It was much faster than a carriage ride, and the few times Bev had "opened her up" were quite exhilarating.

By the time Bev turned the auto down a dirt road that according to the whitewashed sign led to Holly Farm, Phil felt covered in dirt and was certain she had swallowed more than one insect.

At the end of the lane, a white wood-framed farmhouse nestled in a copse of trees overlooking a small lake where several ducks swam lazily in the sun.

Behind the house, a red-painted horse barn was surrounded by several outbuildings, paddocks, and an oval training track that cut across a flat green field. It was an impressive setup.

Bev stopped the Packard at the side of the house and honked the horn, which sent several chickens squawking and flapping to safety.

Bev turned off the engine and waved at a man who stood in the yard, arms akimbo, watching them.

Phil opened her door and lowered her feet to the ground, holding on to the Packard for support.

"I feel like I'm still vibrating," Lily said, climbing carefully out of the back.

"So do I," Phil said, and tested her balance by letting go of the door.

"Look alive, greenhorns." Bev was already out of the motorcar and pulling off her cap, goggles, and duster; she threw them on the seat before striding up the path to meet the man.

"She's wearing a split skirt," Phil said. "How clever. I'll order one for each of us."

"Mr. Preswick will not approve," Lily said seriously, but there was mischief in her eyes.

"He and the rest of the world. Men have such strange notions about women. They countenance our affairs but not our trousers."

Phil wasn't so naïve to think she could totally flout convention. Bev could be as modern as she liked, but that wasn't Phil's style. Phil would be eccentric but not brash. Intriguing but not vulgar. The path to success was a very thin line.

"Phil, this is Henry Cable, our trainer," Bev said. "Henry, meet the Countess of Dunbridge."

Henry's eyes bugged and he scrubbed the cap from his head, uncovering sandy waving hair.

"How do you do, Henry."

"Fine, ma'am."

Bev laughed.

Phil didn't think it was just the country air that was making Bev so animated. She had a sneaking suspicion that Henry Cable might have something to do with it. Bev's "bit of rough," as Phil's father might say.

"You shoulda let us know you were coming. Half the boys are over to Belmont preparing for the training sessions. Crazy track is a right-hander. Don't get why they do that. Not really fair to ask a horse to run both ways." He licked his lips. "But don't you worry. Thunder's a prince; he'll leave them all in the dust."

"We mean to come up to the stable. I can't wait to show him off," Bev said. "But first we must—really must—rid ourselves of dust and dirt."

"That'll be fine. I think you'll be pleased that the lads have kept it up in spite of Mr. Reggie being dead and all."

He nodded to Phil. "Nice to meet you, ma'am." He turned and strode back up the path to the barn and stable.

Bev took Phil's arm. "I'm parched."

"Bev?" Phil asked.

Bev grinned. "Isn't he just delicious? But I think he's afraid of me."

"He has every right to be. You're not . . . ?"

"Heavens no. He's rough-and-tumble, but he smells of horses."

Phil shook her head at Bev's expression. "What's to eat? I'm famished."

They unloaded the Packard and carried everything into the farmhouse kitchen.

While Lily unpacked the hamper, Phil had a quick cleanup in the bathroom which, she was happy to see, had running water. She'd been imagining a pump at the sink and a chamber pot under the bed.

They had a quick snack, washed down by a glass of a cabernet Bev said came from a California winery. Phil was suspicious at first, but it turned out to be full-bodied and well aged, so much so that they decided on a second glass before making their way to the stables to inspect the horses.

"It's just a short walk," Bev said as they started up the path to the barn. "Much easier than taking the car, and looking like a fool while I try to handle the crank. We'll get them to start us up when we go back to the city."

When they reached the barnyard, Phil stopped to look around. It was a very sophisticated setup—and expensive, she thought, with several paddocks and a railed training track that cut a perfect oval through a field of lush green grasses. All bright paint, whitewash, and new money. Several men came out of the barn to greet them.

One of them stepped forward. "Mrs. Reynolds." He dragged his cap from his head. "Don't know if you remember me. Sid. Sid Murphy. It's just that me and the boys"—he stopped to include them in a quick arm sweep—"all feel real bad about Mr. Reynolds."

The four other men, all small and sparse like Sid, Phil noticed, pulled off their caps and mumbled their condolences. In comparison to the fresh clean look of the buildings, this was a motley crew. And they looked like they'd been in a brawl, and as she got closer, she was certain they had actually been fighting, with black eyes and swollen jaws and bruises everywhere.

"Thank you, Sid," Bev said. "Gentlemen. These are my friends Phil and Lily."

Sid and the others nodded again.

"I've come to see how Devil's Thunder is doing."

"Fine, ma'am. Running real good." He looked at the others.

"Fast," said one of the men behind him, and the others nodded.

"Sorry you had to come all this way," Sid said. "Freddy and Bobby were out yesterday. They coulda told you things are going fine." His brows creased, his fingers kneaded his cap. "Unless you think we oughta not run him, on account of Reggie and all, but he's ripe. It'd be a shame—but you oughta talk to Henry about that."

"Of course we'll run him," Bev said. "It's what Reggie would want. But since I'll be running the stables from now on, I thought I should come tell you that I've decided everything is a go."

The men's mouths fell open just like those mechanical banks that flipped pennies into a tank.

Behind her, Lily snorted, conveying a myriad of opinions about Bev's uncharacteristic good sense. Even Phil blinked. This was a new Bev.

"Let's take a look, shall we?" Bev strode into the barn; Sid hesitated then hurried after her. The other jockeys stepped back to let Phil and Lily pass, then crowded in behind.

They followed Sid and Bev down a long corridor covered in straw. There were at least twenty stalls, the names of horses written above half of them. Some were empty as yet. It looked like Reggie had been planning on expanding his stock. Which also didn't jibe with his leaving the country.

What had Marguerite implied? That Reggie cared more for his horses than for his women? And if the stables were any indication of that, Marguerite was correct.

"Are all of these Reggie's horses?" Phil asked.

"Yes, ma'am," Sid said. "We have a couple of new colts, but they're still down in Virginia at the stud farm."

"Ah, there he is." Bev hurried over to a large stall at the end of the row. Devil's Thunder snorted and tossed his head as they approached. The horse in the next stall poked his head out.

Phil looked from one to the other and laughed. "You have a perfectly matched pair."

"Phil, these are not carriage horses."

"I know, but look how alike they are. If you had two more just like these, imagine how splendid your arrival at the opera would be."

Bev laughed. "Imagine the outrage of the Four Hundred."

"My, but they are beautiful creatures."

Henry came out of a back room office and hurried toward them.

Sid moved away.

"I didn't hear you come in," he said. "Or I would've been out to meet you." Devil's Thunder danced back in his stall, but the horse in the next stall snuffled and stretched his neck toward them. Henry ran his hand down that horse's nose.

"This here's Binkie's Boy, ain't that right, Boy-o?" He gave the horse's shoulder a resounding pat. "He and Thunder had the same sire, different dames. Reggie was hoping to clean up with both of them on the circuit, but it ain't gonna happen.

"Thunder is a bit high-strung, but he's the fastest horse I can remember seeing. Boy-o will make back what he was bought for, and then some. He's fast enough, but he won't win any of the big ones. Just like his mama, starts fast, can't finish."

"Sounds more like a man than a woman," Bev said sotto voce.

"But somehow they always make it the woman's fault," Phil retorted.

Henry moved on to the next stall. "Now this here's Filly's Cert. She's a two-year-old. We're running her on the straight today to see how she does. It'll be her first race up here."

Filly's Cert pressed her nose into Lily's shoulder. Instead of screeching and jumping away, Lily laughed and reached up to stroke her nose. The filly nuzzled her and Lily spoke to her, but Phil didn't understand the words, not English or Spanish or French. How many languages did the girl speak?

While Bev and Henry discussed the horse and the race, Phil motioned Lily to follow her down the rows of horses. She stopped to look in a stall at a roan whose right foreleg was plastered.

Lily grasped the half door and stood on tiptoe to look inside. "Pfft, she'll come up lame if they run her."

Henry came up beside her. "Her name's Carolina, and that's

what I told Mr. Freddy when he came out yesterday," he said, stroking the filly. "But he says if she's better, to try her out at Belmont. Without Mr. Reggie to say different . . ." He trailed off.

"Well, you have me to say," Bev told him. She stood on tiptoe and looked into the stall. "Poor thing. Why's her leg bandaged?"

"Buck shins. She oughta be all right if we rest her."

"Well, if she's not fit, scratch her from the roster."

"Yes, ma'am." Henry walked away and went into the tack room.

Phil came up to Bev. "I would have never guessed."

"Guessed what?"

"That you would be so . . ."

"So what? Sensible? To listen to my trainer about the condition of a horse? Freddy only cares about the business. Reggie only cared about winning. Bobby"—she shrugged—"only cared about pleasing Reggie.

"But look at these beauties. Sleek, fast, proud. Amazing animals. I enjoy racing as much as the next person, but it can be cruel. Life can be cruel," she added in a much quieter voice.

"Men are cruel," Lily said. "They'll run them to death. Then kill them when they can't run at all." She seemed to realize what she'd said. "Forgive me, madam. I forgot myself again."

"Not at all," Phil said. "We three are in perfect agreement. Racing is a beautiful thing to watch but can be tragic for the participants."

"Yes."

"Now I have work for you to do," Phil said, taking Lily aside. "See if you can find out which of the men drove for Reggie and if any of them know who drove for him on the fateful day, and where he's gone off to. The police may have already been here asking questions, they'll be nervous, so be subtle. And be safe."

Lily gave her a look and sashayed away.

"She's something else," Bev said. "Where on earth did you find her?"

"It's a long story. Shall we repair to the house for some refreshment and I will tell you while we do a little rifling?"

"An excellent idea. You know, Freddy called yesterday, but he didn't mention coming out here, or anything about the upcoming race. I dare say he didn't want to bother me. They never do. Reggie dragged me to race after race but never asked my opinion about anything important."

"It never enters their brains that we might be able to think for ourselves," Phil agreed.

"But we can . . . when given the chance."

Phil laughed. "Next thing I know you'll be out carrying a sign and demanding the vote."

Bev sputtered. "I think not. I'm a frivolous socialite at heart. But I could take more of an interest in my livelihood. Indeed, I'm afraid I must."

"Like running the stables?"

"Reggie said to depend on Freddy and Bobby. And they're obviously doing fine, and happily so, without me. But I don't know. Do I really want to leave the running of everything to them while I go running off to . . . where? Doing what? With Reggie gone, the fun times don't seem so fun."

Now here was a change in her old friend. "Do you know anything about managing a racing stable?"

"No. But how hard can it be?" Bev frowned, then linked Phil's arm in hers. "All this thinking has made me thirsty. Where is Lily?"

"She'll be along in a bit." And hopefully with a few tidbits of useful information.

"Aren't you afraid to leave her with all those men?" Bev asked as they made the trek back down to the farmhouse. "Jockeys and stable boys are not the best bred men."

Phil thought of Lily's stiletto, gartered at her thigh. "I think she'll be fine."

"And Henry will be close by to make sure they don't forget themselves."

When they reached the house, Phil opened a second bottle of wine, carried it and two glasses into Reggie's office, a small wood-paneled room with an overlarge desk and an underlarge window. The one glaring mistake in an otherwise charming country retreat.

Not only was the room dark, it smelled of stale cigars. Phil put down the bottle and glasses and cleared a space on a side table for the plate of bread and cheese Bev was carrying.

Bev poured out the wine and they stood in the center of the floor sipping and looking around the room.

"Is there a safe here also?"

"I would expect so." Bev put down her glass and began inspecting the paneling for secret openings. They eventually found it in the closet, a narrow cubicle with room for only a huge standing safe and several jackets hung above.

Phil laughed. "No need to hide this. A thief would have to use dynamite to get inside. I don't suppose it has the same combination as the other?"

Bev shrugged. "We hardly ever came out here. I wasn't even sure there was a safe. God only knows what we'll find."

True, thought Phil. If they did find anything, she hoped it led the police away from Bev to somewhere else. But it didn't seem likely.

As it turned out, the combination was the same. And the contents were also the same. Nonexistent, except for one packet of trifolded papers.

"Why have this huge safe with nothing to put in it?" Bev wondered. "No, don't tell me. Whatever he kept here, he took it with him, to start over in Argentina with that—" Bev yanked the packet of envelopes from the safe, dislodging something beneath them. It fell to the floor with a noticeable *ping*.

Bev reached down and lifted it to the light.

"A key," Phil said. Bev held it closer to the lamp. "Lincoln Safe Deposit Company. That's on Forty-Second Street. Hmm. We'll stop by there on our way home tomorrow. I suddenly need to know if I have anything left." She slipped the key into the pocket of her divided skirt.

"Excellent idea." Phil was more than just a little curious herself.

With Phil leaning over her shoulder, Bev pulled the rubber band from the stack and opened the first paper.

"Deed to the farm. Thank you, Reggie." The others turned out to be various deeds and agreements and bills of ownership for several horses, including Devil's Thunder.

Well, it was a start. "Bev, you still own the brownstone. You didn't sign it over to Reggie?"

"I may be flighty at times, but I'm not crazy."

"That's a relief," said Phil and went back to her search.

They moved on to the desk drawers, but at the end of another hour they'd only found more IOUs, more bills, and more depressing bank statements. Reginald Reynolds was seriously in debt. But it would take Mr. Carmichael and an accountant to figure out just what could be done.

They gathered all the papers into a tapestry valise and returned to the kitchen.

Phil was beginning to worry about Lily when she heard an exchange of lively whispers just outside. She looked out the window to see Lily pulling a reluctant jockey up the steps.

Phil went out to meet them.

Seeing her, he pulled away his hand and snatched the cap from his head.

"Madam," Lily said, "this is Rico. He has news I think you should hear."

14

"Shouldn't we go into the house, then, where we can be more . . . private?" Phil said to Rico who hovered nervously in the shadows of the eaves.

He was a small man and lightweight even for a jockey. It gave him the appearance of a child. And probably easily dismissed because of it.

The stable boys and jockeys would probably be a wealth of information. More likely to be around when any plans or deals were going down and just as likely to be ignored.

Another round of urgent whispers between Lily and Rico, in Spanish if Phil was correct.

"He says he can't speak in front of Mrs. Reynolds."

"Ah." Phil considered telling them that Bev knew all about Reggie's peccadilloes, but on the other hand, did she? And perhaps is wasn't about not wanting to hurt her but that he didn't trust her? Was there more to come, and was Bev a part of it?

Phil held up a finger for them to wait and went into the kitchen, where Bev was unwrapping packages from the hamper. "I need to speak with Lily for a moment. Will you be here?"

"Yes. I thought I would make us a bit of dinner, my culinary skills being what they are."

"Wonderful. I'll just take her upstairs for a minute and join you as soon as we're through."

"She hasn't already gotten herself in trouble has she?"

"No, nothing like that. I won't be long," Phil said breezily, and closed the door. She put a finger to her lips and motioned Lily and Rico to come inside. They tiptoed down the hall and up the stairs to the bedroom Lily would be using for the night.

"Now," Phil said, "we should be quite comfortable here. Rico, pull up that chair and sit down. Lily and I will sit on the bed."

He gave a jerky nod and pulled the chair over to face them. He sat down, elbows propped on his knees and his cap dangling from his hands. For several seconds, Phil and Lily were granted only a view of the top of his curly dark head.

"Well, go on, then," Lily finally prompted.

He looked up. His eye was purple and his bottom lip was swollen. "There's big trouble, miss—madam."

"Yes, don't worry about that. What kind of big trouble?"

"Eddie took the rail into town that day to drive for Mr. Reggie."

"Eddie? He works here?"

Rico darted a glance at Lily. Nodded. "He's a jockey; he is supposed to ride Devil's Thunder in the big race."

"Pardon me, but it seems a long way to travel to serve as chauffeur for a drive to the docks."

"Mr. Reggie, he pays very well, extra. Jockeys don't always make so much money. There are many jockeys but not so many people drive a motorcar."

"And did Eddie drive?"

"No, he go all the way and then they tell him they don't need him. Say there was a mistake and he should prepare himself for the race, not driving Mr. Reggie. But to leave his driving uniform. They pay him anyway, so he does, then he stays in town and—"

Rico stopped to look quickly around. "He goes to a bar where jockeys go, has a few drinks, a little fun. He don't know what happens to Mr. Reggie until he gets back here the next morning.

"Then the police come. They pull us out into the yard, they're not nice. We are all scared. *Muy asustado.*"

Rico licked his lips. Ran the rim of his cap through nervous fingers. "They ask if anybody drove Mr. Reggie that day. Nobody says. We tell them we all work here all day.

"We tell them to ask the people at the garage in town. Mr. Reggie uses them a lot. More than us.

"But they don't leave. The big cop—"

"Detective Sergeant Atkins?" Phil asked.

Rico shrugged. "The big one, he sends men inside to search everywhere in all our things, they're in there a long time. Then he take us into the corral and we can't see nothing of what the others are doing.

"The big cop and another guy take us one by one away from the others and question us. They're pretty rough."

"Is that how you got that split lip?"

A jerk of his head. "Then someone shouts and the big man goes into the bunkhouse. He comes out with—" Rico took a slow breath. "They find Eddie's coat all crumpled up and it's got blood on the front."

Phil smiled reassuringly. "And did they arrest Eddie?"

"Go on, Rico," Lily said. "My mistress is okay. *Confianza.*"

"No. When we see them come, Eddie runs 'cause we know how police work. They'll say he was there and they'll take him away until after the race, because the race is big money. And some people they don't want Thunder to win."

Definitely turning into something more than a lovers' triangle, Phil thought. "Then what happened?"

Another jerk of Rico's head. "Then Bobby and Mr. Beecham come running up the driveway. Bobby's fighting mad. Mr. Beecham's pretty upset, but he tries to talk to the big one. He says he can't believe that Eddie would hurt Mr. Reynolds, but the big guy doesn't listen. He says they got a tip." Rico snorted. "Then he just rounds up his men and says we'll all go to jail if we don't turn Eddie in.

"Then Bobby and Mr. Beecham get into it. And Mr. Beecham tell Bobby it's his fault and he's a big crook. And he's gonna tell Henry not to let him around the horses no more. And they had to hold Bobby back to keep him from knocking him down.

"But missus, Eddie didn't kill nobody. When he came back he didn't have his driving coat with him."

"That you saw," Phil added.

Rico's fists clenched.

Lily said something to him, and he let out a long breath. Looked at her. Ran the back of his hand across his mouth.

"He didn't have no coat when he came back. I saw him. We all did. There weren't no coat in the stable. We clean it three times a week, Mr. Reggie makes us. And blood attracts flies and animals. We woulda known if it was there. If somebody put that coat there, it weren't Eddie."

"Do you know where Eddie is?"

Rico shrugged. "He's lying low, afraid they'll do him for the murder or worse."

"What could be worse than being arrested for murder?"

"Make him do things like throw a race or hurt one of the horses. Then he won't be able to get work, he'll be a . . . *paria*."

"Pariah. I see." And indeed she did. In America, gambling at the racetracks was notorious for corruption. Was it any surprise? Just look at people like Reggie.

"He's scared. He wants to run, but he's supposed to ride Thunder in the big race over at Belmont. Nobody rides that horse like Eddie. Mr. Reggie promised him a bonus if he wins. Thunder ran real good last week at Jamaica. Eddie made a good bonus then. He's got a girl."

He cut his eyes toward Lily.

Lily rolled her eyes at Phil.

"He's saving up to marry her, he wants to buy a farm." Rico shook his head. "Who would want to farm when he could be a jockey? Lily here says you will help Eddie. He didn't kill Mr. Reggie. None of us did."

"Who do you think did murder him?"

Rico lowered his head, bothered his cap. "Some men."

Ah, thought Phil. *Now we begin to get somewhere.*

"What men?"

"I don't know, but they want him to do things. We hear things in the stables. Before and after races. They never mind us. Most of us don't speak English so good; if we do, we keep our mouths shut.

"They know we won't squeal. We are . . . *como si dice, olvidado*?"

"Forgotten," Lily said, and her voice was so sad that for a moment Phil forgot about the murder and the jockeys while she contemplated her maid.

"Do you think Mr. Reynolds wanted Eddie to lose the race?" That would be a good motive for murder, Phil thought. But she couldn't see someone like Reggie offering to throw a race. Reggie reveled in the glory of winning or the admiration of his peers. Losers don't get the limelight.

Unless it was a matter of life and death. Were they threatening him, or Bev?

"I don't know. But they say someone told him to make sure Thunder pulls up short. A . . ." A quick consultation with Lily.

"Rumor," she said

"Well, Mrs. Reynolds is running things now," Phil said. "I'm sure she won't allow anything like that to happen."

"They powerful men, ma'am."

The door opened. "What are you two doing?" Bev looked from Lily to Phil and then her eyes came to rest on Rico.

He popped out of the chair. "Sorry, missus. I didn't mean to—" He danced past her and ran down the stairs.

"What on earth is going on?"

"Is dinner ready, Bev? Come downstairs and I'll tell you all about it while we eat. Lily, stay in the house, please."

Lily frowned at her but didn't argue. Just lightly touched the side of her skirt, letting Phil know she was prepared to protect herself and her mistress.

Phil didn't tell Bev *all* about it. But she did give enough information about "some men" being seen here talking to Reggie.

And she wondered, innocently, for Bev's sake, if there could be any side bets, or possibly, just possibly, maybe someone who wanted Reggie to throw the race.

Bev seemed genuinely appalled by the idea and adamant that Reggie would never throw a race. He was all about winning. "But what are we to do about Eddie? If they find him, he'll go to jail, and if they don't, who will ride Devil's Thunder?"

"I'm sure Henry or Sid is working on contingency plans."

"That must have been why Freddy came out yesterday. I'll give him a ring as soon as we get back to town."

"No."

Bev frowned. "Why not? He was Reggie's business adviser."

"Because, dear friend, I think it's best to keep our own counsel until we know more, and that includes your father."

"Father? What could he possibly have to do with Reggie's murder? He didn't like Reggie, but—Oh, Phil, you're not implying that you think he might have murdered Reggie?"

"I'm not implying anything. I'm telling you to keep your head. Everything you say will get back to Detective Sergeant Atkins. Or"—Phil smiled—"the Fireplug. So just don't say anything."

"You're so clever, Phil."

Yes, she was. It was the only way she had survived the turbulent waters of high society. And she didn't come to America to be thwarted by a bunch of ex-prizefighters and turf men.

"Well, I'm off to bed," Bev said. "Training starts in the early hours in the morning, and I want to see for myself what's going on. Sleep in if you want."

"I wouldn't miss it for the world." They walked upstairs arm in arm.

"Don't worry, Bev. We'll get to the end of this."

"I know you will."

Phil left Bev at her bedroom door. How easily "we" had become "you."

No matter. Tonight she had something that took priority over Reggie's death and Bev's possible relation to it.

While Lily brushed her hair, Phil asked, "How did you convince Rico to come talk to me?"

Lily shrugged.

"Lily, do I need to warn you about getting involved with men?"

"No, madam."

Was that because she already had been involved with men, or was innocent, or had been warned before?

"Excellent. Men can be quite wonderful in their way, but only if you are first, prepared, and second, can be discreet. Understood?"

"Yes."

"And if by chance you find yourself in a predicament—of any kind—or if something makes you unhappy or afraid, you'll come to me, no matter what it is. You won't run off?"

Lily stared at Phil's reflection in the mirror. Then moved to kneel beside her so that Phil by necessity had to look down at her. "I will never leave you."

Phil laughed softly. "May it be so, if it makes you happy. But one day you may want a life totally your own."

"Oh, no, madam. If I were to go, who would torment Preswick?"

Who, indeed? "Mr. Preswick to you, miss."

Between the drive and the wine and Rico's tale of the missing jockey, Phil expected to fall asleep right away. But her mind had other intentions. Bev was right, she did need to get to the end of this so she could get started on the rest of her life.

But they seemed no closer to finding Reggie's murderer than ever.

Now, only a week into her American experience, what had originally appeared to be suicide or a lover's quarrel had grown to include a jealous wife, an angry father, and horse racing, which added a whole new world of possibilities from gambling debts to missing jockeys.

Bobby? Freddy? Henry? Bobby was Reggie's "right-hand man," at least according to Bobby. Freddy, his friend, business manager, and only relative. Henry, his trainer whose reputation depended on winning horses. It could be any of them or none of them.

It just didn't seem that anyone had anything to gain from Reggie's death . . . except maybe Bev. But Bev, despite all good sense, seemed to have loved the man.

Mimi? It might as well be Mrs. Tappington-Jones or the Austrian attaché. Phil smiled at the thought. The upcoming race had been a big topic of conversation at the Tappington-Jones dinner. Even the ladies seemed eager to attend.

What could any of them have to gain by losing a race?

Money, of course. Which tilted the suspect list toward those who gambled. The jockeys might be paid to pull a horse, but could they earn enough to live on if their reputation was wrecked? Or, in Eddie's case, to buy a farm? But Reggie had already promised him a big bonus if he won.

If he'd been approached by someone else to throw the race, and Reggie had found out about it and threatened to fire him, would he kill him? Perhaps, but that was taking a big chance and look where it landed him—on the run with no chance of affecting the outcome of the race.

This was infuriating.

Phil had been to Ascot and Epson Downs, but she'd sat in the clubhouse with the other elite ladies, who made their own discreet bets, while the gentleman disappeared to gamble their fortunes and their fate on favorites and long shots and sheer good or bad luck. Though she'd never witnessed it firsthand, she knew there was an enormous thriving community of bookmakers who ran the show from the cheap seats. Gambling was big business.

She yawned. Turned over. Her last thought was . . . if Eddie often drove when Reggie was with Mimi, how could Mimi not recognize him? Unless they were in on it together . . .

* * *

The sun was just coming up when Phil awoke to the sound of neighing horses and the calls of stable boys. It took a few minutes to recall that she was at Holly Farm and this morning they were watching the training runs. She sat up and became aware of someone moving around her room.

"Lily?"

"Yes, my lady."

My lady? Was this Lily feeling contrite? Because of Phil's questions last night? Or had something else happened after she'd retired?

Enough. It was like her mind was stuck in the center of a maze, so many paths to choose from. Only one led out to freedom . . . and a nice cup of coffee.

She inhaled. Someone was brewing coffee.

"If madam wishes to see the horses before they are finished, then madam should rouse herself."

"Madam" guffawed and sat up. "Something simple for watching the training run."

"You are a countess."

And becoming less so by the minute, Phil thought. She was enjoying it immensely.

"True, but don't take too long. I already hear Bev moving about downstairs, and coffee beckons. I think when we get back to town we should order those split skirts for both of us. Imagine the freedom of being able to stride down the sidewalks of Manhattan like any gentleman."

"I don't think Mr. Preswick would approve."

"We will be discreet."

"Bah, discreet. Mrs. Reynolds is not discreet."

"No, she isn't and she's under suspicion of murder. The thing about discretion, my dear, is it's like a magician's screen. All calm and ordinary on the outside, while a world of incredible things thrives behind it." Phil stood and faced Lily, who was holding out a white tucked shirtwaist for Phil to put on.

"I think being discreet is a big bore."

Phil thrust her arms through the sleeves and turned to be buttoned up. "Yes, so do I. But it can't be helped. And decorum is a perfect disguise." Phil held on to Lily's shoulders for balance as she stepped into her tweed skirt.

"Ah, a perfect outfit for a day in the country," Phil said, and went downstairs.

Bev was in the kitchen pouring coffee into a thermos.

"My, you're industrious this morning," Phil said.

"I want to see them put Devil's Thunder through his paces." She was dressed in another split-skirt ensemble. "I forget that I love the stables. I think I should have been a man. I even ride astride sometimes. Do you?"

"I've had occasion to."

"I haven't ridden in ages. Maybe we'll come out after the races. We keep a couple of hunters here, though neither of us ever hunted. Barbaric, if you ask me."

Phil nodded in agreement, but she wondered about this new Bev. Not only did she seem just as at home here as in the company of Reggie's decadent friends, she seemed excited about taking over the enterprise.

"I suppose I must follow you to the rail to get a cup of that?" Phil indicated the thermos.

"Well, you could sit here like a slug and have Lily make you a fresh pot."

"And miss Devil's Thunder? Never."

They walked up the road to the track, Lily following a step behind, carrying a hamper of thermos, cups, and condiments and a folding camp table. There was another touring car parked near the barn. And a man standing at the rail talking to Henry.

"Freddy's here," Bev said, and strode toward them.

Several horses were being led in and out of the stables. Others were being put through their paces in the paddocks. Rico was leading Carolina out of one of the paddocks. He saw them and tucked his head in acknowledgment.

"Lily, why don't you check on Carolina's condition. If anyone asks, I sent you."

"Yes, my lady."

"Wait. Leave the hamper." Phil took it and watched Lily hurry toward Rico and the horse.

"You're not playing matchmaker, I hope," Bev said.

"Absolutely not, but she's not inexperienced with horses. And she was concerned about racing her too soon."

"Redoubtable maid, your Lily."

"Indeed. I may have to make her my secretary."

"Freddy!" Bev called.

Freddy turned and waved, his serious expression turning into a broad smile.

"I had no idea you wanted to come out to the stables," he said, taking both her hands and kissing her cheek. "I would have driven you out. Morning, Lady Dunbridge. I see that Bev didn't manage to overturn you in her wild machinations."

"She was the spirit of driving acumen."

Bev gave him a saucy smile. "I drive more safely than you or Reggie ever do. Besides, we can't all fit in your roadster, and Reggie would roll over in his grave if I let you drive the new Packard."

She laughed. "Dear old thing, even Marguerite drives better than you do."

Freddy chuckled. "Alas, it's true."

A cloud passed over his face. "Reggie treated that car like that thoroughbred." He smiled at Bev.

Bev sniffed and patted his arm. "Besides, you don't have to cater to me. I know the mayor needs you. I'm surprised he let you get away today."

Freddy chuckled. "The mayor is a member of the Turf and Field Club. I suspect he wanted me to make sure things are proceeding to schedule." He watched Henry lead Devil's Thunder across the yard. He was accompanied by one of the jockeys Phil had seen yesterday.

He was a beauty, Phil thought. Well balanced with a deep chest, well-angled shoulders; he displayed a muscularity of near perfection just walking toward the exercise field.

"Besides," Freddy continued, "I told him I'd be back by ten o'clock. So we'd better get started if I'm to see any of the training."

"Well," Phil exclaimed, "I can't wait to see him in action."

Everyone, including the other jockeys and stable boys, collected at the rail to watch.

"Who are they planning to mount with Eddie gone?" Bev asked.

"It looks like Pete," Freddy said.

But when Henry hoisted the jockey into the saddle, Devil's Thunder reared; the jockey barely held his seat as Thunder pranced and tossed his head. It was inevitable—Thunder bucked. Pete fell off the side and scrambled away.

Henry looked around. "Coco!"

A jockey sitting at the end of the rail slid to the ground and walked reluctantly toward the horse. Thunder whinnied, danced away. Finally Henry and another stable boy held the horse long enough for Coco to mount. He lasted only a few seconds. Devil's Thunder tossed his head, twisted his body, one way and then the other. Coco fell off and landed hard.

He barely managed to roll away as hooves came down near his head.

Phil looked at Bev. Bev shrugged back.

Henry looked along the rail to the other jockeys. Phil could feel several of them shrink.

"Sid!"

Sid looked at the others, jumped from the rail. Thunder turned in a circle while they tried to hold him steady for Sid to mount.

"I told them he wouldn't accept another rider," a new voice said behind them.

Phil turned to see Bobby Mullins drop his cigar to the ground, grind it out with his heel, and open the gate to the track.

"Bobby, stay out of it," Freddy called after him.

Bobby didn't even slow down as he stomped toward the agitated horse and rider.

"Damn fool, doesn't know a damn thing about horses, but he insists on butting in. I don't know why Reggie kept him around. I'd better go referee."

Freddy strode over to the gate.

"Do you think I should intercede?" Bev asked Phil.

"No time like the present. But what are you going to say?"

"I have no idea." Bev hurried after Freddy. Phil followed and joined Lily and Rico by the gate to the track.

Bev was talking to the men, but their concentration seemed more on the horse than what she was saying. Well, no one said taking over what until today had been a man's business was going to be easy.

"He wants Eddie," said Rico.

Phil nodded. Sid had managed to mount Thunder, and for a second, the horse seemed to accept him. Sid turned him toward the starting line. He took several measured steps, then he reared on his hind legs. Sid toppled off and landed on the ground on his back.

Phil winced.

Sid scrambled to his feet and backed away from the horse, who calmly watched until Sid retreated to the other side of the rail.

Henry, Freddy, and Bobby huddled together, clearly arguing.

Being ignored by the others, Bev strode over to where Phil was standing. "Well, this is going nowhere. Bobby's insisting they'll ruin Thunder if they keep trying different jockeys. Henry says he'll adjust to a new jockey in time for the race. Freddy's worried about the repercussions if they have to scratch the most talked-about horse of the season."

"What repercussions?"

"I have no idea. I guess I'll need to bone up on breeding and betting if I mean to make a start." She sighed, and they turned to watch the three men.

It was a very animated discussion, which ended with Bobby throwing up his hands and walking away.

"Rico!" Henry called.

Rico jumped.

"Get over here."

Rico looked toward heaven and quickly crossed himself.

"Be careful," Lily said.

"Yes," Phil said. "Do be careful."

Rico walked reluctantly onto the track. Stopped to stroke the horse and talk to him.

"What's he saying?"

"He's telling him he understands, and he respects him, and please not to throw him."

"Ah."

Henry hoisted Rico into the saddle. Thunder danced and tossed his head but eventually calmed down, and Henry led horse and rider to a white starting line chalked out on the dirt surface.

"I can never get used to this," Bev said, looking from left to right.

"What?" asked Phil.

"Running clockwise, all the rest of the tracks here run counter."

"Odd," Phil said, and leaned forward to watch.

Freddy came to stand beside them, but Bobby had taken a place as far away as possible.

"What was that all about?" Phil asked.

"Just Bobby muscling his way in over his head. Thought we should wait for Eddie to return to run Devil's Thunder. But if Eddie returns, he'll be arrested for murder. Sorry, Bev, but that's what is going to happen. We need to get another rider on Thunder as soon as possible. Any delay could be disastrous."

To the horse or to those who had already placed bets on the winner? Phil wondered.

Thunder was fast, no doubt about that. And Rico held his seat, but there was something slapdash, not quite synchronous between horse and rider. *He isn't Eddie*, Phil thought.

Henry stopped his watch and took a look. Shook his head.

Rico walked Devil's Thunder around waiting for the verdict.

"We'll try him again later," Henry called. Rico continued to walk the horse, then led him back to the paddock. Henry walked over to them. Sighed. "Not close to his time at Jamaica. Of course it's a new rider and no competition. I'll run him again this afternoon with Boy-o and Dander, see if he does better. You want me to keep Rico on him?"

Freddy shrugged. "Try him."

Henry nodded, started to go.

"I mean, if it's okay with Mrs. Reynolds," Freddy added.

Henry turned, not quite wiping the smile off his face before he asked, "Is that okay with you, Mrs. Reynolds?"

"Certainly, let's see how it goes," said Bev.

Freddy glanced at his watch. "I've got to get back to town. No rest for the wicked, you know. Will you ladies be okay on your own?"

"Yes, you dear fussbudget, we'll manage to bumble along somehow." Bev kissed his cheek. "Do you have time for breakfast before you go?"

"I wish, but no. I have to be downtown by ten. I'll just make it if I leave now."

"And speed like the very devil," Bev said. "Do be careful, Freddy."

"I will, and don't worry about any of the paperwork in the office, if you even looked at it. I'll go through everything next time I'm out."

"Well," Bev said as she watched Freddy crank up his roadster and leave for town. "What do you say we scramble up some eggs and have a real country breakfast before we go back to town?"

"Fine," Phil said, distracted. The others had returned to their duties, but Bobby stood leaning against the rail dropping the ash of a newly lit cigar onto the track. He was scowling. Still angry at being voted down about who would jockey Devil's Thunder?

It seemed to Phil that the turf war being played here was not among the horses but by the men in charge.

15

Now that the initial running of Devil's Thunder was over and their stomachs were full, they loaded the hamper and returned the luggage to the Packard.

They would go straight back to Manhattan and stop by the Liberty Safe Deposit Company, and probably find another empty safe. Then they would spend another quiet evening at home. These mourning customs were just not fair.

Phil didn't envy Bev. Mourning was hard enough, but when your husband had been murdered and you had been a suspect no matter for how short a time, it was going to be difficult to reinsert yourself into society.

They all donned their dusters and goggles, just as a black van pulled out of the backyard and rumbled down the drive.

"Oh, damn," Bev said. "That's probably Henry going to the feed store. I should have flagged him down to give us a crank."

Phil gave her a patient look. "Get in." She lifted the crank out of its mounting and walked around to the front of the car. One crank and the engine caught.

She climbed into the front seat. "Drive," she ordered.

Bev pulled out the throttle. "You're amazing, Phil. Where did you learn how to do that?"

Phil smiled. "A delightfully wicked Parisian auto racer. I'll tell you the story one day."

Bev made a wide sweep, honked the horn, and tore down the dirt path toward home. It was a beautiful day and Phil leaned back to enjoy the passing scenery.

They'd gone less than a mile when Phil heard another motor behind them. She turned and saw a black van barreling toward them.

Lily turned, too. "It is the police!" she cried.

"No, not a Black Maria, a delivery truck of some sort."

Bev watched. "What are they doing?"

Before Phil could yell an answer, they were hit from behind. Phil was thrown to the floor.

"Hold on," Bev yelled, and the touring auto shot forward.

Phil scrambled back onto her seat. The van had dropped behind, but only far enough to swerve to the left to overtake them.

Bev looked over her shoulder, then swerved out of his way. The tires rumbled along the grassy verge, and Phil waited for the inevitable blowout and loss of control.

But Bev managed to gain the pavement, and the auto shot ahead.

"We're gaining on them," Phil yelled, and slumped back in her seat, just in time to see a farm tractor bouncing out between rows of corn.

"Bev, watch out!"

The tractor was crossing the road in front of them. The driver didn't even seem to notice the auto speeding toward him.

Phil squeezed her eyes shut, expecting a crash. Felt Bev swerve. Then they were going faster than before.

"Wahoo!" yelled Bev.

Indeed, thought Phil, adjusting her hat. She looked back to make sure Lily was okay. Lily was clutching the hamper with white knuckles. But she was safe.

The van was stuck behind the farmer, and two men were standing in the middle of the road shaking fists at each other.

Phil sat back and didn't bother to complain as they sped back to the city. That had not been an impatient roadster behind them. Someone had tried to run them off the road. And she thought she knew who.

"Was that Henry driving that truck?" she yelled out to Bev.

Bev's head snapped toward her. "Don't be ridiculous. All these farms have vans."

Phil wasn't so sure. The timing was very coincidental. Too coincidental. But why?

They managed to make it back across the bridge and to Forty-Second Street without further mishap, and Bev stopped the Packard safely in front of the Lincoln Safe Deposit Company and began pulling off her goggles and gloves.

"Where is my purse?" Phil said, checking the seat beside her.

"You didn't leave it at the farm?"

"No. It must have fallen to the floor during *la chasse*." Phil opened the door, then dropped to her hands and knees to search the floorboards, trying to ignore the memory of the last time she'd crawled into this very auto . . . looking for a purse.

"I see it." She pulled it toward her, but the strap had become wedged between the floor box and the steering column.

She pulled gently at the delicate ribbon, but it didn't budge, wiggled it and stretched it until it finally popped free.

"Success!" She clutched it in her hand and began inching her way back. But she had dislodged something more than her purse string.

She picked up a small, square piece of paper. A candy wrapper had suffered the same fate as her purse string.

She crawled back and stretched her feet to the pavement. When she stood up, Bev and Lily were watching her with indescribably comic expressions.

"Here it is," Phil said blithely, and stuffed purse and candy wrapper in her duster pocket. "Shall we go inside?"

The building was very much like any other financial institution, with marble columns and a heavy front door, guarded by an uniformed attendant. They checked in at the reception desk and were led across the marble floor to a wall of bars that reached to the ceiling. A second attendant unlocked a door in the bars, waited for them to pass through, then locked the door behind them. Phil could feel Lily pressing closer to her.

He opened another heavy vault door and they entered a large room completely lined with locked boxes ranging from the size of a shoe box to ones almost as large as a full room and several small tables and chairs for viewing the contents of the boxes.

The guard led them to Bev's box and waited while she fished the key from her purse and unlocked the vault, before returning to his place by the door.

Bev pulled the box out and placed it on one of the tables. For a few seconds the three of them just stared at it. Then Bev stuck out a tentative hand. Moved the latch over, opened the lid a few inches, and slammed the lid closed.

Please no cut-off ears or any other body parts that the villains in dime novels seemed to be enamored of, Phil prayed.

Bev motioned for Phil and Lily to come closer.

"Don't act surprised," she whispered.

She slowly opened the top. Inside were stacks of bills.

"This is where the money went," Phil whispered. "How much do you think is there?"

"Must be thousands," Bev whispered back.

And far more than Daniel Sloane would have paid Reggie for the diary.

"Why didn't he take it with him?" Bev asked, breaking into Phil's train of thought. "Do you think whoever killed him was after this?"

"Possibly."

"Well, we're not leaving it here."

"No," Phil agreed.

"Lily, you mustn't say anything about this," Phil said.

Lily shook her head, her eye's wide. "On my mother's grave."

So she was an orphan, thought Phil and returned her thoughts to the current problem.

Bev opened her purse and started putting the packets of bills inside.

"Not there," Phil said, looking at the flimsy strap. "We'll have to wear it out."

"Oh, Phil, you're brilliant, just like when we stole the brace of birds from the larder."

"But hopefully not as greasy." Phil turned her back to the guard.

Among the three of them, they managed to hide all of the bundles inside their shirtwaists.

Bev reset the lock and returned the box to the shelf. She slipped the key down her décolleté. "We're ready now."

The attendant unlocked the vault door and the three of them followed him back the way they had come.

They had just reached the street when an urchin raced past them. He tore the purse from Bev's wrist and ran off down the street before any of them could react.

Lily started off in pursuit, but Phil stopped her by the expediency of grabbing her skirt. "Let him go."

"Can we please just get out of here?" Bev asked

"Yes," Phil agreed. "Before the police can be summoned. Get into the auto." She grabbed the crank and started the car. She jumped inside just as a policeman ran around the corner.

"Whew," Bev said as they made their way up Park Avenue. "What the heck is going on?"

"I don't know." But she'd have to figure it out soon. The curious incidents were beginning to mount up. Surely there was worse to come.

They returned to the brownstone and walked into bedlam.

"What happened?" cried Bev as Tuttle rushed toward her, dodging scullery maids, parlor maids, and footmen. He'd seemed to forget he was holding a dustpan filled with shards of broken glass.

"The police, madam," Tuttle said, and quickly put the cleaning utensils on a nearby table. "They arrived this morning with a warrant to search the premises. They've made a mess of things. No respect or care. We were trying to right it before you returned, but it's taken rather longer than we wished."

Bev pushed him aside and marched into the parlor. Pillows were on the floor, a vase had broken and jagged pieces covered the carpet. Pictures hung askew on the walls.

Phil had barely caught up to her when Bev spun around and left the room.

"Is everything like this?" Bev demanded from Tuttle.

"The parlor and the library. Mr. Reynolds's dressing rooms are the worst. I've taken the liberty of calling your father, and he is at the precinct station filing a formal complaint."

"Grrr," Bev said, and stomped down the hall to the library, Phil at her heels and Lily following close behind. If the parlor was a mess, the library was in shambles. Books had been pulled from the shelves and left where they fell, the bindings bent, pages torn. Papers had fallen from the desk and the locked drawers had been ripped open.

"How dare they?" Bev cried. "How dare they? I'll have Atkins's head for this."

Phil stepped up beside her. "I don't think Detective Atkins was responsible for this. It must be that Becker fellow. Atkins would never have let this happen."

"Well, whoever it was will pay."

"Why?"

Bev's head snapped toward Phil. "What do you mean?"

"Why search here? Now? You had already been the victim of an attempted burglary. You told Detective Atkins that nothing to your knowledge was missing. So what are they looking for? Certainly not clues. One keeps the crime scene intact so as not to disturb any possible clues. Besides, Atkins already went over the library."

"Did they take anything?" Bev asked Tuttle.

"They carried away some papers, madam. I couldn't tell what."

"Is the rest of the house like this?"

"Just the rooms I mentioned." Tuttle turned to Phil. "When they started on your room, Mr. Preswick barred the door and they knocked him down."

"Is he hurt?" Phil asked.

"He got a knock on the head. He's down in my sitting room. Cook put a plaster on it and fixed him some sweet tea for the shock.

"I have to say, my lady, he manned the bastions like a much younger man. He told Sergeant Becker that it was the Countess of Dunbridge's room and his superiors would hear about it from the highest office.

"That gave them pause, I can tell you. They left shortly after that."

"Well, bully for Preswick. I'd better go check on him, if I might."

"Of course, my lady. This way, if you please."

"Pardon me, Bev. I'll be right back. Lily, please stay with Mrs. Reynolds in the library."

Lily curtseyed. "Yes, my lady."

But Phil was too worried about Preswick to notice.

She found him seated in Tuttle's wingback chair, a plaster on his forehead and the cook, Mrs. O'Mallon, plying him with tea.

He tried to get up when Phil entered the room, but the sturdy lady pushed him back down again.

"No offense, my lady, but he's had a shake-up and has no business being on his feet."

"I couldn't agree more," Phil said as she swept into the room. "Well done, Preswick."

"Thank you, my lady."

"Did they summon a doctor for you?"

"No, my lady, it isn't necessary. Mrs. O'Mallon has taken quite good care of me."

"Just what any other good Christian would do."

"I do appreciate it, Mrs. O'Mallon. I would be lost without

Preswick." Phil pulled up a wooden chair. "Do you feel like telling me what happened?"

Preswick straightened a little. "Yes, my lady. It was around ten this morning when there was a knock at the front door, mind you. The front door. Tuttle answered it, but I heard the commotion and came up to see. The head police said he had a warrant to search the library, and his men rushed in. It looked like a raid—" He cut his eyes toward Mrs. O'Mallon. "That I've been told goes on in some of the lower drinking establishments."

"Ah," Phil said. "Did they say what they were looking for?"

"Not that I heard. I don't think they even knew, because they were indiscriminate about where they looked. But when they proceeded upstairs, well, it was the outside of enough. Tuttle and I barred the way, and finally the sergeant called them off. They left without so much as a by-your-leave, and leaving the residence in shambles.

"The staff has been trying to put things to rights before Mrs. Reynolds returned."

Phil stood.

Preswick frowned. "My lady. Begging pardon, but something seems to be askew in your dress."

Phil glanced down at her shirtwaist and the odd lumps that had rearranged themselves on the ride home.

"Dress in haste, um, repent at leisure," she extemporized, gaining a severe look from Preswick. "Something I will remedy forthwith." As soon as she divested herself of Bev's money.

"You get some rest. We're going to have busy days ahead. Thank you, Mrs. O'Mallon, for taking such good care of my dear friend."

"Aw, don't think nothing of it," said Mrs. O'Mallon, blushing.

Phil went back upstairs to consult with Tuttle. "I need a boy to deliver a message. Do we have such a person?"

"Yes, my lady."

"Good, I'll just be a minute." She had to force herself not to lift her skirts and run up the stairs to her bedroom. Things were getting out of hand. Two murders, a purse snatching, her butler roughed up by the metropolitan police. She needed to get to the bottom of this before someone she cared for got seriously hurt.

Bev and Lily whirled around when Phil opened the door to the library. The safe was open and they both were in various states of dishabille. Both gasped, followed by audible sighs of relief.

"I'm not certain the safe is the best place to hide this," she said, reaching into her shirtwaist and pulling out a bundle of bills.

"Well, I'm not wearing it next to my person until the race next week."

"The race. Of course."

"Reggie must have meant to place this on Thunder." Bev sat down suddenly.

"Bev," Phil said, depositing the last of the money in the safe and turning around. "Why would he leave this amount of money if he was absconding to South America?"

Bev slumped on the desk. "I don't know. It doesn't make sense. Maybe he wasn't leaving me after all?" she asked hopefully.

"My dear, I'm afraid that ship has sailed. Better you acknowledge it once and for all."

"I know. And truthfully, the only part that really hurts is my pride. So why do you think he left that money?"

"My guess is he didn't plan to."

"Maybe he didn't have time to retrieve it."

Phil didn't honor that guess with more than a skeptical look.

"He stole it?" Lily ventured, then clapped both hands over her mouth.

Bev and Phil both turned to stare at her.

"Or stole it," Phil echoed. "In which case, these things that are happening could be caused by someone who wants their money back."

Bev shook her head. "He wouldn't." She kept shaking her head. "That would mean—No there must be another answer."

"In that case we better do something about figuring it out, and quickly."

"You're scaring me, Phil."

It's about time, Phil thought.

"I just don't understand what's happening." Bev's words ended on a sob. "My husband is dead, there was a murdered man found in my library. The horse that was going to make us rich now doesn't have a rider. My house is in shambles, Freddy and Bobby are fighting. And I'm going to spend the next two years twiddling my thumbs, getting older. And I don't know what to do to stop it."

"Neither do I," Phil said. "But I know someone who might." She reached for a pen and paper, jotted down a quick note, and folded it over.

She rang for Tuttle, who appeared immediately.

She handed him the missive. "I'm not sure of the address."

Tuttle raised an eyebrow as he read the name on the paper. "The boy will know where to take it."

"Good, tell him to wait for an answer. Preswick will take care of him when he returns."

Tuttle bowed and left to instruct the messenger.

Phil watched him leave. What was done was done. They needed help.

And there was only person she thought she might be able to trust.

16

It was four o'clock when the Reynoldses' town carriage stopped at the entrance of Central Park, and the Countess of Dunbridge stepped down to the sidewalk.

She had changed into a beige walking suit and a matching coat with walnut trim and buttons. Her hat had just enough of a veil to shadow her appearance without blocking her view or making her look like the dowager she was.

John Atkins was there, standing next to the stone wall and looking more dapper than a policeman should look.

Phil took a fortifying breath, hoping to heaven she was doing the right thing. And also hoping that her demeanor was as well put together as her attire, she went to meet him.

Atkins offered her his arm and they strolled like any other couple down the walk and into the luxurious landscape. Any other day, Phil would have enjoyed the walk immensely and perhaps even the company, but today was pure business.

"Thank you for agreeing to meet me."

"Did I have a choice? It sounded rather like a summons."

"Did it? Old habits."

"Habits that you intend to modify anytime soon?"

"Perhaps."

"Fair enough. But let me say right away that if you're here to complain to me about Sergeant Becker's clumsy search of the Reynolds brownstone, Mr. Sloane has already made his feelings known."

"But you said he wouldn't bother us again."

"Evidently I was wrong."

She frowned at him. A man who could admit he was wrong? *Now here was a unique specimen.*

"His men were also out to Bev's farm."

"And how do you know this?"

She'd walked into that one. "We drove out."

"I knew I shouldn't have released the Packard. Didn't I tell you not to leave town?"

"You did, but Bev felt that she needed to keep apprised of the business."

"Assert her authority, you mean."

"Well, yes, that too. The police had been there looking for a jockey."

"Eddie Johnson. He's wanted for the murder of Reggie Reynolds."

"He didn't do it."

"They found—"

"Yes, I know. His bloody driving coat, but he said he didn't drive that day. He'd left his driving coat with the car."

"And you know this how?"

"I asked." Phil had stopped walking in her agitation, and he nudged her onward.

"I appreciate your enthusiasm, but if you could be a little less expressive . . . It would be frowned on if it were to get back to my superiors that I was meddling in things that were none of my concern."

"I beg your pardon," Phil said as her cheeks heated with chagrin. "I do know better, Detective Sergeant. A slip in my breeding."

"Is that what your behavior has been?" he said, bestowing a smile on her that reverberated through her person. "Who told you they turned the jockey away?"

She smiled. "I'm not at liberty to say."

Now he stopped. "If you know something for certain, telling me could help the man considerably."

"Or get him locked away for something he didn't do so your Mr. Becker can take credit for the arrest."

"And heat for removing the most favored jockey from the most favored horse of next week's race."

"I don't understand."

"Thank heaven for that."

"You'll not explain it to me?"

"No. I've already said too much."

"So you can't help?"

"Shall we sit down, Lady Dunbridge? There's a nice view of the pond from here." He guided her over to a bench among the trees that was a little removed from the bustle of the winding path.

"This is lovely," she said on a sigh, momentarily forgetting the dire reason for her being here.

"It is," he agreed. He was looking at the water as if gaining peace from its still surface. And she felt a twinge of sympathy for an apparently honest man trying to work in a corrupt world. She didn't envy him, but she did need his help.

"Lady Dunbridge, you would do better to stay out of this. Perhaps take your friend Mrs. Reynolds to the country. Newport is very popular, as is Saratoga if you want to be near the races."

"You told her not to leave town, now you're telling us to flee? Why? Are you expecting trouble? Does that mean you no longer suspect her of killing Reggie? And what about the man in the library? Who killed him?"

"I'm not even sure the two deaths are related."

"How could they not be? They happened within a similar time frame, and the second occurred in the dead man's library. How could they not be related?"

"You must not have gotten to that chapter in your studies yet."

"I don't profess to be a professional, but I care for my friends, and since it's obvious no one can be trusted—"

"No one?"

"I'm trusting you, somewhat. Don't disappoint me."

"Spoken like true royalty."

"I didn't marry the king, merely an earl; that makes me peerage."

"I stand corrected." He was acting obnoxiously formal, but his eyes were laughing. He shifted on the bench to look at her. "You are something, Lady Dunbridge."

"So it's been said."

He laughed out loud at that. "And you're very observant."

"Comes from years of surviving in London society."

He cocked his head.

"The more you know and how careful you are with what you do with the information, the more secure your place in society. I suspect that you know that very well."

"Huh."

"Of course you do. The trick is to always keep the upper hand."

"You wouldn't do anything foolish, would you?"

"Me?" She laughed. "Always. But not in this particular case. How can I help?"

He took off his hat, placed it on his knee, looked around as if he thought someone might be hiding in the trees listening to their conversation.

When he didn't say anything, she started for him. "I've been thinking for a while that this might be more than a lovers' quarrel or a jealous triangle."

He nodded. "Possibly, but he was shot with a twenty-three-caliber pocket pistol. The same as Mrs. Reynolds's pistol."

"But those are very common."

"But the bullet that killed the man in the library and the one taken from Mr. Reynolds's body were shot from the same pistol."

"How can you tell?"

"By certain markings on the bullets, though it is not always accepted as evidence in a court of law."

Thank heavens for that, Phil thought against her will. "Detective Sergeant, Bev didn't shoot Reggie, so either he had it with him, or someone stole it, shot him with it, and . . ." She frowned. "Returned it to the library?"

"Or she gave it to someone to do the job for her, then shot him when he returned for payment."

"You don't believe that."

"Not really. It seems a lot of trouble to go to. And why use her own weapon, then return it to the library to be found by the police? I suspect that beneath that dramatic façade, Mrs. Reynolds is not as dumb as she seems."

"No, she isn't. So what is your theory?"

He raised an eyebrow.

"Can't you give me a hint?"

"So you can put yourself in harm's way? Haven't you had enough?"

She'd had more than enough and her future was like a train pulling away from the station without her. Soon to be moving too fast to board.

She knitted her brows. She hadn't asked to meet him just to have him not answer her questions.

But if the gun he found on the library floor was the gun that killed Reggie, then . . .

"I know! Reggie took the pistol with him for some reason, the thief wrestles it away from him, shoots him, comes back and breaks into the library to steal whatever he was looking for, then leaves the gun to frame Bev."

"But not until someone else shoots him?" Atkins threw his head back and groaned. "I should take those forensic books away from you."

"But someone has to do something. I won't see my friend blamed for something she didn't do."

"Stay out of it. Because you don't, and I repeat, don't want to draw any more attention from Charles Becker than you already have. He'll figure out a way to soak every penny from both you and Mrs. Reynolds, and Daniel Sloane, too."

"Oh, dear."

"But if you leave it alone, he may be done with the two of you. So I would—as we say in police parlance—lie low and don't make waves."

"I understand. But is there nothing to be done about him and his cronies?"

Atkins leaned forward, resting his elbows on his knees and staring down at the grass at his feet. "I was a young beat cop when Mr. Roosevelt became commissioner back in '95. He was a great man, had real plans to clean up the force. It was rife with corruption and violence then."

It seemed to Phil not much had changed, but she held her tongue.

"It was an uphill battle, none of the old-timers wanted change, they were cleaning up with graft and corruption. Fortunes were made squeezing the small shop owners, the saloons, even the big guns who had something to hide.

"He worked hard, gave hope to some of us that the police could be a vehicle for change. They fought him at every step. Two years later he left to become assistant secretary of the navy, then vice president, now president. And things here have reverted to the old ways."

"Leaving you and the other reformers at the mercy of a corrupt head."

He leaned down and plucked a dandelion ball from the grass, shook it, releasing the delicate winged seeds into the air. They watched the tiny seeds float away.

"Such that it is."

"But surely—"

He sat up straighter. "I don't expect you'd be interested. I just told you this in order to give you some idea of what you're up against. Becker searched the brownstone for a purpose. He may have been looking for something specific or it might just be a ploy to intimidate Mrs. Reynolds. Whatever it is, you can believe it's something nefarious.

"Keep a wide berth of him, Lady Dunbridge."

"Is that what you do?"

He laughed softly. "No and look where it's gotten me."

"And might someday get you fired, or killed. I don't envy you. Though I must say, it got you here. Sitting on a park bench with a countess is not the worst thing that could happen to a man."

He did laugh now. "You *are* something else. It's getting late. I have to get back and so should you."

"You think Reggie was killed because he crossed some powerful men? Or just the local police?"

"People in power don't tend to kill the goose with the golden eggs."

"So I should look closer to home?"

"You should mind your own business and go about entering New York society."

"So you don't intend to help us. Therefore I might as well not tell you about nearly being forced off the road on our way back or that Bev's purse was snatched."

"Did you report this to the police?"

"I'm reporting it to you."

"Tell me."

She did, leaving out the part about the money. She saw no reason to muddy the waters and leave themselves open to another raid by the "authorities." And really, the fewer people who knew about the money they'd found, the better.

"I'll see what I can find out and be discreet as possible. But don't be surprised if you find yourselves in the newspapers tomorrow. There are always reporters hanging about the streets. Now I must go."

He stood and reluctantly so did she. What a waste of a lovely afternoon in a beautiful park with an attractive man.

They walked in silence until they were back on the street.

Bentley was still parked where she had left him. She stopped to admire the new Plaza Hotel. "Isn't it lovely? They say they have wonderful apartments there. I think it would be a nice place to live. Across from the park."

"I'm sure it would be—and very expensive."

She smiled. "No matter, so am I."

Bentley opened the door and let down the steps.

"Thank you, Detective Sergeant Atkins. You've been most helpful."

"It was my pleasure, but . . ." He took her hand and leaned over it. "I wouldn't broadcast the fact that we met this afternoon."

"No indeed. Good day."

She didn't really know what to think of John Atkins. He was convincing in his desire to reform the department. But there was a short distance between convincing and conniving. She'd navigated London society by knowing the difference.

The one time she'd succumbed to confessions with her best friend about a harmless flirtation with someone other than the earl, her new husband, the story came out in the *Tattler* the following week, which sent her off to Dunbridge Castle in disgrace, while the earl continued his exploits without criticism.

She'd learned her lesson, only instead of becoming a docile, obedient wife, she just became more discreet.

The brownstone was eerily quiet when Phil returned after her meeting with Atkins, though she was happy to see it returned to its normal state.

"Mrs. Reynolds and Mr. Sloane are in the library, my lady," Tuttle informed her.

Phil walked down the hall wondering what Bev had divulged to her father about their trip and their brushes with disaster.

"Aha, there you are," said Bev, coming through the door. "I'd wondered where you ran off to, Phil."

"Emergency shopping for Lily."

"You should have sent one of the footmen."

"I think it might have had an embarrassing effect on a gentleman," she said, preventing further discussion.

"Oh." She turned to her father. "Well, is it an insurmountable mess? Am I broke?"

"No, my dear, and even if there is no ready cash—"

"You don't need to worry about that, we—"

Phil shot Bev a quelling look. "We can certainly make do on what I have until things are straightened out."

"That's right," Bev said, looking chagrined.

"Neither of you is to worry about any of this. I won't let you starve. Now, I have to go. I have an engagement for this evening, but make sure Tuttle double-checks the locks tonight. And have the footmen keep watch in shifts."

"We'll be fine, dearest." Bev stood on tiptoe to kiss his cheek and he made for the door. "But are you sure you can't stay? Freddy and Marguerite are coming for cocktails."

"Sorry, I can't. Do send them my best regards."

"Lady Dun—Philomena."

"Daniel."

Bev turned to face Phil. "Is it Daniel and Philomena now?"

"We decided there was just too much Lady Dunbridge–Mr. Sloane to make conversation comfortable."

"You wouldn't want to make Hilda Tappington-Jones jealous. She can be merciless when provoked."

Phil laughed. "I wouldn't think of trying to steal your father or Mr. Tappington-Jones from her."

"Oh, good, it wouldn't do to have you as my mother-in-law."

"Heaven forbid."

"I should change if you're entertaining," Phil said.

"I don't think you have time. Freddy said he needed to discuss a point of business."

"About . . . ?"

"He didn't say, but I'm sure it's about Thunder and next week's race. It's the only thing on people's minds. Even Tuttle mentioned it."

The doorbell echoed from the foyer.

Phil smoothed her skirt and she and Bev went to greet their guests.

While Marguerite and Bev kissed and asked about each other's health, Phil unpinned her hat and set it on the side table.

"Good evening. I'm afraid I arrived back here only a moment ago. I had to rid myself of this hat."

"Think nothing of it," Freddy said. "We just dropped by because I need to discuss some things with Bev."

They went into the parlor.

Marguerite sat down beside her. "Shopping?"

"What?" Phil asked distractedly. Freddy had taken Bev to the side. He was speaking in low tones, but Phil managed to pick out "Devil's Thunder," "Bobby," and "Henry" from the discussion. "I beg your pardon?"

"I asked if you had been shopping. There must be so many things you wish to do now that you're in New York."

"Yes. My maid was separated from her trunks at the docks before we sailed."

"—think it's a mistake to keep him around—"

"So it was necessary to purchase her an entire new wardrobe."

"—what he's been up to with the horses—"

"And as much as I depend on Preswick, when it comes to buying certain items, I felt I needed to go myself."

"—was a prizefighter—"

"I ran later than I meant to."

"—I can't be watching the stables every minute—"

"Oh, dear," Marguerite said, as Bev and Freddy's voices rose. "I confess I can't wait for the end of race season. All this hoopla over a few minutes of excitement. Personally, I can't think of anything duller than watching horses run around and around in a circle and having men talk nonstop about 'horseflesh' and 'betting odds' at every gathering. Not to mention that between his work at the mayor's office and trying to keep Reggie's enterprises running smoothly, Freddy's constantly tired and short-tempered, poor man. I suggested we stay home tonight, but some Austrian diplomat is in town and he couldn't say no."

"I wonder if it's Herr Schimmer. I met him at the Tappington-Smiths' dinner the other night. Charming man. I knew his predecessor."

"Please tell me he isn't addicted to racing and sports."

"He was . . . very polite."

"Well, that's something, I suppose. At least the clubhouse at the new Belmont track has wonderful food. And we all wear our best finery to be oohed and ahed over."

"That's very important," Phil said with just a touch of irony that went over Marguerite's head.

Bev hurried over. "Phil, I need your advice. You don't mind if we talk business for one more second, do you, Marguerite?"

Marguerite smiled wanly. "Would it make a difference?"

"No, you old grump. Freddy thinks I should fire Bobby Mullins."

"As I told Bev, he's a shady character. But she has such a soft heart."

Phil swore that Marguerite growled under her breath.

"We can't depend on him not to start throwing races and handicapping horses to his own advantage. He was known to do such things when he was fighting. And there's no reason to think he won't start it again now that Reggie's not around to keep him in line."

"Really?" asked Phil. "I thought he was Reggie's right-hand man."

"He may have been. But he isn't family, and I don't think we can trust him."

"I know," Bev said. "But I hate to do that. Reggie's will said to leave him in charge of the running of the stables."

"Because Reggie, pardon me for saying it, couldn't see beyond Bobby's toadying up to him all the time."

"Not to mention that Bobby introduced him to Mimi," Marguerite added.

"Bobby did?" Bev said. "How did Bobby know Mimi?"

"He's a lowlife," Freddy said. "You'd be surprised who his associates are. Henry knows more about horses than Bobby could ever learn. I know he isn't happy with him either."

Bev cast a look toward Phil.

Freddy gave her a patient smile. "You can't expect Countess Dunbridge to know the ins and outs of stable management. It isn't fair to her."

"I think perhaps Bev should sleep on it," Phil said. "Then if she decides to fire him, she can do so."

"Bev, I understand your sense of loyalty and it's to be admired, but Bobby is a hothead. If he gets angry or cornered, he's liable to get nasty. He may even try to hurt the horses."

Phil's head snapped toward Freddy. It was similar to the story of Silver Blaze, where the trainer was planning to lame the favored winner, and close enough to be suspicious. She shook herself; her imagination was running wild.

"I think you should leave it to me and Henry."

"Maybe he's right, Phil."

Perhaps he was. Phil didn't know anything about the business or about Reggie's and Bobby's relationship. But she hated to see Bev being pushed into something she wasn't sure of.

"Freddy's just trying to help, Bev," Marguerite said. "And you have to admit, he's kept Reggie's business in order."

Bev clearly didn't know if he did or didn't. Still, Phil was all for Bev taking control of her life.

"You don't really mean to take over the running of the stables, do you?"

"Well, yes."

"What on earth for? Do you have any idea how much time

and energy it would take? Just look at Freddy. Have you ever seen such dark circles under his eyes?"

"But he also has his City Hall job. Anyway, I like the horses."

"And bookkeeping, payroll, operating expenses?" Freddy asked.

He said it kindly, but it raised Phil's hackles. And as far as bookkeeping, surely running a stable couldn't be more complicated than running a household. Though she had to admit that so far she'd seen no evidence of Bev attempting to run hers.

"I can't believe this," Bev said. "There's just one unpleasantness after another. Reggie murdered. Dead man in my library. Police ransacking the house. Trucks. I just want it to all go away."

"Well, I can at least take this burden off your shoulders."

"Fine, Freddy. Whatever you think is best. I'm sick of the whole thing."

"Well, then, we should be going," Marguerite said. "I'm rather eager to meet Herr Schimmer." She took out a mint from her bag, popped it into her mouth, and smiled slyly.

Well, well, thought Phil.

Marguerite gave Bev a kiss. "You should take some powders and get some sleep. Things will look better once everything has died down."

"Easy for you to say. You're on your way to dinner at the Ogdens'."

"My poor Bev." Another kiss and the couple was gone.

"Are you sure that's what you wanted to do?" Phil asked, picking up Marguerite's candy wrapper from the table and dropping it in the wastepaper basket. "What happened to running things yourself?"

Bev sank onto the settee. "I don't know. Last night it seemed like such a good idea. But today the 'men' wouldn't even listen to me. And Freddy sounded so sure of Bobby's perfidy." She shrugged. "Was that just another incidence of male one-upmanship?"

"Possibly. You forget, I don't know Freddy and only met Reggie once."

"I don't know what to think. He was so adamant about what Reggie would want and what was best. And he seemed so certain that Bobby would cheat. And one thing I know about Reggie, he wanted to win, but fair and square." Bev sighed. "He didn't mind cheating on his wife, but he drew the line at the track.

"Let's have dinner served in here on trays. What's the point of changing into more black?"

17

Phil changed for dinner even though she and Bev would be dining alone. She returned wearing one of her new Paul Poiret tea gowns. It was exquisite, draped purple chiffon over a blue-embroidered underdress and fringed with tiny golden beads, much too elegant for dinner on a tray with a widow, but she felt Bev could use some cheering up.

Bev's mouth opened in silent admiration. "You look . . . absolutely Greek."

"A young designer I discovered at the House of Worth. I expect great things from him. Do you like it?"

"I adore it. And no corset?"

"Corsets are soon to be a thing of the past. We'll order you one. You can wear it at home when there are no prying eyes."

"Is this the fashion in London?"

"Not quite, though I imagine it will be all the rage in a year or two. But you know me. Always one step ahead."

"You are. And we'll order one or two, maybe three first thing tomorrow."

They ate in silence, each caught up in her own thoughts. Phil felt for Bev's predicament. It was early days and her friend should have to worry only above receiving condolence calls and choosing mourning clothes. Not murder, corrupt police, car chases, and running a business.

After the dinner trays were removed, they settled down to endure a long quiet evening at home. Bev passed the time by flipping through one magazine after another, and Phil, finding a deck of cards in a side table, set out building a house of cards on the games table.

At length, Bev stood, walked to the window, came back, and sat down again. "Oh, Phil, what am I going to do?"

"About?"

"Everything. This is interminable. I feel like a prisoner in my own home. If they would just find Reggie's murderer."

"It's barely been a week."

"How did you stand it?"

How? Every day filled her with resentment that she should have to give up her life because of a man who cared nothing for her. How? "By gritting my teeth, wearing blackest black in society. And being extremely discreet when I wasn't."

"You didn't keep strict mourning?"

Phil shrugged. "Most of the time. But Bev, you've never been known for being discreet."

Bev threw herself down on the couch. "I'm never going to make it."

Phil completely agreed. And there was no real reason except etiquette that said she should.

Bev shot up. "What was that?"

"Really, Bev, it's the doorbell."

Another ring, longer this time, followed by heavy, insistent knocking.

"Good heavens. It can't be the police!" Bev looked quickly around the room as if she thought she might flee.

Phil arranged her skirts and tried to look disinterested.

"Where is she?" echoed from the foyer.

Not the police. "I believe we're about to be visited by Mr. Mullins."

"Oh, Lord." Bev grabbed a magazine and pretended to read.

Phil stood and headed for the door, hoping to stave him off. She didn't get very far. Bobby burst into the parlor, followed immediately by a remonstrating Tuttle.

Bobby stormed over to where Bev was seated.

"Is it true, then? Are you firing me?"

Bev threw her magazine and pretense aside and stood to face him.

"Bobby, calm down, have a seat and let's discuss this."

Mullins snatched the bowler off his head, leaving his hair matted and wild; obviously he hadn't been concentrating on his toilette. He glanced around and dragged a chair over to face the settee. Bev sat. Bobby sat. Phil and Tuttle stood over the two in case one or the other needed to be restrained.

"Freddy telephoned. Told me my services were no long needed. Didn't have the guts to tell me to my face."

Phil winced. For someone who worked in government, Freddy hadn't bothered with diplomacy.

"I didn't believe him. How could you go and do something like that? Reggie told me to take care of the stables if anything happened to him. I promised him."

"Bobby, please. I know it must be a disappointment, but Freddy thinks it's best if there is only one manager deciding the direction of the stables."

"He's right. But it shouldn't be him. He doesn't know nothing about horses except how to bet on 'em. He don't care about establishing stables or a stud farm. But Reggie did."

"Oh, Bobby, Reggie only cared for where his next thrill came from."

"That's not true, Mrs. Reynolds. You know it's not. Freddy might have led him astray, but he knew what was what and came around in the end."

Phil's ears pricked up. Freddy led Reggie astray? From all she'd heard, it was the other way around. Came around in the end? That had an ominous ring.

"Freddy Beecham is out for what he can get, any way he can get it, and you don't want to be a part of that. Reggie wouldn't want you to do that."

"Bobby, I'm sorry. But it's been decided."

Bobby shook his head. For a terrible moment Phil was afraid

they'd have to call the footmen to bodily remove him from the room.

"Look. I'm gonna tell you straight. Reggie owed a lot of money, fixing up the farm and building the training track, the horses. It all cost a lot more than he figured."

"I gave him plenty," Bev said, an edge to her voice.

"Well, he tried to double it, but he got scorched. He was going to win it all back with Devil's Thunder. Somebody killed him before he could. I'll go, but don't blame me when it all comes tumbling down."

He stood, fists clenched, hulking over Bev like an angry gargoyle.

"I'm sorry."

"Not as sorry as you're gonna be. Remember that."

He brushed past Phil and Tuttle. Tuttle, recovering, quickly followed him. Phil had to run to catch up.

"Bobby, wait."

He barely hesitated.

"Do you know something concrete, or are you threatening Mrs. Reynolds?"

"Threatening? Lady, Reggie was my best friend. What kind of man do you think I am?" And with that he stormed out of the house.

What kind, indeed, Phil wondered as she returned to the parlor.

"I feel terrible," Bev said. "But it's like Freddy said. The man was a prizefighter. Not the most scrupulous of creatures. To be in charge of my fortune, or what's left of it . . . What was Reggie thinking? Am I wrong to trust in Freddy? Phil, say something."

"I think we must be missing something, Bev." *And it's time I put my mind to finding out what it is.*

That night, after sending Bev to bed with a sleeping powder, Phil called her two servants together.

Lily took her usual place next to the stack of books with a pad and pencil placed in front of her. Preswick refused to sit until Lily pulled his chair from the hallway and placed it at the study table.

Phil paced the room while the other two waited patiently for her to begin.

"Time is passing. We need to take this dilemma by the horns and shake it until we get some answers."

"Yes, my lady," Preswick said.

Lily merely picked up her pen. "Ouch." She shot Preswick an angry look. "Yes, my lady."

"Excellent. Now, this is what we know. And it only goes this far. No one else is to know anything, because, quite frankly, I have no idea whom we can trust.

"What we know is Reggie is dead. Possibly shot with Bev's pistol. A man was found dead in the library, also shot with Bev's pistol. At least Detective Sergeant Atkins thinks so." She glanced at Lily to make sure she was getting this all down.

Lily finished writing and looked up. "She shot both of them?"

"A logical conclusion, except that the man in the library, according to Tuttle, must have been shot before Reggie was shot, not after as I have been assuming."

"So how did the pistol get back in the library?" Preswick asked, finally unbending to enter into the investigation.

"Exactly, because the library was kept locked and Bev didn't have the key."

"So she says," Lily said.

"So she says, and so says Tuttle."

"Who is a loyal servant to the family," added Preswick.

"So she might have shot a burglar before leaving the house to come to the docks. Locked the library door with a key that presumably doesn't exist. Killed Reggie and somehow got back into the library without anyone seeing her and threw the pistol on the floor for the police to find."

"That would be a stupid thing to do," Lily said.

"Indeed." Phil took another turn to the window and back. "Bev is flighty, and sometimes silly, but she isn't stupid. And I really don't think she's a murderess. And evidently John Atkins didn't either, or he would have arrested her.

"We've been thinking in terms of a lovers' triangle, or an unknown killer with an as yet unknown motive."

"The jockey Eddie," Lily said.

"Perhaps, but why? And how would he—or for that matter Bev or Mimi LaPonte—be connected to the dead man, a local crook?"

"What was the dead man doing in the library, my lady?" Preswick said.

"Stealing something," Lily said, and added, "my lady."

Phil put her hand to her forehead. "I think we can dispense with the 'my lady' while we're investigating, don't you? I never noticed before how it clutters a conversation."

"Yes, my—yes," Preswick said.

"Everyone gambles, at least a little," Phil said. "I plan on putting something down on Devil's Thunder if we ever make it to the races. It would be disloyal not to."

"People lose their fortunes through ill luck."

"True, Preswick. But I don't see how gambling could play into the two murders."

"What if the dead man was putting the squeeze on Mr. Reynolds?"

"Lily, you will not use phrases of that ilk in the presence of your mistress or any person of quality. You should not use it at all," Preswick admonished her.

"They said it in the kitchen. Is it slang, then?"

"Yes, my dear, it is." Phil smiled at Preswick. "I told you she was a quick learner."

Preswick's countenance didn't change, but she'd known him long enough to see that he was becoming proud of the girl.

"So he comes in to squeeze Reggie," Phil began. "Reggie shoots him? Then later shoots himself? Then how does the pistol get back to the library?"

"If there were two of them like we thought at first, they came in to steal the money, got in a fight, and one of them killed the other."

"Then takes the money or whatever it was, follows Reggie, kills him, and then returns here and breaks in again to put the gun back?"

Lily sighed. "That would be stupid, too. Besides, they didn't break in." She slumped back. "None of this makes sense."

"No it doesn't. But it will . . . eventually."

It was late when Phil called an end to their speculations. Lily closed the notebook on a yawn. Tuttle rose stiffly from his chair and returned it to the hall before bidding them good night.

Neither Lily nor Phil spoke while Lily brushed out Phil's hair and helped her into bed. They'd speculated, analyzed, made a list of events, a list of clues, a list of possible suspects and motives. There were too many of each. And yet each time they tried to whittle them down, a new idea arose to prevent them. What they all needed was a good night's sleep and a fresh brain.

But Preswick would be at his superfluous post first thing in the morning. And Lily would be up even before that. Phil knew she had a lot to do tomorrow, she just wasn't sure what.

It had been a long, exhausting day, and Phil fell asleep immediately. She awoke just as quickly. Sat bolt upright in her bed. A thought had awakened her, an elusive scent in her memory. A reason for killing Reggie that she couldn't grasp. A sense that they had been looking at the crime scene from the inside out, when it should have been the other way around.

Then all thoughts dissipated like John Atkins's dandelion, and she fell back asleep and dreamt of flowers.

Phil didn't expect to find Bev at the breakfast table the next morning. Tuttle, however, was waiting for her with the newspapers turned to page six.

"Mrs. Beverly Reynolds and Lady Philomena Amesbury,

Countess of Dunbridge, who is visiting Mrs. Reynolds from England," the article began, "were set upon by ruffians as they exited the Lincoln Safe Deposit Company yesterday a little after two o'clock. Mrs. Reynolds's purse was stolen. No one was injured."

"Outrageous," Phil said. "It took less than two minutes for the entire episode to occur." Either Detective Sergeant Atkins was correct about the journalists or he'd leaked the information himself. "Well, at least the town will have something other than murder to gossip about for a refreshing change."

"Yes, my lady."

"Oh, I am sorry, Tuttle," Phil said, noticing he was holding the coffeepot at the ready.

While he poured her coffee, she scanned the rest of the headlines, turned to the sports and racing news and perused the latest results of the Jamaica races. There was a small item about Reggie's death and the state of betting on Devil's Thunder. The odds were still favoring Thunder, with a horse named Shadow Boxer the next favorite at 10–1.

She put the paper aside and went to the buffet to fill her plate with eggs, bacon, and tomato. Tuttle set a stand of toast next to her plate.

"I expect Mrs. Reynolds will sleep in this morning," Phil said.

"Yes, my lady."

"Good. She needs her rest."

"Yes, my lady."

Phil sighed. Somehow here in America, hearing "my lady" after every other word seemed absurdly out of place.

The front bell sounded and a minute later a footman came to the door of the dining room and motioned to Tuttle.

"Pardon me, my lady."

"Of course, Tuttle, but if it's Bobby Mullins, please send him away. Mrs. Reynolds has had quite enough upset from that quarter." Phil reached for a piece of toast. The brownstone was becoming quite as busy as Victoria Station.

"Miss LaPonte is at the door, demanding to see you or Mrs. Reynolds."

"Good heavens, show her in."

Tuttle bowed and withdrew, but returned almost immediately, Mildred Potts, pressing behind him, somewhat like a racehorse at the starting line. As soon as she was inside, she rushed to where Phil was seated.

"Good morning," exclaimed Phil. "Miss LaPonte, won't you be seated. Have you breakfasted? Coffee, perhaps?"

Mimi shook her head energetically, cut a look toward Tuttle.

"Thank you, Tuttle, that will be all."

Tuttle hesitated, then left the room.

"Do sit down," Phil said, marveling at the transformation of the woman before her. She might be doing a melodrama at Drury Lane as the grieving widow. She was dressed in a drab black gown and a black picture hat with equally black plume and veil that Phil remembered seeing as a part of her Florodora costume.

Fortunately, she was holding a black handkerchief in one hand and a tapestry bag in the other, or Phil had no doubt that she would have entered wringing her hands and thrown herself at Phil's feet.

"Please." Phil gestured to the chair and hoped that Tuttle would have the good sense to keep his mistress from making a surprise appearance.

"I don't have time to socialize, Lady Dun . . . whatever. I heard what the coppers did over here, and somebody broke into my rooms while I was performing last night. They left it in a terrible shambles."

"How awful. Do you think it was the police?"

"I don't know. Nobody saw them and they didn't leave no calling card."

Mimi had moved far enough to stand behind the chair but made no move to sit down.

"I need to talk to Mrs. Reynolds, but that stiff shirt wouldn't let me in."

"So you asked for me, very wise. What seems to be the problem?"

"They're gonna kill me."

But not before you kill the mother tongue, thought Phil, and kept her sympathetic expression in place. "Who is going to kill you?"

"I don't know. I don't know who Reggie told."

Oh, Lord, thought Phil. It *was* more than a lovers' triangle. "Well, sit down and tell me all about it."

Mimi looked around the room, then pulled out the chair and sat down, keeping the bag in her lap.

Phil poured a cup of coffee and placed it before her. She stared at it as if it might be poisoned. Her whole demeanor was getting a bit tiresome.

"Now Miss LaPonte, why would someone want to kill you? Perhaps we can figure out who it is."

Mimi blinked several times. Her lip quivered.

Phil realized she was sincerely frightened and relented. "Now my dear, tell all."

Mimi sniffed. "The book."

Phil sat very still, determined not to show excitement. The book that Reggie had promised to Daniel Sloane? It must be. Surely he hadn't been killed over a tell-all bit of gossip. Or had he? Was Mimi's life really in jeopardy?

"It was just a joke at first, you know?"

Phil made encouraging murmurs.

"Me and Reggie. We'd be with people and they'd go beyond the line . . ." She paused for a reminiscent smile. "Sometimes Reg and I did, too."

Spare me the details, Phil thought.

"At first it was just me, writing like a diary. Ya know, in case I became famous and had to write my memoirs. People can do the craziest things. And I wrote 'em all down. Then I'd read them to Reggie and he laughed like they was the funniest things he'd ever heard. And said to keep it up. It was a gold mine."

A gold mine? Mildred Potts was the "lady" who wrote the scandal book? The mind boggled.

"So I did. Sometimes he'd tell me about things he's seen or heard and we'd laugh till we was about to bust. Then after a while Reggie, he gets on the bandwagon, so to speak, and he starts writing stuff down, too.

"Sometimes I wrote about Mrs. Reynolds. She's no saint, no matter what people think. I didn't let Reggie know about those."

Really, Phil would be amazed if anyone thought Bev a saint; still she held her peace. Was Mimi LaPonte, Mildred Potts, about to try a little blackmail? Well, wouldn't she be surprised.

"I felt a little bad about that, 'cause I think we could probably have been friends if I hadn'ta stolen her husband."

Phil seriously doubted it.

"And I'm thinking how's it all gonna end. With my name up on the marquee of some big Broadway theater and all the stories of my love affairs and people I partied with."

An automobile backfired outside, and Mimi squeaked. "They're gonna kill me."

"Because of a few risqué stories? That doesn't seem likely. Who knows about the book?"

"Nobody. Reggie said we wasn't to tell. I didn't see what the big deal was. Some of the things were pretty funny and I thought people might get a kick out of them, you know?"

Phil nodded, wondering how much the woman was going to ask for.

"Then Reggie started writing down things that happened when I wasn't around. And he said it was our insurance policy. Sometimes he'd talk like that, and it would give me the willies.

"Now Reggie's been killed, and Bobby's disappeared, and there's—"

"Wait. Bobby's disappeared? Are you sure?"

"Yes. He'd said he'd accompany me to the theater on account of those threats, but he didn't come."

"It's still quite early. Are you sure he isn't just running late?"

"I'm sure, I tell you. No one's seen him at his lodgings or down at the pub. I think they musta killed him, too. I gotta get out of town. You have to help me."

"Calm yourself. We saw Mr. Mullins last night. He was angry at something that happened at the stables. Maybe he just, um, 'tied one on,' I believe is the expression, and is sleeping it off somewhere."

Mimi shook her head. "They killed Bobby, too. They musta found out I gave him the book for safekeeping after they killed Reggie."

"Who is *they*?"

"I tell ya, I don't know. Some rich pooh-bah that don't want his wife gettin' into trouble. We got real juicy stories in it. Some of these fine ladies sure know how to get rambunctious.

"I'm gonna be next. They're probably waiting for me outside your door."

And to Phil's discredit, her first thought was, *We can't possibly withstand another murder so close to home.*

"I need to get out of town. I want five thousand dollars."

Ah, now it comes. "Miss Potts, I'm afraid you've wasted your time. Poor Bev doesn't have a cent to her name. Reggie spent it all. And I . . . well, I just arrived from England. I have no banking arrangements set up as yet. I'm afraid you'll have to take your book elsewhere." Phil smiled ruefully but couldn't keep from holding her breath. She wanted that book. "I'm sorry. Perhaps one of your other subjects will be able to help you."

"I bet Mr. Sloane would pay to keep his daughter's name out of the papers." A determined half smile quivered on Mimi's lips.

Phil almost felt sorry for her. Almost. "I'm afraid Mr. Sloane is quite used to seeing his daughter's name in print."

Mimi gave up all pretense. "You have to take it." She fumbled in the bag pulled out a red leather-bound notebook.

Phil pushed back her chair and rose. "I'm sorry, Miss Potts, I'd like to help, but unfortunately it is out of the question."

"A thousand, then," Mimi said, jumping up to stop Phil's exit.

"A thousand and you can have it. Burn it or sell it to one of them scandal sheets, I don't care. I don't want it."

"Then why don't you burn it?"

"Reggie said to guard it with my life, but I thought he was just saying that."

"Who is 'they,' Mildred?"

"The men who Reggie wrote about."

And now the plot thickens. This book was not just about ladies but also about gentlemen behaving badly. Reggie must have had real knowledge that could be dangerous. And Phil wanted that notebook.

"Sit down, Miss Potts. I cannot in good conscience let you go out to an uncertain fate."

Mimi sat. Phil buzzed for Tuttle and asked him to send for Lily.

Lily appeared two minutes later. Phil took her aside and explained quietly what she needed and cued Lily on what to bring. Lily curtseyed and withdrew.

"Where will you go?" Phil asked, just to pass the time until Lily returned.

"Home, maybe. If my parents will take me back. I don't know."

"Ah, and where is home?"

"Why do you want to know? Are you going to tell them?"

"Just making conversation, my dear. I don't know who they are."

"Well, I don't either, but Reggie did and now he's dead."

Lily returned, trying not to sound out of breath, and handed Phil her purse. Instead of withdrawing, the girl positioned herself behind Phil's chair as a petite but somewhat fierce centurion.

Phil reached into her purse and brought out a handful of bills. Counted them out. Exactly two hundred dollars as she'd requested, which she could ill afford, but she had no choice. "It's all I have at my disposal. It should get you home to wherever."

Mimi reached for the bills.

"First the diary."

Mimi reluctantly handed it over. Phil flipped through it until she ascertained that it might indeed be valuable. She gave Mimi the bills; Mimi shoved them into the tapestry bag and stood up.

"I hope they don't come after you, your ladyship. You've saved my life." She backed away, then turned and ran for the door.

Phil stayed where she was until she heard the front door open and close.

"You know, Lily, if we ever find ourselves in dire straits, which I doubt, but if we do, I might make a career on the stage."

18

Tuttle came back into the room, and Phil slipped the book to her lap. "Thank you, Tuttle. You did the right thing bringing her here. We needn't bother informing Mrs. Reynolds of her visit."

Tuttle merely dipped his chin, but Phil knew he was brimming with curiosity and perhaps had been listening at keyholes.

"She wanted money. I gave her a little something. I don't think she'll be bothering us again."

"Very good, my lady. Would you care for more coffee?"

"No, Tuttle, that will be all."

"Now," Phil said to Lily as soon as the door closed behind him, "take this upstairs and keep it out of sight until I can get up to read it. And don't let Bev know what has occurred."

Lily curtseyed. Phil handed her the book and she slipped it beneath her apron. "And don't peek."

"No, madam."

Phil finished her coffee, trying to appear normal when she really wanted to lift her skirts and race up the stairs to find out if Mildred had indeed written something that would have inspired someone to kill Reggie and then go after her.

It might come to nothing, along the lines of Mr. A.P. was seen leaving the premises of Mrs. C. in the wee hours before dawn by an observant a lamplighter, et cetera. Hardly motive for murder, unless perhaps you were Mrs. C.'s husband. And even then it seemed far-fetched.

Most likely Mildred had been receiving emotional but empty

threats by members of Reggie's loyal admirers, and Phil had wasted two hundred dollars she didn't have to spare.

She finished her breakfast, and since Bev had still not made an appearance, she climbed the stairs to her own bedroom.

Lily was waiting for her. The diary, however, was nowhere in sight.

"Where—?" Phil began.

Lily lifted the side of her skirt and pulled the book from her garter. "I was afraid to put it down."

"Who knew garters could be so useful," Phil said, trying not to smile. "Well, let's take a look and see if it's as volatile as Mildred Potts believes."

They spent an hour reading Mildred's thoughts on the other actresses. *Connie has to use bust lifters to fill out her dress. I bet the managers didn't know that when they hired her. Can you imagine watching her undress? Quelle surprise for some unsuspecting gentleman . . .*

Her derision of the upper class. *Mrs. Adela Freeland got rip-snorting drunk the other nights at H.T.'s and fell over the ottoman. By the time the boys hauled her up, everyone had seen that she wasn't wearing . . .*

Reflections on Bev Reynolds. *I wanted to go to the races but Beverly was going with him. She's such a bitch. And I bet she's frigid. I'd love to see them at night, I bet she won't do half the things . . .*

Phil skimmed a few more entries. She didn't think any of what they'd read was relevant to "Who Killed Reggie and the Library Stranger?" Mimi had said that Reggie had made entries, and she was tempted just to look ahead for those, but she didn't want to be accused (not that there was anyone to accuse her) of not being thorough.

Poor Pansy Grantley has been sent to the country. Not knocked up at her age but something worse. Drugs. The family found her in a stupor last night on the front doorstep of their Fifth Avenue mansion and shipped her off in the middle of the night. All over town by today. Bye-bye place in society . . .

Dandy Rollins . . . —The Mrs. Rollins at Hilda's dinner party? Too delicious—*was complaining about how her servants were being paid to spy on her. She didn't say who's paying them. Probably one of those pornography magazines. Everybody knows her ladies' suffrage get-togethers are—let's just say they're not about suffering. No men allowed??? Eww. Give me a man any day. I wonder what else her servants know . . .*

Lily lost interest and wandered to the window, but since it only looked out to the roof of the brownstone next door, she was soon back again. "This is a waste of time. Who cares what old randy Dandy Rollins does at her meetings?"

"No one, but here's something." Phil perused the bottom third of the page that Mimi had written hurriedly. A closer look showed that it was as much in anger as in haste.

"What?"

"It's about Bev."

Lily came to read over her shoulder.

Well, of all the nerve. Beverly shows up at the Haymarket with Otto Klein. Of course she sees Reggie and me. At first she ignores me, but then Reggie wants to leave, like he's embarrassed to be seen with me. Then what does that bitch do but takes Otto upstairs like a common whore. Reggie sees red and goes after them. I see redder and go after Reggie. And there they are going at it up against the wall of one of the best private rooms of the best after-hours clubs in Manhattan. No class. Don't see what Reggie, or Otto, for that matter, sees in her . . .

"Doesn't take much to know what they see in her," Lily said.

"However, I doubt if Bev or her father would want this spread about."

Phil closed the book. Maybe she shouldn't keep reading. At least not in front of Lily.

Lily fisted her hands on her hips. "Afraid to see what else she says . . . my lady?"

"I was trying not to shock your delicate sensibilities."

"I won't be shocked," Lily said.

"Very well." Phil reopened the book and turned to the next page. "What's this?" *Reggie is so angry. He's angry all the time now. It's that damn horse. Reggie says he's the best there is, but ever since he was entered at Belmont, Reggie's been on a tear. Bobby and Freddy are at odds over the training and Reggie's threatening to get rid of one of them or the other if they can't get along. I hope it's Freddy. No gumption, that one.*

Phil skimmed over the next entry. Nearly a whole page of Mildred's ramblings about the inconveniences of taking the trolley to the theater and about some actress who got her hat mixed up with Mildred's.

And then another about Reggie. She read aloud. "'*Down at the Haymarket tonight. I just wanted to dance, but Reggie keeps at Bobby for not "taking care" of the boy who's some kind of runner for that policeman. I told Reggie not to get involved with him. A bully and he'll bleed us dry.*'"

Policeman? Not Atkins, surely; it must be Becker.

Then he grabbed the kid by his collar and told him to let em know that he knows what they're up to and they wouldn't get away with it. Reggie's got guards on Devil's Thunder. I guess so nobody tampers with him. They drugged McMaster's Easy Money last year and it did more than slow him down. Died on his way back to Virginia. I don't want the same to happen to D's Thunder, but I'm getting sick to death of the damn beast. He's all they talk about. He gets more attention than I do.

Join Bev's club, thought Phil. The two of them could commiserate over Reggie's lack of attention.

"I don't blame him," Lily said. "All that actress does is gripe, gripe, gripe."

Could the two murders possibly have been over a horse? Is that why Freddy fired Bobby?

Or was this just a diary of a grasping, demanding mistress? A tell-all, maybe, but not scandalous enough for blackmail, unless Phil had missed something. Why did Reggie tell Mimi this book would be their insurance policy?

Two pages later, Mimi's entry made her think twice about her first impression. *Reggie came tonight all pissed off. I thought at first it was something his wife did, cause he got real rough with me. I like it a bit rough sometimes, but he nearly gave me a black eye. And they'd fine me for sure if I showed up at the theater with a shiner. Anyway, afterward, we had a couple of drinks and he said he didn't want to go out anywhere, cause he felt like committing murder.*

Wasn't sure I wanted to stay in because I didn't want to be that handy if he acted on that whim. But after a while I calmed him down. I know how to work magic on a man, Reggie's like putty when I get to going. "Fools," he says. "I'm gonna make them pay, baby, oh yeah, I'm gonna make em pay," he says.

Leastways he didn't make me pay and hopefully things'll look better once this big race is over.

It continued on in this vein until Phil came upon blank pages. She thumbed through a few more. Nothing. Nothing about leaving for South America or any plans for their future. She leafed through the remaining pages, just to make sure she didn't miss anything. All of them were empty until she got to the last page. It appeared to be stuck to the flyleaf, but the top corner was bent down. Carefully, Phil tugged at the paper, and the page opened to reveal two more pages. And . . .

Lists. Column after column. Written in a neat hand grouped together in several batches with an enumeration of ten to twelve sets of initials and accompanying numbers. Each was headed by a capitalized letter and a date from the last twelve months. Or more to the point, four groups from last fall and two from the past month and a half. And if Phil was not mistaken, they coincided with the racing season.

There was no title head or explanation. But even at a glance she could see that some of the initials appeared in more than one group.

"The initials must stand for people's names," she said to Lily. "The numbers could be—"

"Money," Lily said confidently.

"I agree. People who owed Reggie money, or gambling debts Reggie owed to them. He called them fools. Because he was planning to abscond and never repay them?"

Phil huffed out a sigh. "I have no idea who these people might be. Though one or two do seem familiar. T-J appeared numerous times. I wouldn't have suspected Mr. Tappington-Jones of underhanded dealings. Because these must be underhanded."

"Why?" Lily asked.

"Because respected people use qualified bookmakers."

"Oh."

"We'll have to enlist Bev to help us with the rest of these initials. Though I think we will withhold some of the nastier parts about her and Reggie."

"Yes, madam. I don't like this Mildred person. She is . . . *maligno*."

"Malicious, yes, quite. So we'll keep these things to ourselves. As for the rest . . ." Phil looked at Lily and knew they were thinking the same thing. Those little tidbits of knowledge might come in handy as leverage in her future life. Not that she'd ever resort to out-and-out blackmail.

"Actually, fetch me pen and paper. I'll copy down the lists and tell Bev we found them stuck in a magazine. A little subterfuge will keep from hurting her feelings and protect her father from certain things he really doesn't need to know. Being able to share the lists will prevent us from having to figure this out on our own."

Phil copied all the lists with accompanying marks and scrawls from Reggie.

In total, the lists contained twenty-four different set of initials, at least seven of which were repeated, some four or five times, all with various amounts written next to them. They hid the diary in Phil's jewelry case and Phil slipped the key down her chemise, before folding the list into her pocket and going downstairs.

Hoping any condolence callers had condoled and left, she entered the parlor to find Mrs. Tappington-Jones taking her leave.

"Oh, there you are, Lady Dunbridge. I just dropped by with a message from Mrs. Alice Langham requesting your presence at her ball tonight. She would have come herself, but she just returned from London and is up to her ears in preparation. But learning that you were here, she insisted that I deliver her invitation."

Bev stirred. "Just sealed the deal to marry her daughter off to Lord Abington and is holding a victory dance."

"Oh, Bev, you're so droll," said Mrs. Tappington-Jones. "And I just hate that you won't be able to attend. But it will pass before you know it, and you'll once more be out in society."

Bev groaned and clutched a throw pillow to her stomach.

"Here is the invitation." Mrs. Tappington-Jones handed Phil a pristine white envelope. "Mr. Tappington-Jones and I will be honored to take you in our carriage."

"I appreciate the invitation and the offer, but I feel I can't leave Bev."

"Nonsense. Mrs. Langham particularly requested your presence. It seems the Austrian cultural attaché specifically asked if you'd be there."

"You must go, Phil," Bev said. "And tell me every juicy morsel of gossip when you return. Or else I really will die of boredom."

"In that case, I'd be delighted to attend. I'll send my RSVP immediately."

She wrote out a quick reply and Mrs. Tappington-Jones was soon on her way.

Phil sat down. "I know you think I'm languishing here with you Bev, but it isn't true. Society will wait."

"I know. I just don't want you to miss out on any of the important events. The Langhams are industrialists. Nouveau, not old money, but you don't mind, do you?"

"Good heavens no, I've had enough of lineage to last several lifetimes." She moved closer to Bev. "But there is something I want to ask you about . . . I found some initials and numbers and I thought you might be able to tell me who these people are."

She took out the paper and opened it.

"What is this? This isn't Reggie's writing."

"No, unfortunately I had a little accident, which made it illegible. Fortunately, I was able to quickly copy it. I think it's lists of people's initials."

"I see. Well. G.G. could be George Gould. We don't really run in his circles; Father does. It could be Gerald Girard. I'm not sure what he does. Something with shoes, I believe.

"P.B. . . . the first thing that comes to mind is Paddy Boyle, but what would he be doing on a list with Gould or even Girard? He's a real character and incredibly entertaining. He's some kind of liaison, I think, for something not quite legal, a real lowlife type. Or it could be Paul Barnes, he works with Freddy in the mayor's office and is on the board of directors at some insurance company. He's more likely to be part of a group that includes either G.G."

It went on this way until several rows from the end. "T-J, that's an easy one."

"Tappington-Jones. I noticed that, but twenty K. Would Reggie borrow from him?"

"He might try, but Arthur is as closed-fisted as he is ham-fisted. Why do you think his wife looks elsewhere for her affection?" Bev frowned over the sheet. "You found this list in the library?"

"Hmm," Phil said, deflecting to a passable observation. "Could it be some kind of register. Maybe of taking bets?"

"God knows they're all into racing. Find me a man who isn't into racing, and I'd marry him . . . if I weren't in mourning. Devil's Thunder does attract big money. We built our own training track at Holly Farm and acquired several colts from winnings."

"T-J shows up several times, and if you add up the amounts, that's a lot of money to win or lose or even loan."

"Bets?" Bev asked.

"I'm thinking so. Could that be the money in the safety-deposit bank? They gave money to Reggie to bet for them?"

"No. They have bookmakers for that. I know Reggie did a few things on the side, but no, that doesn't make sense. Especially not this early in the game." Bev sighed, tapped her chin. "Besides, I think Mr. Barnes is on the Turf Commission And come to think of it, so is Arthur."

"Which leaves us nowhere," Phil said. "If we only knew who the rest of these people are, and if the money in the safety-deposit box is theirs or Reggie's."

"Well, you might be able to find out at the Langham ball tonight. There's a T.L. on the list. It might be Thomas Langham. He's your host and there will be others among the guests there."

But of course. Just like London society, Manhattan society was small and elite. Loans or bets or blackmail, she wondered how she would slip, "Are you involved in something illegal?" into the small talk of the evening.

"In that case, I'd better ring for Lily and prepare for the ball. And don't look so glum. I'm attending merely to find answers, not to enjoy myself."

But between the list and what she might find out tonight, she might have a brilliant idea in the morning.

19

Phil was sitting in her boudoir reading Mildred's diary when the maid announced the arrival of the Tappington-Joneses. She quickly slipped the diary under her pillow—a safe enough place for the next few hours—and hurried downstairs.

She'd dressed in an exquisitely expensive ball gown, silver stitched with swirls of silver sequins, and an overdress of pink chiffon, caught up in a metallic belt above the waist. Its short sleeves, finished by two pink-and-sliver tassels, gave just a hint of playfulness to the ensemble.

It was designed not to bowl over the other guests but to reassure them. Impeccably tasteful, elegant, and—for Lady Dunbridge, anyway—quite demure.

She might not be the object of male ogling tonight, but the ladies would approve. And as any intelligent woman knew, the door to society was opened and closed by the wives of important men.

Not exactly in keeping with her guest-of-a-house-in-mourning status, but she had no intention of playing that game again. And if anyone commented negatively on that fact, there would be another lady who would be sympathetic toward her situation. After all, she'd just finished her own period of mourning.

Poor Bev, on the other hand, had taken her widow's weeds to her father's rooms for a quiet dinner.

Mr. Tappington-Jones was all amiability, but Phil had to concentrate not to let the initials she'd seen color the way she conversed. She wanted to grab him by the lapels of his evening dress and shake him. Demand he tell her what his initials were doing in Mimi's tell-all book. Unfortunately, that might work with an errant husband, but as far as investigation techniques went, she was certain that wrinkling your escort wouldn't pass muster.

Patience, she reminded herself. Tonight was to gather information, not to force someone's hand. She smiled inwardly. Lady Dunbridge, lady spy. It did have a certain cachet.

The Langham mansion, for mansion it was, was ostentatiously perched on the corner of Fifth Avenue and Fifty-Fifth Street. With three stories of French doors and tiny balconies and columns along the ground-floor landing, it looked like a stone wedding cake, whose decoration reminded Phil not of confection but of the crenellation on medieval ramparts.

Phil and Hilda ascended the steps arm in arm, with Mr. Tappington-Jones behind, making Phil think of a sheepherder as he navigated between his wife's train and Phil's billowing chiffon.

She took a fortifying breath. Her debut appearance in New York, and she was thinking about the list. She'd memorized many of the initials. Now to give them a name and a face.

She expected to identify at least a few. Though as Bev had pointed out more than once as they perused the sheets of paper, they could be the initials of upstarts or lowlifes who had nothing to do with the society she'd be keeping this evening.

Phil didn't believe that. Not with the amounts of money—if it was money—after each set of initials. She was trying not to make assumptions without evidence. One of the many pitfalls Dr. Gross had warned of in his criminal investigations book. Still . . .

"Lady Dunbridge. How lovely that you were able to come."

Phil nodded to her hostess, a tall, thin woman who looked like she might bend in the wind. "Mrs. Langham, I was delighted to receive your invitation."

She turned to Mr. Langham. He was a short, heavily joweled man, with thinning hair pomaded forward in an awkward and entirely unsuccessful attempt to cover his shiny pate.

As he bowed over her hand, he flicked a quick look to Mr. Tappington-Jones down the line.

If only she could read thoughts. . . .

She moved into the hall, Hilda Tappington-Jones by her side. Mr. Tappington-Jones accompanied them as far as the first two groups of people for Phil's introduction, then excused himself.

The ballroom was already crowded, but Phil saw Marguerite Beecham standing with several women at the edge of the dance floor. An orchestra was playing somewhere at the far end of the room. The walls of the ballroom were filled with large oil paintings probably bought in Europe from the looks of the subject matter. *Money and a modicum of taste,* Phil thought and turned so Hilda could introduce her to another group of ladies.

She'd halfway expected a repeat of the dinner party, not in players but in attitude. But she must have made some friends at the Tappington-Jones dinner because her welcome was warm, interested, with only a few holdouts reserving judgment as to her suitability. Perhaps this time, her reputation had preceded her in a useful way.

She'd managed to work her way around the room and stood talking with the Langhams, taking particular note of Thomas and filing it away for she didn't know what, when her hand was claimed by Herr Schimmer.

He bowed. "May I have the honor of this waltz?"

Phil put down her champagne glass and he led her to the floor.

"How nice to see you, Herr Schimmer."

"Likewise. I was hoping you would be here." He took her hand and back and they moved effortlessly across the floor. He smelled of champagne and masculinity, aftershave and—

"Ah, a pleasure to have such a partner."

Phil recollected herself. "Have you been busy while here, Herr Schimmer?"

"Quite."

"Have Mr. Tappington-Jones and friends whisked you off to the track and kept you from your work?"

He smiled. She imagined he was quite good-looking beneath that beard, and she found herself wondering what those lips looked like when not partially concealed by his mustache. He was an excellent waltzer. And better still, he could carry on a conversation while twirling around a crowded ballroom. She was impressed.

"I think gentlemen must get an extra excitement being at the rail so close to the actual event instead of sitting with the ladies in the stands. And placing a wager here and there, no doubt." She smiled coyly up at him. He was several inches taller than she, the prefect proportions for dancing.

He smiled back at her. "Here and there. These Americans are much more cavalier than we Austrians about throwing their money after fast horses, sometimes to their detriment."

Phil immediately forgot about his attractiveness.

"Oh, dear. Did someone lose heavily? Not you, I hope." She let her eyes roll up. "Some of them have formidable wives. Though I suppose they manage to keep their losses hidden."

"I suppose. Though I doubt the earl could keep his losses from you."

She thought his look was much too penetrating.

"Pardon me, I didn't mean to be impertinent."

"Not at all. The earl didn't even try. But in England my money wasn't my own, so it didn't really matter to me if he won or lost."

"Alas. A law that will perhaps someday change."

"Perhaps."

The waltz ended and he returned her to the group of ladies. Their numbers and identities had changed. New introductions were made and conversation continued. Phil had little time for gossip, as her hand was immediately claimed for another dance.

So she twirled around the floor while she kept an eye out for the men she did know or had good reason to suspect were on the list. She danced with several of them, who doggedly stuck to the weather and her impressions of Manhattan no matter how hard she tried to lead the conversation to the track.

She also danced with both Thomas Langham and Arthur Tappington-Jones, but neither of them seemed to be able to carry on more than a monosyllabic conversation while concentrating on the dance steps. And again with the attaché, who was her most attentive and coordinated partner of the evening.

She'd met several gentlemen tonight whose initials were on the list. Of course it could be coincidental. Still, whenever she wasn't dancing, her gaze invariably wandered across the room. Anyone watching would be forgiven for thinking she was waiting for a secret lover.

Alas, not a lover, but a clue.

Halfway through the night she saw Marguerite sitting on one of the sofas around the perimeter. And she could tell, even from this distance, the poor girl was looking pale.

"Excuse me," Phil said, meaning to ask Marguerite if she was unwell.

As she crossed the room, she saw Thomas Langham nod to someone. A common salutation, except that as he continued toward the door, he was joined by Arthur Tappington-Jones. Off for a cigar and a brandy in the pool room, no doubt. On the other hand . . .

Before she could decide whether to continue to Marguerite or follow them, Herr Schimmer appeared at the edge of the ballroom and followed the two men out.

He might merely be joining the other men for a cigar, though she knew the attaché used a pipe. It left a faint aroma of a distinctive tobacco about his person. She'd noticed it at the Tappington-Joneses' dinner and again tonight. Faint, intriguing, inviting you to move just a little closer, let your guard down ever so slightly.

But she had no intention of letting her guard down tonight.

This migration from the ballroom might be completely

innocent, but she needed to know. Dropping her intention to help Marguerite, she, too, sidled toward the door and stepped out into the foyer. Only the usual footmen were there, and a few men and women returning from or going to the withdrawing rooms. She followed two ladies up the stairs to the landing, which curved left and right, with a central main hallway that stretched toward the back of the house.

When they turned left toward what was obviously the ladies' withdrawing room, Phil continued down the main hallway, where she thought the smoking room and billiard room might be located and would be the most obvious destination of the men who had just left the ballroom.

It was darker in this corridor. Sconces cast sprays of light up the walls between an assortment of tables, cabinets, and objets d'art that lined the way. She paused and listened, thought she heard voices at the end of the hall.

She moved closer. A door farther along opened and closed. She stepped back out of the light and made a hasty retreat into an alcove, where she squeezed in between the wall and a marble statue of an athletic Greek youth. Then held her breath as Freddy Beecham strode quickly toward the stairs. Not the stride of a man eager to return to the dancing, but a man out of temper. He took the stairs almost at a run.

She was tempted to follow him, but she was more tempted to find out what had made him so angry.

She peered down the corridor, now deserted again, and slipped out of her hiding place. Slowly she made her way forward, pausing to listen outside the door he had just exited.

There was no way she could hear what they were saying without entering.

And wouldn't that just put a damper on whatever urgent proceedings were going on inside?

But there was an adjacent room. She hurried toward it and tried the handle. It turned easily. She took a deep breath and stepped inside. It was a small sitting room, dimly lit by several wall sconces turned low. At the far side was a pair of French doors that opened to a small balcony.

Perfect. That would at least get her closer to the conversation, especially if the windows to the room next door were open . . . The possibilities were endless.

She crept forward, gently turned the door knob, and eased the door open, cringing slightly as it rasped on the doorjamb. She could hear an argument going on next door. Did she dare go out onto the balcony? Were they also out on the accompanying balcony?

She hugged the wall, afraid to move forward but not willing to go back.

"I tell you, it's under control."

"Can you guarantee that in spite of what happened?"

"What are you saying, man? We had nothing to do with that."

"The hell you didn't. Now rumor has it that there's going to be a crackdown on the whole industry. There's trouble ahead."

"You're off your bean. There's always rumors. No reason to think this is any different."

"I heard it, too. And after what happened to—"

"Don't be such an old woman. I know for a fact that . . ."

Phil eased herself closer, peered cautiously around the edge of the door. Caught the unmistakable whiff of an exotic tobacco.

She froze. Slowly, slowly turned her head.

He was standing in the shadows, only the glow from his pipe illuminating the trim reddish beard.

She eased away. His head turned and he brought his finger to his lips. Then as nonchalantly as the last moment was tense, he tapped his pipe on the balcony rail, returned it to his pocket, and stepped silently across the space to the door.

Phil inched her way back into the room. He stepped inside and closed the French doors behind them.

"Ah, Lady Dunbridge," said Herr Schimmer softly. "You have caught me attempting to have a few moments with my pipe."

"I believe, sir, there is a smoking room on this floor."

"Yes, but I care not for the brands these Americans smoke. I prefer a special blend in fresh air so as not to have the lesser mixes interfering with my enjoyment." He chuckled in a deprecating way. "One of my little idiosyncrasies."

Phil thought he might have more than he was letting on, but she wasn't ready to call him on them. Not yet.

He took her elbow and, without a word, ushered her gently but firmly across the room and into the hallway.

"You, however, seem to have lost your way." He led her back toward the stairs as he talked. "Ah, I believe that is what you are looking for," he said as several ladies came out of the withdrawing room.

Chagrined, she could only thank him and go inside.

She stood just beyond the door, wondering how long it would take before it was safe to leave. After a few minutes, she stepped out into the hallway and caught a glimpse of Mr. Langham in the foyer below as he said good-bye to some departing guests.

The meeting was over. It was irritating to have been caught by the attaché, but she had learned a few things. Certain men were worried about some clandestine enterprise they were carrying on, and that someone, presumably some arm of the government or racing commission, was investigating.

She returned to the ballroom, meaning to go directly to Marguerite and offer to accompany her home, but Mrs. Tappington-Jones waylaid her and introduced her to one of the aldermen of New York, who asked her to dance. After that she was immediately taken up by another gentleman with equally high recommendations.

Evidently, they all intended to pay their regards to the visiting countess as a part of the duties of their stations.

An hour later, her feet hurt, her shoes were scuffed from clumsy feet, and Phil was longing for bed.

She saw Marguerite still sitting on the sofa and talking earnestly to Freddy, and she joined them. Marguerite was extremely pale.

"Whatever is the matter? Do you feel unwell?"

"Just the heat. I really must go home. I don't want to embarrass myself by fainting on Mrs. Langham's carpet."

"Indeed. Why don't I come with you? Just let me inform Hilda that we're leaving. Freddy?"

"What? Of course. I'll have them send for my carriage." He left Marguerite sitting there. Phil promptly sat down next to her. "Do you have a vinaigrette?"

"No. No I'll be fine."

Within minutes they were in the Beechams' carriage, heading uptown.

It took awhile to go the few blocks due to an overturned milk cart that had caused traffic to stop in four directions. But after that was overcome, the drive was direct. They let Phil out at her doorstep.

"Don't see me in," Phil said. "Take Marguerite home and put her to bed. Are you sure you don't need me?"

"I'm fine, really, but thank you."

She was surprised to see Preswick waiting for her in the foyer. "My dear man, you shouldn't have waited up. I hadn't intended to stay this long." The case clock was just chiming quarter past two. "You go on to bed. And we'll have a strategy meeting tomorrow."

"Yes, my lady."

Though she noticed he stood at the bottom of the stairs until she could no longer see him. Dear man.

The hall lights were turned down low.

She turned the knob to her room. And was surprised to find it totally dark inside. She'd told Lily not to wait up; she must have forgotten to leave a light on for Phil.

She groped her way inside, just recognized a faint sweet smell of tobacco before a hand clamped over her mouth, as the door was eased shut.

"Don't move, don't make a sound." He was holding her against his body, his arm immovable.

She tried to shake her head, but it was impossible. He was holding her so tight against him she could barely breathe. Her mind seemed to have stopped working. Part of it was saying *Herr Schimmer.* The other was stultified with fear that she'd interrupted a burglar. Actually, both were terrifying. Why would Herr Schimmer break into her room?

And how had he broken in? Then she felt a breeze coming through the open window. Gradually, her eyes became accustomed to the dark, and she was able to see that the window was indeed open. But Lily would have never left the window open.

Déjà vu. The intruder must have gotten in that way.

But how could he possibly have climbed the walls to the second floor? He'd been at the ball just . . . when had she seen him last? If it really was Herr Schimmer. And who else could it be? The pipe tobacco. The arms that had held her waltzing . . .

She tried to wrench away.

"Stop fighting me, Countess. I won't hurt you."

This was not Herr Schimmer. That was an American accent.

She held perfectly still.

"I'll move my hand if you promise me not to scream."

She nodded as best she could.

Why had she told Lily not to wait up for her? If she *had* obeyed her. A horrifying thought rose in her mind. If he had hurt her maid, she would . . . would . . . do something.

"Lily is fast asleep in your dressing room, and if you don't want to wake her and cause me all sorts of grief and her some discomfort while she watches me slit your throat, you'll keep quiet."

He let go of her mouth.

She collapsed against him. "Who are you?"

"Shhh," he said in her ear, and it was almost a caress.

"Could you please let me go? You're wrinkling my gown."

"And a lovely gown it is. I don't trust you not to run, Countess. Besides, I'm rather enjoying this."

"What do you want?"

He chuckled softly, lifting the tendrils of hair on her neck. "Actually, I have it already."

The diary. He had the diary? What was so important about the dratted book? But she knew. The list. It must have something to do with the men tonight. But how had he known about it? And what did it mean? And if Herr Schimmer was still at the ball, who was this?

"I don't have the slightest idea what you're talking about."

"Good try. But since I already have what I need, it doesn't really work. Though I must say, you've done quite well so far. Better than expected."

"So far? How do you know what I've been doing?"

"I've been watching you."

"I knew it."

"Keep your voice down. I really don't want you to wake anyone up."

She lowered her voice. "I knew someone had been watching me. I thought it was the police."

"Them, too."

She tried to shift so that she could see his face, but he tightened his grip.

"I've torn out the list. You must try to forget everything you might have gleaned from it. Forget that you've ever seen it. I'll take it from here.

"I did leave you the rest of the book. It's back under your pillow. Really, Countess, your pillow?"

"It always worked with my governess."

He laughed quietly, standing so close, she could feel his breath on her cheek.

"Now this is what you'll do. When someone comes to ask for it—and they will, make no doubt—give it to them. Do not resist. They'll stop at nothing until it's in their possession. So hand it over. I wouldn't want you to meet an untimely demise; I'd rather like to get to know you better."

She felt him shift slightly and it set off fire in her skin.

"I see you've been reading Sherlock Holmes."

Phil glanced toward the table where the Holmes book sat on top of the stack of books.

"Did you enjoy the Silver Blaze story?"

Phil's breath caught. "Very much."

"I thought you would."

"How did you—?"

"Unfortunately, as much as I would like to stay, I must get these pages to the proper, shall we say, eyes."

He released his hold, turned her around and, to her astonishment, kissed her . . . deeply, passionately, and much too quickly.

Then he was gone. She was hardly aware that his hands had released her and she was free. But she couldn't move.

He, however, was moving toward the window. She stretched out an ineffective hand to stop him, when he leaped to the sill and jumped.

She made a sound and rushed to the window. Grabbed the sill and looked out. Thrust her body forward until she was afraid she would pitch to the ground below. The drop was straight down, not a ledge or tree or anything to break his fall.

It was impossible. The only way out would be the roof of the brownstone next door. But it was a good six feet away. No one could possibly . . .

Not even Mr. X—because Mr. X he must be—could have made that leap. Could he?

She peered into the darkness and saw a moving shadow gliding across the roofs.

She touched her lips where the taste and feel of his kiss still lingered. And she remembered something else. The kiss. The clean-shaved skin. Herr Schimmer wore a beard. But if not Schimmer, who was he?

She kept watching long after he'd disappeared into the night.

Then she turned on the lamp and pulled the diary from under her pillow.

He had left the diary, like he said. The last pages were gone. In their place he'd left a note.

Sweet dreams, Countess, until we meet again.

20

"I think I met the elusive Mr. X last night." Phil sat up in bed and waved away the coffee tray that Lily was about to set down.

She pushed back the covers. "I'll have coffee while you do my hair. Many things to do today."

"Yes, madam." Lily followed her over to the dressing table, set down the tray, and poured Phil a cup of coffee.

"Who is this Mr. X, then?"

"Well, I'm not sure exactly. But I think he is the Austrian cultural attaché."

"No. How is that possible?"

"I don't know. Nor why he should be. What I do know is that when I arrived home last night, my room was dark."

"I left the lamp on for your return just as you said."

"I am quite sure you did. Because as I stepped inside I got a whiff of pipe tobacco. And . . ." She shook her head. "And then I was grabbed from behind, his hand clamped over my mouth."

"Are you hurt? I will sleep on the floor tonight. If he comes again I shall slit his throat."

Phil resisted a shudder. "No slitting of throats. We've had quite enough murder around here."

"But why do you think it was that Austrian?"

"Because once my initial shock and fright receded, the experience was rather like waltzing with the attaché."

"He was that awkward?"

Phil smiled. "*Au contraire*. Not awkward at all. In fact, rather . . . exhilarating."

Lily rolled her eyes. "Did he steal your jewels?"

"Strangely, no. He stole the list from Mimi's diary. And told me when someone comes and asks for the book to give it to him without question because they were very dangerous."

"Who is he? Why did he want the list?"

"I have no idea. Except he said the oddest thing right before he left." She decided to keep the kiss to herself. It might inspire Lily to reach for her knife at the least provocation. "He saw the Sherlock Holmes book. And asked me how I enjoyed the story of Silver Blaze. I told him I liked it, and he said, 'I thought you would.'

"How did he know we had read that particular story? I never mentioned it in the attaché's presence. In fact, I don't believe I mentioned it to anyone."

"Well, I didn't."

"Of course not."

"Sorcery."

Phil looked at her maid in surprise. "Certainly not, but I did have the oddest notion."

"What is that, madam?"

"It's absurd."

"What is?"

"Remember the old man in the bookshop I told you about? He recommended the story to me."

"The old gentleman in the shabby suit?"

"That's the one."

"But you said the attaché was a handsome younger man."

"But could he be both?"

"Like a spirit!" Lily's hand rose automatically, she snatched it down. A warding-off sign or a sign of the cross?

"I was thinking more along the lines of Mr. Doyle's Sherlock Holmes. He often used disguises in his investigations."

"Why would the Austrian attaché and an old man be interested in Mr. Reynolds's murder?"

"He—they—whoever were interested in the list. And the list—"

"Is gone," Lily said.

"But the copy isn't," said Phil. "I'd put it in my skirt pocket earlier today. In the excitement of my intruder, I forgot about it. Then much later I woke up and remembered. I was afraid he'd found it, too, but it was still in my pocket. Et voilà." She reached beneath her pillow and pulled out several sheets of folded paper.

"But why did the old man come to the bookstore?"

"I think he was giving me a clue. Pointing me in the right direction."

"What direction?"

"Devil's Thunder. Bring me that copy of the mystery stories."

Lily fetched the book, her face full of puzzlement.

"The Silver Blaze story is about a stolen horse," Phil said as she flipped through the pages. "Let's see. Holmes and Watson go to find this missing horse, Silver Blaze."

"But Devil's Thunder isn't missing."

"No. Not yet, anyway. But the jockey is. And what about the dog that didn't bark in the night?"

"I didn't see a dog at the stables."

"Nor did I." Phil ran her finger along the page. "But it wasn't about the dog."

Lily just frowned at her.

"The dog didn't bark because he knew the thief."

Lily's frowned increased. "No one stole Thunder."

"No," Phil said. "But I'm sure the lists and the horse are somehow tied to some nefarious doings at the stables. Someone who has access to the horses. Now if we can figure out how the initials and Devil's Thunder and Silver Blaze come together . . . It's daunting. But I have no doubt that between you and Bev and I we will get to the bottom of this."

Phil pushed the covers away. "I think my lilac faille morning dress. I can't think of a single reason to avoid any more of poor Bev's condolence calls."

"But how are we to find out? It makes no sense."

Phil shooed her toward the dressing room and began unbraiding her hair.

"No, It doesn't, not yet, but I have no doubt it will."

Lily returned with the lilac gown. "So then what happened?"

"They covered Silver Blaze's mark with shoe polish to hide his true identity."

"Not with Silver Blaze, with the intruder?"

"Oh. He left."

"How? How did he get in in the first place?"

"Ah, through the window."

"But it's too far to the ground."

"He came and went, clever man, over the rooftops."

"Oh, *mon Dieu*."

"Quite. Let's keep this visit to ourselves. No use alarming Bev or the others. I don't think he'll be back now that he's gotten what he wants." And if he was tempted to come back, Phil certainly wouldn't want them to be interrupted.

Silver Blaze. The old man had specifically mentioned that story. Not a friendly recommendation. He wanted her to read it. Because he wasn't just a charming old man; he was a devious younger man who was manipulating events. She didn't know why. Or which side he was on. But she intended to find out as sure as she intended to solve Reggie's murder.

In the Silver Blaze story, they had a missing horse and a dead trainer. What they had here was a dead owner, a missing jockey, and a list of initials, but no missing horse.

Missing horse . . . missing horse . . .

Things were beginning to come together. Something was still missing, if she could just figure it out.

She reached for the Holmes volume. A little light reading while her mind went to work.

Bev and Phil had barely finished breakfast and settled themselves in the parlor when the door opened and Tuttle announced John Atkins.

Bev groaned. Phil stood to meet him. "Well, this is a surprise,

Detective Sergeant. Do you come bearing news?" she asked as she tried to quell the undercurrent of anxiety that his visit was causing. "Won't you be seated?"

He crossed the room, nodded to Bev, and sat down. "I do have news, rather unpleasant, I'm afraid. Mimi LaPonte was found beaten and close to death yesterday."

"Yesterday?" Phil squeaked. She cleared her throat. "How on earth?"

"I thought perhaps you might tell me."

Phil raised an eyebrow, her stomach was threatening mutiny.

"How would we know anything about that woman?" Bev snapped.

"Because she was found in the gated park across from this brownstone. Would either of you know why she might be there?"

"Good heavens no," Bev said. "Why on earth would she be out there? She wouldn't dare show her face here."

Atkins changed his focus to Phil. She glanced at Bev, who was staring at her hands, so Phil took the opportunity to give the detective a pointed look.

"Detective Sergeant, Mrs. Reynolds is expecting condolence calls any minute, perhaps we could step into another room to discuss this."

A flicker of annoyance, then understanding. "If you wish."

Bev looked up. "Phil?"

"I'll return shortly. No need to worry. This way, Detective Sergeant."

He followed her out to the foyer, and she was momentarily stymied. The servants would still be cleaning the breakfast room. She had no desire to be in the library in the company of John Atkins. "Tuttle, is the morning room being used?"

"No, my lady." He led the way down the hall, past the library to the morning room. When Tuttle had left, she turned to face Atkins.

He walked past her to look out into the garden, which was quite nice, though she couldn't imagine how sunlight managed to squeeze past the surrounding buildings. She watched his back as he continued to ignore her.

And she wondered how she could ever have thought that John Atkins might be Mr. X. He was tall, strong, muscular, not finely honed, and agile like a cat. John Atkins would never be accused of skulking. He would make a bold entrance, dominate a room, and leave by the door, daring anyone to stop him, not jump out the window and disappear into the night.

He turned abruptly and she barely had time to wipe the smile from her lips. "Now what's this about Mimi LaPonte?" she asked.

"She was attacked right across the street from this brownstone. Left for dead. Fortunately, a nanny and her charges found her yesterday afternoon as they went for their afternoon walk. The children were traumatized. It wasn't pretty."

Phil sank onto the nearest chair. She must have been set upon as she left from meeting with Phil.

"Was she robbed?"

"Hard to tell. But I'd say yes. She had no money on her and her purse was gone." He cleared his throat. "Her clothes were . . . mussed."

"She'd been—?"

"We don't think so. It appeared more like they were searching for something on her person. But strangely, she was dressed in black. Heavy mourning.

"Did she come here yesterday, Lady Dunbridge?"

She had to tell him. But when she did, she'd have to tell him about the book and the list, and she didn't dare.

"I thought you were off the case."

"The other case, but Mimi was found in my precinct. I'm on this case. And I think it's time you told me the truth."

Phil considered. Obviously Mimi's diary was no secret, that must be what they were after. Or the two hundred dollars Phil had given her. But how could she tell him about the money without divulging that Mimi had given her the book only to have the list stolen? If he asked for it outright she would know that she'd been wrong to trust him after all. And if he didn't?

Well, the list had been stolen and she couldn't show him the other parts. Bev would never forgive her, nor would her father. He'd would probably insist on searching the brownstone, and that would put poor Bev right over the edge.

"Lady Dunbridge?"

She sat on the rattan chair. "She did come here. Yesterday morning. But Bev—Mrs. Reynolds doesn't know."

He cocked his head.

"Do sit down, it's hard to think with you hulking over me like that."

"I beg your pardon," he said. Ironically, Phil suspected. He pulled the mate of her chair to face her and sat down. He was just as intimidating when they were eye level. Though she could be, too.

"Why didn't you tell her?"

"Because you've seen how she is. Bev was made for fun, not tragedy. And she's very fragile at the moment."

"I find that hard to believe of either of you ladies."

"Well, it's true of Bev nonetheless."

"Countesses are made of sterner stuff?"

"Needs must . . ."

". . . when the devil drives," he finished. "And what devil is driving you, Lady Dunbridge?"

"At the moment, finding out who murdered Reggie and the man in the library and putting this behind both of us."

"I see. And before?"

"Society, Detective Sergeant."

"And the earl?"

"The earl is history. And he died of natural causes, I assure you."

He coughed out a laugh. "I didn't suppose otherwise. Now tell me about this visit yesterday."

"She came in the morning, Mrs. Reynolds was still in bed.

She said she needed money, because they were going to kill her, and she needed to leave town."

"Did she say who 'they' were?"

"No. At first I just assumed that they were some of Reggie's fans. She'd gotten several bouquets at the theater that had threatening cards attached."

"She told you this yesterday?"

Phil sighed. "No. I visited her there and saw them myself."

"You what?"

"Well, you weren't doing anything about it. I know you're fettered by superiors and corruption, but I'm not. So I decided to try to find out for myself if Reggie was really planning to run off with Mimi. It was the least I could do for Bev."

"We know he was."

"We know he was carrying two steamer tickets. We don't know that he was taking Mimi."

"Her trunks were on the steamer."

"Well, if you had shared that information . . . As it was, I had to learn that from Bobby Mullins."

"You talked to him, too?"

"As it happens. He works for Mr. Reynolds, if you recall."

Phil thought Atkins had a remarkable face. Most people went red with anger, but not Atkins; he went white.

"It was a very misjudged thing to do. It could have been dangerous, not to mention interfering with an investigation."

"Well, I wasn't molested, and as far as I can see, pinning the murder on some defenseless jockey is hardly investigating."

She knew it was a low blow but, really, she hadn't come all the way to America just to be told what she could and could not do. She could have stayed in England for that.

"Now, I think it goes deeper than a few hysterical fans."

"Would you like to elaborate?"

Not really. She didn't want him racing off to inform his superiors. From what she had learned so far, they might be part of whatever was going on. Certainly Charles Becker must be.

"About racing."

He looked up sharply. "Why do you say that?"

"Don't you think it, too?"

He scratched his head. "You know, Lady Dunbridge, you're an infuriating woman."

"It's a gift."

"You need to mind your own business."

"I assure you, sir, this is my business. And, quite frankly, I don't see how you can expect me to cooperate when you refuse to give me the same courtesy."

"Then I'll tell you something. If Mimi LaPonte dies, you will be complicit."

For a full minute she stared at him. "Ridiculous. She came to me for help. Though now that I think about it, I have an idea she thought she was being followed, and that's why she was dressed in widow's weeds."

"Whew. When I first arrived, I was afraid it was Mrs. Reynolds. And when I discovered who it was . . . I've never seen a mistress in mourning."

"Rather in poor taste," Phil said. "I thought that myself at first. But I think she was using it as a disguise, the complete black, the heavy veil, someone might mistake her for Bev if they were watching the house. Good heavens, you don't think they were after Bev?"

He looked taken aback for a second. Phil was sure she did, too. The possibility of Bev actually being murdered had never entered her mind. Until now.

"So she came and asked for money and you gave it to her."

Alack, the man was tenacious. Just how much could she safely tell him? "As I said."

"And you gave her money out of the goodness of your heart."

"Something like that."

"Or perhaps she was trying on a spot of blackmail?"

"My life is an open book."

"I doubt it, but I was thinking of Mrs. Reynolds."

"Bev's life is well known. I don't think any scandal Mimi might dig up would turn heads."

"Not even if Mimi actually saw Mrs. Reynolds shoot her husband? Now that she herself is in the clear, she might see this as a means of squeezing Mrs. Reynolds for money."

"I assure you, I merely gave her enough money to get back to Idaho or Iowa or one of your states"—she waved her hand vaguely in the air—"out there somewhere."

"And she gave you nothing in return."

"Peace of mind, Inspector? Sorry—Det—"

"Never mind. Did she tell you anything about why they—whoever they are—wanted to kill her?"

Phil shook her head. *Should* she tell him about the book? If he was indeed honest, he could get to the bottom of this. But he'd demand to see it. And if he caved to that Becker character or to the mayor or even Mr. Tappington-Jones, Daniel Sloane wouldn't have the power to tie his hands.

"I don't know that I can trust you with the truth."

It was his turn to stare. He did, then he got angry—angrier than before. He stood abruptly and walked to the window and back. Took a controlled breath, while Phil tried to decide whether to run or capitulate.

"Let me rephrase that. I don't think you're dishonest, but I'm not sure you can hold out against the corruption that, in spite of the reforms your Mr. Roosevelt pushed, is still running rampant."

"I can, I have, I will."

"Lord, you are stubborn. Why do you do it?"

"Like you said, I'm stubborn. I think you can understand that." He gave her a half smile. He was very attractive when he smiled.

"Ugh. Very well. She had a diary. She wanted to sell it."

He sat down. "And you bought it?"

Phil shrugged. "It exchanged hands."

"You realize you have no right to it. You must turn it over."

Her intruder's words echoed in her mind. *If they come for the book, let them have it, they're very dangerous.*

And would be even more so after they got the diary and didn't find what they were looking for. Because she knew with certainty "they" didn't really care about Bev's raucous sex habits or Mrs. What's-her-name's lack of underwear or any of the other little peccadilloes Mimi described. Those might cause some short-lived gossip and humiliation, but would soon be forgotten. No, she wouldn't hand it over quite yet.

"Well, that could be a problem."

"More problem for you, if you don't."

"I can't. It was stolen."

Up and out of the chair again. Honestly, the man was like a volcano on the verge of erupting.

"It's the truth. I took it to my room. It was stolen while I was out. And you can't go around asking questions and accusing the servants."

"And why is that?"

"Because of course they didn't take it."

"Then who did?"

She could kick herself. Why had she let his righteous indignation gull her into telling him about the diary in the first place? He could take it right to Becker for all she knew. If the names on the lists meant something nefarious, as she thought they did, they would pay plenty to get the list back. Or kill for them instead.

And she wasn't about to turn Mr. X in until she knew exactly what he was up to. "I don't know. Just that he came in through my bedroom window and left the same way."

21

Atkins insisted on searching the grounds beneath Phil's window. She let him. No reason to tell him about the roof. Imagine what the neighbors would think to have policemen tramping over their heads while looking for clues.

Besides, what if her nocturnal visitor wanted to return and ran into a gaggle of policemen waiting for him instead of her?

So she watched from the window as he poked around the garden, then continued the—unbeknownst to him—futile search in the narrow patch of ground between two brownstones.

"What's he doing?" Bev asked when she joined Phil in the morning room.

"A rather long story, which I'll tell you as soon as he leaves."

Bev looked sidelong at Phil, then smiled. "Phil, are you up to your old tricks?"

"I believe I might be, but I think the intrepid detective has given up for now." But not for long if she knew John Atkins.

"Did you find anything?" she asked innocently once he'd scraped his feet on the mat and reentered through the French doors.

"No, I did not," he said, giving her a penetrating look.

"Oh," she said and left it at that.

She saw him out and came back to where Bev was stretched out along the wicker love seat. "I forget how nice this room is," Bev said. "I never seem to get back here."

"Finished with your condolence calls for the day?"

"I expect there will be more later this afternoon. By then I intend to be fortified with a nip of something in my tea. Now what gives? Why was he searching the garden?"

Phil pushed Bev's feet aside and sat down next to her. "I had a visitor last night after I returned from the ball."

Bev sat up. "You *are* up to your old tricks." She sighed. "Lucky you."

"Not exactly. He unfortunately was not after me, but after Mimi's book."

"Mimi's book? What are you talking about?"

"I wasn't going to tell you. I knew it would just upset you. But yesterday morning Mimi came here. She needed money and wanted to sell me this book she had. She told me it would be very valuable. That's where I got the lists."

"Why didn't you tell me?"

"Because I knew you would be upset at seeing her, and frankly I wanted to find out what she knew before you could kick her out."

"Is that why she was attacked in the park?"

"I think it might be, though you should be careful if you do go out."

"Why?"

"She was wearing all black with a heavy veil."

"The nerve of that hussy. Oh. Oh, no."

"Just a precaution."

"They want that list?"

"I believe so."

"Then why didn't you just hand it over to Atkins and let him deal with it?"

"One small problem. The list was stolen."

"At the ball? Why on earth would you take it there? Oh, Phil. You weren't going to try on a spot of blackmail yourself?"

"Don't be ridiculous." She'd be much more subtle than out-and-out blackmail. "From my room."

Bev's eyes rounded, her lips pursed, and Phil couldn't help but think of those dolls you won at the carnival. "You took a thief to your room?"

Phil sighed. "Bev, sometimes I think you've drowned your brain in martinis. He broke in, stole the list. Kissed me, which I didn't tell Detective Sergeant Atkins, and which I might add was the highlight of my trip so far, no offense. And left through the window."

"Good Lord. How exciting."

"It was, and now I know the list is to the key to this whole thing."

"And he took it?" Bev looked baffled.

"He did."

"Then how are we ever going to know who killed Reggie?"

"Because he didn't get the copy I made."

Phil rang for Tuttle and asked him to send Lily to her. She arrived promptly, looking as starched and trained as any lady's maid. Phil felt a little burst of pride. "Lily, get paper and a pen from the writing desk."

Lily brought several sheets of paper and a pen. Phil spread the sheets out side-by-side on the tea table. "Okay, let's see what we have here."

"It's pretty clear that the numbers at the top of each group are dates."

Bev bit her bottom lip. "A meeting? The social clubs meet once a week. Businesses, board meetings. Hell, the mah-jongg club."

"But don't they usually meet at the same time on the same day? Lily, see if you can find a calendar." Lily, who had just pulled up a chair, popped up.

"There's one in the top drawer of the writing table," Bev told her.

Lily rummaged in the overstuffed drawer and came back with a piece of cardboard with a picture of a cherubic girl in a frilly pink dress and bow holding a square of the current month.

Phil raised an eyebrow at Bev.

"Don't look at me. It was an advertisement for something, I don't remember what."

"Olson Plumbing," Phil read, and turned the frilly girl calendar facedown to find a calendar for the whole year on the other side. She looked at an earlier date from a month back. And next to it, an A, a P, and a B.

"Look at the dates. The last recorded one is tomorrow. The others are from earlier this year and presumably from last year." She looked more closely. "With a gap between November and April. Bev, when is racing season here?"

"From April through November." Bev looked at the sheet. Sat straighter, looked at Phil.

"You're right. Racing dates."

"And the initials might be a cartel of betting, perhaps?"

"The numbers after the initials might be how much they bet," Bev said. "My goodness, some of them chanced fortunes."

"But are these race dates? And if so, what are these initials after the dates? They're different from the names below." Sometimes two letters, sometimes three or four. Phil had originally thought they might stand for the leader or the coordinator. "Here's the date for tomorrow. And the initials BP—Belmont Park?"

"Where were the races last month?"

Bev frowned. "Let's see, the season started at Aqueduct."

"Aqueduct. That's it," Phil said, and wrote it next to that list.

She found another A from November and checked it off. "Is there a track with the initials SB?"

"Sheepshead Bay."

"Did Devil's Thunder run there?"

"I don't really remember."

"It was last September," Phil said.

"Oh, yes. He didn't. It was a heat wave, miserable, and Reggie and Henry scratched him. The purse wasn't that big. We went off to Newport to escape the weather. And he ran at Saratoga before that. Is there an S?"

Phil sighed. "No. What about J?"

"Jamaica."

"All these initials are racetracks."

"That makes sense." Bev stood, walked to the window and

back. "Everything about Reggie was the racetrack. I don't know. Maybe he was trying to get people to back him or something."

"Did he make book?"

Bev shrugged. "I don't have the slightest. Why would he? Bobby would know. Freddy wouldn't approve. He works in the mayor's office and has to worry about his reputation."

"I met the mayor the other night. Is he an avid horseman?"

"Yes, among other things."

Phil leaned on her elbows and contemplated the list. It was daunting, but she just needed to keep putting the pieces together until everything was in place and the puzzle was revealed.

"Bev, I saw a stack of old racing forms in the library."

Bev jumped up. "I'll get them."

She hurried out of the room and returned a moment later with her arms full.

She dumped them on the love seat next to Phil and brushed her hands off. "They smell like old cigars. So where do we begin?"

"With this month and work back."

The first date she looked for was fourth from the top and the race at Aqueduct.

She laid it out on the table, and Lily and Bev crowded to both sides to look over her shoulders.

"What are we looking for?" Bev asked.

"What C might be," Phil said, running her finger along the page. "See, A and C. The date, the weather good, first race, two-year-olds. Purse amount. No C's. It must be a horse or a horse's owner. There was a W. Curtis who owned a horse in the first race. The horse was named Roscoe. And he didn't win."

She moved to the next race . . . and the next.

"This is hopeless," Bev said. "What time is it? I'm ringing for tea."

"Eureka!" exclaimed Phil. "Sixth race, Charger. Won by a head on eight-to-one odds."

"Charger? Let me see that." Bev read the details. "I remember this. I wasn't there, but when Reggie got home he was really angry. I thought maybe he and that—well, I suppose I should be nice since she's in the hospital. I thought he and Mildred had a fight. But it was about a horse. Charger nosed out the favorite in the last few seconds.

"Now I wish I had paid attention. Let me think." Bev pulled the form toward her, ran her finger down the list of entered horses. Tapped the paper with her finger. "Lester. He was the favorite. Reggie said the jockey had pulled him short at the end."

"Good."

"That he pulled short?"

"No, I think we may have found our connection." Phil laid the form aside, riffled through a few more. The next date came up several forms later. Now that she knew what she was looking for, it took less time to find the next one. "JP. Not J. P. Morgan, as you might think, but Jamaica Racetrack. A horse named Pride edged out the favorite by a head."

Sheepshead Bay. Another also-ran eked out a victory.

It took a good half hour to decipher all the initials, but at the end Phil had a pretty clear picture of what the lists were.

"In all of these races, the favorite didn't win." Phil glanced at Bev.

"The favorites don't always win," Bev said. "And if you're thinking Reggie was planning to lose tomorrow's race, forget it. He would never let any of his horses lose on purpose. Reggie wanted to win. It was everything to him." Bev's eyes misted over.

"But with Reggie no longer here to oversee things . . ."

"Henry would never let that happen. He's the best trainer on the East Coast."

"What about Freddy or Bobby?"

"Freddy mainly deals with the business end. And I think he's more into cards and pool than horses. Bobby? You heard him. He really was Reggie's right-hand man. At least when it came to racing, wenching, and gaming."

Not much to recommend him, Phil thought. "Was he a successful prizefighter?"

Bev shrugged. "I have no idea. But he's not that old, so maybe his career was cut short."

Or maybe he was caught throwing fights and was forced to retire, Phil thought.

"Regardless, tomorrow's date and track are penciled in on the list. And since Devil's Thunder is favored to win, I think we should make plans to be at the racetrack early and make sure Rico isn't planning on pulling him short."

"He wouldn't!" Lily exclaimed. "Madam. My lady."

"Lily, sometimes people—"

"Aren't what they seem," Lily finished for her. "But some are." She hesitated. "Some are better."

"He may be under tremendous pressure. I believe these people can be very persuasive."

Bev cried out, "Oh, my God. Do you think they killed Reggie because he refused to let Devil's Thunder lose?"

"It's very possible." And Phil had a feeling that she wasn't the only one who thought so. People were after that list. Phil just hoped the man who had ended up with it was going to use it for good.

And she needed to figure out what to do with her copy of the list and the book. Because none of them would be safe until she either turned it over to whoever came to ask for it, or prove to him the list was truly destroyed. How on earth would she accomplish that? And would they be safe even then?

22

For the first time in as long as she could remember, Philomena Amesbury, Countess of Dunbridge, was awake before her maid came to rouse her. She felt like something was going to happen today. That the events that had occurred since her arrival in America would all soon come to a head.

And whether it spoke of tragedy or freedom, she was anxious to see it through. "Through" as in finished. She'd had enough of murder, jealousy, disloyalty, policemen; and if she might miss the strange incident of the mystery man in the night, well, it would be the price she would pay for getting on with her life.

So Lily, bringing in a tray of coffee, found her sitting at her dressing table, brushing out her own hair.

Phil expected Lily to comment on her early rising, but the girl merely set down the tray, poured out the coffee, and took the brush from her mistress's hand.

When her coiffure was finished and stuck with enough pins to keep it in place through the most vigorous drive to the track, Lily stepped back. "And what will madam be wearing to the track today?"

Phil smiled in spite of her preoccupation. "I see that Preswick has been continuing your training."

"Yes, my lady."

"A quandary. One generally dresses for the track. However today . . . I think the light blue lawn. Elegant enough for the clubhouse and not too much skirt if I must run for my life."

Lily went into the dressing room to fetch the dress and Phil sipped her coffee, wondering if she should have a plan or if this could possibly turn out to be merely an ordinary day at the races.

She stepped into the dress and turned for Lily to do the buttons. "You told Preswick that he is to accompany us today?"

"Yes, my lady. He is waiting downstairs."

"Excellent." Phil studied herself in the mirror. She was pleased by her appearance. Her dress was from the House of Worth; it fit perfectly and fell in soft folds to the floor. Phil reached down and grasped a handful of skirt. The fabric arced up easily and formed a graceful curve on her side. She dropped the skirt and the hem fell back into place. Really, the man was a genius.

She started when Lily appeared by her side.

"Do not worry, my lady. I will protect you with my life."

Phil swallowed. "Well, thank you, Lily, but let us hope that won't be necessary." She frowned pensively. "Do not do anything to jeopardize your own safety. Do you understand?"

At first Lily didn't answer.

"That is an order, Lily."

"Yes, madam."

"Then bring me my hat and let us go."

Preswick and Tuttle were waiting for them downstairs, both looking as butlery as ever, except that Preswick wore an oversized driving coat over his black suit. He held a spotless black bowler under one arm. Phil hoped he didn't insist on wearing it while they were driving. He would lose it for certain.

Cook had packed them a picnic. "In case the food out there at the track isn't up to snuff."

"As if it was a muddy track in the back of beyond and not the most elegant and exclusive park in the country," Bev whispered to Phil and then thanked Cook for her thoughtfulness.

They donned their dusters over their dresses, tied scarves over their hats and, at least on Phil's part, hoped for the best.

They were followed out of the house by Tuttle and several

other servants, carrying makeup cases, emergency supplies, and food and drink, leaving barely enough room for Preswick and Lily to crowd into the backseat. Bentley cranked up the Packard, and with a longing look at the travelers, waved them farewell.

They were early enough so the streets were clear except for early morning deliveries, and the trip took far less time than it had the week before. They went directly to the track and parked alongside several other motorcars in a flat, grassy field.

"You should have been here for the grand opening," Bev said as they removed their driving coats and Lily and Preswick unloaded the car. "There were so many automobiles and carriages, not to mention the trolleys and the railroad. What a nightmare."

Phil folded her gloves and slid them into her duster pocket. When she pulled out her hand, a square of paper was stuck to her finger. The candy wrapper she'd found on the auto's floor must have stuck to the pocket lining. She crumpled it, passed it over to Lily to dispose of and licked the peppermint off her fingers.

She frowned. "Bev, didn't you say Reggie never let Freddy drive the Packard?"

"Never let anyone but the drivers and me. Why?"

"Just curious." She was more than curious, though she resisted letting her mind go down the path that was beckoning.

"It is beautiful," Phil agreed, as they started across the lawn toward the entrance.

"It is, and I'm sorry that your first glimpse of it is through the clubhouse. The main entrance is quite spectacular. The Field and Turf Club is housed in this beautiful old mansion, and the walks are lined with . . ."

Phil let Bev prattle on. Indeed, the park was incredible from what she could see. Wonderfully landscaped with an impressive array of buildings.

They entered an underground walkway, a wide tunnel able to accommodate hundreds, where each footstep left an echo ringing in their ears.

"And on the left under those trees is the saddling paddock," Bev continued as they came out of the tunnel onto more grassy lawn and an iron gate. They walked around two buildings to another entrance, this one flanked by four large columns.

"And this is the clubhouse. Isn't it grand? I swear it rivals the best of the European courses."

It was an impressive three-story, light brick and limestone building more like a mansion than a viewing station. Two terraces stretched across the front, a perfect shady spot for watching the race.

They walked through the columns and up the steps.

"Do you mind if we drop Preswick and Lily off in the clubhouse, and then I think we should go directly to the stables to make sure things are running according to plan."

"You mean to make sure Devil's Thunder is fine."

"Yes."

Bev had ordered a private room, where they left Preswick to unpack opera glasses, parasols, and other paraphernalia that Bev swore they couldn't do without. Bev and Phil took Lily to the ladies' retiring room to repair their toilettes.

"You stick close to Preswick today, Lily," Phil said as Lily recurled tendrils around Phil's cheek. "I don't want to lose you in the crowd."

"Yes, my lady." Lily moved over to help Bev place an elaborate hat of plumes and jewels and braid over her coiffure.

"Very nice. That will be all," Phil said. "You and Preswick go find yourself some tea. He'll take proper care of you. Do not go down to the stables on your own."

Lily's eyes traveled upward as Phil knew they would, but the girl managed to stop them before it became a full eye roll.

"I am quite serious. Promise me. We don't know who we can trust."

"We can tr-r-rust R-r-rico."

"I hope we can. But best not to get him involved in anything that he isn't involved in. You know how the police are."

"Yes, my lady. They are r-r-r-ogues."

"Unfortunately, some are. Promise."

"Yes, my lady." Lily curtseyed, and after gathering up combs, brushes, atomizers, and pins, she withdrew.

"She's a gem," Bev said, admiring herself in the mirror. "If a little odd."

"Yes, and I thought she'd managed to get rid of that habit of rolling her *r*'s when upset."

"I hadn't noticed that before. Is she upset?"

"Aren't you?"

"Rather. I just can't believe that all this is happening."

They took an elevator, a novel experience for Phil, down to the first floor.

"The stables are this way," Bev told her. They passed between the track and the grandstand, an enormous building painted green and tan.

"It holds eleven thousand they say and has eateries and private boxes and all manner of things for the public. I've never actually been in it, nor in the field stand next to it. Reggie insisted on rubbing elbows with the elite during the actual races.

"The only time he came over here was to lay a bet. The bookmakers have a separate area under the grandstand. Can you imagine, there were over three hundred legitimate bookmakers here opening day. The hurdlers had to stand out in the weather."

"What an education I'm getting," Phil said, having to change her stride to keep up with Bev's suddenly quicker one. "What are hurdlers?"

"The ones who don't keep enough funds to actually pay out on winners and have to jump the fence to get away from angry bettors."

"Ha, too bad I didn't come to America years ago. What a wonderfully colorful atmosphere."

Bev sighed. "I still think we should have placed the money in the safety-deposit box on Devil's Thunder."

"Perhaps, but if it was illegally gained . . ." Or if Devil's Thunder was fated to lose the race . . . Phil was certain they were both thinking the same thing, though they were loath to admit it. And how on earth were they going to stop it?

Bev began walking faster. "The stables are up ahead. There are forty of them, all laid out in neat rows. They can accommodate up to nine hundred horses. Holly Farm horses are housed in one of the southeast stables."

Phil listened to her friend rattle on. She'd hadn't heard Bev wax so excitedly about anything since she'd learned they were going to have a male nude model for Monsieur André's art class. Though she imagined it might be nerves as well as enthusiasm.

They passed into a grid of white wooden buildings that must be the stables. A whole village of carefully laid out spacious stables with outside covered porticos where the horses could be exercised during inclement weather. Bev fell silent as her pace quickened and her urgency to get to Holly Farm's stables increased.

They passed several stables before they came to the one occupied by Holly Farm. Bev led the way through an entrance at one end of the rectangular building and into a wide aisle between two rows of stalls.

Phil could see Freddy and Henry talking at the far end. Henry looked up and saw them. Freddy turned and after a moment of surprise strode toward them.

"My goodness, this is a surprise. What are you doing here so early?"

"I just came to check on Devil's Thunder and the others. What are *you* doing here so early?"

"Doing absolutely the same. We should have coordinated our efforts. No need for us both to be here."

Henry had returned to the stall and Freddy pulled Bev aside. "Actually, I felt I needed to be here. Henry called to say Bobby has been skulking about. It may be nothing, but I don't trust him. He may be here out of habit, but he might be up to something. So I came out to help Henry make sure he doesn't get near the horses."

"You don't think he would hurt them?" Bev didn't wait for an answer, but brushed past him and headed toward Thunder's stall.

Freddy hurried after her. Phil hurried after him.

Henry had tethered Devil's Thunder to the back corner of his stall while he checked the horse's hocks.

"Is he okay?" Bev asked, peering into the stall.

Phil came up beside her and looked inside. The horse seemed to be fine, though it was hard to tell between the uneven lighting and Henry's body blocking her view.

Henry stood up and came over to the half door. "Everything is looking good. He's in fine fettle and ready to run. Just leave it to us." He turned back to his work.

"And did you settle on Rico as the jockey?" Bev persisted.

Henry mumbled something, but since he was facing the horse his answer was lost on them.

"He seems preoccupied," Bev whispered.

"I do get that impression," Phil said, looking around. Everything seemed normal.

Two stable boys passed so closely, sloshing water from heavy metal pails, that Freddy pulled Phil and Bev out of the way.

"Busy place during the races and dirty. I hope you didn't soil your frocks."

"Are you're saying we're a nuisance?" Bev asked.

"Not at all," Freddy said, "but the horses do get rather highstrung before a race and Henry likes to keep things as strictly to a routine as possible."

"I understand," Bev said. She took another look down the row of stalls. "We're leaving now, Henry."

Henry straightened up, pulled on the brim of his cap.

"Only three racing today?"

"Yes, ma'am. Devil's Thunder, Dander, and Filly's Cert. Scratched Carolina 'cause of her shins. We left her and Binkie's Boy back at the farm. I've got a couple of the boys putting them through their paces."

"Why isn't Binkie's Boy running?" Phil asked.

Henry straightened up. "We ran him at Jamaica last week. Giving him time off."

Jamaica last week, thought Phil. And could have kicked herself. She'd been looking for horses racing against Devil's Thunder. Was it possible that Reggie's other horses had been running in those races? She'd checked on Thunder but hadn't thought to check further. This investigation business was not as easy as Sir Arthur made it appear.

"Well, carry on," said Bev.

"Are you breakfasting at the clubhouse?" Freddy said. "I'll join you there later if I may."

"Please do. Is Marguerite coming out?" Bev asked.

"Not today. She's been afflicted with a headache for several days now. A brief respite of country air would do her good, but she says she'll wait for Newport."

"Hey, you there!" he called out to one of the boys. "Excuse me, ladies."

Bev and Phil watched him stride down the stall.

"He looks rather out of place here, doesn't he?" Bev said. "Neat as a pin as they say."

"Yes," Phil said, but she wasn't really paying attention. She wasn't thinking about murder, but how even now that Bev was the owner of these horses, the men still dismissed her as being in the way.

At the moment Bev was just a third wheel. But if she intended to keep the stables going, she'd have to take more interest in their day-to-day running.

As they were leaving, she saw two men talking in the shadow of one of the large oaks that shaded the grounds. Phil recognized

Rico, but when he looked up and saw her, the other man moved away out of viewing. In that second Phil could have sworn it was Bobby Mullins, and if he was talking to Rico who was riding Devil's Thunder today, he had to be up to no good.

It had been arranged the night before that once Phil and Bev were established in the clubhouse, Preswick and Lily should have a few hours off to amuse themselves. Phil had given Preswick money for the occasion, which he tried not to take, saying that he had plenty of coins saved up from his salary.

Phil had no doubt of that, the man hardly ever took his days off. Nonetheless, she ordered him to not only take the money but to treat himself and Lily, emphasizing that it might be the first entertainment that Lily had seen in a long time, if ever. Even Preswick's butler heart couldn't hold out against that one. He took the money. Now Phil would have to tell him to keep Lily from the stables and apprise him of the situation.

Phil and Bev had a delightful breakfast of omelets and fresh fruit, though Phil barely tasted it, she was so preoccupied with the coming day.

After breakfast they strolled in the gardens surrounding Manice mansion, where the Turf and Field Club made its home. It was a lovely garden and delightful to be out in the fresh air of the country. And yet Phil wasn't enjoying herself as she debated whether or not to tell Freddy that she'd seen Bobby and Rico together. But should she trust Freddy?

The thought stopped her right in front of an azalea bush. Is that why Reggie was dead? He'd trusted the wrong man? Or woman? He'd figured out that Bobby had been fixing the races and was going to fire him, or perhaps even testify against him?

Bobby might have killed Reggie to keep him from talking. He was a good friend of Mimi's. Maybe he knew about the lists. Perhaps he and Mimi had planned it together. Though that didn't make sense. Mimi was willing to sell the evidence. Perhaps because it didn't point to Bobby. There hadn't been a B.M. anywhere.

Because it hadn't happened yet? This might be the first time one of Reggie's horses was going to throw a race. And considering the excitement over the thoroughbred, there was a lot of money to be made. But then what did all those names on the list mean?

And if Bobby was involved, who was his accomplice in the stables? The missing Eddie? If he was missing and not dead. Or Rico. Rico had been willing to speak to her, but had he told the truth or had he been told what to say?

All she had was questions. Why hadn't she confided in John Atkins? How on earth did she propose to stop a fixed race and find a murderer on her own?

"Phil, if I'd known you were so partial to nature, I would have taken you to the botanical gardens."

"What? Oh, the azaleas, they're lovely, aren't they?"

"I guess. Though rather past their full bloom." Bev huffed a long sigh. "Oh, Lord, there is Mrs. Osbourne, in the most egregious platter hat with the fruit and pheasants. Maybe she won't—too late. She's seen us." Bev plastered on a smile, remembering to look sweet, slightly bewildered, but brave as a grieving widow should.

"Ah, Mrs. Reynolds and Lady Dunbridge. What a surprise to see you here."

"Yes, I thought the best way to honor Reggie's memory was to carry on what he loved best."

Phil watched in admiration as Bev kindly nodded through Mrs. Osbourne's condolences and the introduction of her two friends, both sporting hats larger even than Mrs. Osbourne's. Then Bev introduced them to Lady Dunbridge.

"She's been such a support in my grief," Bev said tearfully. "I don't know what I would have done without her. Now, you must forgive us, Mrs. Osbourne. It was so delightful to see you, but we promised to meet Reggie's cousin Freddy Beecham for a late breakfast. He's practically taken over running Reggie's business. Such a help."

"Is Marguerite here?" Mrs. Osbourne asked. "She was looking very unwell at the Langham's ball the other night. Didn't you think, Lady Dunbridge?"

"Rather pale, yes."

"Ah, well, perhaps she's finally in a family way? I know she was hoping for some little ones for a while now."

"Oh, she hasn't said. She's been concerned for me and I've been too selfish to ask about her." Bev, in a bit of unseen prestidigitation, produced a hankie and lifted it to her eye.

Mrs. Osbourne looked sympathetic. "Not at all, out of sadness may come some joy."

Her two friends murmured and nodded. The movement of their hats reminded Phil of an arcade game.

"I'm sure you'll return the favor when she needs you."

"Of course," Bev said. "So nice to see you."

"Delightful seeing you again, Mrs. Osbourne," Phil added. "And meeting you ladies." She nodded. They nodded. And she and Bev withdrew as quickly as they could without appearing to sprint across the garden.

"This is harder than I thought," Bev said. "The looks, the pretend sympathy, but really thinking that I should be home weeping into a soggy handkerchief. Hypocrites."

They didn't go back to the clubhouse right away but turned into a wide walkway lined by tall trees.

"It's like a vast park as well as racetrack," Phil said.

"Lovely, isn't it. When the cigar smoke, the shouting, the running back and forth to make bets get to be too much, it's nice to have a place to escape to."

Phil looked at her old friend. "Are you tiring of the fast life, Bev?"

Bev shrugged slightly. "Look where it got me."

"You're the owner of a successful racing stable."

"True. Maybe I'll retire to the country with my horses."

Phil laughed. "Not just yet."

"That's also true. We have to discover Reggie's killer first."

Phil slipped her arm in Bev's. "That's not what I meant at all." But they both knew it was true. None of them could get on with their lives until the killer was caught.

23

"I didn't place a penny on any of the races," Bev said as they made their way back toward the clubhouse.

"It's not too late," Phil said. "We can go mix with the hoi polloi beneath the grandstand seats."

"I suppose so. But it's just not the same without Reggie."

"I was thinking it would get us closer to the race."

"Oh, Phil, are you sure about this? How can we ever stop it, if Rico pulls short? And if we tell the judges, Holly Farm's reputation will be ruined. I need champagne."

By the time they reached the clubhouse, the bugle blared announcing the first race, and Phil and Bev hurriedly took their seats.

The horses were led from the paddock, parading past the crowd as they headed for the starting line, their jockeys clad in the colors of the individual stables.

Some went docilely, walked straight for the starting line without hesitation. Others danced, reared back with nostrils flaring, or balked altogether as the trainers pulled on their leads.

It took a bit of maneuvering before all were standing behind the line.

Below the clubhouse, people gathered along the rail in order to get a closer view and witness firsthand as the horses crossed the finish line. Bev reminded her that the horses would be starting at their right instead of left, running the "wrong way" around the track. To Phil that was the "correct" way, since in England the races were always held in a clockwise direction.

The tape was stretched across the track, the flag was raised, the jockeys crouched forward, knees bent as if they were about to soar over their horse's head. The flag sliced downward through the air and the race began.

Phil watched through her opera glasses as they thundered down the stretch, followed them into the first curve.

The spectators were all focused on the race, most quiet, but some urging their favorites on with yells and waving arms. A few became so animated that they looked as if they were trying to ride the horses themselves.

It was amazing to watch, the strong gleaming flanks of the horses as they rounded the turn, their power propelled by delicate ankles. The jockeys leaning as far forward as they might, looking like colorful birds that had alit briefly only to find a journey already in progress.

Bev had stood and watched intently as horses took the lead or fell behind. Phil was almost as entertained by her friend's absorption as she was by the race itself.

A few minutes later, it was over. The favorite passed over the finish line a good two lengths ahead of the nearest competitor.

Spectators below them crowded around the judges' stand to get a close look at the presentation of awards or hurried to collect their winnings or put money on the next race.

In the clubhouse, conversations took up where they'd left off, drinks were ordered, laughter abounded. At most of the tables, ladies and gentlemen were chatting among themselves and sipping on punch or champagne or tea, their fashion as varied as the jockeys' colors. The hats alone could rival Ascot.

There were a few faces Phil recognized from the ball or from the Tappington-Joneses' dinner. Arthur Tappington-Jones was talking to a group of men. Hilda Tappington-Jones was sitting with Mrs. Osbourne and her friends, and next to Hilda was Daniel Sloane.

Phil didn't see Herr Schimmer anywhere. But if he wasn't in the clubhouse, where was he? Actually, who might he be today? He could be anyone. Anywhere.

She also didn't see John Atkins, not that he would be a member of the clubhouse. She lifted her opera glasses and turned her attention to the rail, where men and women stood three or four deep as they prepared for the next race. She spotted Lily and Preswick crowded in among the crowd in front. Still no Atkins or anyone who might be Mr. X.

The hum of the crowd grew, and people began to return to their places as the next race was called. The names of horses and riders were placed on the result board in front of the clubhouse. The next heat of horses were paraded past the spectators to take their places for the next race.

The race began; Phil sat forward to watch. This race was almost neck and neck to the finish, when at the last minute a bay filly named Lady Linda pulled out a nose to cross ahead of a chestnut named Filodo.

Phil looked back to where Lily and Preswick had been standing. They were no longer there. She searched the surrounding area. Maybe they'd put a few dollars on the winner. That should make their day. She looked toward the grandstand and caught a glimpse of them, but they weren't going to the grandstand and they were not alone.

They were being pulled along by a boy. Phil lifted the opera glasses to get a better look. Not a boy, one of the jockeys.

Phil tried to see which one it was. It couldn't be Rico. There was one more race before the handicap-added race where Devil's Thunder was favored to win. Rico would already be dressed in his silks, making his way to the saddling paddock.

Sid? He was scheduled to ride Filly's Cert in the ninth. One of the others? And what could he possibly want with her servants?

Her first instinct was to go after them, but what could be amiss that Preswick couldn't take care of? Still, she trained her opera glasses on them as they moved farther away. They must be going to the stables. But why? What could be wrong that involved her two servants?

Phil craned her neck, but Preswick and Lily disappeared as the crowd swelled and traffic increased between the stands, the lawn, and the betting ring.

Bev handed Phil a glass of champagne. "Maybe we're wrong about this."

Phil took the glass, nodded to one of the ladies she'd met as she passed by their table. "Do you really think that?"

"I don't know. Why is all this happening? Why would Henry and the others jeopardize their jobs and their futures for one race?"

"Bev, I'm sorry, but you can't wish this away. "Your husband is dead, your main jockey is missing, and a murderer is still on the loose. Henry—or someone else—may not think he has a choice."

"But it might not have anything to do with murder. Just greed."

And if it was? If it turned out that Reggie's death actually had nothing to do with racing at all, they would return to Bev and Mildred Potts as suspects. And none of them could afford that.

The next post parade began at last.

Bev put down her champagne glass and picked up her field glasses. "Those are our colors, purple and gold. Embarrassingly regal, but that was Reggie for you. Do you see? There's Devil's Thunder. Number Eight."

Phil raised her opera glasses and leaned forward to get a better look. She scanned along the horses until she found Thunder. He was certainly a beauty, but among all those other prime specimens, he didn't stand out as much as Phil had expected. Then she found the jockey. He was looking the other way, but even from where she sat, even with the distance, and through the lens of the opera glasses, she could tell it wasn't Rico.

"Bev—"

"Hush. Come on, Thunder," Bev breathed.

They weren't even up to the starting tape and already Bev was fixated. So was Phil, but for another reason.

The jockey wasn't Rico, or any of the other jockeys she'd seen at the farm. Had they brought in an outsider at the last minute?

"Bev, who is the jockey?"

"Rico, I presume."

"Look again."

Bev raised her binoculars. Lowered them again. "I think . . . that's Eddie Johnson. But they'll arrest him for sure, once the race is over, if not before. And look, there's Freddy. At the rail. Do you think he knows? He really should have warned us."

And where were Lily and Preswick? Phil scanned the crowd, stopped, came back to where Freddy and Arthur Tappington-Jones stood at the rail. They were facing each other, not the track. Tappington-Jones was gesticulating. Freddie was fumbling with something in his hand.

His hand came to his mouth, then he crumpled something and it dropped to the ground. One of his dratted peppermints.

The peppermints. Reggie never let him drive the Packard. With sudden blinding clarity, she knew what he had done.

"I'll be back directly," Phil said.

"But the race is starting. Where are you going?"

Phil just waved; she was walking as quickly as possible toward the exit.

She reached the rail near where Freddy had been standing, but he'd moved closer to the finish line. The horses thundered past her on the first turn.

Keeping one eye on the track, she sidled closer to the two men. She didn't have a plan; she just knew she couldn't let Freddy out of her sight.

Whether Eddie won the race or not, they were bound to arrest him before he left the track. He'd go to jail if she was wrong.

The horses were coming around the last turn into the straightaway. Freddy and Tappington-Jones were standing shoulder to shoulder, eyes fixed on the approaching horses.

Phil could see the purple and gold colors in the lead, and excitement raced through her. "Come on, Devil's Thunder," she said sotto voce. "Win this for Bev."

Thunder crossed the line easily, and the crowd erupted in cheers. Phil stuttered to a stop. He'd won. He hadn't lost. Rico hadn't pulled him short. *Stupid*, because Rico wasn't riding him.

Had the plan been foiled?

Freddy was standing totally still, his hands gripping the rail, staring at the finish line almost as if he couldn't believe what had just happened.

Tappington-Jones gave Freddy a look so full of malice that Phil couldn't have missed it even at the distance they were separated. He moved in closer and Freddy cowered back.

Tappington-Jones strode away. Freddy just watched him, then turned from the rail, weaving fast through the crowd, mindless of those he jostled and pushing those who didn't move quickly enough out of his way.

Phil didn't think twice about following him. She held out little hope that he was headed to the betting ring to collect his winnings with the rest of the crowd. He didn't look like a man who had just won. He looked like a man who had just been threatened and might be running for his life.

Pieces of information were beginning to fall into place, but most were still swirling around in her mind. They would have to wait. Phil couldn't concentrate on the puzzle because keeping Freddy in sight was becoming more and more difficult as people surged toward the grandstand.

For a frantic moment, Phil lost sight of him, but she was pretty sure where he was going. She kept moving toward the stables.

She spied him up ahead. Freddy began to run. She had no choice; she sped after him.

He turned down the alleyway between two stable rows. And Phil slowed down in order not to be seen if he turned around. She intended to follow this to its conclusion no matter what it was.

Freddy was two buildings ahead when a man stepped out of a side pathway in front of her. Phil threw herself back against the wall, out of sight.

Not just any man. It was Herr Schimmer. She hadn't seen him all day, until now. It looked like she might have an ally after all. Or an additional enemy.

She quickly unpinned her hat and snatched it from her head, letting it fall to the ground, then she pulled back her hair and carefully peeked around the building.

Freddy had reached the far end of the pathway; Herr Schimmer was half a building behind him.

Phil took off after them, then was stopped as several horses were led from the stable blocking her view of the two men. She tried to get around them, but they seemed intent on barring her way.

A hand grasped her elbow. "This way." She was being propelled along and pushed into an empty stall.

Damn and her hatpin was on the straw-covered ground along with her hat.

She whirled around and let out a sigh of relief. "Detective Sergeant Atkins. I've never been so glad to see you in my life."

"The pleasure is mine. What the hell are you doing?"

"Following Freddy Beecham, who is headed to the stables, I assume to accost whoever substituted Eddie Johnson in the race. Or to kill him."

"What?"

"Eddie Johnson just rode Devil's Thunder in that race."

"We know this, and he will most likely be arrested before he even dismounts."

"Eddie didn't kill Reggie."

"Is that why you are following Beecham?"

"Don't be dimwitted. They planned to put in another jockey to ride Devil's Thunder. I think to make him throw the race. But Eddie somehow managed to get on that horse and win. This isn't over yet. Plus my maid and butler may be in danger. So I suggest you don't dally."

She slipped past him, and finding the horses and men gone, she lifted her skirts and ran.

She rounded the corner to the Holly Farm stable and ran headlong into Rico, who was running toward them.

"Hurry, miss. He's going to kill Eddie."

"Freddy?" Phil demanded.

"Yes."

"Where is Lily?"

"In the stable. Come please." Rico turned back to the stable.

"Go back and wait at the clubhouse," Atkins ordered.

"Don't thwart me. I just got this maid trained." Phil ran after Rico.

"Dammit, Lady Dunbridge." A few strides and he'd caught up to her.

Rico didn't slow down when they reached the stable but ran headlong into the interior just as a shot rang out. Phil followed but came to an astonished stop. Eddie was lying on the stable floor. Two men were scuffling, fighting over a pistol that waved wildly in the air. One of them was Freddy Beecham and the other was—

"Preswick?"

"My lady." Preswick dropped his fists as he automatically assumed butler mode. And in that second, Freddy grabbed the gun and turned it on him.

"Crazy old man," he cried. "I was stopping this murderer from getting away."

Behind him, Devil's Thunder calmly looked over the half wall. How had he gotten back to the stable so quickly? Surely they had a presentation ceremony after the biggest race of the day.

Atkins skidded to a stop beside Phil, his police revolver in his hand.

"Mr. Beecham, put down the pistol and go stand over there

by the empty horse stall." Atkins indicated the space opposite Devil Thunder's stall and knelt by the motionless Eddie.

"You killed him," Rico cried. "You wanted Eddie to throw the race and he wouldn't. He was going to tell."

"Balderdash," Freddy said. "These boys were in cahoots to throw the race. When Reggie refused, they killed him."

"Eddie isn't dead," Atkins said. "Preswick, can you manage to run out and find a constable? Tell him to ring for an ambulance and send in some additional men."

"But of course." Preswick straightened his tie and trotted out of the stable.

Phil looked around. Several stable boys had taken cover in one of the empty stalls. Now their heads peered over the top of the stall door like ducks in a shooting gallery. Herr Schimmer was nowhere to be seen, but there were stairs going up to a loft where the jockeys stayed when they were at the track. Was he up there listening?

As far as she could figure out, they were at an impasse. Did Eddie kill Reggie? Why was Tappington-Jones so angry at Freddy? And why had Freddy run straight here and shot Eddie, who wouldn't have been able to run far wearing shiny purple and gold racing colors.The sound of hoofs . . . Bev appeared in the doorway leading Devil's Thunder.

Phil's eyes widened. If Bev was leading Devil's Thunder, the Devil's Thunder in the stall had to be . . . Binkie's Boy?

Bev pulled up short. "What is going on here? Where's Henry? I had to bring Thunder back by myself. Where's Eddie? Oh, my goodness. What's wrong with him? Oh, my God."

Bev screamed. Devil's Thunder, the one she was leading, tossed his head and reared. Freddy grabbed Bev. But instead of pulling her out of harm's way, he wrenched her arm and pulled her against his chest.

Atkins moved, but Freddy pressed the pistol to her head. "Stay back. Just stay back, and no one will get hurt."

"Rather late for that, don't you think, Beecham? Don't make it any worse. Put the gun down."

Freddy shook his head. "It wasn't my fault."

"All you and Henry and Sid," Rico said.

The gun barrel moved from Bev's head to Rico.

Rico threw himself to the side as the pistol went off. And with the explosion came a curdling cry from the rafters as Bobby Mullins hurtled through the air, his beefy form swinging from a bale wench. He hit Freddy full force, knocking him to the ground. Before he could recover, Bobby yanked him to his feet and hit him so hard that it knocked him into Devil's Thunder, who shied. Freddy lost his balance, staggered back, and fell on his butt, just as Thunder's right fore hoof came down on his leg.

Freddy screamed. Atkins grabbed Thunder's rein and backed him away.

So the man knows his way around a horse, Phil thought. *Impressive.*

Bobby wasn't finished, but Atkins grabbed him by the coat collar as he rushed the writhing man and pulled him back. "Stop it or I'll throw you in jail just for the hell of it."

"He killed Reggie!" Bobby said. "He killed him and then fired me so I couldn't stop him cheating."

Bev had started toward Freddy but stopped. "Freddy? Is it true?"

Freddy turned his face away.

"Freddy?" Bev lunged for him. This time it was Phil who grabbed her gown to stop her.

"I could kill you. I could—" Bev succumbed to tears.

Freddy stretched out a beseeching hand. "I didn't do it. I didn't kill Reggie. I swear it, Bev, you've got to believe me."

"Liar," Bev cried. "How could you? Reggie was good to you."

"I didn't," Freddy sobbed.

Phil could almost believe him, he sounded so sincere. Then his eyes flicked toward the stalls. Not to the one where Binkie's

Boy was calmly munching on a pail of feed, but to the stall where the stable boys were cautiously watching.

All little men. Jockeys were small. Freddy was tall and overweight.

How could she have been so obtuse?

The driver had killed Reggie all right, disguised as Eddie, with Eddie's duster planted to be found by the police. Or possibly even planted by them.

Freddy could never have fit into the diminutive jockey's driving coat, but someone else could.

"Please, please you've got to believe me."

"He's telling the truth for once," Phil said, pushing down her nausea and disbelief. All eyes turned to her. "He was an accessory, probably even planned it, but he didn't actually shoot Reggie." Phil turned to face the row of stable boys. "Did he, Marguerite?"

There was an audible gasp.

Slowly, one of the "boys" straightened. Pulled off his hat, and a braid of long golden blond hair fell over one shoulder.

Marguerite Beecham glanced toward her husband rocking in pain on the floor. "Really, Freddy, can't you do anything right?"

She swung the stall door open and stepped out, revealing a small pistol held in her delicate hand.

"You?" asked Bev, barely above a whisper. "I don't understand."

Marguerite exhaled a weary sigh. "Of course you don't, dear Bev. We're broke. Freddy is in debt. Gambled every last penny. Didn't you, Freddy? We were going to lose everything, the house, our place in society. Such as it is. I'd never be able to hold my head up again. They promised if Freddy would just fix this one race, they'd forgive everything and we could breathe again at last.

"One little race. And you couldn't even do that right, could you, Freddy?"

Bev's face twisted. "No, Marguerite. No."

Atkins roused himself. "Put the gun down, Mrs. Beecham."

"Do as he says," Bev pleaded. "Don't make it any worse."

"Worse? It couldn't get worse."

Bev raised both fists. "I hate you. You won't get away with it."

Marguerite laughed. "Don't you think I know that? Just think of the scandal." She lifted the pistol to her head and pulled the trigger.

The sound ricocheted through the stable. The horses shied, someone screamed, and the others stood rooted where they stood.

Then Atkins broke and rushed to kneel by Marguerite's body. He stood almost immediately. Shook his head.

Bev sobbed, Freddy hid his face in his hands, and Preswick returned with several policemen, who quickly secured the prisoner.

"Rico," Phil said, "where is Lily?"

"She's upstairs, guarding the prisoners."

"What prisoners?" Atkins asked.

"Henry and Sid."

"Them, too?" asked Phil.

"And how do you fit into this?" Atkins asked Rico.

"Me? I helped stop them."

"By harboring a murder suspect?"

Rico sucked in his breath.

"But not the murderer," Phil reminded him. "Really, Detective Sergeant. It's only fair to listen to his story before you make a judgment." Phil rushed over to the stairs, calling out, "Lily, are you all right up there?"

A faint, "Yes mad—my lady."

Phil hiked up her skirts and fairly ran upstairs and found herself in a loft with several narrow beds and Henry and Sid, both tied and gagged, Sid dressed in nothing but his long johns, and Lily holding them at bay with her stiletto.

Phil heard a flurry of new arrivals downstairs, John Atkins barking orders, then heavy footsteps on the stairs.

Phil motioned Lily to put her knife away. Lily returned it beneath her skirts in one graceful movement, just as John Atkins reached the second floor.

"It wasn't us," Henry said right away. "We didn't have anything to do with it."

"Pfft." Lily said. "Guilty as sin."

Atkins lifted an eyebrow and nodded to her, then bellowed down the stairs, "I need a couple of you men up here."

Phil looked around. In the excitement, she'd forgotten the one person who was conspicuously missing. She'd seen him following Freddy.

So where was he now? And whose side was he on?

24

Two constables dragged Henry and the half-clothed Sid to their feet and took them downstairs. After an intent but unreadable look at Phil, Atkins gestured for her and Lily to precede him down the stairs.

They were greeted with a scene straight out of a stage melodrama.

The handsome wounded hero lying on the floor while his sweetheart knelt beside him, wringing her hands over his fate. Only in this case the hero was a villain and Bev looked like she wanted to wring his neck. Fortunately, there was a guard standing at Freddy's head.

Nearby, the villain's villainous wife's body was covered by a saddle blanket.

Eddie was still on the ground, but sitting up. The gold of his left sleeve had turned deep red, and Preswick was wrapping a white bandage, formerly the trim of Bev's petticoat, around his arm. Phil recognized the Valenciennes lace. Rico was coming out of a stall where the real Devil's Thunder was now being rubbed down by a stable boy.

The constable pushed Henry and Sid against the wall. "What do you want to do with these two?"

Atkins slowly looked from one to the other.

Bobby snatched up his hat where it had fallen and pushed it back on his head. "It was Freddy. I oughta—"

Atkins stretched out his arm. "You oughta cool down or I'll take you in, too."

"You know they won't arrest Beecham. He works for Tammany. He's in deep. Somebody oughta teach him a lesson."

"But not you, Bobby."

Phil moved up to him. "Not Bobby, Detective Sergeant, but you. You know you have to do it soon, or they'll take the case from you and sweep it all under the proverbial carpet."

Atkins turned a formidable frown on her.

"Don't get all huffy, Detective, you know it's true."

One side of his mouth tightened.

A smile, perchance?

"Detective sergeants don't get huffy, Lady Dunbridge. I really can't tell you what we do. It would be unfit for a lady's ears." Then he cocked his head. "I know you're dying of curiosity and quite frankly so am I. And you are perfectly correct. Once these people leave my jurisdiction, it will be out of my hands."

"Shall I make tea?" Preswick said. "I believe there is a kitchen and provisions upstairs."

Atkins just looked at him, possibly dumbfounded.

"An excellent butler," Phil told him. "That would be lovely, Preswick. Lily?"

Lily curtseyed and followed Preswick back up the stairs.

So while Preswick made tea, Freddy groaned on the ground and Eddie told his story. It was much the same as Rico had relayed to them at the farm, with a few more damning details.

"I went in to drive for Mr. Reggie. He liked to have a driver . . ." He cut a glance at Bev. "Sometimes. But when I got to the house that morning, Mr. Freddy was waiting for me outside. He said Mr. Reggie had changed his mind, that he wouldn't be needing me, but he would need my driving coat.

"I thought that sounded funny 'cause Mr. Reggie had his own driving coats, several of them. But . . ." Eddie shrugged, winced.

"You weren't in a position to say no."

"No, sir. Then he paid me a hundred bucks and told me to enjoy myself. Which I did, which was stupid. I know that now, 'cause when I got back to the stables all hell had broken loose."

Atkins kept a steady gaze on Eddie. "Then how did your bloody clothes end up in your bunk at the farm?"

"He was framed!" yelled Bobby.

"Thank you, Mr. Mullins."

"They weren't there before Mr. Freddy and Bobby here met at the farm," Rico said. "Then the police came and found them."

"Hmmm," John Atkins said. Phil knew just what he was thinking.

Atkins turned to Bobby.

"Don't look at me. I didn't know what Beecham was up to. I was Reggie's right-hand man. I wouldn't've never hurt him. But him"—Bobby jabbed a beefy finger at Freddy—"they musta got to him."

"Who is they?"

Bobby squeezed his lips together, cut his eyes toward the other policeman.

He was afraid to speak, afraid that it would get back to the corrupt powers that be. Did that include Mr. Tappington-Jones? And how many others? Phil bet Reggie's last list would tell her.

And Mr. X? How did he fit into all of this?

"What is it, Lady Dunbridge?" Atkins asked. "Did you think of something?"

"Uh, no." She wasn't quite willing to share what she was thinking. Mr. X was obviously not an Austrian attaché or an old-book collector. She didn't know what he was, but villain or hero, she wasn't ready to share him . . . not even with John Atkins.

Bev marched over to Freddy. "I hope you . . . you despicable piece of . . ." Bev stepped back and kicked his broken leg.

Freddy howled.

"And your wife." She kicked him again and no one tried to stop her. "You killed my husband. Your cousin. Your friend. A man who helped you, introduced you to people you'd never meet on your own, loaned you money when you'd lost at cards. He was good to you."

Phil put a supporting arm around Bev. Even if she didn't need it, it would serve just as well to restrain her.

"Good to me? He was a stingy bastard. How can you defend him? He cheated on you. Spent your money. He never intended you to have the stable or his money. He was going to leave you."

"So you and Marguerite killed Mr. Reynolds in order to fix the race," Phil said. "Why not just let him go to South America?"

"Lady Dunbridge," Atkins warned.

She cocked her head. "Sorry, I didn't mean to butt in, Inspector Detective Sergeant."

He let that pass, as she knew he would. "Well, Freddy?"

"I'm not saying anything until I see my lawyer."

Atkins raised an eyebrow. "Fine, if you live that long. Racketeering has a very long arm. And so does accessory to murder."

Freddy tried to push himself up on his elbow but fell back with a groan. "You have to protect me. They'll kill me."

The same thing that Mimi had said. That day Phil had thought she meant Reggie's admirers, now she knew she'd been talking about the men the list could indict. And they had almost succeeded. A sobering thought.

They were bound to find out Phil had the book, even though the lists had been stolen. And now she and Bev would be targets. She would have to do something to remedy that situation.

"They wouldn't leave me alone. I was desperate." Freddy's voice broke with a sob.

"You're not only a traitor and a murderer," Bev cried, "you're a spineless worm."

"Hurrah, Bev," Phil said under her breath.

"And I hope they hang you for it."

Before Phil could interject "electric chair," Bev turned back. "And furthermore . . . why the hell did you use my pistol? So you could frame me for Reggie's murder? You lowdown—"

"I expect," Atkins said, coming to her other side, "if you were convicted of murder, you wouldn't be entitled to the inheritance, and Freddy boy here, being next of kin, would. And that would leave him in a position to continue fixing races for, let's just say, certain members of society."

What little color was left in Freddy's face completely drained away. "I don't . . . know what you're talking about . . . I need a doctor . . . I need protection."

"The hell you do," Bobby said. "I oughta kill you myself. I'm a witness. You tried to kill Eddie here because he wouldn't throw the race. You framed him for murder. Then you talked Henry into doing a switcheroo."

Bobby slapped his knees. But Phil didn't think it was out of laughter. Bobby Mullins could easily kill Freddy with his bare hands. A handy man to have on your side.

It *was* laughter. "Damn, we outfoxed you. Pulled a double switch. Thanks to Rico and the little lady and your butler, ma'am.

"I say we leave him right here. I'm sure he has friends who will be out looking for him soon. They can take care of him."

"No! No! You can't leave me here."

An ambulance brigade burst into the room. Atkins motioned to one of the constables. "Go with them and have them take Mr. Beecham straight to the Tombs infirmary. Let's see how he likes seeing how the other half lives."

The constable's eyes widened.

"I'll clear it with your captain. And give you train fare home."

"Yes, sir."

"And, Constable, don't let him escape."

"No, sir."

"Eddie, do you need—?"

"No, sir, I'll get the vet to look at me later."

"But Eddie," Bev said, "you need to be looked at by a proper physician. I want you to have the best of care. You're my head jockey."

"I believe," Atkins interjected, "that he is in no danger and will feel more comfortable around people he can trust."

"You mean someone might try to—?" asked Bev.

Atkins gave her a look that said "stop talking."

And for once, Bev did.

"Higgins, you and this constable here take these other two over to the Maria and accompany them to the precinct for questioning."

"Yes, sir. Come on, you two." Higgins and the constable hauled Henry and Sid out the door.

"And now, Lady Dunbridge, I have a few questions for you."

"Indeed, Detective Sergeant. Won't you come into my parlor?" She gestured to the stairs, where overhead she could hear footsteps of Lily and Preswick making tea.

The stable boys were left in charge of grooming Devil's Thunder with the added instructions of "guard him with your life, boyo-s," from Bobby.

Preswick served tea in an assortment of mugs while everyone sat around a rickety wooden table and Lily served cheap and slightly stale biscuits from a chipped plate.

"Bobby," Bev said, "we must get a better grade of biscuits for our boys. Make a line item or whatever you do for that."

Bobby grinned, for the first time Phil had seen. He had more than one missing tooth. "Yes, ma'am."

"To begin with," Atkins said, accepting one of the biscuits and looking dubiously at it, before putting it down. "How did your maid and butler become involved in this capture?"

"You'd best ask them," Phil said. "When I saw them earlier, they were watching the race."

Atkins motioned Preswick and Lily over. "Preswick, would you like to begin?"

Preswick glanced at Phil.

"Preswick, that was not actually a request."

"Sir." Preswick straightened to his mightiest butler demeanor. "Lily and I were watching the race when Rico here"—he paused to nod over at Rico, who was sitting next to Eddie, who was lying on one of the cots—"comes up to us and says they've got terrible trouble at the stables and could we please come."

"We had to do it," interjected Lily.

"Of course you did," Phil said. "We always help those in need." She smiled at the detective.

He smiled back—ironically.

"When we arrived," Preswick continued, "Rico brought us not to the stables but to the field where the transport wagons are parked. Rico said Henry had scratched him from the race and was replacing him with that Sid person. That's when he realized that they weren't planning to race Devil's Thunder at all."

"Because Sid couldn't keep his seat on Thunder," Bev said.

Silver Blaze, thought Phil. Mr. X had guided her toward the answer because he needed her help to get inside information. But where was he?

"He was here," Lily whispered as if reading her thoughts.

Phil looked a question.

"Your mystery man, with the beard. He made Bobby swing down on the rope." Lily grinned. "He didn't want to do it. But he wouldn't let me. He said to thank you for the list."

"Where did he go?"

Lily shrugged. "He just left . . . like a spirit."

"Is that correct, Rico?" Atkins demanded.

Phil brought her attention back to the story.

"Yes, sir. Me and Mr. Bobby got a plan, but we needed more help to make it work."

Atkins narrowed his eyes at Mullins.

"Perfectly legit," Bobby said. "Devil's Thunder's name is in the program and Devil's Thunder ran. And I substituted Eddie at the last minute. Weighed him in and everything. All aboveboard."

"Uh-huh," Atkins said, but he looked impressed.

"But Sid was wearing the only set of colors we could get to, so we had to, uh, appropriate them. And we had to get Henry out of the way so we could substitute Thunder for Binkie's Boy. That's when Rico had this idea that Lily and Mr. Preswick here would help.

"After that, it was a piece of cake. I gotta tell ya, your ladyship, these two are a mightily fearsome team."

"Indeed."

"I sent the stable boys out and the rest as they say is history." Bobby broke into a full snaggletoothed grin.

"History? I would like to hear it, if you don't mind," Atkins said.

"Oh, yeah." Bobby told them how they'd overtaken Henry, relieved Sid of his colors, and stashed the two men upstairs with Lily as guard. Then they brought in Devil's Thunder from the transport wagon and saddled him. Rico just had time to attach his number and get him to the paddock in time for the post parade.

"I was sweatin', I can tell ya," Bobby said. "And he won like I knew he would even with all the rushing around. And I knew that was gonna make some folks awful mad. So I handed Thunder over to Mrs. Reynolds here to accept the purse and hightailed Eddie back to the stables to hide. I went upstairs to check on Lily and the prisoners, and that's when I heard the commotion downstairs. I looked down and Freddy was fighting Preswick here, who held his own pretty damn well.

"It was touch and go, but in the confusion I jumped on the stall half wall, grabbed the bale wench, and knocked down Freddy. I'm still pretty agile, if I do say so myself."

Phil thought his entrance had more resemblance to a swinging bear than an acrobat, but she would never say so.

Next to her, Lily snorted.

"Thank you, Bobby, for the clarification. And now, Lady Dunbridge, how did you find your way here in time for the grand finale?"

"Sheer luck. When the race started, I noticed that Rico wasn't riding and I also noticed that my servants, who had been standing at the rail at the start, were no longer there. I went down to find them. Instead I saw Freddy standing at the rail with Mr. Tappington-Jones."

Atkins blinked at that, though he showed no other surprise.

"When Devil's Thunder won, instead of being elated, Freddy seemed angry. Tappington-Jones certainly was."

"And how could you tell this at such a distance?"

"My opera glasses, of course. I'd been watching the race through them. I believe that Tappington-Jones may have threatened Freddy, because Freddy stepped back and then turned and almost ran in the direction of the stables. And I—I believe the phrase is 'smelling a rat'—followed."

"A rat. You smelled a rat," Atkins repeated incredulously.

"Actually, it was a peppermint."

Atkins took a controlled breath. She hurried on. "I'd found a candy wrapper in Reggie's auto. Something your men failed to find, I might add. Reggie never let Freddie drive it. And when I saw Freddy drop his candy wrapper on the ground while he was watching the race, it suddenly made sense."

"Of course it did. A candy wrapper."

But she had forgotten, much to her chagrin and a near fatal outcome, that Marguerite was also an avid peppermint enthusiast. Never mind, it had come out all right after all.

"And I might have been soon enough to prevent Eddie from being shot if you hadn't stopped me. Why were you following me? Or was it Freddy you were following?"

"You. And I have to thank you. I didn't see Freddy from where I was standing."

"But you did see me."

"It isn't often that you see an English countess, with her skirts lifted, racing down the lawn at a racetrack. I couldn't resist."

"Well, we're lucky that it all ended as well as it did."

"Ended for you and Mrs. Reynolds, hopefully, but just beginning for Freddy Beecham."

They soon broke up. A doctor had been found by one of the stable boys, and while he examined Eddie, the rest of them descended the stairs.

Atkins turned to Bev. "I'll visit in a day or two, if I may, when I receive more news about Mr. Beecham and the state of the investigation."

"But of course, Detective Sergeant Atkins. I'll be looking forward to your visit."

Phil resisted the impulse to roll her eyes. Lily didn't resist at all, and Phil almost laughed out loud.

"Bobby, make yourself available."

"I'll be at Holly Farm," Bobby said, and dragged his much maligned bowler from his head. "That is if Mrs. Reynolds wants me to stay on."

"Stay on?" Bev said. "You're my manager and you'd better start looking around for a new trainer. I don't want Henry or Sid back on the premises."

"Yes, ma'am."

"Now, if that's settled, I'd like to get back to the city. I think champagne is in order."

They walked back to the clubhouse, packed up their things, and headed for the Packard. Bev walked on one side of Phil and Lily on the other while Preswick walked behind carrying the hamper, the blankets, and other paraphernalia. Lily looked over her shoulder and ran back, took some pillows and a frilly tablecloth from his arms and raced back.

Phil looked a question at her.

Lily shrugged. "He looked silly, and besides he is too old to carry so much."

"He certainly didn't look old this afternoon."

"No, this afternoon he was a hero. But do not tell him I said so."

"I wouldn't think of it," Phil said, and put her arm in Bev's. "Champagne is definitely in order."

25

John Atkins appeared the next afternoon.

"We've learned much more since I saw you last," he said.

"Freddy confessed to everything?"

"Oh, yes."

Phil tried not to think about the electric chair waiting for him in Sing Sing.

"He was more than willing to tell all once he was offered a lesser sentence, though I don't see what protection he could possibly expect in prison, where he most certainly will be going.

"I know you are both eager to see the end of this and I doubt that either of you will have to testify. Basically, Mr. Beecham got in heavy debt to certain people who told him they'd call it even if he could fix the Devil's Thunder race. And if he didn't, they'd call in his debts and ruin him . . . or worse.

"He knew Mr. Reynolds would refuse."

"He did?" Bev asked hopefully.

"Yes. Evidently Reggie was honest . . . . at least when it came to the track."

"See, Phil, I told you."

"Yes, dear." Phil didn't dare look up and catch Atkins's eye.

"Reggie wouldn't budge, so Beecham brought in a thug to persuade him. But when he threatened Reggie, Reggie pulled out a pistol from the desk, your pistol, and shot him.

"Beecham panicked, convinced Reggie that 'they'—and we still don't know who they are—would kill Reggie to get their way and said his only way to survive was to flee.

"They set it up to look like a burglary, a falling-out of thieves, if you will. Beecham promised to get rid of the gun and take care of the police investigation. He told Reggie to take Mimi and go to South America. Beecham would stay in the States and send his horses down when he'd settled somewhere and was ready to start breeding again."

Phil couldn't help it—she let her eyes roll to the ceiling.

"Exactly," Atkins agreed.

"Then when Eddie arrived to drive them to the docks to meet the SS *Oceanic,* Freddy intercepted him and sent him on his way. He planned to dress in Eddie's coat, goggles, and hat."

"But they're much too small," Phil interjected.

"Enter the dutiful wife, who was the perfect size for them. They knew Mr. Reynolds was carrying a suitcase of money, which Mrs. Beecham handed off to her husband while Mr. Reynolds was inside Miss Potts's apartment.

"And now here is something I'm sure one of you can elucidate for me. There is no evidence of any money in the Beechams' possession."

"Which probably means, Detective Sergeant," said Phil, "that it is back in the possession of its owner."

Atkins held up his hand. "Let us agree to leave it there."

"Indeed."

"But how did they manage it?" Bev asked.

"When they were at the docks, Mrs. Beecham took the opportunity to leave the auto, ostensibly to clear the way, but she doubled back, shot Reggie as he was getting out of the car—according to Miss Potts—to go look for his driver. Reggie fell back against Mimi, obstructing her view, and Mrs. Beecham disappeared into the crowd before anyone realized what had happened.

"Then later Freddy hid Eddie's clothes back at the stables where he knew they'd be found," Phil said.

"The villain," Bev said.

"So the broken library window was actually . . . Freddy returning the pistol to frame Bev?" Phil concluded.

Atkins nodded. "He didn't even have to break in. Just tossed it though the broken pane and left. Dastardly, to be sure."

It certainly was, thought Phil.

Atkins left soon after that. He hadn't asked about any lists, which Phil could only assume meant he didn't know about them. And quite frankly, he was safer without the knowledge. Now what was she going to do to save herself and Bev?

When Phil came downstairs for breakfast the next morning, Bev was already eating, and Daniel Sloane was sitting next to her, nursing a cup of coffee. He stood when Phil entered.

"There you are, Phil. Get yourself some breakfast and come hear the news."

Phil helped herself from the sideboard and sat down.

"Father brought the morning papers. Show her, Papa."

Daniel Sloane opened the paper to the second page and handed it to Phil. "I managed to keep Reggie's name out of most of them, but I'm afraid Freddy's name is front and center."

A notice that Freddy had been arrested for race fixing and murder. Phil read on, then looked up. "'His wife, distraught at hearing of her husband's perfidy, took her own life'?"

"Well, no need to drag her family through the muck," Sloane said. "It will be bad enough for them."

"But read the article below it," Bev said.

It was a small paragraph stating that Mr. Tappington-Jones had been taken in by the authorities for questioning concerning horse race fixing. Phil wondered what authorities, certainly not Sergeant Becker.

"This is very unusual. I don't know if you are aware, Philomena, but Tappington-Jones is fairly high up in the Tammany organization."

"I didn't. But if he's been arrested . . ."

"Not arrested yet, but the mere fact that they actually brought him in for questioning bodes ill for many of his associates. Heads will fall."

"Not yours," Bev said, alarmed.

"Good heavens, no," Sloane said. "You should know me better than that. But there will be some unpleasantness." He held up his hand. "Not with me, have no fear. But it is possible that both the Beechams' and Reggie's pasts may be freely aired."

"I see. Well, I'm sure I don't care."

"But I do. I've decided that a trip to Europe is in order. Just you and me."

"Europe? You hate ocean crossings," Bev said.

"Indeed I do, but I have my own reasons for desiring a time away."

"Hilda?"

"Yes, she, too, will be leaving for a trip abroad quite soon, I understand."

Bev and Phil exchanged amused looks.

"Oh, it does sound good." Bev frowned. "But Phil just got here. I don't think she wants to go back so soon, and I couldn't leave her all alone. I haven't done a thing for her except get her involved in racketeering and murder."

"Don't worry about me," Phil said. She would worry about herself, as it seemed she must. "The Continent will do you both good. And," she added knowingly, "they're very much au courant on their ideas about mourning there. You'll have a lovely time."

"I plan to close up the brownstone while we're gone. I think you should sell it outright. So many unpleasant memories," Daniel said to Bev.

"But where will Phil live?"

"Actually, I've been thinking that the newly opened Plaza Hotel sounds like just the place for me. And right across from the park, too."

"That sounds like an excellent idea," Sloane said. "Bev, dear, why don't you run upstairs and tell Elmira the news and that she should start packing immediately. I'll just keep Philomena company while she finishes her breakfast."

As soon as the door closed behind Bev, her father took a crisp white envelope from his breast pocket. "I was asked to deliver this to you, Philomena. It seems you have friends in high places."

"Me?" Phil said, opening the envelope.

Inside was vellum stationery. An official-looking seal but no lines of formal address, merely . . .

Madam,

For your services in the investigation of the recent case and with the understanding that you will soon be looking for permanent residence within the city, we'd like to offer you an apartment at the Plaza Hotel gratis for a year and hope to be allowed to call on your services again. We are certain that others will also come to depend on your impeccable discretion.

Once again, thank you for your aid.

Sincerely,

The name had been written and struck through until it was indecipherable. Phil turned it over, looked at the back, and found nothing official. She moved it in front of her face, not even a whiff of pipe tobacco.

For her services? It was not from the New York police department; they would have a letterhead. But whom? And why didn't they just identify themselves. She put the letter back in the envelope and slipped it into her pocket.

"Where did you get this?"

"A friend of mine, a rather important man in the government and not tainted by local politics, asked me to make certain you received it." He smiled into his fist. "And to persuade you to accept the offer."

"The Plaza, that would be nice."

"Good, then it's decided." Sloane finished his coffee. "Though there is one more matter that needs to be considered. There have been rumors that Reggie made a list of subscribers to a certain 'betting club.' Just things I've heard down at the publishing house, you understand. And that was why Mimi LaPonte was attacked in the park outside our door."

Phil placed her napkin on the table. "She came here that day to try to sell what appeared to be her diary. I didn't tell Bev at the time because I didn't want her to be upset. I felt sorry for the woman, so I gave her some money and never gave it another thought." She hurried on. "It turned out to be nothing more than the peccadilloes of certain society ladies and several actresses."

"And stories about my daughter?"

"A few."

"And a certain list?"

She took a breath. "Yes. The list was stolen, but I made a copy."

"Then it must be destroyed."

"Yes, it must."

"These men will stop at nothing to get that list, though perhaps it's too late to save them."

Phil nodded. "However, they may not know that."

"Agreed. They must think that Reggie had it, and it may still be in our possession, which puts us all in danger."

"I agree," Phil said. "And to that end, I have an idea that should put both matters to rest. Though you may think it a bit extreme."

Half an hour later, Phil came downstairs carrying a book covered in brown paper. She met Daniel Sloane in the library.

"Is everything of value out of the room?"

"Except the carpet, and that I'm willing to sacrifice."

"Ready?"

He nodded and walked behind the desk. He ran a loving hand

over the top, and for a moment Phil wanted to say never mind we'll find another way. But this was the best way. The thug Tappington-Jones had sent to shake down Reggie had been found with his hand in the drawer of the desk. All the newspapers had reported on it.

Sloane opened one drawer, then reached in to the cavity of the side drawer. There was a click and the inkstand released. Phil turned it to reveal the secret compartment.

She hesitated. With a final wistful look, she slipped the book inside, then turned the inkstand until it clicked again.

Daniel stepped away from the desk, his expression tight. "Ready?"

Phil dragged two wastepaper baskets filled with wadded paper under the desk. Daniel took a can from where it had been placed by the windowsill.

"Step back," he said.

She did. "Be careful."

Daniel unscrewed the top and poured liquid over the top of the beautiful oak wood. Poured a ring of liquid around the legs, then emptied the rest into the wastepaper baskets.

"Go."

Phil hurried to the door, just as a whoosh echoed behind her. Then Daniel was pushing her into the hallway.

Lock the door," he said. "I'll call the fire department."

Alarm spread through the house. Tuttle tried to open the door, but Daniel stopped him. "It's better to leave it contained. The fire brigade is on its way."

At that moment, fire engine bells could be heard ringing from afar, getting louder. Daniel went out to meet them.

"It seems to be contained to the library," he yelled, and the brigade pulled the heavy fire hose down the narrow air shaft between the brownstones.

The breaking of glass. A larger whoosh.

Phil swallowed. She hoped Daniel hadn't overdone things.

It was over in less than an hour.

"Looks like a case of arson," the fire chief said.

"I agree," Daniel told him seriously. "As a newspaperman and publisher, I'm often the target of anger and revenge." He sighed as if resigned to his fate. "An unfortunate part of life. Thank you so much."

"You want us to investigate?"

"No, I'm planning on closing up the house. Selling, actually. I don't want my daughter subjected to this kind of criminality anymore."

He reached into his wallet, pulled out several large bills. "This is for you, and this is to buy the lads a few beers."

"Thank you, sir." The fire chief touched his hat and went out to help his men roll up the hose.

Daniel walked away and stood in front of the now open library door. Phil came to stand beside him.

The acrid smell of smoke mixed with gasoline permeated the drenched furnishings of the library. The two chairs were beyond repair. The ceiling was covered in black soot, and the few books that hadn't been removed from the shelves earlier were swollen with water and ash.

And in the center of the room, the three-hundred-year-old desk was a pile of embers. And beneath it, nothing but a charred hole where the carpet had been.

He stepped away and pulled the door closed. "Well, it had to be done. The rest of the house is unscathed. You and Bev will be able to stay here for the time being. I'll keep the staff on until it's sold, then try to get them all jobs elsewhere."

"I'm sorry," Phil said. "I couldn't think of another way."

"Don't be. This is the best way to put this chapter to bed. Now I have an article to write and a few calls to make. I'll say good day."

The papers reported the fire the next day. "The fire brigade was called to a brownstone at 6 East Sixty-Eighth Street, former residence of Daniel Sloane, currently occupied by his daughter,

Beverly Reynolds. The quick response of the engine company contained the fire to the library, and while most things were saved, an antique desk and what was purported to be a newly acquired manuscript that had been stored inside were completely destroyed. Said Mr. Sloane, 'The desk was a family heirloom and will be missed, but the manuscript is irreplaceable. I had just purchased it, intending to publish it next fall. The diary of a woman about town. I had only read a few pages when the fire broke out, but it promised to be a hilarious roman à clef on the foibles of some of the local society members when their manners were down. Alas, now we'll never see it. Unfortunately, it was destroyed in its entirety. Though sad not to have been able to read more, I'm certain some ladies will be glad to know that their misadventures are still their own.' "

"Well," Phil said.

"He's rather brilliant, isn't he?" Bev said.

"I now know from whom you get your audacity."

But the real news was the roundup of several prominent businessmen and politicians for questioning concerning race fixing and racketeering.

"By a special task force," Phil read. "So not Charlie Becker and his friends at City Hall."

"Who, then?"

"The racing commission?"

"Perhaps." Bev sighed. "Well, I suppose I must get back to packing. Father has booked passage for us at the end of the week."

Phil nodded. She knew Bev had mixed feelings about leaving. She really did have a knack for handling a breeding farm. But it would be better for her reputation and her safety until this was all cleared up. And the farm would be here when she returned.

"You'll be back in time for the fall season. And you'll have all new gowns from the best houses in Europe. You'll be the toast of the town."

"I will be, won't I?"

"Absolutely. And you have Bobby to manage the farm while you're gone and Mr. Carmichael to keep him on the straight and narrow."

"Yes, that's one less thing to worry about." Bev stood and started to leave, but turned back to Phil. "Oh, I almost forgot." She reached into her pocket and pulled out two keys, which she dangled in the air. "I would take it as big favor if you would keep the Packard running while I'm gone."

"Are you certain?"

"I wouldn't trust anyone else with it."

"Then I'd be delighted to."

"Wonderful." She dropped the keys into Phil's hand. "Phil, I don't know how to thank you. I was supposed to help get you settled in Manhattan, and you ended up saving my bacon."

"I was happy to oblige, my dear friend. Now go pick out which hats you're taking, but not too many. I have the perfect milliner on rue Guimard."

Bev laughed, then grew serious. "I know Reggie wasn't part of the betting scandal, and was running for his life, but why with her, why not me?"

"Because you'd be safer without him. And he did leave you everything."

"You're not just saying that to make me feel better?"

"Would I do that?"

Bev shrugged. "I don't know, but you've always made me feel better."

"Well, believe me." *After all, it might be the truth.* "Now let's go finish packing."

A few days later, Phil and Lily stood across the street from the Plaza Hotel, the park at their backs and the gleaming new hotel rising nineteen stories before them.

"It's magnificent, isn't it?"

"Yes, madam."

Things were looking up. She had living accommodations in a beautiful new hotel, the use of Bev's yellow Packard . . .

A boy suddenly appeared at her side. "Here, miss, a gentleman asked me to deliver it to ya."

Phil took the note. "Thank you." She reached in her purse for a coin, but when she went to hand it to him, he was already gone. A frisson of interest ran up her spine and she turned around to see him disappearing into the trees.

"Hmm." She opened the envelope, unfolded the single sheet.

Enjoy your new digs. See you soon, Countess. was scrawled elegantly across the page. There was no signature, but she knew whom it was from. And a frisson of something much more exciting than interest ran up her spine.

She put the note in her purse.

"A home, an automobile, and—do you still have the . . ."

Lily patted the side of her skirt. "Right here, madam."

"Excellent. Though I did hate to sacrifice Mr. Locard's treatise to the fire. I'm sure we'll be able to find another copy. Now, come, the future awaits us, and Lady Dunbridge is happy to oblige."